CATALYST

HIDDEN PLANET BOOK TWO

ANNA CARVEN

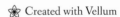

CHAPTER ONE

IMRIL THE LIGHTBRINGER, Overlord of Khira and destroyer of half his cursed race, opened his eyes and hissed.

Pain engulfed the entire left side of his body, from the planes of his face right down to the soles of his feet. He sat up in alarm and found himself surrounded by a pool of hot silver liquid.

He recognized it at once. *Ilverium*. Living metal. The mysterious, tech-infused substance that beat right through the heart of the Ancestor's dark ship.

"No!" he screamed, fearing the liquid metal would enter his body and consume him at any moment, forever tethering his soul to the *Destroyer*.

That was his worst nightmare; to be chosen as the new Master of that deranged sentient ship, doomed to orbit Khira until he went mad and the dark ship consumed him.

In desperation, he scuttled backward, his fingers touching the edge of the silver pool.

White-hot agony shot through his hands as the stuff burned through his scales, leaving his pale skin exposed.

Trembling, he rose to his feet. His joints were stiff, and by Za's forked tongue, he was *weak*. Barefoot and in terrible pain, he staggered across to the other side of the cavern, finding an area where the metallic sludge hadn't yet covered the ground.

He blinked.

Wait... this is not the Hythra. Where am I?

Bit by bit, the memories returned. The *Hythra* had once imprisoned his brother, Mael, but that was a very long time ago. Mael was free now.

And so was he.

Relief mingled with confusion as he took stock of his surroundings. He ignored the pain shooting down his side and tried to remember why he was in this forsaken place.

Rough stone walls soared above him, illuminated by a soft orange glow. Sharp spears of stone hung from the roof, glistening with moisture and tiny crystals.

He was in some sort of cave.

Imril followed the liquid metal as it snaked along the rough ground in a slow trickle. It had to be coming from somewhere. He stared into the distance, blinking furiously against the heat and smoke. His *saccadae*—second eyelids—slid over his eyes, and suddenly he could see clearly.

The gently sloping floor of the cave extended upward into a vast chamber that ended abruptly, giving way to a massive pit. At the center of the pit, lava spat and smoldered, releasing a constant plume of black smoke that turned the air acrid and obscured his vision, making him cough.

This wasn't any old cave, but a tunnel inside Za itself. He was inside the belly of the great volcano that had once threatened Khira with its fury, spewing forth ash and fire until the entire planet was blanketed in a dark cloud.

And he hadn't just been asleep, he'd been in deep hibernation, recovering from near-mortal injuries and terrible sickness.

Infected with a virus strong enough to bring even *him* to his knees.

Imril cursed long and hard as the full weight of his buried

memories came crashing down upon him. A terrible emptiness spread through him as he realized what he'd lost.

Everything.

His people were gone.

So were his enemies.

This could have all been avoided.

Fucking younglings. He'd *warned* his people not to go down that path, but they'd gone ahead and used their Naaga servants to create the ultimate killing weapon.

Deathkiss.

A virus that was deadly to even the immortal Drakhin.

The fatality rate was catastrophic—nine out of ten Drakhin who contracted the virus would die. So many of the second generation—those Drakhin who were more biologically *competent* than him but weaker—had succumbed to the illness quickly, dying off in droves. The others—those who tested negative—had left the planet, hastily sent away by Imril in Drakhin ships.

Where had they gone?

He didn't know.

Already infected, Imril had stayed behind to fight.

Ah, he missed some of them deeply; his War Counsellor Orin, his Technology Advisors Righel and Zemian, and Squadron Commander Tykhe, amongst others.

And then there was noble, shining, *deceptive* Nykithus, who he'd treated like his own son...

Who had delivered the ultimate betrayal, right into the heart of Imril's stronghold.

If he found out that Nykithus was still alive, Imril would tear the bastard's wings from his back and stuff them down his throat. Then he would burn him to a crisp.

Filled with a strange mixture of fury and humiliation and grief, he stalked down the cave, his untrimmed claws digging into the compacted earth. He would never understand how he hadn't noticed the signs until it was too late, but thinking back on it now, it all made sense.

Nykithus had always loved power a little too much, and his acting skills were exceptional. He'd brought *Deathkiss* into Imril's eyrie, right under his fucking nose.

By the time they realized what had happened, Nykithus was long gone, and Imril was murderous. Infected and full of rage, he'd flown to Nykithus's domain, Ton Malhur, and rained destruction upon Nykithus's armies, but they'd been ready, and they'd fought back with their cursed vir-weapons, wounding him badly.

In the end, he'd been left with no choice but to retreat.

With battle-wounds covering much of his body and his armor damaged beyond repair, he'd flown to the other side of the planet, trying to get as far away from the chaos as possible. Sick, weak, desperate, and wary of being followed, he'd swooped down into the Crater of Za, hoping the agonizingly hot, spitting core would deter his pursuers.

The last thing he remembered was crawling into the tunnel, lying down on the stone floor to rest, closing his eyes briefly, and then...

Sleep. Blessed sleep.

How long had he been out? Hundreds of revolutions? *Thousands?* Did it even matter?

If not for the hot metal jolting him awake, he might have slept for a long time yet... perhaps forever.

Maybe that would have been preferable to this cursed awakening.

The only thing that drove him now was the desire for revenge. He would kill the one who had wrought this senseless destruction, and he would make sure he died the most painful, agonizing death. Then the cursed Universe could swallow him up and eat his cursed bones for all he cared.

But first, he had to get out of here.

Imril stared through the smoke and saw a familiar outline

embedded in the rock. A massive thing of dark grey metal was slowly sinking into the lava pit.

Could it be?

Impossible.

There was no mistaking that shape, that *color*, the sheer size of the thing. It was the Ancestor's cursed ship, the *Hythra*, and it was slowly disintegrating.

That explained the pool of molten liquid.

So the great Destroyer had finally been brought down? Who could possibly be powerful enough to pull that dark, sentient, *insane* ship out of her orbit and crash her into the biggest fucking volcano on the planet?

Even now, so many revolutions after he'd escaped from that floating metal prison, the sight of it made him want to retch.

This was the ship where he'd been created, tortured, and shaped into a monster.

For a moment, he stood as still as a statue, paralyzed, his heart racing. A torrent of painful memories flooded his mind.

Mother.

It was so long ago, but he could still remember the feeling of holding her in his arms, of kissing her dewy violet skin, of running his fingers through her dark hair as he wept.

As Mael wept.

Imril shook his head, fighting the unexpected rawness of those memories. He thought he'd buried them deep, but then again, he'd hadn't been this vulnerable in a very long time.

You can't afford to do this now. Move!

He started to run, slowly at first, then faster and faster, ignoring the pain that shot through every cell of his ancient body. Vicious hunger rose up inside him, almost bringing him to his knees with its ferocity. How long had it been since he'd last fed? He was so depleted of *vir* that his body was on the verge of shutting down. His limbs were heavy, and a fog of fatigue clouded his mind, threatening to lull him back into sleep.

Forget the *Hythra,* forget sleep, he had to get out of here now. There would be time to figure things out later, but right now, he needed to feed.

Grunting with exertion, Imril unfurled his leathery wings, his wing-bones cracking from disuse. He ran toward the edge of the lava pit, demanding speed from his aching legs, and if he was anything but Drakhin, it would have been a suicide mission.

But he was one of the original twins, and he'd survived much, much worse.

So he jumped.

Fell.

Beat the hot air with all his might.

And rose slowly, painfully, caught between death and freedom.

Fly, idiot. Fly.

He had no choice now. If his control slipped, he would fall to his death. He might be the Lightbringer, but even he would not survive the intense heat of Za's deadly lava pit.

Up he went, each laborious beat of his wings sending an agonizing bolt of pain down his left side. As he rose, he saw the wreck of the *Hythra.* It was almost unrecognizable now, having sunk halfway into the vast lava pit, its massive body disappearing from sight as it was blanketed by a thick haze of smoke.

The ship was slowly melting.

The cursed *Hythra.* The last link to the dreaded Ancestor, the Dark One, the mad bastard who had tried to remake Imril and his brother, Mael, in his very own image, who had imprisoned them upon that cursed ship and tortured them for hundreds of revolutions. Now the ship was becoming one with the world it had held in its dark thrall for so many orbits.

Good fucking riddance.

If Imril weren't in so much pain, he might appreciate the

irony of it all, but every shred of his energy was focused on getting out of the cursed pit. As he reached the top of the crater, a blessed gust of hot wind swirled past, carrying him up over the edge. He angled his wings, catching the slipstream...

And soared.

Even when he was in this much pain, when he was this *weak*, the feeling of rising on a swift current of air with the cold wind hitting his face... it was exhilarating.

He lived for this feeling.

No matter how bad things got, the sky would always be his refuge, his sanctuary.

Imril stared down upon the world he had once ruled, recognizing the vast wetlands of the Ardu-Sai. The sun was setting, casting a golden glow across the rippling surface of the water.

A forgotten corner of the world, it was as far away from his eyrie as one could possibly get. The Ardu-Sai was the domain of the primitive Vradhu, the original inhabitants of the land. Drakhin rarely bothered to come here, unless they were searching for that most mythical of creatures—a Vradhu female.

Every Drakhin desired a female, but only a few had ever found their *lukara*. Vradhu females were potentially compatible, but the Vradhu were very, very good at hiding and protecting them. After the short, bloody war against the Drakhin, which the Vradhu lost miserably, the violet-skinned ones had retreated into the Ardu-Sai, concealing themselves in the dark, thorny *sekkhoi* forests.

Ah, if only he had a *vir*-rich female now...

Imril tried to remember where he might even begin to hunt for a Vradhu clan in this place, but he was too weak to think straight. All of his energy went into flying. The wind currents carried him well enough, but he had to beat his wings now and then in order to maintain his course. With time, it would all come back to him, but right now, he just had to *fly*.

It was excruciating. His wings trembled. Imril's desperation grew, and he wondered if he would make it back to his eyrie without falling into the vast waterplains below.

He needed *vir,* but the odds of finding a Source in this part of the world were slim to none.

Perhaps he could find a Naaga... *if* there were any blue ones left in this part of the world. To be this depleted, this hungry... it was sheer torture.

Imril banked to the left, following the wide waters until he reached a point where they started to narrow. He turned toward land, tracking along a winding river that was lined with dead, skeletal trees. Abruptly, the water ended, giving way to a dense tract of forest that quickly rose into undulating hills and valleys.

Everywhere he looked, trees were dropping their leaves, turning vivid shades of brown and orange and red, leaving skeletal branches behind.

Then he saw it.

There. In the distance, a soft golden glow rose through the canopy. It became brighter as he drew nearer, flickering like a naked flame.

He would know that glow anywhere.

Vir.

Beautiful, intoxicating *vir,* burning more brightly than he'd ever seen before. Exactly what he needed. There were creatures milling about in that clearing below, and they radiated pure, strong *vir.* It was as if the cosmos had answered his wishes.

His hunger spiked.

Imril twisted out of the slipstream and circled, staying high so they wouldn't see him.

With his acute vision, he could make out even the tiniest details.

The purple-skinned ones he recognized immediately. They were Vradhu warriors; wily, vicious fighters who wielded heavy war-spears and were experts at camouflage. The barbs in their tails were laced with a deadly poison that made even the fiercest Drakhin think twice before challenging them.

Vradhu venom was one of the deadliest known substances on Khira... and then there was the poison of their cursed Breeders, which was even *more* toxic than the barbs. The Breeders were a mystery. He had never encountered one of them face-to-face.

But the ones down below were Hunters, not Breeders.

Why were the Vradhu out here in the open, allowing themselves to be seen from above? Perhaps they had grown complacent because there were no more Drakhin to terrorize them.

Imril wasn't really interested in the Vradhu right now.

No, he was far more interested in the tailless, wingless, brown-skinned creatures that milled around a thicket of thorny bushes, collecting small shiny orange fruits. Two legs, two arms, smooth skin, soft hair ranging in color from almost-white to black, differing in texture from straight to very curly. Several of the creatures had pale brown, almost-white skin, whereas others were were dark. Most were in-between.

Such variation in pigment. How fascinating.

Collectively, the golden glow of their auras was dazzling.

What are they?

He'd never seen this species before in his life, and he'd been on this planet for thousands of revolutions. There had only ever been two intelligent species on Khira: Drakhin, and Vradhu.

Three, if one counted the Naaga.

So these creatures would have to be...

Aliens?

Whatever they were, it didn't matter. He needed one, *now*.

Imril growled as his hunger became unbearable, turning him into little more than a mindless beast. He would stop at nothing until he fed; he would not hesitate to kill to get the *vir* he so desperately needed.

It was survival, nothing more.

Surrendering to his basest instincts, he studied the strange creatures below, trying to decide which one to take.

One of them stood a slight distance apart from the rest, completely oblivious to him as he angled his wings, preparing to strike. Its dark hair was arranged atop its head in neatly knotted rows, and it wore a light green tunic that made it stand out from the others.

Was it just his imagination, or did the creature's *vir* burn just a little more brightly than the others? It didn't matter, really. He needed to feed, and this creature had strayed away from its pack.

Easy prey.

Mine.

He swooped.

CHAPTER TWO

ESANIA LOOKED up at the darkening sky, marveling at how it had turned such a spectacular shade of violet. On Khira, the sunsets were shades of purple and maroon, not fiery orange like they were on the Old Planet, Earth. No, here they more closely resembled a good Mars sunset, a sight she didn't miss one bit.

A warm breeze swept past, rippling the light fabric of her sea-green tunic, flicking the ends of her braids.

In the distance, five of her attendants picked tiny edible orange berries under the watchful eyes of their violet-skinned guards. Esania had intentionally separated herself from the group, choosing to pick berries several meters away, because she knew the women felt uncomfortable in her presence, and she just wasn't in the mood for stiff, awkward conversation.

When one of the Vradhu guards followed her, she'd waved him away, wanting to be alone for just a few precious minutes. By now she was well aware of the dangers of the Ardu-Sai, but he hadn't gone far—only a few steps away—and the purple-skinned warrior could move like lightning if he wanted to.

Besides, one of the mercenaries, Zahra, was standing watch on a small rocky outcrop, her hand on her particle gun.

The modified human was a fierce, wily fighter, and with her illegal bio-implants, she was much stronger than Esania.

They were protected.

What was the worst that could happen?

Just a few minutes.

So she could breathe.

So she could *think*.

There was something about tribal living that she found utterly stifling. All those people—Vradhu, human, bionic-human—living in such close proximity, sheltering in communal structures made of wood and stone.

She wasn't used to it.

For a moment, she visualized her past life on Mars, where she'd been a Primean senator, one of the elected delegates of the powerful State Council. Everything had been orderly, sanitized, predictable. She'd been in *control*.

Then, with the revelation of a single secret, her life had fallen apart, making her question *everything*.

Esania plucked another of the berries from its thorny bush —a round thing the size of her thumbnail—and studied it closely, struck by its strangeness, its *alienness*; the way its smooth red skin took on a metallic sheen in the dim light. *Tchirrin,* the Vradhu called them. For some reason, these particular fruits were bitter during the heat of the day and sweet in the evening, which was when the Vradhu and the humans would come down to the valley to collect them by the basket-load. They could be eaten fresh or roasted over an open fire until the purple flesh became soft and gooey inside.

Strange.

Everything on Khira was *strange,* and almost everything appeared to have thorns, even the inhabitants.

A sudden burst of sunlight hit her face, a last gasp from the setting sun as it slipped below the the horizon, cloaking the valley in deep shadow.

The sun was setting on Khira, and it was spectacular, a

sight as powerful and *alien* as the striking ink-faced warriors who called themselves Vradhu.

Oh, and they just happened to have tails; long, black, dextrous things with *poison barbs* at the end. Calexa, the captain of their doomed escape-transport, had told her about that particular quirk... amongst other things.

Crazy woman. Esania shuddered. Calexa Acura made no effort to hide the fact that she'd formed an intimate relationship with not just one, but *two* of the intimidating aliens.

Ares and Ares's clone. With wings.

She shuddered.

Calexa was rather proud of her Vradhu conquests.

Calexa had never said anything, and Esania was too cultured to ask, but... how was such a union even possible?

That Calexa, she was mad.

Only a human would even think of doing something so ridiculous...

No, don't think like that.

Esania stifled her typically Primean instincts, trying not to fall into old patterns of thinking. They weren't in the Serakhine anymore, and Calexa was free to choose who she involved herself with. Esania should probably respect it, even if she didn't understand it.

Of *course* she didn't understand it. After all, Esania's kind were forbidden from seeking carnal pleasures.

Well, that was the official line, but slowly, she'd learned that Primeans weren't as enlightened as they pretended to be. The constraints of Primean culture hadn't stopped that asshole, Deputy Commander Kivik, from impregnating one of her girls.

He'd *forced* her, and somehow, Sara's contraceptive implant had failed.

What were the chances of that? Statistically, a million-in-one.

What a mess.

Serakhine law was not influenced by emotion. Serakhine law was absolute. The man, the woman, and her unborn child would be sentenced to death. Those that aided and abetted— no matter what their station—would be sentenced to a life of hard labor on Kalluq-3.

If caught, all of the women in her entourage would be found guilty. They'd helped to conceal Sara's pregnancy for months.

Primeans were notoriously obsessive about protecting the purity of the genetic pool, and cross-species coupling was a Capital One offense, so that moron Kivik had tried to cover up the entire thing, with near-disastrous results.

That was why Esania had and her attendants had escaped on a dark-market mercenary transport run by a crew of unhinged bionically enhanced female mercenaries. In order to conceal her identity, she'd taken the moniker 'S'. It was, for want of a better word, *complicated*.

Then things had gone horribly wrong. Out of nowhere, a Paxnath raider ship had attacked, and Esania had her suspicions about its origins. They'd had no choice but to enter the Silverstream, an uncharted parallel dimension where ships frequently went missing.

Now she knew what happened to said ships when they went *missing*.

That's how they'd ended up here on this wild, primitive planet, where there wasn't a shred of civilization to be found.

Esania sighed as she dropped a handful of berries into the small woven basket that hung at her side. It occurred to her that they might never leave this place.

She could die here. If some venomous plant or creature didn't get her, then perhaps she'd succumb to some terrible disease or infection.

There was no advanced medical care here, after all.

A shrill whistle split the air, and the Vradhu warrior watching over her gestured, making a V sign with his fingers.

"*Kaala*," he called, sounding a little bored. In Vradhu, the word meant *let's go*. Esania knew only a few basic words in their language, and *kaala* was one of them. Infuriatingly, they liked to use it a *lot*, in the most gratingly insistent tone.

Grumpy bastards. Vradhu warriors were a proud, surly lot, and apparently, they didn't stoop to such menial tasks as collecting berries. It was their job to stand guard while the women worked.

Huh. What archaic nonsense.

Esania snorted as she made her way down the rocky slope, wet fern-shaped leaves brushing against her boots. She wasn't used to being ordered around by *anyone*, but here she had no choice but to go with it. They were on an unfamiliar planet, surrounded by dangerous flora and fauna, and for reasons she didn't truly understand, these Vradhu had chosen to separate from their tribe and protect them.

She suspected it had something to do with Calexa and her unlikely union with Ares, but she didn't really understand what had happened on the *Hythra,* and the *Medusa's* crew were being infuriatingly cryptic.

At that moment, something made her look up. It wasn't anything she could put her finger on, but more of a *feeling*. A tingling sensation ran over her scalp and down the back of her neck...

Whoosh.

A fierce gust of wind engulfed her from above. She felt it before she heard it. Suddenly, she was inside a vacuum devoid of sound and movement.

There was only pressure.

Immense pressure.

The Vradhu guard was shouting, but she couldn't hear him.

Whomp. Whomp.

The air around her became a torrent, a battering ram, smashing down upon her from above. Esania reflexively turned around brought her hands up over her head, ducking down as she tried to run. The cured ends of her braids whipped around her face, stinging her cheeks.

Three of the Vradhu peeled off from the main group, running toward her, their war-spears raised high, their black-and-purple faces twisting into expressions of pure fury.

One of them—the leader—was Calexa's fearsome lover, the one called Ares, who had emerged from the wreck of the *Hythra* sporting a pair of menacing black wings.

He sprinted toward her, a terrible war-cry erupting from his throat.

"Esania, get down!" From her vantage point, Zahra aimed her gun.

Esania dropped to the ground.

Zahra fired.

Blam!

Time slowed to a standstill. She scrambled to her feet.

Steeling herself, she looked up...

And saw a horror that was supposed to have died with the doomed alien ship.

Drakhin!

Only this one was different.

Massive pale wings blotted out the remaining daylight.

She gasped.

It—*he*—was completely naked. She knew the Drakhin was a *he*, because with *that* body, he couldn't possibly be anything else.

Power. He was sheer power. Broad, powerful shoulders, pale arms bulging with corded muscle, sculpted chest and rippling stomach, massive...

Oh, my.

A certain part of his anatomy was on full view, and it was... *impressive.* She had to force herself to look away.

A pale winged demon was bearing down on her, possibly to kill her, and all she could do was stare at his cock.

Move, idiot.

To her dismay, the blast from Zahra's particle gun hadn't even grazed the alien. Why had Zahra missed?

Too close. With growing horror, Esania understood. From where Zahra was standing, it was a risky shot.

Her attacker was too close to her. Zahra could easily have killed her.

A fearsome pair of golden eyes stared down at her, and for a moment, she was utterly transfixed.

She wanted time to freeze so she could simply stare at the impossible creature, but he moved so fast he became a blur.

Heading straight for her.

Move!

But she wasn't fast enough.

A flash of white split the darkness as a huge pair of arms surrounded her, holding her so tightly the breath was pushed out of her chest.

She tried to fight, tried to resist, but it was futile. The creature that had captured her was impossibly strong; his arms felt like folded steel around her waist.

Esania's self-control shattered.

She screamed.

Impossibly, the creature relented, hissing in pain as he released her. A long spear protruded from his calf. *How?* Behind him, the Vradhu were screaming their visceral war-chants. One of them must have attacked him!

Move!

Esania didn't waste time. She pushed his arms away and ran as fast as she could, stumbling over the uneven ground. The Vradhu surged in her wake, hissing loudly as they surrounded the Drakhin.

Were they going to kill him?

She wasn't planning on sticking around to find out.

CHAPTER THREE

IMRIL'S VISION blurred then sharpened as he dropped into a steep dive. The air rushed around him, becoming a deafening roar in his ears as he gained velocity.

It was as if he were staring down a dark tunnel, transfixed by the light at the end. All he could see was that mesmerizing *vir*, growing brighter and brighter, driving him completely mad as he swooped.

It was his for the taking.

At the very last moment, the creature turned and looked up, an expression of sheer horror crossing its face.

The strangest, most vivid green eyes stared back at him, widening in fear as he took a deep breath and extended his arms, preparing to grab his prize.

The Vradhu were running, their spears raised.

Blam! A blast of energy hit him in his chest, sending excruciating pain through his body, but it didn't stop him. He was already in descent.

Imril drew on the last reserves of his strength and beat his wings. The creature tried to run, but Imril was already there, his wings whipping up a small vortex that sent small leaves and twigs flying into the air.

His feet hit the ground.

His hands closed around the creature's waist and he inhaled its *vir,* absorbing just just a small taste as it radiated off the creature's slender body.

Got you.

As tendrils of golden energy flowed into Imril's body, he stiffened, his eyes rolling back into his head. For a brief moment, all he saw was her golden aura.

What is this?

He had never tasted *vir* this sweet in his entire life, and he had lived for a very long time.

Could it be...?

Powerful. Intoxicating. *Dangerous...* for the Source. It took all of his self-control to avoid completely draining the creature right then and there. With a single touch, he could so easily kill this fragile thing, and as hungry as he was, he knew that once he laid his hands on its bare skin, once he tapped into its *vir* directly, he wouldn't be able to stop.

No, he needed to draw from it in a controlled manner, in a place where he could separate himself when he needed to, slowly, gradually, letting the Source build up its reserves between feedings.

It would take several feedings until he was back to full strength.

A soft gasp escaped the creature's throat, and with great effort, he stayed his hand, disgust welling up inside him at his loss of control.

And he realized that his cock had gone hard, and *that* hadn't happened in a very long time, and when it had, the reaction had never been as strong as *this*.

Control yourself. You need to get out of here first.

A strange choice lay before him. He could drain the creature completely—right here, right now—and make his escape, or he could take it with him.

A risk.

But what a reward if he pulled it off.

A *vir*-slave with energy so rich and potent it made him swoon. Just the tiniest taste, and he was already addicted.

Imril didn't know how he did it, but somehow he held back from touching its light brown skin. Right now, he was so hungry for *vir* that he feared he might kill the creature if he fed outright.

No, he couldn't feed here.

First, he—*they*—needed to get away.

He could do it without harming it. Just the tiny amount of energy he'd already taken was enough to give him the strength to get away. This creature... it was *exceptional*. He hadn't tasted anything as powerful, *ever*.

Now all he needed to do was get them airborne...

He pulled the creature against him, and its strange clothing created the thinnest of barriers between them, preventing him from draining it completely. For that, he needed skin-to-skin contact.

Still, he inhaled what he could of its *vir*, reveling in the sheer purity of it as the golden energy surrounded him, giving him just enough strength to take to the skies once more.

But then the creature screamed, a shrill, piercing sound that savaged his sharp hearing. It fought, and for such a small, soft skinned being, it was surprisingly strong.

Thud!

Something pierced his calf, something sharp and heavy, sending a fresh bolt of agony through his body. His arms loosened, and the creature slipped out of his grasp.

How had he missed its approach? Clearly, he'd been far too distracted by his alluring catch.

Thud!

A body slammed into him with incredible force. He didn't even have time to fold his wings properly before he was sent reeling, and it took all his strength to roll to one side and right himself. Grunting in pain, he spun and came face to face with a winged Vradhu.

Winged Vradhu? Impossible!

But there was no time to ask questions. Imril lunged to one side, narrowly avoiding a vicious war-spear that shot past his left cheek. The Vradhu attacked, whipping out its tail and extending its barb.

Imril growled as he danced away. Vradhu venom was bad news. "You dare attack me?" Drawing upon memories of a different time, when a Vradhu warrior wouldn't dare attack a Drakhin at first sight, he spoke in fluent Vradhu. "Don't you know me?"

"I know you, *Imril,*" the Vradhu grated as he sank the poisonous barb into Imril's side. "Do not think you can take whatever you want just because you are the so-called Light-bringer. Things have changed since you disappeared."

"Oof." Well now, *that* was unexpected. This warrior was fearless; a real insolent bastard. Imril gasped and wrapped his hands around the Vradhu's tail, trying to dislodge the barb. Blood seeped through his fingers; cold, sticky, cerulean-hued—his own. After sleeping for so long in Za's smoldering belly, he was surprised that any blood flowed through his veins at all.

Hunters closed in on him from both sides as the *vir*-creature scrambled backward, a look of abject terror on its face.

Careful. In his weakened state, they could do him some serious damage. He had to shake them off before they realized how weak he really was.

Screwed if you do, screwed if you don't.

He channelled his *vir.* Normally, it was a raging torrent, plentiful and easy to tap into, but now it had become a trickle, probably less than a thousandth of his full power.

And that was only what he'd taken from the alien.

Because he hadn't fed for so very long. Because the Naaga servants that once supplied him with a continuous flow of *vir* were no longer there.

Because the last time he'd taken the *vir* of a Vradhu female, he'd endured the vicious scratches of her nails across his face when he'd spurned her advances.

Because before the war, *everybody* had wanted to seduce the Lightbringer, yet none of them pleased him.

"You should be more cautious, Vradhu." He took a deep breath and summoned a small ball of *vir*, a desperate plan forming in his mind. "You are a thousand cycles too young to be taking me on, bastard." With a grunt, he ripped the Vradhu's tail-barb out of his side and quickly placed his hand over the wound. "Ugh." He hissed in pain as he released a small burst of power, cauterizing the flesh. The burn would sequester the poison and stop it from spreading into his bloodstream, where it could quickly kill him. He would have to cut out the dead flesh later—before it turned septic and gave him blood poisoning—but first he had to get out of this mess.

He might be exceptionally long-lived, but he wasn't invincible. Far from it.

Come on. He drew upon thousands of revolutions of ancient knowledge, turning the meager trickle of power into something terrible and potent.

Thank you, sweet little thing.

It would never know it, but the strange brown-skinned creature had just saved his life.

The air around him started to crackle, and he felt the familiar warmth of his power. The Vradhu shouted warnings to their tribesmen, telling them to *get back* and *protect the women.*

They knew what was coming. They knew what he was. Oh, they *knew.*

He dropped to his knees and touched the ground with his palms.

Boom!

Power radiated out from his hands, throwing the Vradhu back. The fearless one that had stung him received the full brunt of the blast, and the smell of charred flesh rose into the air.

They were fortunate he wasn't at his full power, because he would have annihilated them all.

Imril hissed as the worst kind of agony shot through his side, adding to the pain from his metal burns. Somehow, he found the strength to rise to his feet, and he channeled the last shreds of his power into his legs, propelling himself toward the *vir*-creature, who had also been thrown to the ground.

Boom!

A blast of energy hit him in the side, something that felt similar to his own power.

He hissed as another alien ran forward, this one possessing pale skin and a braided tail of brown hair. It had a weapon in its hand; some sort of blast-device. The alien screamed at him as it prepared to fire again, but Imril staggered forward, grunting in pain, drawing on the last reserves of his strength until he reached his original target.

His attacker hesitated.

He reached down, fighting through the agony.

Got you.

The *vir*-creature shrieked, waving its slender claw-less hands, an expression of horror spreading across its face. It tried to scramble backward, but Imril was there before it had a chance to rise to its feet.

He grabbed it by the waist, and only the thin fabric of its tunic prevented him from touching its skin.

It screamed. The alien with the weapon screamed too, but didn't dare fire, obviously not wanting to harm his captive.

Now he just needed to get airborne, out of range of the Vradhu war-spears. Once he was high enough, there was nothing they could do, and it wouldn't matter how weak he was... as long as he had his prize. With a great roar, Imril spread his wings wide, beating faster and faster, generating a powerful gust of wind that threw the Vradhu back. Before they had a chance to react, he launched himself up into the clear violet sky, clutching his prize tightly.

The creature pummeled him in the chest with its small fists, kicking wildly, fighting him with every fiber of its being. A sharp elbow landed in his side where the Vradhu barb had stuck him, and Imril hissed in pain.

Still, he didn't stop moving his wings. That he could do in his sleep. Flying was as natural to him as breathing.

Higher they went, higher and higher, until the Vradhu were small specks in the wild landscape below, powerless to do anything but stare up at Imril as he escaped with his catch.

And the higher they went, the less the brown-skinned alien fought. Perhaps it understood that one wrong move could make him let go, sending it plummeting to the ground below.

Still, it gave one last defiant kick as he broke through a bank of wispy clouds, and if he weren't half-dead and exhausted, he might have summoned the energy to be irritated.

But how could he be annoyed when he was surrounded by the blissful, intoxicating cloud of its *vir*? Instead of growling, Imril wrapped his arms and legs around its body to stop it from flailing.

"Stop," he whispered in his native Drakhin, and to his relief, the creature ceased.

If it had continued to fight, he would have been at risk of dropping it—he was that weak.

Instead, it froze in his arms, staring at the terrain below as the trees and waterways and undulating hills grew smaller and smaller.

Fear gave its *vir* a bitter tinge. Of course, it made sense that a land-dwelling creature would be so afraid of flying. Imril couldn't imagine what it would be like to be wingless.

To be stripped of the ability to fly was a fate worse than death. Even when he was so weak he could barely walk, he could still fly.

For as long as he drew breath, he would fly.

They soared over mountain ranges and lakes and wide grass-plains, and all the while, Imril absorbed just the tiniest amount of its golden energy; the *vir* that naturally radiated from its body. Gradually, the creature relaxed, its limbs losing some of their stiffness as it became used to the sensation. With the cool wind rushing past his ears and the creature's warm, slender body held tightly against him, Imril was almost lulled into a state of contentment.

But still, he was exhausted, and each wingbeat was getting harder and harder, reducing in amplitude as he tried to ignore the pain in his side. Perhaps a little of the Vradhu poison was working its way into his system.

Imril had no choice. Simply inhaling her *vir* wasn't enough. He was going to have to tap into that glorious energy, and the only way to do that was to touch its bare skin. *Careful.* He was going to have to exercise the greatest amount of self control to avoid killing it.

Make it quick. Not too much.

He just needed to take enough strength to get out of the Ardu-Sai, away from Vradhu and the ever-present threat of the vicious, deadly kratok.

Now he recalled why the Drakhin hadn't really bothered with this remote wilderness.

Kratok were a serious pain-in-the-ass, and if they encountered one right now, they were dead.

Slowly, he snaked one hand through the creature's intricately knotted hair until he reached the elegant curve of its neck. Taking a deep breath, he extended his fingers and touched its bare skin for the very first time.

Boom.

What he felt beneath his fingertips blew his ancient mind.

This Source... so rich, so pure it almost terrified him. This kind of perfection should not exist.

"Sweet thing. Where did you come from?" he murmured

as its *vir* flowed into him, filling him with euphoria... and power.

And then it struck him.

This incredible creature was *female*.

What species it was, he had no idea, but she was definitely not of this world.

Yes, even Imril the Lightbringer could still be surprised from time to time.

He absorbed her essence hungrily, desperately, forgetting self-control, not caring that she whimpered in horror, her cries growing weaker and weaker as he made her golden energy his own. He was a long way from being back to full strength, but as he tapped into her *vir*, his wingbeats became stronger, his flight smoother, his vision clearer.

He broke through a bank of thick white clouds, exulting in the feeling of pure freedom.

But like all things, the feeling was only temporary.

She grew limp in his arms, whimpering softly.

Shit.

He'd drained her almost to the point of unconsciousness, and the air up here was thinner, less oxygenated.

Stop.

He had to stop, but it was oh-so hard. She was a drug, this soft, sweet, otherworldly creature, and now that he'd had his first taste, he wondered if anything else would ever feel as good.

Don't kill her, idiot!

He was on the edge now, dancing between salvation and the darkness of his cursed ancestry.

CHAPTER FOUR

WHOMP. Whomp.

Her feet left the ground. The creature beat its powerful wings one, two, *three* times, and they ascended, shooting up into the darkening sky. At first, his movements were uneven, but then a gust of wind blew past, and he began to fly more smoothly, quickly gaining altitude.

Her back was to him. He held her aggressively, triumphantly. *Savagely.*

Something in her snapped, and she went wild, kicking, screaming, fighting with all her strength until the futility of it all hit her right in the gut.

Stop.

He whispered something to her in a language that was utterly alien, eliciting a cold, dark ripple of terror—an emotion Esania had never felt to this extent, not even when Kivik's bots and goons had assembled at her gates.

And for some reason, his voice—deep and male and *rough* —sounded as if it hadn't been used in a thousand years.

Her legs swayed in thin air as they went higher, higher, higher...

She dared to look down. Ares-with-wings lay on the

ground unmoving, and several Vradhu quickly surrounded him.

Was he critically injured? *Dead?*

Her heartbeat quickened. Her breaths came faster and faster; short, sharp, rasping gasps. At this rate, she was at risk of hyperventilating.

Stop it! Calm down! Pull yourself together!

She couldn't afford to panic.

With great effort, she pushed aside her emotions. A feeling of detachment came over her as she stared at the scene below.

The people below were shouting, gesturing, running toward the spot she'd been plucked from, their faces growing smaller and smaller until they became tiny flecks in a sea of violet and black shadows.

Then they were *gone*, and the lush Ardu-Sai stretched out before her, wild and terrifying.

She saw the lay of the land, saw a serpentine river glistening as it was caressed one last time by the rays of the dying sun, saw her reality disappear yet again, turning into a nightmare a thousand times worse than the one she'd left behind.

Once again, sheer panic threatened to burst forth. Esania only barely kept it in check.

She was helpless and utterly terrified, and she *hated* it.

The man-creature-*thing* wrapped his legs around her lower body, restraining her completely. There was something strangely reassuring about his powerful hold on her—at least she wouldn't fall to her death, because he was gripping her so damn tightly.

The air grew thin and cold, rushing past her face. She struggled to breathe as they went higher still, and Esania could no longer make out the landscape below, because night had fallen, and Khira's moon was tiny and didn't cast much light.

They shot upward through a thin veil of clouds and moisture hit her face. She couldn't breathe. She started to shiver.

The *creature* curled one large hand around the base of her neck where her skin was exposed....

And for the second time, he touched her bare skin.

His fingers—yes, they were *definitely* fingers—sent a ripple across her skin; a tingling, electric, burning sensation that quickly spread outwards, engulfing her entire body.

But his hands... they were ice cold. How could any living creature be this cold?

What is this?

It wasn't unpleasant.

It was strangely pleasurable, in fact.

And suddenly, despite the cold air and his frigid touch, she felt warm.

Her limbs, stiff with fear, grew heavy and limp. The longer he kept his hand on her neck, the weaker she felt, but maybe it was the lack of oxygen that was making her feel giddy.

He inhaled deeply and whispered something dark and seductive and utterly incomprehensible in that rough, deep voice of his. Instead of making her panic, the sound of his voice lulled her into a languorous state.

What the hell has he done to me?

She couldn't help it; she closed her eyes...

And soared up into the unknown, not knowing what would become of her human attendants—the women whose fates she was solely responsible for—not knowing whether she would live or die.

A monster of Khira had her now, and his touch was lulling her into a state of detached euphoria, melting away her terror.

Why wasn't she afraid? It shouldn't feel good like this. With great effort, Esania opened her eyes and stared straight ahead. They had reached the edge of the sky, where the stars bled into the darkness.

If she were human, she'd probably be unconscious right now, because human hearts and lungs and red blood cells were adapted to very specific conditions on Earth, but she wasn't human. She was *Primean*, and so she stayed awake a little bit longer, just long enough to see the very edge of this dangerous world.

Whoosh.

Suddenly, his wings were around her, wrapping her in a pale cocoon. His hand left her neck, and Esania screamed.

But no sound came out.

So weak. What was this feeling? She couldn't do anything. She was drained to the point where she was almost unconscious.

His powerful body twisted, and he inverted.

One-hundred-percent *upside-down.*

They plummeted.

And Esania promptly blacked out.

CHAPTER FIVE

WITH GREAT EFFORT, Imril removed his hand from her neck, even though he was far from satisfied. He couldn't risk killing her. She was that most rare and valuable of things—a Source.

And possibly something more...

He became still, stretching his wings out so that they glided on a current of cold air. For a moment, he just hung there, listening to the rush of the wind; listening for...

There.

She still breathed. She moved.

His Source was still alive, although barely conscious.

Relief coursed through him.

Without thinking, Imril inverted. He had to get back down into the oxygenated zones before she stopped breathing.

He shifted his weight, plummeting back toward the face of Khira, holding his prize tightly, even as he took the utmost care not to press his bare skin directly against hers.

Careful.

He could use her again and again. She would be his servant, just like the pale-eyed Naaga that had roamed the halls of his eyrie high above the waves, above the shores of his island.

Were his Naaga servants still alive? Had they kept *Eleia* running in his absence?

The air became warmer as Imril reached the lower atmosphere. He tightened his grip on the female, and the only thing preventing him from draining her further was the thin material that separated his hands from her firm flesh.

He flew on, taking her farther away from the Vradhu, all the while having to restrain himself from touching her bare skin again as her aura surrounded him.

It was so heady and intoxicating that several times, Imril almost passed out.

Then he realized that his prize had indeed passed out.

Shit.

He had to find a place to rest, because in her current state, she wouldn't last very long.

CHAPTER SIX

IMRIL TWISTED his body until they were upright again and snapped his wings open, catching a gust of wind. He held the creature tightly as they were jerked violently out of freefall, angling his wings to catch the slipstream.

For a moment, he hovered on the wind, looking down upon his vast world. Soft starlight fell upon him from above, and for the first time, he realized something.

The Shadowring was gone.

Of course it was. The Dagger had crashed, tearing down the dark mist that had obscured their planet from the rest of the Universe for aeons.

But... *how?*

What had happened on Khira while he'd been in his deep slumber? Dark fragments of memories swirled through his mind.

His wings drooped from sheer exhaustion. Every single beat was agony, and his right wing didn't work as well as the left, causing him to tilt to one side. Perhaps one of his wing-bones was broken.

He was injured, sick, and completely depleted of vir. The plague had spread from eyrie to eyrie, wiping out thousands of

Drakhin, ravaging Imril's body with terrible ulcers and filling his lungs with poison so that he could barely breathe.

That mad bastard, Nykithus... he had opened a chest of horrors. A pathogen that killed only Drakhin could only have its origins in one place.

Still, Imril was one of the original Twins, and he was stronger than all the others. He would survive this, but right now, he felt so damn weak. He'd been flying for such a long time, and his wings were so damn tired.

He started to fall...

He squeezed his Source, taking care not to touch her bare skin. "Wake up," he growled. "You are not permitted to die on me."

Nothing. The alien lay limp in his arms, her eyes closed, her expression serene.

At least she breathed.

And she still radiated *vir*. That meant she was still alive, just unconscious.

Just a little bit more.

Her shimmering golden aura tempted him so badly. It was like those potent substances some of the Drakhin used to ingest to achieve a state of euphoria—a *drug*.

It took all of his self control to stop himself from touching her again. At this rate, he was going to end up addicted.

Imril flew on, gaining speed as he crested a ridge of snow-capped mountains—the Isskar range. He caught sight of a vast lake in the distance, and remembered that it had once been home to a minor Lord called Kunlo.

He'd met the bastard once, only briefly, and found him tiresome. Afraid to speak their true minds, the lesser Drakhin all used to grovel around him.

Was Kunlo still alive? He doubted it.

But Kunlo's eyrie was there, rising through the mists above the glassy surface of the lake. It was small compared to Imril's great tower in the sea, and it lacked *Eleia's* architectural elegance, but it would do for now.

Kunlo's eyrie was nothing more than a squat grey tower perched on a tall stone pillar, with five narrow spires ascending from the roof, the largest of which rose from the center like a cursed *sekkhoi* thorn.

Ugly thing.

Imril would have much preferred to take her to his own eyrie, but that was on the other side of the world, and she was fading fast.

So Kunlo's tower it was, and she had better respond to his care, because he wasn't yet back to full strength, and he needed her *vir*.

Perhaps when he was fully recovered, he would go back and capture more of those soft-skinned brown creatures. He would keep an entire stable of them, drawing on their *vir* as he pleased. Unlike the other Drakhin, Imril was not a cruel master. He'd always taken care of his servants.

He'd even grown quite fond of some of them.

As long as she gave him what he needed, he would treat her well.

Now she just needed to survive.

CHAPTER SEVEN

ESANIA CAME AWAKE SLOWLY. Her head was fuzzy, her eyes were gritty, and she could feel the beginnings of a terrible migraine coming on.

Bright light flooded her vision. She looked up and saw a riot of glittering color. An ornate ceiling stretched above her, and she had to blink several times to fully process what she was seeing.

What is this?

Then it hit her.

They were *gemstones*. Thousands of tiny glittering gemstones, arranged in the most intricate designs. Starbursts, swirls, fractals.

Am I dreaming?

She was lying in some sort of bed, still dressed in her original clothes. In a daze, she glanced to either side of her and saw folded wings.

Wings?

Black, hard, curving wings. With menacing claws at the ends. Esania's heart hammered as it took her a moment to realize that they weren't *real* wings, but carvings that encircled a massive oval-shaped bed frame.

She stretched her arms and legs. There was nothing on the bed, not even a thin sheet to cover herself with, but the surface beneath her was impossibly soft and comfortable.

Glancing to one side, she saw a polished stone floor that extended out as far as her eyes could see.

Where am I?

She was in a large room, a light, airy space with ornately arched ceilings and walls of smooth white stone. The construction was more sophisticated than anything else she'd seen on this planet.

She definitely wasn't in Vradhu territory anymore.

Overhead, sunlight streamed in through high windows. One of them appeared to be broken, allowing a balmy breeze to enter the room. To her right were a pair of massive black doors, decorated with incredibly detailed carvings of flowers and foliage. Big grey metal bolts studded the borders, giving Esania the impression these doors could have been found on Earth during medieval times.

What am I doing here?

She shook her head. At first her thoughts were a slow, fuzzy trickle, but then realization struck her, and Esania gasped.

She sat up in alarm as the terrifying memories returned. She'd been abducted by a monster of Khira; a pale, winged, flying demon. He'd taken her up high, where the air had become cold and thin, making her grow lightheaded from the lack of oxygen.

Then he'd done something to her; something that had made her drowsy and weak.

She'd passed out.

Esania took a deep, shuddering breath. For the first time in her life, she felt like bursting into tears.

Don't be ridiculous. Pull yourself together.

Humans cried. Primeans didn't. She was going to get

through this. She was going to use facts and cool-headed logic to get herself out of this mess.

Ha. Look at where her so-called *decisions* had led her. From the Serakhine to a Fiveways mercenary ship, to this forsaken planet on the other side of the Netherverse. Even the most sophisticated behavioral prediction algorithms couldn't have accounted for cause and effect and the utterly *human* emotions she'd experienced when she'd found out that Sara was pregnant.

Somehow, her integration score had never accounted for her own vulnerabilities, but none of that mattered anymore, because deep down, she knew that what she'd done was *right*. Did being right always lead to justice? In the real Universe, probably not. But she could damn well fight for it, all the same.

She might be the prisoner of a pale, winged alien who could suck the strength right out of her with just a touch, but at least she was alive.

Clearly, she was of some value to him, because he could so easily have killed her.

Trembling, Esania rose to her knees, trying to get a better view of her surroundings, which were partly obscured by the strange black wing-carvings of the bed frame.

Something flickered in the distance; a large, imposing figure of shimmering white and gold.

Her heart skipped a beat.

He's here!

"You..." She froze, momentarily forgetting to breathe. He sat so still that at first she'd thought he was a statue, but no, he was very much alive.

CHAPTER EIGHT

A MONSTER SAT across from her in a high-backed chair, watching her with cold golden eyes. It had taken her a while to notice him, because he didn't move, didn't blink, didn't say a word. He could have been made of stone for all she knew.

Except that something flickered over his eyes; a clear membrane much like a lizard's third eyelid.

She shuddered, even as she took the chance to *really* look at her captor for the first time.

She'd caught brief glimpses his kind before, on the doomed ship called the *Hythra*. A silver-skinned monster just like him had appeared and fought viciously against the Corrupted, the zombie-like creatures that had materialized in the bowels of the cursed ship.

Later, she'd learned that the monster was Calexa's Ares, momentarily transformed by the sentient ship into something utterly alien, utterly terrifying.

But no, this monster was different.

He was a study in warm shades of white and gold. His pupils were narrow slits, his irises perfect amber, and his pale wings—pearlescent, cream-colored, dazzling—were folded behind him, extending into a special recess that was carved into the chair.

Beautiful, and yet he was harder, colder, and more terrifying than the other. *Crystalline*.

Was he a celestial thing... a god of some sort?

Don't be ridiculous. He's no god. He's just an alien.

A feeling of horror coursed through her as she remembered the chilling sensation of his fingers on the back of her neck. It was almost as if he'd been a dead thing, sucking the life right out of her.

Esania got the feeling this creature had been around for a very long time, and there was no doubt in her mind that he was dangerous.

He didn't move, didn't make a sound.

How eerie.

His almost-white skin glittered like the gemstones on the roof, and as Esania studied him closely, she realized that what she'd thought was smooth skin was actually made up of tiny shimmering scales. A shadow fell across the room then—a passing cloud, perhaps—and the light streaming in from above turned dim. For a moment, his scales took on an amethyst hue, as if his true skin were purple underneath all those glittering scales.

Then the sunlight broke through again, illuminating his hard face.

Mesmerizing her just a little bit.

Esania was not a superstitious person—she was Primean, after all—but in that instant, she could very well believe in gods and monsters and demons, because the creature, man, *thing* standing before her looked like he came from the depths of Earth's imaginary hell.

Not heaven, because things that dwelled in heaven supposedly didn't have scales and claw-tipped wings and ice-cold hands that could suck the life right out of you.

As she stared at him, a flicker of a smile appeared at one corner of his mouth. It was the only sign of life in his mask-like face.

Smiling? After he'd *captured* her? After he'd taken her energy without even asking?

She felt violated somehow.

"You *bastard*..." The words slipped from her mouth before she could stop them.

The alien's smile grew wider, revealing long, pointed teeth. There was no warmth in that smile. Rather, it was dipped in arrogance and laced with cruelty.

And limned with just a touch of dark amusement.

Fear kicked in and sealed Esania's lips shut. Her heart hammered in her chest. Her mouth went dry. She'd never been this afraid in her life, not even when Kivik had sent his death squad to her door.

In the Serakhine, she'd had power.

Here, she was *nothing*.

And a monster sat across from her, and she knew nothing about him or his world. Her heart sank as she glanced at the solid double doors. It was pointless to even think of trying to escape. So what if she managed to get past this strange creature? She had no idea what lay in wait for her outside. How far away was she from Calexa and the Vradhu pack? Even if she got past the walls of this place, there was no way she survive out there in the wilds of Khira with only her limited knowledge of the terrain and its flora and fauna.

Trapped by walls.

Trapped by nature.

Angry but powerless.

Afraid.

"*Misurash.*" His voice shocked the hell out of her when he finally spoke. It was a deep baritone; smooth and decadent a little bit *cultured.*

He was dressed now, wearing a simple black sleeveless tunic that revealed bare white arms rippling with corded muscle. The garment contrasted deeply with his golden hair, which cascaded over his shoulders; a lustrous untamed mane.

He raised his hand, which was covered by a black glove, and made an imperious gesture. They might not share the same language, but the meaning was obvious. *Stay there.*

Esania bristled. Nobody told her what to do, ever. In the Serakhine, she'd been a freewoman, a *senator* with a near-perfect integration score. She answered only to Primean law. *Her* law.

I am not going to let this creature assume superiority over me.

"What do you want from me?" She spoke Primean, forcing herself to sound cool and composed, knowing very well that he couldn't understand a word she said.

Abruptly, he stood, his eyes never leaving her face. His wings shifted slightly but remained folded against his back. He was barefoot. He had three toes. He moved silently, fluidly, with the grace of a natural predator.

Esania rose to her knees, intending to get out of the bed. The raised wing-edges made it so hard to get out from the sides, so she would have to exit from the foot of the bed. Seriously, who designed such a ridiculous thing? As she navigated across the soft surface, she desperately tried to hide the fact that her legs were trembling. She was barefoot too, her boots nowhere to be seen. Had he taken them off while she slept? Why did she find that thought so unnerving?

At least she still wore her tunic and thermal undersuit, although she had no way of knowing if he might have removed them at some point too.

As she straightened in indignation, her vision grew dim. She swayed on her knees. Why was she so damn weak? It was maddening.

"*Attu misurash,*" he growled, a whipcrack of a command.

Stay?

Huh. As if she were a trained pet.

This is crazy. This can't be happening to me!

Panic kicked down the doors of her composure. Sweat broke out on her face. She started to hyperventilate, becoming lightheaded, and suddenly, she was on the verge of blacking out. The dazzling ceiling played tricks with her mind as her knees threatened to give way.

Crap. She didn't want to show weakness in front of her captor, but her body betrayed her.

She swayed.

He moved, pale wings flashing.

Whoosh.

Suddenly, he was on his knees before her... on the *bed!* Strong hands curled around her upper arms, preventing her from falling. She was glad he wore gloves, because the last thing she wanted was to feel his icy fingers against her bare skin.

Maybe that was why he wore the gloves; to avoid draining her energy. Could it be that he was actually trying to be considerate of her, or was she just a commodity, to be taken care of because she served some purpose?

Esania shuddered.

His fingers hurt as they into her flesh, as if he didn't know that holding her so tightly would cause her discomfort.

He didn't know anything about her kind at all, did he?

Unable to break out of his iron grip, she had no choice but to look up, meeting his eyes. A faint golden glow suffused his gaze, hinting at untapped power.

Only now, up close, did she really get a sense of how massive he was. His broad, muscular chest stretched the dark fabric of his shirt. The muscles in his arms flexed, and she got the sense he could break her in two if he really wanted to.

Hadn't he been seriously wounded by the Vradhu earlier? Where was the evidence of those injuries now?

She caught a tendril of his scent. Musk, spice, and something else she couldn't identify. To her surprise, he radiated warmth.

Suddenly, he seemed very much *alive,* and the way he looked at her...

Such intense curiosity, but there was also a certain arrogance in his expression, as if to say: *I own you now. You have no power here.*

A chill settled in the pit of her stomach. What was the expression her human servants used?

You're totally screwed.

Before Esania could respond, he leaned forward until their faces were almost touching and inhaled deeply, closing his eyes.

What is this?

Was he trembling?

Esania stiffened. He was doing that thing again. She could *feel* it. The bastard was actually draining her energy just by being close to her. He was a black hole, a living vortex, sucking the life right out of her.

A vampiric, reptilian alien.

If he was a black hole, then she was the stars.

"Stop it," she whispered. She searched for a word, *any* word, and faintly recalled something Calexa said to the Vradhu in that horrible sounding language— Naaga. *"Bogu." Stop.*

"Ah." He exhaled and froze, tipping his head back so the light gilded his dazzling face. To her relief, their lips were no longer almost touching. His eyes opened slowly, and maybe it was just her imagination, but the golden glow of his irises seemed just a little more intense.

"I'm fine," she snapped, trying to wrench herself out of his grasp. "Let me go."

He refused.

"*Attu misurash*," he growled, impatience creeping into his voice. Slowly, he lowered her, and Esania had no choice but to go with him, because her legs felt like jelly, and she was on the verge of blacking out.

As soon as she was comfortably seated on the mattress, he let go. Esania rocked backward, propping herself up on her elbows, gaping at the creature. Almost instantly, she started to feel better, her vision clearing as her body recovered from the effort of standing. The alien remained on his knees. He looked down at her, a slight frown disturbing his pale mouth.

Now he looked perplexed.

"What do you *want*?" Esania couldn't help it. Fear, frustration, indignation—all of it seeped into in her voice.

She hadn't come all this way with her entire human retinue just to end up dead in some strange alien's chambers. Theoretically, the women didn't need her protection anymore —they were as far from the Serakhine and its death squads as they could ever hope to get—but she still felt responsible for her people, especially Sara, who had suffered the most.

Opinionated but good-hearted Sara, who carried Kivik's child.

How far along was she now? Around four months? Esania *had* to make it back to the Vradhu settlement to witness the child's birth, to make sure everything went to plan, to make sure Sara had all the help she needed.

To make sure she was *safe*.

If only she could communicate with this alien and somehow convince him to let her go.

Stars, this was so *frustrating*.

"Don't touch me," she blurted in her native tongue as she held her hands up in front of her, defensively crossing her arms and desperately hoping he could understand her gestures, her tone. "Just don't. Please. *Bogu!*"

To her surprise, the alien raised his gloved hands and

showed her his palms, attempting to placate her. *I'm not going to touch you.*

Huh. That was progress, of sorts.

For a moment, they just stared at each other, unmoving, unblinking.

I need to communicate with him... somehow.

This was her chance to test him, to see what his true intentions were.

Esania took a deep breath and put her hand to her mouth. She made a scooping motion with her fingers and gestured toward her mouth.

Food. Water. She desperately needed to get something in her belly.

In truth, she was parched. Starving. Lightheaded.

Maybe that was why she felt so weak.

"Food!" She made a fist and pretended to chew on it as if it were a chicken leg. He had the sharp teeth of a predator. Did he not chew things from time to time? Or else what were those menacing looking teeth for?

The creature's golden brows drew together in a frown.

"My species needs to eat and drink," she said slowly, patting her stomach. "Just like the *Vradhu.*" He had to understand that word, right? She faintly recalled him exchanging barbs with Ares in the melodic Vradhu tongue. In fact, he looked rather similar to a Vradhu. He had same powerful warrior's frame; tall, broad, and rippling with corded muscle. Even his facial features bore an uncanny resemblance to the Vradhu. He possessed the same slanted eyes, broad nose, and full, sensual lips.

But there was one major difference. He didn't have a tail.

The alien narrowed his eyes. "Vradhu?" He pointed at her. "*Antu?*" He chuckled, then shook his head. "*Tey Vradhu.*"

"Of course I'm not Vradhu, but I need to *eat*, and I'm getting tired of repeating myself." Esania shook her head, her frustration growing. Her stomach growled in protest. Her dry throat begged for water. She didn't know the Naaga words for food or water. How frustrating.

The alien rose to his feet, shaking his head. To Esania's disappointment, he gave her a cold look then stepped up off the bed, turning his back on her. At a loss, she stared at his back, at the elegant lines of his folded wings as he started to walk away.

"You can't leave," she pleaded, something she'd never done before in her life. "Wait, don't go."

Fuck.

She never swore, either.

Esania needed to catch his attention, even if it meant grabbing him by the arm—putting herself at risk. She tried to rise to her feet again. The alien looked over his shoulder and shot her a stern look.

"*Misurash,*" he snapped.

Stay.

This time, his voice was laced with an unmistakable warning.

She'd never heard this tone from him before; it was cold and desolate and utterly frightening.

She froze, becoming acutely aware of the fact that this alien could easily kill her.

He strode across to the massive doors and pressed his palm against them, his movements powerful and deliberate. Everything about him radiated power; the way he walked, the way he spoke, the way he looked at her.

The doors swung open and the alien disappeared, leaving Esania alone on a strange bed in a decadent, light-filled room, feeling so weak she could barely lift a finger.

Thoughts of escape and survival flitted through her mind, but once again, her body betrayed her, and she closed her eyes as she collapsed into the bed.

So tired.

I'll just close my eyes... just for a moment...

Suddenly, she was helpless against the powerful lull of sleep.

Sleep was an escape from this frightening new world, where being Primean meant nothing at all, and deadly creatures stalked the earth and reigned in the skies.

But like most things, sleep was only temporary.

CHAPTER NINE

IMRIL TREMBLED as he strode down Lord Kunlo's decaying corridor, his long legs eating up the cold stone floor. He walked away as fast as he could, wanting to put some distance between himself and the female.

The further he walked, the more uneven his movements became, because he no longer needed to mask his pain. The wound in his side still burned something fierce. He'd cut out the dead flesh and packed it with a wad of soft fabric he'd torn from one of Kunlo's shirts, but it would be a while yet before it was completely healed.

Then there was the matter of the infernal hole in his calf, where the Vradhu spear had stuck him.

He cursed under his breath. It was embarrassing to think that he'd almost been undone by those wild, barbaric fighters.

And it was unbelievable that even now, he couldn't forget about the female and her magnificent *vir*.

One more touch. That's all it would have taken for him to kill her. She was already terribly weakened, yet as he'd set her back down on the bed, he'd strayed *too* close, and the golden energy surrounding her had come into contact with his vortex.

She radiated life. He absorbed it.

Like some reckless fledgling Drakhin, he'd inhaled her essence, filling his empty soul with her warmth.

It felt so good that he could have kept on doing it for an eternity, but then he'd looked into her green eyes as she'd pleaded with him in her strange melodic language.

Desperation. Anger. *Fear.*

She was filled with fury, and yet she was terrified of him.

As soon as he'd tasted the fear in her *vir*, it was like a bucket of ice water had been thrown over him. Her fear reminded him of unspeakable things; shadows of memories that lingered at the edge of his consciousness, too terrible to fully realize.

And yet despite her fear, she'd been defiant, daring to question him, *challenge* him.

None of his servants had ever been like this. Even the Vradhu females who had attempted to win his favor hadn't displayed this much resistance... well, except for Akania, the very last Vradhu he'd spurned before the war.

This soft brown-skinned creature didn't yet understand that she was his, didn't adopt the customary mannerisms of the servile Naaga—*don't make eye contact unless permitted, don't speak unless spoken to, and never, ever contradict your Masters.*

Of course, Imril was far too old to bother with most of that nonsense. The younglings had liked their pomp and ceremony. He preferred simplicity.

He exited the corridor and passed through a covered walkway, catching sight of the wide, glittering lake. From memory, the Drakhin had given it a name—*Sarhil.*

Kunlo had been crazy to live all the way out here in this remote, isolated place on the edge of the Ardu-Sai. The lordling was long gone, most likely killed by the Plague, his eyrie abandoned. Nature had taken hold in his absence, lining the walls and floors with swathes of blue and green moss. Twisting vines and roots snaked through broken windows and dislodged doors, curling around intricate statues and carvings that had been created by skilled Naaga craftsmen.

The entire place was in a state of advanced decay, and Imril had imprisoned his creature—his *Source*—in the only room that retained some semblance of its original grandeur.

Well ventilated and high enough to sit above the encroaching mists of the lake, the spire room was the perfect place to keep her, and thankfully it wasn't hideously decorated like the rest of Kunlo's crumbling eyrie.

Now he just needed to find her something to eat. How could he have forgotten that most land-based creatures needed to consume *other* land-based creatures in order to survive?

Sleeping in Za's Crater must have made him dull-witted. Even he ate on occasion, although that was more for pleasure rather than any real necessity.

The alien, on the other hand... her lips were cracked and dry, her belly lean, her cheeks a little too gaunt. Hunger had been with her long before he snatched her away from the Vradhu pack.

He would have to go in search of food and water.

Imril rounded a corner and paused mid-stride. A sound caught his attention, and it was so faint he might have been imagining things, but his acute hearing had never fooled him before.

It came from a crumbling doorway that led into to the shadows. Beyond the pale stone archways, he caught a glimpse of a wide, dark room.

Shhkt.

There it was again, that faint shuffling noise. He walked inside the room, his feet stirring up dust on the stone floor. Imril sighed. "If you try and escape now, I'll hear you, and then there will be consequences. Plus, you are not permitted to escape. I have taken up residence in this eyrie." He spoke in Naaga, because that was the only language the servants had ever known. They weren't permitted to speak any other tongue. "Show yourself." The last part was unmistakably a command. If the creature was what he thought it was, it would have no choice but to come out.

No Naaga could resist an order from him. It was just the way they were designed.

It was the way *he* was designed.

He waited.

Sure enough, after a brief hesitation, a slender blue figure emerged from behind an oversized fallen statue of a Drakhin. Imril's gaze flicked briefly toward the statue and he made a soft sound of distaste in the back of his throat. Gaudy thing. Why had the younger lords been so obsessed with capturing their likenesses in stone? The face had crumbled off, so it was impossible to see who the statue was supposed to represent.

"M-master?" The Naaga walked forward and prostrated himself at Imril's feet, not daring to look up.

Imril sighed. "Oh, get up *samare*. I am too old to bother with useless etiquette."

The Naaga made a high-pitched sound; an expression of surprise. Slowly, he raised his feathered head. "My Lord. I am at your command." As the Naaga took him in, his white eyes widened in recognition, but the servant didn't dare speak what was on his mind.

Of course the Naaga recognized Imril. No other Drakhin possessed his coloring. He was the pale-skinned demon, the light to counter the darkness that was his ill-tempered twin, Mael.

He was the Lightbringer, the Ancestor's son.

An abomination.

What crap.

Really, all of that was just exaggeration and nonsense.

His unique coloring was the result of a pigment deficiency in his scales, nothing more, nothing less. Imril might be one of the oldest living creatures on Khira, but he wasn't a god or a demon.

And his empire was in ruins.

The servant rose to his feet, and Imril took note of the number tattooed into the his forehead.

357.

One of the third generation. That explained the faint silver aura of *vir* that surrounded him. This Naaga would have seen a few things in his lifetime. Normally, Imril wouldn't have hesitated to feed from him, but now all he could think of was the intoxicating golden *vir* that had rolled off the female, a hundred times sweeter and more potent than this poor wretch's energy.

After one taste of that glorious soul-energy, he was ruined. Nothing else would satisfy him now.

This could become a problem, if he let it.

Would the other brown-skinned creatures have the same effect on him, or was it just this particular female? Was her *vir* different somehow? Perhaps he'd have to capture another one and find out.

"Do you wish to feed, my Lord?" The Naaga bared its neck in the customary pose of submission, averting his eyes.

For some reason, that only irritated Imril, but he couldn't refuse the offer. Hunger roiled through his chest, down his arms, and right into the tips of his scale-covered fingers. He reached down and curled his fingers around the Naaga's neck, drawing the servant's *vir* into his body. Compared to the female's brilliant energy, the Naaga's *vir* felt cold and dull.

Imril fed without relish, without joy, without emotion, treating it as a simple exchange between Master and servant. The Naaga's *vir* wasn't nearly as plentiful as the female's, either. It was like a trickle in a dry creek bed compared to her glorious torrent.

This feeding was *nothing* compared to what he could have with her.

As soon as he finished, he waved 357 away. The servant moved back, keeping a respectful distance.

"What are you called, *samare*?" *Samare. Survivor.* Words held meaning; they were a form of power.

"I am referred to by my number, Lord."

"Was that Kunlo's preference? *Tch.*" Crude bastard. Far too often, the younger lords had treated their servants like disposable objects. For every Naaga they'd killed, they thought they could just clone another one. "Think back, *samare.* You had a name once."

For a moment, the Naaga closed his eyes, and although his features showed no emotion, Imril got the sense he was feeling wistful.

"Rau," he said at last, his voice cracking. "My name is Rau."

"Rau... Ah. Now I remember." Imril searched the labyrinthine twists and turns of his rusty memory. There was too much clutter in his mind. Sometimes he wished he could just erase it all and start afresh. "You used to belong to Vakry, didn't you? How did you end up in Kunlo's possession?"

"First Master lost a wager," Rau sighed. "Second Master selected me as his prize."

"For your *vir*?"

"Kunlo didn't have a *vir*-slave of his own until he acquired me."

"And how often did he feed from you?"

"Daily." A dark shadow crossed the servant's face. For a Naaga, he showed a little *too* much emotion.

"That would have been exhausting."

"Yes, it was." Rau's dark expression turned into one of surprise. "I was weak and undernourished. He rarely gave me enough time to replenish myself and food was scarce."

Imril made a sympathetic noise deep in his throat. "The Power is like a drug to some. They take beyond what is reasonable, especially when they do not understand it. I presume Kunlo is long gone, because you do not look malnourished to me."

"Kunlo is dead." The Naaga nodded solemnly.

"And what revolution is this, Rau?"

"We are currently in the middle of the one-thousandth, four-hundredth and thirty-sixth revolution around the sun since you and your brother fell to Khira, my Lord."

Revolution 1436. So he had been in hibernation for a little under three hundred full revs. It could have been worse.

"And what has happened in that time?"

"I-I am not sure, my Lord. I have not left this place."

"Three hundred revs, and you have not sought to venture out into the greater world?"

"I have everything I need to survive here. The lake water is clean and the *sarukark* are plentiful. The dangerous forest beasts are unable to reach the eyrie. This existence... it is better than what I had before." Rau looked up at him with trusting eyes, simply accepting that Imril was his Master now. Perhaps the thought even gave him some sort of feeling of security.

Imril sighed. "There is a female in the great spire room. Get her clean water for drinking, fresh *sarukark* meat, and whatever fruits or other things you consume in this place. Do it quickly, because she is weak." He thought for a moment. "Then you can arrange for her to bathe, but she is not to leave the spire room. Let me make this clear, Rau. She is my prisoner and my property."

"Yes, Master."

"She is not to be harmed in any way. She is to be protected at all costs. If anything happens to her, or if there are any problems, you tell me straight away."

"Yes, Master."

"And Rau?"

"Yes, Master?"

"Start teaching her how to speak Naaga. The quicker she learns, the easier it will be for all of us. You are not, by any chance, a language implant surgeon, are you?"

"That was not my discipline, Lord."

Even if Rau was trained in fitting the devices, there was no way a language implant could be done in these dilapidated facilities, so the alien—whatever it was—would just have to learn Naaga the old fashioned way. "What *is* your discipline, Rau?"

"I am a Housemaster."

"That is good to know." Naaga could be trained in any discipline, but experienced Housemasters, who were responsible for the general running and upkeep of an eyrie, were rare. "Then your first task is to tend to the female and replenish her *vir* as quickly as possible. I expect her to be ready in three darklights. The next time I go in there to feed, I want her to be strong, Rau. Feed her. Let her bathe. Clothe her. Give her everything she needs to feel comfortable. I imagine she will be experiencing some level of distress at her predicament. Try and get her to relax." With time, the creature would learn that Imril wasn't a threat to her. He just needed to feed.

"Yes, my Lord." This time, Imril's orders were received with almost a certain amount of relish... but no, he was just imagining things. Naaga weren't supposed to feel any emotions. A good Naaga was like a sponge, ready to absorb whatever emotion the Master was feeling, ready to respond to its Master's needs without having to ask questions.

A good Naaga was a mirror of its Master's soul.

"Master, am I permitted to speak a thought?"

"You're full of surprises, Rau. Next time, don't ask. Even when I'm in a bad mood, I will not kill you for having a thought."

"It is good to know that the Lightbringer is finally ready to take a mate."

Imril's good mood evaporated then, and it must have shown, because Rau flinched in anticipation, fear crossing his milky white eyes.

No, this Naaga was definitely capable of feeling emotion.

Imril went very still. "You are mistaken, Naaga. She is not

Vradhu, and I have not taken her as my mate. Now get out of my sight."

For some reason, Rau's words got under his skin.

The servant bowed deeply and scurried out, and Imril knew he would take good care of the female, because no Naaga had ever disobeyed him.

They were biologically programmed to obey his word.

That was simply the way the Ancestor had designed them, and the sound of Imril and Mael's voices were powerfully imprinted upon their genetic memory.

So Rau would never disobey him, *ever*.

Words were power.

Imril was going to take back his world, one Naaga servant at a time.

And if he found out that Nykithus was still alive...

The bastard would learn the price of betrayal, in the most painful of ways.

CHAPTER TEN

WATER.

Esania woke to the sound of water being poured into a glass.

Am I dreaming?

No, there was a tray on the bed beside her, and on it was a silver cup and a jug and a dish laden with some sort of gelatinous pink meat.

The meat was sliced into delicate strips, which were arranged in a perfect circle that reminded her of that Earthian delicacy, *sashimi*.

Her stomach growled.

She looked up, half expecting to see the shimmering winged monster again, but instead she was greeted by a blue-skinned Naaga.

It—she couldn't tell whether it was male or female—stared back at her with an unnerving white gaze, its featureless eyes devoid of any pupil or iris.

She froze. "Don't touch me," she warned, crossing her arms defensively. She'd seen the Naaga on the *Hythra* before the massive destroyer had crashed down to the surface of Khira. One of the blue creatures had almost killed Calexa.

The Naaga shrugged and spread its hands wide. Then it pointed at the water and food. "*Tevch,*" it said, then left.

"Wait..." But before Esania could say anything, the Naaga disappeared through a small side-door that swung shut with a resounding clang.

Huh. She hadn't noticed that door before.

There would be time to examine it later. Right now, she just needed to *eat*.

She chugged down the water, finished one glass, then poured herself another, and another. It was cool and pure and refreshing, and just about the best thing she'd ever tasted.

Then she turned to the meat. What was it? Protein, obviously. But would it make her sick? On this one, she would just have to trust that her enhanced Primean immune system and bioenhanced liver—capable of eliminating toxins at a much faster rate than humans—would be able to protect her.

It wouldn't make sense that her strange alien captor would want to poison her.

There was a utensil on the side; a long, elegant two-pronged fork made of a shiny metal that looked like a cross between copper and gold. Esania stared at it for a moment, blinking. She shook her head as the surreal nature of her surroundings—the ornate bed, the soaring ceilings, the pristine polished floors—hit her like a punch in the gut. And this small detail, this perfectly formed *instrument*... After living in the forest for weeks, it was so strange to be holding something so finely crafted.

Wherever she was, she wasn't in Vradhu territory anymore. This was a sophisticated, highly advanced civilization.

Drakhin.

And now she was eating mysterious pink flesh with a Drakhin fork. At least it didn't smell bad.

Her stomach rumbled again, and her mouth began to

water. Without a second thought, Esania picked up a piece of the strange meat with her fork and ate.

Hmm...

Cool. Firm. Slightly sweet, yet fishy.

Not unpleasant, though.

And definitely raw.

Slowly, her energy returned. She finished her food, drank down the jug of water, and got up off the bed, walking barefoot across the cool stone floor. Really, it was a pleasant space, bright and airy and just the right temperature, reminding her of the temperature-controlled garden-spaces of the Serakhine, where the artificial sun had provided them with warmth at a constant twenty-four degrees Celsius all year round.

She wanted to look outside, to get a sense of her surroundings, but really, those windows were too damn high. What kind of person made a room with windows one couldn't see out of?

Esania's blood ran cold as she realized what this deceptively pleasant room *really* was—a prison.

She ran her palm along the wall, feeling its rough-yet-smooth surface, feeling for any cracks or weaknesses or defects, until she came to a small irregularity; a part of the wall that shifted slightly beneath her fingers.

She pushed against it, and white dust fell to the floor.

What is this?

She pushed again, and bits of stone flaked away, revealing a faint outline. It looked like a part of the wall was loose, and perhaps she could just pry it away like a puzzle piece, revealing whatever was out there.

Esania almost broke into a run as she returned to the bed and retrieved the copper-gold fork. She inserted its thin prongs into a crack above the defect and pulled.

One, two, three. Three tugs and a chunk of wall the size of her fist fell away, revealing...

Another chunk.

Painstakingly, she removed this too, then another one, inserting her fork into the narrow space and jimmying the thing until the chunks slid toward her. At least there was enough space between the solid wall and the pieces, as if someone had designed them to be removed this way.

It was slow, repetitive work, but Esania was driven by desperation and the Primean obsessiveness that kicked in every time she started a task.

She wouldn't rest until she was finished.

By the time she reached the last piece, she was breathless and sweating, her body reminding her that she wasn't yet fully recovered.

Imagine if the Drakhin walked in and saw her now; clutching a metal fork, her face and arms covered in white dust, wall-rocks scattered around her feet.

Exhausted.

Again.

She didn't care. She *had* to know what was on the other side.

A small cavity had opened up in the wall now, just large and wide enough to admit her head.

What is this thing?

Why have something like this in the seamless wall, and why go to such lengths to conceal it? It was almost as if someone had been slowly carving out sections of the wall with a small implement... perhaps they'd been trying to escape.

She shuddered.

Esania took a deep breath and removed the final piece, a flat stone the size of her fist.

Bright sunlight shot through the wall, nearly blinding her. It was followed by a gust of cool, crisp breeze. She blinked the dust from her eyes and peered outside.

And froze.

The first thing she saw was the brilliant blue sky of Khira, stretching out into eternity. She stared out into the distance and saw the hazy blue outline of a mountain range. A vast canopy of trees stretched out alongside it, shades of red and orange and brown and green coalescing to form a brilliant patchwork of color.

Large bodies of water were scattered amongst the trees, shimmering in the bright sunlight so that they appeared almost silver. Esania angled her head, trying to look directly downwards, but it was impossible. The opening was too small.

But she could see the shimmering body of water that surrounded the tower. A massive lake surrounded her, stretching all the way to the foot of the mountain range.

Spectacular.

A prison with a spectacular view. If the lake surrounded this tower on all sides, then there was no way she could escape.

As the wind whipped at the ends of her braids, a terrible realization struck her. Judging from how far into the distance she could see, she was very, very high up indeed.

"*Tu kyi naka?*" A sharp voice jolted her out of her observations, and she yanked her head out of the hole, spinning around. The blue servant stood in the center of the room, eyes narrowed, arms folded in front of him—well, at least she *thought* it was a he—in a distinctly disapproving manner.

Esania tightened her grip around the fork. "I was just taking a look," she said slowly, knowing she was caught in the act and there was nothing she could do about it. She shrugged. What was the big scary Drakhin going to do if he found out? Punish her?

There was no escaping from this tower. Not through the hole in the wall, anyway. That was a certain route to death.

A suicide route...

Unless one had wings.

To her surprise, the Naaga just muttered something under his breath and scurried across the room, pushing her out of the way. He gathered up the wall-pieces and put them back in perfect order, as if he'd done this a hundred times before.

With a sigh, he retrieved something from inside his white tunic—a tubelike metal device—and sucked up the dust until not a single speck was left on the glistening surface. His movements were fast and efficient, and the whole mess was cleaned up in just a few seconds.

The Naaga pointed to the other side of the room. A clear-walled tub filled to the brim with water had materialized out of nowhere. Fresh, crisply folded garments were arranged on the bed.

"*Pardu,*" he said, the meaning obvious.

Bathe.

They exchanged a look. The Naaga tapped his foot. There was an air of mild exasperation about him, even though his elegant features conveyed very little emotion.

"Don't worry, I get it." Esania turned away from the wall, brushing the white dust off her arms. That earned her a sharp look from the Naaga.

Oops.

He'd just cleaned the floor. She made a gesture of apology with her hand. "You're not going to stay here while I have a bath, are you?"

The Naaga dropped to his knees and cleaned up the rest of her mess.

"Let me guess. The mighty Drakhin wants me cleaned up and dressed to his liking before he's willing to come in here again?"

No answer. Of course, Esania wasn't expecting one, but speaking her mind helped her to feel as if she still retained some semblance of control.

So why did she feel like she was the sacrificial virgin all of a sudden?

The Naaga stood. Esania waved him away. *Go.*

He walked straight past her without any acknowledgment whatsoever, disappearing through the little door on the other side of the room.

She didn't know whether to feel offended or relieved. Briefly, she contemplated not bathing at all just to spite the infuriating Drakhin, but the water looked so inviting, and she hadn't had a proper bath since...

Well, in longer than she could remember.

If she was going to be the servant, energy source, *whatever*, then at least she would be a clean one.

CHAPTER ELEVEN

THREE DAYS.

Esania counted the number of times light and darkness had graced the windows overhead as she lay in her bed, wearing the soft white dress the Naaga had provided her with.

Three days passed and still there was no sign of the Drakhin. The Naaga servant—she'd since learned that he was called Rau—came and went, leaving food and water, snapping terse one-word commands. Berries, salty leaves, raw meat, nuts. Not unpleasant, but not the tastiest fare either. At least she wasn't starving anymore, and none of it had killed her... yet.

Occasionally, Rau would point something out to her, then say the word in his language, as if he were expecting her to learn these things.

He *wanted* her to learn his language.

So she was here for the long run, then.

Once a day, the clear bathtub would mysteriously appear, only to disappear after she was finished bathing, and always when she wasn't looking.

How does he do that?

She'd long since given up trying to figure it out. Rau was *very* good at his job. The Naaga was the consummate attendant. Efficient, unobtrusive, quiet. Her girls could learn a thing or two from him, only they weren't *her* girls anymore. Technically, the humans she'd rescued from the Fiveways were now all freewomen.

Did any of them actually miss her now that she was gone? Esania hadn't been the warmest of bosses, but she had saved their lives. Surely that counted for something, and hopefully, the Vradhu were searching for her. Ares-with-wings seemed to be her only hope of rescue, but he was injured, possibly dead.

And what could he do against a pale, winged monster who wielded raw energy from his hands?

What could *she* do?

Esania slid off the bed and padded across the room, heading for the small door in the wall. Three days of rest and nourishment had done wonders, and she almost felt back to her normal self again. The bone-crushing weariness was gone, and there was no way she was going to become lightheaded or black out again.

The way she'd been with the Drakhin last time... it was almost embarrassing.

She pressed her palm against the black door as she reached it, wondering what was on the other side. Both this one and the massive double doors were locked; she knew this because she'd inspected them countless times.

Three days, and she was growing restless, wondering what was going to happen next.

Perhaps she should ambush Rau when he came through that little door and make a run for it...

What a stupid idea. Besides, she didn't mind the blue guy. He'd given her everything she needed and hadn't hurt her in the slightest.

She couldn't imagine bashing him in the face or knocking him out. Primeans of her station had no need for violence.

Voom. The door opened suddenly, and she stepped back, letting Rau pass.

The Naaga glared at her, bidding her to follow. "*Nug,*" he said. There was something in his arms; a garment of some sort.

He seemed to be in a hurry.

He seemed tense.

Something was about to happen, and she guessed it had everything to do with the Drakhin.

"He's coming to feed, isn't he?" She eyed the garment in Rau's hands with suspicion. "And I'm supposed to wear that and get down on my knees and give him exactly what he expects."

Just the thought of being *on tap* for this energy sucking monster was enough to make her nauseated. Angry, too, that she couldn't do anything about it.

How utterly demeaning.

Rau thrust the garment in her face. It was a jacket of some sort, made of shimmering golden fabric that was similar in color of the Drakhin's hair.

"No thanks." Esania tossed it on the bed. "It's too warm for that." Now that she'd recovered, it was time to push back a little, to refuse the status quo.

To her surprise, Rau didn't force her to do anything. He just gave her a cryptic look and slipped away, as soundless and unobtrusive as ever, ignoring her completely as he disappeared through his little side door.

It swung closed with a certain sense of finality, leaving her alone in silence to await her fate.

If the all-powerful Drakhin wanted to take her life-force, she had no way of stopping him. Beyond simple gestures, she had no way of communicating with him.

And there was no escape from this high tower in the sky.

No, this wasn't a battle she was going to win by force or daring escapades. If she was going to survive, she was going to have to learn the Drakhin's weaknesses...

And manipulate them.

Stars, how was she even supposed to *begin* to do that?

CHAPTER TWELVE

"SHE IS READY FOR YOU, my Lord."

"You gave her something warm to wear?"

"Yes."

"Good. Take your leave, Rau." Imril pressed his hand against the door lever, his trembling fingers betraying the seething hunger within.

For three darklights, he'd rested in the lower halls of Kunlo's decaying fortress, seeking even the tiniest shred of information about the new world outside, staying as far away from the female as possible.

Who ruled now? That fool Nykithus? The thought made him seethe inside.

What had happened to the tens of thousands of Naaga slaves when their masters suddenly died? More importantly, what had happened to the Vradhu mates?

He'd found nothing, just bare walls and vegetation and scattered debris and the half-insane echoes inside his own head.

Still too injured to risk flying, he'd curled up in the crumbling North spire in a light-filled room without windows or walls. Its curving archways were covered in twisting green vines, and a family of small winged *pettichen* had taken up residence in one of the alcoves.

Twitatwitawhoo. Occasionally, the small black creatures would irritate him with their shrill, high-pitched nattering, but not enough for him to lob an idle blast of power in their direction.

Why should he disturb them when they'd been here first?

Crossing his legs, folding his wings, he'd stared out at the world below, watching as light and shadow fell across the wild forest, keeping perfectly still as small furred creatures and insects skittered across the moss covered floor. The morning mists came and went, coating his body in a fine sheen of moisture, but he was oblivious to it all, submerged deep in the crumbling labyrinth of his memories.

Oh, he was far too old to remember everything in sequence. Memories came and went, some fully formed, some half decayed.

His wounds healed slowly, and several times he had to scrape the dead flesh out of his side to get rid of the Vradhu poison.

Just when he thought he could endure the hunger no longer, Rau had come and informed him the female was back to her full strength.

That was the reason he was here, opening the door, striding into her light-filled chambers, ready to fill himself with the intoxicating nectar from this soft, fragile creature.

Mine.

His prize.

Already, he could see her, smell her, *feel* her.

She sat on end of the bed with her bare feet planted firmly on the floor, dressed in a simple white garment that covered her arms up to her elbows and ended at her knees—the kind that might be worn by a Vradhu female. Rau had sourced it from somewhere deep within Kunlo's storehouses, and Imril found it distinctly pleasing. It was a fraction too large for her, accentuating her slenderness and willowy limbs, its neckline opening to reveal the graceful bones beneath her neck, and just a glimpse of her pert cleavage.

For an alien, she was not... *unpleasant* to look at.

The female sat with her head bowed, not making eye contact even though she was well aware of his presence.

There was a certain insolence written into her pose, as if she were saying: *I will acknowledge you on my terms.*

A soft groan escaped Imril's lips as he walked into the radius of her glorious golden *vir*. It was as rich and plentiful as he'd ever seen it, radiating off her body like mist. He didn't think he'd ever seen a creature with *vir* as powerful as hers.

She was all he needed.

He took a deep breath and inhaled pure energy.

Perfect.

Like a drug.

The sting of his wounds lessened, and his footsteps became more fluid. Power began to fill his *vir*-channels.

And that was only a taste of what was to come.

Suddenly, he didn't care that his entire world had crumbled and turned into ashes and dust, that he had only himself to blame for the ruin of his empire.

He had *her*.

The Source.

And everything would be fine.

He came to a stop in front of her and she looked up, her startling green eyes locking onto his.

Imril froze.

Pure green, the color of a deep forest lake or a new *quinze* leaf at the turn of the season, before Mael had brought down the shadowring and killed that entire species of spectacular plants.

Pure, crystalline green; eyes that were *definitely* not of this world.

But then again, neither was he.

She held him with her gaze, demanding his complete, undivided attention. *How does she do that?*

And then she smiled and placed a hand on her chest. "Esania," she said.

Esania. Her name.

Oh? Now this creature wanted him to know her name? This wasn't how a terrified servant would behave. Just like words, names held power.

He stared down at her but didn't offer his own name in return. Her smile never wavered, and yet it wasn't a friendly smile. Its softness hid hard edges; more of a challenge than a greeting.

Imril wasn't used to such looks from anyone, even other Drakhin.

His eyes narrowed.

Know your place, creature.

Still wearing the gloves he'd found in Kunlo's war room, he reached out and gently stroked the side of her face, a veiled threat if there ever was one.

This time, he wasn't going to touch her until he was ready; until he was sure he could control his feeding.

As expected, her smile disappeared, but then she did something that blew Imril's mind.

She tipped her head to the side ever so slightly and bared her neck.

An act of submission... of trust.

She should not be the one to initiate it. He was supposed to be the one to *demand* this.

How did she know that this tiny action was so provocative, so *powerful?*

Unable to hold back any longer, Imril hissed and tore the black glove from his hand, curling his fingers around her neck.

Her skin was warm, soft, smooth, her neck so delicate and fragile he could snap it with his bare hands.

Her pulse beat beneath his fingers, and it was surprisingly steady.

Then it hit him.

"Ah..." He exhaled slowly as her glorious *vir* surged up through his arm, filling him with the power he'd craved, flowing into the deep well that was his empty soul.

What he'd taken from her before... it was nothing compared to what he was about to drain.

As Imril grew *vir*-drunk on her heady energy, taking more and more of the golden nectar into his body, it occurred to him that he hadn't been the one to initiate this feeding.

She'd *forced* him to lose control.

Just like that.

And the well of her energy was deep, just like his hunger.

Warmth spread through Imril's body as his cells converted living energy into power.

He did not question why he needed *vir* to survive or why his body could transform it into pure energy. He did not wonder why only females of certain species seemed to give off the golden *vir* that every Drakhin craved, and why the Naaga, the *made* race, were only capable of producing bland, silver *vir* that paled in comparison to the rich energy of the females.

There was a time when he used to wonder about such things, but his father, the cursed Ancestor, had left more mysteries than truths, and perhaps some things would never be explained.

As he stared down at her, growing more and more intoxicated, she looked back at him, her green eyes wide and unwavering.

For the first time, he was struck by the intelligence in her gaze.

Where did you come from, sweet thing?

This alien might be soft-skinned and weak, but she was no fool. She knew *exactly* what he was doing to her. Resentment radiated from her, even as Imril's hand tightened around her neck.

Oh, she tried to hide it from him, but she couldn't. He could feel it in her *vir*.

He closed his eyes and took a deep, shuddering breath, trying to convince himself this was like any other feeding; a simple master and servant transaction.

Esania.

She'd told him her name.

His wounds began to heal; he felt the familiar itch as his true skin knitted together. His scales would take longer to grow back, but at least the pain was starting to diminish. Three dark-lights he'd waited for this, putting up with the very specific, excruciating kind of pain that came from a Vradhu barb.

And although he'd fed from Rau, the other one's *vir* just didn't interest him. *This* was what he wanted. Pure, undiluted bliss.

More. Give me more.

As the *vir* flowing into his body reached the sweet point, Imril's senses grew sharper. He became aware of the sound of her breathing; slow, steady, but with an almost imperceptible hitch now and then. He studied her in intense detail, noting the way her round black pupils constricted slightly, watching in fascination as her long, dark eyelashes fluttered against her silky brown skin.

Her features were elegant, symmetrical, *perfect*. A high forehead, straight nose, full lips. Her skin was perfectly smooth, in contrast to his.

Soft. She was softer and more delicate than a female Vradhu, lacking the sharp teeth and claws that made the violet-skinned ones so irritating to deal with.

You're not made for this world, are you, sweet thing?

His cock grew hard, surprising him once again. Maybe he was just drunk on *vir,* but he suspected it was something else.

Her perfect combination of submission and defiance.

It seeded a certain kind of madness within him.

Fuck.

She rubbed her upper arms. Fine spots rose on her brown skin. Her teeth started to knock together. *Chattering.*

What was this sudden reaction?

Too much? Was he going too far?

You need to stop, Drakhin.

He didn't want to kill her.

With great effort, he pulled his hand away, even though he wasn't yet sated, even though he was just starting to feel like his old self again.

Then Imril froze.

Slender fingers curled around his wrist, staying his hand. She stared at him, growing weaker and weaker by the moment.

But she wasn't afraid.

Did she not realize how *dangerous* he was to her right now? Just a fraction more and he could drain her to the point of no return.

Her heart would stop beating. Her body would go cold.

He knew. He'd done this once before.

"Stop," he growled, wrenching his wrist out of her grasp. He took a step backward, power coursing through his veins. It crackled from his fingertips and sent a golden haze across his vision. "I do *not* want to kill you."

Teeth still chattering, she leaned back on her elbows and had the audacity to *smile* at him.

For some reason, that angered Imril. "You would risk your life just to prove a point?" He spoke in his original tongue, the language of the Ancestor, and of course, she couldn't understand a word he said. Rau was supposed to teach her Naaga, but nobody learned a language in three darklights, not without an implant.

And he would never allow her to speak Drakhin, because that was the language of power, spoken by his people alone.

With power snapping and writhing at his fingertips,

responding to his anger, Imril leaned in and picked up the golden jacket Rau had retrieved from some mysterious place. "Never do that again. *Ever*," he snapped, knowing she would at least understand the warning in his tone. He thrust the jacket at her. "Put this on. Warm yourself up."

It was a ceremonial jacket, an old thing, the kind that might be donned by a Vradhu female to preserve warmth after a ritual feeding. It was the younger Drakhin who had invented these strange customs and rituals. Imril didn't care much for such things, but the garment was warm and finely made, and seemed to have survived the ravages of time well enough.

With trembling fingers, she took it and slipped it on.

Imril couldn't help but admire the way the fine golden fabric complimented the warm brown tones of her skin.

Still, he was angry. In that brief moment, she had tempted him, challenged him, and forced him to reveal an important truth.

She was *valuable* to him.

And there was no way for him to punish her, because he needed her in perfect health.

She knew it. She was telling him, loud and clear, that she knew it.

What a risk she had taken. Was this delicate creature actually *mad*?

No, she was calculating.

Her *vir* was softer now, a tantalizing, ephemeral halo that beckoned to him even as he backed away.

"Next time, I won't be so forgiving," he growled, his wings lifting threateningly. "Know your place, servant. Do you really want to die?"

Her eyes never left him, even as he turned his back and left through the wide doors, feeling stronger than he had in a long time.

But nowhere near his full strength.

He needed more *vir*. A *lot* more.

Soon.

Next time, he wouldn't be so reckless.

So this impudent little creature thought she could vex him, huh? He, who had once ruled the greatest civilization that ever existed on this wild, hidden planet?

As he watched her, something shifted deep within his soul, and an ancient rhythm began to pulse through his veins. A dark, primal song spread through every fiber of his being. Instantly, he knew what it was, even though he'd never heard it before.

Could it be...?

Song of the Void Between Worlds.

He had to be imagining things.

So quickly? *This* creature, this alien—he didn't even know what *species* she was—was having this effect on him?

Impossible.

And here she was, looking at him with a secret smile hovering on her lips. This alien thought she could play games with him?

He was going to have to teach her that she wasn't as irreplaceable as she thought. Oh, she was special, all right, but Imril would not allow himself to become dependent on a single Source.

It was too dangerous, especially when she had *this* effect on him.

He turned and stalked out of the room, slamming the doors behind him, activating the lock with a flick of his hand.

Sealing his prisoner inside, even as his cock grew hard at the thought of her.

CHAPTER THIRTEEN

AS THE DOORS SLAMMED SHUT, Esania let out a deep, shuddering sigh. Was it possible to feel drained and angry and smug and terrified and mildly aroused, all at the same time?

Because that's how she felt right now, with the memory of the Drakhin Lord's touch lingering at the base of her neck, where her skin still tingled.

Surreptitiously, she ran her fingers over the area, replaying the moment in her mind's eye. This time, his touch hadn't been painful or forceful. He'd been gentle with her even as he'd sucked her dry.

Like a parasite.

A beautiful, terrifying parasite.

What he'd done to her was hideous, monstrous, and it defied any logical explanation. Extracting pure energy through touch?

It wasn't even *scientific*. It was woo-woo stuff, straight out of the fanciful stories humans made up to entertain themselves.

And to think she'd encouraged him.

What the hell did you just do, woman?

She'd taken a risk, and it had worked... perhaps.

As she'd predicted, the Drakhin had finally come and claimed his dues. He'd pulled the raw energy out of her, drinking it in as if it were water, leaving her shivering and drained, and the look on his face...

He'd enjoyed it.

And surprisingly, so had she, up until the point where he'd taken so much energy from her that he'd pushed her body into a kind of hypothermia.

His hand on her neck had been firm, but not painful, the pads of his fingers smooth and without the scales that covered the rest of his body. When his... *vortex,* or whatever it was, collided with her energy, the feeling was electric.

A dark, irresistible caress.

As he'd stared down at her with those glowing catlike eyes, she'd almost felt...

Aroused?

Impossible.

That would be entering serious Stockholm Syndrome territory, and she was Primean.

She should know better.

Only humans succumbed to things like that.

Esania tucked her hands into the folds of the impossibly soft jacket, reveling in the sumptuous feel of the fabric, even as she desperately tried to get warm. The garment was incredibly well made, although it smelled slightly musty, as if it had been stored away in someone's closet for a very long time.

Crazy Drakhin.

Leaving her here freezing, half-drained and wearing a splendid musty old jacket with a high collar and intricately patterned buttons. It could have come straight out of some history archive on Earth.

Bastard. He thinks I'm his property.

But she'd achieved what she'd set out to do.

He'd needed something from her, and instead of fighting him, she'd *invited* him to feed.

Doing the unexpected.

Throwing him off balance.

Making him realize how valuable she was to him, and no, he didn't want to kill her. She was certain of that now.

Esania curled up into a ball, fighting the shivers that racked her entire body. Her feet were cold. She couldn't even feel her toes anymore. *Numb.*

Numb toes, racing heart, thoughts on fire.

Was she reckless, or stupid, or both?

As weak as she was, Esania forced herself to get up out of bed and pace around on bare feet, trying to generate some warmth. The next time he appeared, she would ask the Drakhin to give her damn boots back. Still shivering, she pulled up the collar of her jacket and tucked her hands into her armpits.

Well, at least her teeth had stopped chattering.

So you've gone ahead and poked the big bad dragon with a stick. What are you going to do now?

She had no choice but to wait. Clearly rattled, he'd left in a huff, shooting her a dark glare as he pulled his wings tightly against his back and slammed the double doors with a vengeance. She had no way of knowing if he'd be back in a few minutes, or hours, or days, or even months.

She had no power here.

But her actions had caused a reaction in him.

Now she just had to wait and see what he would do.

After all, every action had an equal and opposite reaction, didn't it?

CHAPTER FOURTEEN

IMRIL DRIFTED SILENTLY over the clouds, watching for any trace of life below. The dense trees obscured his view of the land, but it didn't matter.

He was hunting for *vir,* and even from up here, his sharp eyes wouldn't miss even the slightest hint of a golden aura. He circled the spot where he'd picked up the creature, *Esania,* searching for any clues as to where the Vradhu and their brown-skinned companions might have gone.

Thanks to Esania, he was stronger now, strong enough to hunt without fear of the Vradhu. He'd found a suit of Drakhin scale-armor in Kunlo's war room, and now the second scales covered every part of him from head to toe, leaving only his eyes and wings uncovered.

No Vradhu barb or war-spear would be able to penetrate his armor, and if he was unlucky enough to encounter a kratok beast, he would be well protected.

As he angled his wings, swooping down toward the forest, Imril growled, unable to get a certain face out of his mind.

Esania.

Such a bold female. It wasn't just her *vir* that was addictive.

That piercing stare. Those mesmerizing, impossibly green eyes, the color of the new leaf-buds on the *quinze* trees, which he'd just seen dotted amongst the forest canopy. Impossibly, even as other parts of the Ardu-Sai died off, the spectacular trees were coming back to life after hundreds of revolutions in hibernation.

Just as he had come back to life—thanks to *her*.

This alien, this *female*... where had she come from?

She reminded him of something, of *someone,* of a time when he knew nothing about the world below and believed everything he was told.

But that was long ago, the memories buried so deep within his consciousness that they were barely a part of him anymore.

He dropped into the clearing, landing feet first, his scale-armor moving in perfect synergy with his body. From memory, Kunlo had been a head shorter than him and thicker in the torso, but Drakhin armor was designed to mold to the wearer's frame, so it had stretched to accommodate his size.

He carried no weapon. He didn't need one.

Power pounded through his body, and really, it wasn't his energy but *hers,* a constant reminder that without *vir*, he was nothing.

He began to walk, folding his wings against his back and following the trail left behind by the Vradhu. Alone, the warriors were impeccable trackers and hunters, and they would have left no trace of their passing, not even a scent. But they had females with them, and they'd obviously left in a hurry.

Imril closed his eyes and took a deep breath, inhaling the scents of the forest. Flowers. Berries. Decaying leaves. Even the pungent smell of some small animal's droppings. The cycle of life and death went on, accelerated now because the sun had appeared for the first time in over three hundred revolutions.

There.

His eyes snapped open as he caught it.

A trace of something otherworldly, easy to identify because it was similar to Esania's scent. He swore he could even detect *her* scent mingled in with the others.

Imril walked across to the place where he'd first put his hands on Esania, a barren patch of land surrounded by straggly *tchirrin* bushes. Evidence of her struggle was still there on the ground; a small cloth pouch filled with bittersweet orange fruits lay in the dust.

The strap was broken. It must have snapped when he'd stolen her away.

Imril picked up the thing, knotted the strap, and hung it around his neck, taking care not to damage the fruits inside. Judging from their smell, they were just at the point of maximum sweetness.

Those who knew him would have shaken their heads in disbelief at the sight; Imril the Lightbringer, dressed in full Drakhin battle-armor, carrying a pouch of sweet *tchirrin* fruit around his neck.

But he'd always been considered strange; he knew the lesser lords had whispered such things behind his back.

The Overlord has been on this world for too long. Age has turned him mad, the same as his cursed brother. Abominations, both of them.

They never would have dared say a word of it to his face.

He'd been known to kill on a whim, and he was too powerful for any of them to seriously consider challenging him —or so he'd thought.

Following his nose, Imril moved across the clearing, heading for a thicket of trees.

His eyes snapped skyward as a familiar sound reached his ears.

Whoosh.

A dark shadow streaked overhead, and his gaze snapped toward the skies. He caught sight of a sleek black ship as it coasted overhead, disappearing into the distance. It was a Drakhin ship, the sort used to transport servants and cargo over long distances. Once, every Drakhin had owned a fleet of the black ships—another gift from the Ancestor's collection of dark technology.

Two more ships streaked past, signifying that this wasn't an ordinary transport mission.

Imril growled.

Deathkiss was supposed to have killed most of the Drakhin lords, and the Naaga couldn't operate the ships on their own... could they?

Whoever it was, perhaps they were here for the same reason. There was a valuable prize in their midst.

He beat his wings, once, twice, three times, and shot up into the sky, gaining speed as a cool gust of wind buffeted him from below. Faster he flew, *faster*, until he caught sight of three black specks in the distance.

The ships.

His prey.

Imril caught them easily, soaring overhead, matching their speed. The three ships flew in a spearhead formation until they started to decelerate, slowly dropping until they hovered over a thick, twisting *sekkhoi* thicket. Imril swooped down and landed on the roof of the first ship, where he crouched and stuck his fingers into a narrow seam, hanging on tightly as hot wind swirled around him.

Instantly, he saw what they were looking for.

A golden glow drifted up through the trees. *Vir.*

He realized what this was—a hunting party. As the ship touched down on the ground, something noxious invaded his senses, making him feel lightheaded and nauseated.

Poison. Where is it coming from?

How did the Naaga have chemical weapons? The scent triggered powerful memories. Suddenly, he was back on the

Hythra, locked in a testing chamber as noxious gas poured in from the vents.

Enraged, he dropped to his knees coughing, choking, cursing his sadistic father. He tried to summon his power, but he was too weak. Thick shackles encircled his wrists, his legs, his neck. His wings were pinned together by a metal wire that pierced through the taut membrane, causing agony every time he moved. Behind him, his broken tail hung limp, the poison barb gone. It had lodged nicely in the bastard's neck, but then Acheros dematerialized, evading the poison by just a heartbeat.

And now he was here, shackled and tortured.

This was the price of defiance. Acheros wanted him broken.

He shook his head, fighting the darkness that threatened to swallow him whole, fighting the urge to destroy everything in his path.

Yes, chemical weapons were definitely an Auka thing. Imril had expressly forbidden their use on Khira, but someone had obviously been developing them in his absence.

He had a good idea who that might be.

Imril glanced to one side and cursed softly under his breath.

An odorless mist poured out of a vent in the transport's side. Imril coughed and his helm responded automatically by shifting and merging with his scale-armor, becoming an airtight filter.

The Ancestor's technology never failed.

As he breathed easier, he looked around and saw a flash of movement in the surrounding forest.

Vradhu. At least half a dozen of them.

The Vradhu started to cough. Several dropped to their knees, gasping, cursing. *Poisoned.*

Angry shouts pierced the commotion, but he couldn't understand the language. Two humans burst through the thicket, fierce females brandishing strange weapons. Like him, they wore armor, but theirs was strange—clunky gear that creaked when they walked. Clearly, these aliens possessed technology that was much more advanced than the simple spears and blades of the Vradhu, but it didn't hold a flame to the mysterious gifts that had been left to the Drakhin by the Ancestor.

Golden *vir* rose from their bodies, thick and powerful, but he wasn't drawn to either of them in the slightest.

His friend Tykhe had once tried to explain this phenomenon to him. It was said that once a Drakhin found his True Source—the one he chose to give his *elgida* to—no other *vir* would satisfy.

His suspicion was confirmed.

Esania had already ruined him.

"Run!" one of the Vradhu shouted, his voice hoarse, but the brown-skinned creatures didn't move. Instead, they glared at the ship, an unspoken challenge in their eyes. The ship landed with a gentle *thud,* and Imril remained crouched on its roof. One of the aliens swiveled on her heel, her eyes widening in recognition as she raised her weapon, pointing it at him. Imril lifted his head and glared back at her.

For a moment, they locked eyes.

Do not attack me. I am not your enemy right now. I can help you.

He shook his head once, making a slicing motion with his hand.

Wait.

The alien shook her head slowly, and he could have *sworn* she rolled her eyes.

With a soft hiss, the ship's hatch opened and dozens of Naaga streamed out, brandishing strange triangular devices that Imril had never seen before.

Imril rose to his feet. "Stop," he said, speaking the language of slaves. *Naaga.* The language of power and submission, that was drilled into their genetic memory.

The only language they knew. They weren't capable of learning other tongues.

To his shock, the Naaga ignored his words.

What is this?

He, the Overlord of Khira, who wasn't used to being ignored, *ever*, had just been dismissed by a group of insolent Naaga. They didn't even spare him a second glance.

How dare they?

Were they defective somehow? Had they not heard him?

He didn't have time to think about it, because the Naaga had almost reached the fallen Vradhu. The females shouted at one another, their voices full of panic.

Boom!

With ruthless efficiency, one of the aliens lifted her weapon and shot the lead Naaga in the head. The noise was deafening, shaking a flock of winged shrieking *gwar* from the treetops above.

Huh. So these aliens could be aggressive too.

The leader fell. The rest advanced.

To the casual observer, it might seem like an insane strategy, but Imril understood. He'd seen Naaga used in war before. Some foolish Drakhin had taken to using the blue servants as diversions, flooding the battlefield with them as war raged in the skies above.

Naaga weren't fighters. They overwhelmed the enemy through sheer numbers.

Naaga were expendable. They could be cloned again and again.

As the toxic gas became thicker, the Vradhu warriors dropped to all fours, coughing violently. Three more aliens appeared from between the trees, wearing protective clothing and helms. Two of them appeared to be male. The female provided cover fire as the males started to help the Vradhu out of the dangerous gas.

Boom. Boom. Boom. Her aim was accurate, but she

couldn't keep up with the advancing Naaga. How many of them were packed into that ship?

A piercing scream split the air. Imril spun in the direction of the noise. An unprotected female—pale-skinned and golden-haired—stood between the Naaga ship and the Vradhu, frozen in terror.

Had she been caught out? How had he not noticed her before?

A large pack of Naaga—around a dozen—emerged from the ship and headed for the female, wielding their strange devices.

To his surprise, the female bent down and picked up something off the ground.

What is she doing?

When she rose, there was a stone in her hand. She lobbed it at a Naaga and screamed a fierce battle-cry, hitting him square in the forehead. A look of dismay crossed her face as the Naaga paused and put a hand to his head, his fingers coming away covered in green blood. But it didn't deter him. He shook his head and continued to advance. The female threw more rocks. The Naaga kept going until he reached her.

She swung a wild punch, but the Naaga got inside her reach and pressed his strange triangular device against her neck.

The alien dropped to her knees, gasping. Her *vir* dimmed.

It was being absorbed by the device!

What kind of infernal technology was this?

Why—*how*—were the Naaga, who literally could *not* use direct violence, operating on their own? Anger rose up within him as he remembered Nykithus's cursed words, spoken over three hundred revolutions ago.

What if we modified them... allowed them to have free will?

He'd suggested... setting the Naaga free.

You don't understand a thing, youngling.

Nykithus's dirty fingerprints were all over this mess. It *had* to be him. Soon Imril was going to have to put the whelp in his place, but first he had to stop this. Imril summoned his power, letting it flow through his arms and into his fingertips. His metal scale-armor conducted a little of the power, sending an electric ripple over his body.

Noticing him for the first time, several of the Naaga turned away from the melee and rushed him. He threw power at them, and they died instantly, falling to the ground with tendrils of smoke rising from their slender blue bodies.

More Naaga appeared in their place, streaming out of the dark ships. Imril leapt off the roof and walked forward, destroying Naaga left right and center, careful not to let his power hit the injured Vradhu.

The rock-throwing female was cut off from her companions, surrounded by a ring of slowly advancing Naaga. The one who'd drained her energy was trying to restrain her with a strange metal device.

No! Imril broke into a run. He reached the Naaga's side and clamped his fingers around the creature's neck, pushing so much power through its slender body that it died on the spot.

The smell of charred flesh rose into the air.

The golden-haired female stared at him in horror.

For a moment, she was perfectly still, her face frozen in an expression of disbelief.

Then she screamed. She screamed and screamed and screamed, her shrill voice assaulting Imril's sensitive hearing to the point where it became agony. Za's curses, these creatures could be *loud*. Unsure how to handle her, he moved behind her and brought his arm around her waist.

"Quiet," he hissed in Drakhin, but she didn't understand. She just kept on screaming.

He was so close to her now that he unwillingly absorbed a small amount of her *vir*. It gave him strength, and yet he found it lacking. It was rich and powerful, but tapping into it almost made him feel ill.

He resolved not to take anything more. Better that he didn't. Half his full strength was enough. There was a reason Imril rarely ever filled himself to capacity. Too much *vir*, and he became dangerous to others. If he fought the Naaga while at full strength, he would take out the aliens and the Vradhu as well.

Besides, she'd already been drained once.

The drift would always happen; he couldn't help that, but it was minuscule compared to what he would have taken from her in a true feeding. She might feel a little tired after being in his presence for too long, but the drift wouldn't harm her.

"Get away, Drakhin. She is ours." One of the Naaga spoke, its voice flat and emotionless.

Imril glared at them. Clearly, the servants were acting upon the orders of another—he suspected Nykithus—but his commands were supposed to override all others. Why hadn't it worked? "You dare to challenge me?"

Imril's rage grew. Beside him, the female clutched a rock tightly in one hand, as if she alone could stop them.

Like Esania, she was bold. He had to admire that, but underneath it all, she was trembling. She tried to hide it, but clearly, she was terrified.

Time to end this. He glared at the Naaga.

"Kneel," he thundered in Naaga. "Know your place, servants."

Unable to resist the compulsion in his voice, several of them obeyed, but to his shock, at least half remained on their feet.

"Kneel," he said again, louder this time.

No effect.

"A resistant breed," Imril muttered, shaking his head in disbelief. What were they going to do next? Try and fight him? They were mad. utterly mad.

More Naaga emerged from the dark ships. Sensing the threat, they moved toward him.

Imril sighed.

There was no other way around it. He was going to have to use massive force.

Careful, now.

He had to control his power. He didn't want to harm the Vradhu or the aliens, especially the female beside him, who would bear the brunt of the blast.

The only way was up.

Left with no other choice, he wrapped one arm around the female's waist and beat his wings, ripping past the trees, going higher, higher, higher...

She kicked and screamed as he broke through the canopy. In contrast with Esania, this one wasn't able to control her emotions very well.

This wingless one didn't seem to appreciate that if he dropped her, it was a long way down.

But Imril wasn't going to drop her. Compared to when he'd captured Esania, he was much stronger now.

"Be still," he hissed, tightening his grip as his irritation rose. A fierce gust of wind swirled past, creating turbulence.

That silenced her for a moment.

Imril hung on the wind, watching, waiting...

When he was satisfied that the Vradhu had all been dragged to safety, he raised his free hand and rained a bolt of pure golden hell down upon their attackers, incinerating everything in sight.

The alien in his arms gasped in horror, going very, very still.

Yes, his power tended to have that effect on people.

Ah, what to do with this one? He was certain now that feeding from her wouldn't give him the same pleasurable sensation, the same exquisite *thrill* that he got when he tapped into Esania's soul.

But if he was going to rebuild his empire, he needed all the power he could get, and perhaps his Source would benefit from having a companion.

He might be a monster, but he wasn't inconsiderate. It was his responsibility to cater for her wellbeing.

So he took the alien away, climbing higher into the cloudless sky, leaving a trail of fire and destruction and ash in his wake.

CHAPTER FIFTEEN

JUDGING from the way the shadows lengthened in her room, it had been several hours since the Drakhin had left her.

Esania waited beside the small door in the wall, listening for any trace of movement. Sooner or later, Rau would come through here, and this time, she wanted to catch a glimpse of what lay beyond.

Just in case she ever needed to... *escape.*

She stared at the door in the wall, almost trying to will it open, but predictably, nothing happened.

If this went on for much longer, she feared the sheer uncertainty of it all would drive her insane.

"*Aaargh!*"

Wait... what's that sound?

Maybe her ears were mistaken, but...

She stiffened, straining to hear. It almost sounded like screaming. *Human* screams.

But that was impossible.

Whoosh.

The massive double doors swung open, and the Drakhin strode through them, his wings flaring as he walked toward Esania's bed. He ignored her completely. There was something—no, *someone*—in his arms; a pale, kicking, screaming *someone*.

Esania knew that voice. The mere sound of it triggered a protective instinct in her that was so powerful she forgot all about her own safety.

"Sara!" Horrified, she ran toward the Drakhin. Bringing Sara here meant only one thing. He'd found the Vradhu clan and stolen her away.

Had he touched her with his bare hands? *Drained* her?

Fury rose up in Esania, white-hot and irrational, like nothing she'd ever experienced before. Part of it was the shock of seeing pregnant Sara in the arms of this dangerous creature, not knowing if he'd touched her and drained her life-force... or that of her unborn child's.

But there was something else to her anger too, a feeling she couldn't quite identify. "Oh, no you don't," she shouted, her voice cracking as she ran toward him, her bare heels pounding on the smooth stone floor. "No you fucking *don't*. You can drain the life out of me, but you do *not* get to touch her."

"You motherfucker! Let go of me!" Sara was as feisty as ever, kicking furiously as the Drakhin carried her across the room. A powerful scream erupted from her throat, but very moment she caught sight of Esania, it faded, and she gasped.

"Ma'am, you're alive! Oh God, what is this place? What does he want with us?" Relief. Fear. Anger. But mostly, fear. Like most humans, Sara wore her emotions on her sleeve.

Esania rushed to the Drakhin's side. Without a second thought, she grabbed hold of his arm, her fingers curling over his massive biceps.

The bare tips of her fingers collided with a surface that was hard and unforgiving, covered in large metal scales that gnashed and writhed with his movements. Strange metal armor covered the Drakhin's entire body, molding seamlessly to his powerful form, making him seem more remote and alien and inaccessible than ever before.

"Let go of her," Esania hissed, pulling on his arm. "Bastard, she's pregnant! Let go."

He ignored her.

Sara kicked and screamed.

The Drakhin kept walking, and Esania went with him, using all of her strength to try and hold him back.

It was futile. His strength was monstrous; she was like an insect clinging to a great, dangerous beast. Still, she held on, a haze of fury clouding her judgment.

Her mind searched for a word, *any* word that would get through to this monster.

"*Bogu!*" she roared as he reached the bed and unceremoniously dumped Sara onto it. The words that came next were spoken in her native tongue, a torrent of anger and distress that she just couldn't hold back. "Who the hell do you think you are, treating my people like this? What the hell are you, you bastard?" She stepped between Sara and the Drakhin. "If you're going to take the energy, you take it from *me* only." Esania tipped her head, showing him her bare neck. She repeatedly stabbed her finger into the center of her chest. "*Me.* Not her. She is not to be touched under any circumstances. You want it? You take here. *Here.*" Her chest heaved up and down as she slapped her sternum, emphasizing her point.

She didn't know *why* he'd returned with Sara in his arms, but she could put two and two together.

He fed on the energy that Esania gave off. Her DNA was 99.9% human, so it made sense that the other women in her group might produce a similar energy.

But he wasn't going to take Sara's energy.

Over her dead *fucking* body.

That was the second time she'd ever said a curse word.

"What are you doing, ma'am?" Sara hissed. "You can't fight him. He's crazy strong. He'll kill you."

Better me than you... and your unborn child.

But the Drakhin didn't want to kill her. She knew that

because she'd intentionally tempted him, *tested* him, and he'd held back.

That knowledge gave her a sliver of power in a hopeless situation.

"Sara, you just back down and do exactly what I say. Quiet now. Get as far away from him as possible."

To Esania's relief, the hotheaded human actually listened.

Esania swallowed as she stared up at the Drakhin. He stood perfectly still, his head cocked slightly to one side, his arms folded, golden eyes blazing.

Dangerous.

She was probably provoking the devil himself, but she didn't care. The whole thing was too far gone now, so she stared right back, studying him in detail. The armor that encased him was gunmetal grey, made up of thousands of interlocking scales, like a futuristic version of chainmail. It left nothing to the imagination, caressing the hard, elegant contours of his body.

She was struck by the sheer perfection of it all.

Really, he was one well built alien.

Idiot, why are you thinking such things at a time like this?

A sleek, curving helm hid his face, revealing nothing but his golden eyes, which pierced right through her.

Stars, he looks so sinister.

Ba-bump. Her heart fluttered.

This was her captor, her tormentor, the energy-vampire that could suck the life out of her with just a touch. She should be deathly afraid, but she wasn't, because she knew she was *right*, and there was a reason she felt so protective of Sara and her baby, almost to the point of obsession.

Primean-human hybrids weren't supposed to exist, but they did.

Sara's baby was special, and needed to be protected at all costs.

Otherwise, all the risks they'd taken would be for nothing.

The Drakhin's wings rose slightly then lowered again, an involuntary movement that she *thought* signified irritation... or perhaps something more sinister.

"Don't touch her, Drakhin," she warned. Slowly, she shrugged off the golden jacket and let it fall to the floor, revealing her bare arms. She lifted her chin suggestively, exposing her neck. Then she took a step forward. "This is all you need."

Impossibly, she felt something.

It started at the tips of her fingers and extended all the way to her chest. A *pull*.

Like a magnet, some invisible force compelled Esania toward the Drakhin. She wasn't imagining it. She actually had to physically resist it.

Was *he* doing this?

Bastard. Stop it. If you want it, you come to me.

She glared at him, drawing on every remaining ounce of strength in her body to resist the pull. His eyes never left her face. It was a dangerous game of cat and mouse she was playing, and it was utterly addictive.

Suddenly, he removed his helm, revealing his arrogant white features.

Gods and demons, just his face alone was enough to blind her. Dazzling scales. Razor-sharp cheekbones. Burning eyes.

This monster was beautiful, she couldn't deny it.

But he was the enemy. She must never forget it.

Behind her, Sara let out a soft gasp of surprise, but the monster didn't even so much as flick his gaze in the human's direction, not even for a millisecond.

His eyes were only for Esania, and although she hated to admit it, that thrilled her as much as it freaked her out.

"*Navush*," he growled, one corner of his mouth curling upwards ever so slightly.

"Na-vush?" she repeated, not knowing what the hell that

meant. "You know, I really wish you and I spoke the same tongue, Drakhin."

He nodded slowly, his expression of faint amusement getting under her skin. *Why* did he make her so angry? She rarely ever let her emotions get the better of her, but for some reason, this creature made her act in the most impulsive, irrational way. Esania wanted to remove that infuriating almost-smile from his face, but she forced herself to remain perfectly still.

The Drakhin stepped forward; big, menacing, unstoppable. "Na-vush." He mimicked her awkward pronunciation. Armor-encased fingers stroked her cheek, a possessive gesture if there ever was one.

Esania stiffened, but deep inside her, something shifted. Her heartbeat went from pounding drums to butterflies. Her insides twisted.

The Drakhin's touch... it was gentle, almost *affectionate*.

With his helm tucked under one arm, he spun around in a ripple of pale wings, disappearing through the main entrance. The heavy doors swung shut behind him with a thud.

Esania counted to ten, then sank to her knees on the cold stone floor, letting out a sigh of relief. Stars, she was trembling, and her hands felt so cold. She turned to Sara.

"What the hell?" Sara blurted, clutching her lower belly protectively. "*Whoa.* What was that all about?" There was a note of admiration in her voice, and she was looking at Esania with a strange expression. "That was *nuts*. I thought he was going to rip your head off."

Imril would never do that. The thought entered her mind unbidden.

"Did he hurt you?" Esania demanded. "Did he touch you with his bare hands? Drain you?"

"No..." Sara shook her head. "He just swooped in and grabbed me, but he didn't hurt me, and he definitely didn't touch me with his bare hands. What, are you trying to tell me that he's some sort of weird pervert?"

"No! He's not a pervert. He's just—"

"Sorry." Sara raised her hands in a placating gesture. "I didn't mean to insult the guy. Your question was a little weird, that's all."

"Sara, this might sound strange, but if a Drakhin ever tries to touch you, you fight, you run, you do everything you can to stop him from draining your energy."

"*Draining?*"

"If it ever happens to you, you'll know what I mean. It's dangerous for them to touch us, *especially* you, in your current state."

"Understood. But your guy, he didn't do anything like that. Actually, he saved me. He didn't attack us, it was those blue creeps. They took us by surprise. Three ships came down from the sky, blasting through the trees. They used poison gas against the Vradhu. There were *so many* of them. I'm not sure, but I... I think they took Rachel."

"Rachel?" Esania was filled with horror as she thought of cocky Rachel being captured by those strange blue aliens. The Naaga seemed to have no empathy whatsoever for other species, and if Rachel gave off *vir* like the rest of them, there was no telling what they might do to her.

"It was absolute chaos. Naaga, Vradhu, all fighting like crazy, but the Vradhu were weakened by the poison. For some reason, it didn't affect us, and so we started fighting back, protecting the Vradhu. I didn't see what happened to Rachel after that. The Naaga were coming straight for me with a bunch of weird machines. They tried to take me onto their ship too, but then *he* appeared out of fucking nowhere. "

"What happened? Was anyone hurt, or... killed?" Dread roiled around in the pit of her belly at that last thought, but she had to ask. Death was only ever two steps away in this unforgiving place.

Sara's expression turned grim. "I... I don't know. This might sound crazy, but the alien did something I can't explain. He shot fire from his hands, and the blue guys... they just *fried*. He took down two of the ships... killed so many of them... but one of the ships got away. It was a total mess." Sara shook her head, her expression becoming distant. "I don't know if the laws of physics are supposed to change on other planets, but what he did... that shouldn't be possible, right? What the hell *is* he?" She started to hyperventilate, her breathing becoming faster and faster as she wrapped her arms protectively around her belly.

Sara was vulnerable enough as it was, but to be carrying a delicate, innocent life inside her, and then to be suddenly abducted by a massive Drakhin without warning...

Suddenly, Sara leaned over the edge of the bed and vomited. Esania rushed to her side, pulling Sara's thick golden hair away from her face.

"It's okay," she whispered, feeling the rawness of Sara's terror. The very same emotion raced through her heart. "You're safe now. He didn't kill you, and when I told him to back off, he did. I've been here for a few days now. They haven't treated me badly, all things considered. I don't think he wants to hurt us. If he wanted to be brutal, he so easily could have."

"S-sorry. It's just that I was remembering the awful smell, and how fucking terrified I was, and this damn morning sickness... Morning sickness is such a bullshit name. It should be called All The Fucking Time sickness." Sara retched again, but there was nothing left in her stomach.

Esania pulled her away from the awful mess. "You're okay, Sara. You're okay. Hold on a moment."

She picked up her golden jacket and used it to clean Sara's face before mopping up the sick on the floor. Then she flung the jacket across the room, as far away as possible. She retrieved a pitcher of water and a silver cup from a small table beside the bed and poured water into the cup. "Here. Drink."

Sara took the cup with trembling hands. "This is weird. You attending to me, I mean. You're—"

"We left the Serakhine a long time ago," Esania said quietly. The vast Mars colony where Primeans had built their civilization was a distant dream; a world of strict rules and hierarchies, designed to preserve peace and order at all costs.

None of that applied here.

"I'm not your employer anymore, Sara. I'm not able to offer you board or food or protection. That was our contract, and now it's been broken, so forget how things were on Mars."

"Seems to me that you're still protecting me, ma'am."

"I'm just doing what's necessary. I've been here a little longer than you. I know a little bit about how he might react to certain things."

"Wh-who is he?"

"His species are called Drakhin. That's all I know."

"He looks like Imril."

"Imril?" Esania's heart skipped a beat. "Who is Imril?"

"A Drakhin who came from the black ship that swallowed us up. The Drakhin of all Drakhin, ruler of his people. Sounds crazy, huh? I don't know if he's real, or a goddamn myth." She shrugged. "A few weeks ago, some of us took a walk with Calexa and Zahra and a couple of the Vradhu warriors. They took us to this weird place, an ancient monument or something. A hologram came out of a stone, showing us vision of these two aliens. One was light, the other dark. Twins. The Vradhu said they came to this planet thousands of years ago and started a civilization. You know what? That guy, he *really* looks like the holo of Imril, right down to the shape of his wings and the missing tail. It's spooky."

"Sara, I highly doubt he's a thousands-of-years-old myth. Physical likenesses happen all the time. If this Imril ever existed, he would have had ancestors. Maybe our guy is one of his descendants." Esania's voice softened as she took in Sara's disheveled appearance. Her blond hair was knotted and tousled, her boots and pants were stained with red dirt, and there were dark circles under her eyes. "Why don't you rest up a bit? I'll keep an eye out. There's a Naaga servant who comes in here every so often. He brings food and water, but he's fairly harmless."

"*Naaga*? Your servant is one of those blue assholes?" Sara's eyes narrowed. "Those guys are *horrible*. You know what they did, right? They blackmailed the Vradhu, threw poison in their waterways, drugged them, and forced them up onto that sentient ship to fight the deranged metal AI-zombies, because apparently, they're too fucking cowardly to fight anyone themselves."

Esania nodded. "Calexa told me the story." At least, Calexa had told her a *version* of it. She was pretty sure the mercenary was omitting a few important details.

"How can you even trust this Naaga?"

"I never said I trusted him. I just don't think he's a threat to us. Trust *me*, Sara."

Sara stared at her as if she were mad, her blue eyes glazing over. Esania had seen that look on humans before. It was the look they got when fear pumped through their veins, the ancient fight-or-flight response overriding any rational thought.

Primeans liked to think they'd evolved beyond those sorts of reactions, but Esania wasn't so sure anymore.

"I hate those weird aliens," Sara blurted. "I don't understand them at all. At least the Vradhu have some sort of sense of honor, but the Naaga give me the creeps. And that Imril... he scares me. What if he's just keeping us here like livestock, waiting until we're fattened up or..."

"Sara!" Esania's voice became a sharp whipcrack of command. "We can't afford to think like this right now. I need you calm and clear-headed, and you need to be strong. For your baby's sake." She squeezed Sara's hand. "Trust me, we're going to find a way out of this mess."

Maybe they would never get off this planet, but there had to be some way to ensure their safety. Not just for Esania and Sara, but *all* of them.

"Uh, Esania, what the hell is that?" Sara was staring at something above, her eyes widening in fear.

A shadow passed overhead.

Then there was a deafening crash.

Sara screamed and Esania shielded the pregnant woman with her body as one of the high windows exploded above their heads, raining shards of glass all around them.

Pain lanced the back of her right arm, followed by a warm trickle of blood.

I've been cut.

The wound was just above her elbow, at the back of her arm. It started to throb, but Esania ignored it, looking up in horror.

Darkness filled the room, swirling all around them, sucking the light from above. Something dropped through the opening; a black figure moving so fast it became a blur.

It dropped to the floor with a resounding thud, and suddenly there was a chill in the air.

The monster that stood before them could have been the dark mirror-image of the Drakhin lord—the so-called *Imril,* according to Sara—but he was lithe where the other was muscular, his features finer, his cheekbones higher, his eyes set at a sharper angle.

Imril was all radiance and sheer power, but this one was darkness incarnate.

Black wings, obsidian skin, eyes like the deepest midnight on Earth.

She couldn't decide which one was more terrifying. Her captor, or this fierce intruder.

"Mael," Sara whispered, her voice trembling. "I *knew* it."

Before Esania had a chance to ask, the massive double doors swung open, and Imril burst through in a whirlwind of metallic scales and pale wings and golden fire.

He's here.

Despite herself, Esania felt a tiny sliver of relief.

Imril went straight for the dark creature, crashing into him with the force of a hurricane.

"Sara, let's go." As Drakhin clashed—*stars, this was such a nightmare!*—Esania tugged her charge off the bed, and they ran across the floor, trying to get as far away from the warring demons as possible.

CHAPTER SIXTEEN

IMRIL SLAMMED his fist into Mael's chest, sending a bolt of power through his twin's body.

"You know that doesn't work on me," Mael hissed, his fangs flashing as he grinned. "You have two of them, and I have none. Why don't you share a little, brother?"

Mael's shadows threatened to engulf him, but Imril retaliated with a burst of power, easily dispersing the shadow.

"I don't share," he hissed. He brought his fist around in a vicious arc and smashed the bastard's face in.

Mael hooked his tail around Imril's neck and squeezed tight, cutting off his air supply. Even as he grew dizzy, Imril noted with some satisfaction that Cerulean blood trickled from Mael's nose.

Serves you right, bastard.

With a grunt, he cocked one leg and delivered a powerful kick to Mael's stomach, sending his twin flying.

Imril rose to his feet, taking deep, gasping breaths. He rubbed his neck and cursed the Shadowbringer for having such an irritatingly powerful grip.

But Imril cursed his twin even more for the loss of his own tail.

He'd gotten even though. In revenge, he'd ripped off Mael's wings.

No wonder the bastard wanted to kill him.

Clutching his stomach, Mael stood, but instead of attacking, he glanced over his shoulder, his black eyes narrowing. Power rolled off his body in waves, but where Imril's power was white-hot light, Mael's was darkness; the complete *absence* of light.

His twin was a living vortex, sucking energy out of the air itself. Wherever he went, Mael sowed darkness.

Something had gone wrong during their conception. Mael had inherited a little too much of the Dark, and Imril channelled excessive amounts of Light.

Energy. He made it, and Mael...

Imril hated to admit it, but he still didn't understand how Mael's fucking power worked. Mael needed *vir* just like any of the other Drakhin, but he could survive without it for very long periods of time.

And whenever they met, their powers simply neutralized one another.

Mael's shadow writhed and stretched out above him like an extension of his dark soul, drifting toward the females.

"No," Imril growled. His wings rose in anger as he dashed across the floor. The females huddled in the corner, Esania standing in front of the golden-haired one with her arms raised defensively, her green eyes burning with conviction.

She was bleeding. He only had to take one quick glance behind him to see that a trickle of crimson blood ran down her arm, and the smell of it—bold, coppery, slightly bitter—was like a drug.

How vulnerable these aliens were.

She was powerless here. Her soft hands and slender frame told him she was no warrior, and yet she protected the other female with every fiber of her being.

For a heartbeat, he locked eyes with her, remembering the

way she'd clung to him so fiercely, the way she'd chastised him, her voice full of fury, as if *she* were the one in charge.

Imril couldn't remember the last time anyone had dared speak to him in such a manner.

He couldn't remember the last time a female wasn't afraid of him.

And now Mael was trying to steal her from him, and unintentionally or not, he'd *hurt* her, and that was unforgivable.

"Listen to me very carefully, Mael," Imril said, his voice going very, very soft. Mael, who knew him best, would understand that tone. And to think there was a time when they once fought side-by-side, back-to-back, protecting each other from the evils of the *Hythra* and their insane father. "They are mine. If you touch even a hair on either of their heads, I will tear your face from your skull and make you eat it, brother."

Mael chuckled, a deep, menacing sound. "You can keep the green-eyed one, brother. Your scent is all over her. I can tell you haven't touched the other."

It was true. Although this new female radiated *vir* as strongly as Esania, her energy just didn't appeal to him. It was like standing in a valley filled with a hundred *tchirrin* bushes, and finding that only one bore sweet fruit.

Esania had ruined him.

This was going to be a problem.

His hand reflexively went to his chest. The small pouch still hung there. Miraculously, it hadn't been damaged during the fight. Mael eyed the thing with curiosity, a mocking smile flickering across his dark lips.

"They are both mine," Imril hissed before Mael could say a word, stepping between his twin and the females. He extended his wings threateningly, blocking his brother's path. He wasn't interested in tapping into the new female's *vir* in the slightest, but he saw how determined Esania was to protect her, and so he would not give her up.

She was part of his domain now, along with Esania—his most *coveted* Esania—and Rau.

A chill engulfed Imril as Mael sent his power toward him, the shadows creeping across the floor, rising around Imril's body like mist. Imril channelled his *vir*, sending it down his arms and into the waiting shadows, filling the dark vortex with his light.

But it wasn't enough.

He was still far from being at full strength, and Mael... well, he didn't know what the fuck Mael had been doing for the last three hundred revs, but he probably hadn't been wasting away, asleep in the pit of a smoldering volcano.

"Back off, Mael. These females are *mine*."

"Not if I steal them from you. I'm pleased though, brother, to find that you're still alive. See, now I thought I could take the pleasure of killing you myself, but really, I can't even do *that*."

"What are you talking about?" He'd forgotten how irritating Mael could be. The Shadowbringer reveled in being cryptic; in speaking in half-truths and metaphors.

"If you relax a little, we can talk. Why do you always have to be so stubborn? You can keep your precious green-eyed creature. Just give me the golden-haired one."

"*Leave!*" Imril roared, losing patience. Mael *always* made him lose his temper. He threw a torrent of power at his twin.

Mael winced, but didn't budge, his shadow rising to counter the light. The bastard was strong, and Imril wasn't yet fully recovered. At this rate, he was going to deplete his small reserves of *vir* entirely.

Still, he threw another blast at Mael, and as his twin sustained the blow, he stepped forward. He was going to have to get inside Mael's range. In his current state, he would eventually lose a power on power battle, no matter how long he held on.

Mael knew this.

Mael was trying to wear him down.

Imril flapped his wings, creating a powerful gust of wind. Mael laughed, and the shadows surrounding him appeared to grow even thicker and denser.

Imril grunted with exertion as he pushed on. His recently healed wound-sites were hurting again, and the torrent of power flowing from his fingertips was becoming weaker.

Keep moving.

He wanted to look over his shoulder and tell Esania and the other female to *run*, but he couldn't afford even the slightest lapse in concentration.

Just keep moving.

He just needed to get within arm's reach of...

He stopped cold.

A familiar sensation radiated up his back; warm, inviting, delicious. Imril stiffened, his eyes widening in disbelief.

It's you?

Of course it was her.

He would know the taste of her *vir* anywhere.

A slender hand snaked its way up the back of his neck, reaching the part his armor didn't cover, touching his true scales; his second skin.

It was enough. All he needed in order to absorb her *vir* was this touch.

Pure sweetness flowed into him, and he drank it in thirstily, absorbing it into his body and sharpening it into power.

"You have trained her so well already, brother?" Mael took several steps back, wrapping himself in a diaphanous raiment of shadow. "I thought I had seen everything, but this..."

Becoming a blur, Mael feinted to the right then went left, darting around Imril and Esania, going straight for the other human, his arm outstretched, his expression becoming rapturous.

"*Nooo!*" Esania howled, and the sheer anguish in her voice

made him want to turn around and hold her, to fight to the death for her.

Imril tensed, preparing to launch himself at Mael once again.

But then he stopped.

Mael had stopped only a few steps away from the golden-haired one. For a moment, they stared at one another, transfixed.

Then the infernal female opened her mouth, bared her teeth, speared Mael with a hateful glare, and started to scream.

It was the very same scream Imril had been forced to endure as they flew through the skies. Not knowing what else to do, he'd lost patience and clamped a hand over her mouth, and she'd had the nerve to *bite* him, although her soft white teeth couldn't make a dent in his armor-scale gloves.

But her shrill, irritating voice could harm his sensitive ears. He suspected she knew it.

Imril flinched. Mael flinched and cursed under his breath.

This was pure torture.

She *really* shouldn't provoke Mael like this. Imril was going to have to...

Suddenly, Esania said something to her in a harsh, commanding voice, and immediately, the screaming stopped.

And Imril secretly loved the way his Source spoke, radiating authority and composure.

"Ah," Mael said smugly.

"Ah, *what?*" Imril said, and his left eyebrow twitched in irritation. *Nobody* could annoy him quite like Mael. "For once, can you drop the cryptic shit, brother?"

Mael turned in their direction, studying Esania in great detail for the very first time. "Huh. *Now* I understand why she protects the other."

"What are you talking about?"

"Did you not notice, brother? Were you too busy soaking yourself in your submissive little female's *vir* to hear the second heartbeat? But you always loved the power games, didn't you?"

"Remind me to kill you in the most agonizing way possible," Imril snarled. "She is not exactly the submissive type, in case you hadn't noticed."

"Oh, I know. Females rarely are, but I enjoy goading you. It's far too easy."

"Mael, your attempts to goad me have always been pathetically misguided and utterly predictable. For once, can you spare me these tedious games and get to the point? What is this *second* heartbeat?" Seething, Imril tried control his anger. Esania was still behind him, but her hand was no longer on his neck. She swayed on her feet. The scent of her blood surrounded him, mingling with her *vir*. What a drug she was. Fearing she might collapse from exhaustion, he took a step backward so they were side by side, so he could catch her in case she wavered.

"It isn't my fault if you're slow-witted at the best of times," Mael said, and Imril wanted so badly to wipe that infuriating smirk off his black lips. "But for once, I will be quiet, because I want you to *listen*."

"What?"

"All that time spent lording over your gilded court has made you *forget*, hasn't it? Your senses have become dull, Imril. For once in your life, just listen." Mael's expression was perfectly sincere. Imril couldn't remember the last time he'd seen his brother like this. Perhaps when they'd been younglings, before they'd discovered the world outside the ship, they might have spoken without pretense and malice, but time had made them old and bitter, and the rift between them had turned into a chasm.

For a moment, Imril forgot about the bad blood and took Mael's advice. He went still and truly *listened*, opening his senses to the sounds that flowed around him.

He heard Esania; the rapid patter of her heart, the uneven

rasp of her breathing. He heard the gentle caress of the wind outside. He heard the soft back-and-forth flicking of Mael's tail. He *smelled* her, her sweet feminine musk tinged with fear, the acrid-yet-addictive smell of her blood. He felt the now-familiar, comforting warmth of her powerful *vir*.

And he heard the golden-haired female's heartbeat too, pounding alongside the faint patter of *another*.

A tiny thing.

Shit.

How had he not picked up on it earlier?

"She is with child," he murmured, a feeling of reverence coming over him. He, who had been created by the most unnatural means, could only dream of such things.

"How observant of you, Lightbringer," Mael hissed.

"Did I ever tell you that sarcasm is the lowest form of wit?"

"Frequently. But it's too much fun to use, especially on you."

Imril became aware that the two females were staring at them with looks of pure apprehension on their faces. Esania tensed, as if trying to anticipate his or Mael's next move.

He didn't want her to feel so afraid. He wanted to reassure her that even though Mael was partly insane, he *knew* Mael, and no matter how crazy his brother was, he would never harm a female who was with child.

A pregnant woman was an incredibly rare phenomenon, a miracle, to be protected at all costs. In Drakhin history, there had been so very *few*. Although he and Mael were incapable of reproducing, the second generation *could*... if they found the right partner.

Chances of such a thing were extremely slim.

This golden-haired human radiated pure, joyous life. He could almost feel the innocence of the tiny being growing inside her.

He shuddered. He'd been so *close* to draining her. If not

for Kunlo's metal armor and the powerful memory of Esania's rich *vir,* keeping him from tapping into her directly...

No *wonder* Esania had protected this female so fiercely.

Part of him wanted to thank Mael for his violent intervention, but he was still on bad terms with his twin after hundreds of revolutions of incessant fighting, so he simply eyed the Shadowbringer warily, trying to figure out his motive.

He glanced at his Source, noticing the pallor in her cheeks, the dark circles under her eyes, the way her jaw trembled ever so slightly.

And yet she stared straight ahead, clear-eyed, fearless, her hands hanging loosely by her sides.

Ready to spring into action at any moment.

Something inside his ancient heart unraveled just then, and for the first time, he saw her as more than just a servant.

He wanted to tell her that she was his now, and that both she and her friend were under *his* protection, but he didn't have the words.

How frustrating.

"You don't even know what she is, do you, brother?" There was Mael again; softly-spoken, insidious.

"What, and you do?"

"I stayed far away from your scorched-earth war, Imril. *I* did not get infected. While you were sleeping, I was watching the skies. I saw my Shadowring torn down. I saw the *Hythra* crash into the Crater of Za. I saw the seasons change and the skies open up and the floods return to the Ardu-Sai. And when I finally reached the crash site of the *Hythra*, I plugged my soul back into those cursed metal cells and stole her memories." He grinned. "*Hythra's* dead, you know. Killed by a Vradhu of all creatures. The *ilverium* cells still retain her memories, though. They're imprinted into the DNA. I stole a fragment. I know everything, and you know nothing." Mockingly, he held out his hand, and a tendril of molten metal emerged from his palm and writhed around before disappearing beneath his shiny obsidian skin. A bitter laugh escaped his lips. "Once you have been bonded, a piece of the monster always remains with you."

For once, Imril didn't challenge his brother's words. He remembered the moment when they'd finished their duel, both thinking they'd lost, and *Hythra* had chosen his brother as its new Master.

How Mael had screamed and fought.

And what chaos he'd wrought when he finally broke free of the cursed ship and landed on Khira. He and Imril had fought again and again and again, light and darkness locked in an endless cycle of violence and destruction.

The Shadowring... that had been Mael's doing too.

"I will make you a deal," Mael said, his lips still curved in that dark, infuriating smile. Bringer of shadows, keeper of secrets, sower of chaos. That was Mael. "Keep the females together until the birth. Make sure the golden-haired one has everything she needs, and keep her safe. I will not touch her until I deem her to be ready; until it is safe to do so, but when she has had her child, I will come for her. She is to be mine."

Such certainty... is she his...?

No. Impossible.

Beside him, Esania stiffened, and she shot Mael an eviscerating glare, as if she understood perfectly well what he was saying.

"I refuse," Imril said flatly, taking a step forward. The power rippled around his fingers; he was ready to turn it into a death-blast if Mael made a move. "She is under my protection."

"Then we are going to have a big fucking problem." Mael and his shadows became a dark blur as he moved across the floor, and suddenly the Shadowbringer was standing close to the pregnant female, so close he could probably almost inhale her *vir*.

But not quite. He stayed just outside the radius of absorption.

Imril cursed under his breath. "Don't you dare lay a hand on her, Mael."

Esania started to move, but Imril put a hand on her shoulder. He turned and met her gaze. *Stay*.

She glared at him, breathing heavily. A torrent of harsh words dropped from her lips, and she grabbed his wrist, pointing at Mael, a furious, imperious expression crossing her features.

Her eyes blazed. He didn't understand a word she was saying, but he swore she was telling him to kill Mael.

No, not telling him; she was *ordering* him.

Imril's eyes widened.

Mael chuckled.

Za's curses, this female was stubborn.

If the situation weren't so serious, Imril might have found it terribly amusing. Here he was, the Overlord, the Lightbringer, the destroyer of half his cursed race, the one who had torn Mael's wings from his very back, being ordered to kill his brother by an impudent female.

And he still wore a bag of *tchirrin* berries around his damn neck.

All traces of her exhaustion had disappeared, and her *vir* glowed brightly, as if fueled by the strength of her anger alone. She reached out and grabbed the back of his neck, lending him her power once again.

Glorious *vir* filled the deep chasm inside him. Imril's arousal flared, and his monstrous heart swelled with an emotion he hadn't felt in a very long time.

He hadn't thought he was capable of feeling this way again.

This is where it starts.

Strangely, her *vir* seemed stronger and more plentiful than last time. Her stamina was impressive.

Imril channelled her energy into power, building up a massive charge within his body, concentrating the energy into a single focus, ready to be unleashed if Mael made just the slightest misstep.

The air around him began to crackle. His fingers tingled. His vision took on a golden tinge, and he knew his eyes would be blazing with pent-up energy.

"I warned you, Mael." His voice reverberated with power.

Mael ignored Imril completely, a strange look flitting across his face.

Did Mael's expression... soften just now?

Stranger things had happened.

Suddenly, his twin said something, and it took Imril a moment to register that he was speaking in another language.

Silence descended upon the room. Above them, the wind eddied and swirled, entering through the broken window. Esania's eyes widened in disbelief.

Silence.

Then the pregnant one replied, meeting Mael's gaze for the first time, her voice tremulous.

Imril couldn't understand her question.

Esania was shaking her head.

"*You,*" Mael replied simply. His Shadow pooled on the floor, becoming a dark circle that radiated outwards, swirling at their feet.

Alarmed, Esania stepped forward, moving into Mael's radius so that her *vir* naturally drifted toward him. She was acting on instinct, sacrificing her own safety for that of her friend's, and she didn't know what she was doing.

One more step, and she would touch the Shadow, and if she did that, Mael could kill her with a thought... if he so wished.

He might just do it, too, just to spite Imril. He would never forgive Imril for taking his wings, depriving him of the joy of flight.

Mael reached out and tasted a little of Esania's *vir*. Her eyes went wide in shock as he drew the golden energy into his body, smiling. It twisted in the air before flowing into his hand, just like that.

Slowly, deliberately, he turned, and met Imril's gaze.

He inhaled deeply. "Yours, brother?"

And smiled.

Something inside Imril snapped. He moved past Esania and attacked Mael, wrapping his hand around his twin's neck, using his wings to propel himself forward, slamming Mael against the wall.

He squeezed. Mael gasped, his black eyes widening.

Imril's hand crackled with the power. It bled from his eyes and even his nose and mouth, turning his breath golden. "Do not do that again. *Ever*."

"Y-you're quite taken with this one." Mael coughed even as Imril tightened his grip, his power burning into the scale-hardened flesh of his twin's neck. His brother didn't wear any Drakhin armor. In typical Mael fashion, he'd turned up bare-chested, wearing only his shadows and a pair of loose black pants.

"It seems I am." Perhaps he was only just realizing it, but the euphoria he felt when touching Esania's soul... he didn't want to share it with anyone else.

Drakhin didn't share their *vir*-slaves, but this was different.

She'd brought him back to life.

She'd quickly understood what he needed and offered herself freely, vexing him in the process.

She protected her own.

She wasn't afraid of him.

And when Mael showed up uninvited, she'd quickly become his ally, even though she couldn't understand a word of what was being spoken.

Quick. Clever. Brave.

What kind of female was this? Where had she come from?

"Already so obsessed, and you don't even know what she is. I'll tell you, brother. They are *human*, and just like our father, just like us, they are not of this world. If you don't release me right now, I will thrust my shadow into her mortal body and kill her in an instant."

Imril growled, but released Mael at once, fully believing his brother's threat.

"Just give me a moment so I can speak with my female," Mael said quietly. "Then I will be gone."

"How do you know their language?"

"*Earthian*, Imril. That's what it's called. It took me a long time to reach the Crater of Za, to climb into that infernally hot cesspit and steal a tendril of knowledge from the *Hythra*. I have her memories now. The *Hythra* understood Earthian. *Tch.*" He shook his head. "Her last Master, that Vradhu lunatic, didn't understand how to use her vast intelligence properly. She could have made things so much easier for him. Perhaps I should give it to you." Something appeared in Mael's palm, a writhing blob of dark grey *Ilverium*.

A small drop of the dead destroyer.

"What are you talking about?"

Before Imril could react, Mael pressed his palm against his forehead.

Hot molten metal writhed against his bare scales, forming thousands of tiny needle-like points that penetrated his skin, burrowing through his forehead, lancing his skull, twisting into his brain.

He screamed and dropped to his knees as pure agony engulfed him.

Mael laughed. "There you are, brother. Thank me later, when you have taken back your hollow fucking empire."

Imril's vision grew dim. Voices swirled around him, but only Esania's urgent, steady voice cut through the fog.

"...Imril, get up, please!"

How does she know my name?

He swayed...

Wait... I can understand her?

And had just a fraction of a heartbeat to curse his own weakness before his vision went dark, leaving his shattered empire at Chaos's mercy.

CHAPTER SEVENTEEN

"DON'T WORRY, I'm not going to kill him. Right now, I probably couldn't, even if I wanted to." The obsidian-skinned Drakhin spoke perfect Earthian, without any discernible accent.

Esania stared at him in shock, not quite believing her ears. *How?*

"I just need him to be quiet for a while." He *tsked* and shook his head. "My brother can be a tad overbearing, as you've probably realized by now." Despite his menacing appearance, the Drakhin actually seemed to relax as Imril slumped down onto the cold stone floor, the remaining tendrils of liquid metal disappearing beneath the lavender-white skin of his forehead.

Esania dropped to her knees beside Imril. "What have you done to him?"

The Drakhin waved his hand dismissively before he peeled himself off the wall, rubbing his neck and wincing. "You'll see when he wakes up. I don't want to kill him... not *yet*." He grinned viciously.

"Y-you're Mael, aren't you?" Sara stood with her back

against the wall, her blue eyes never leaving the Drakhin's face.

"Yes, I am. Do me a favor, humans. When he wakes from his slumber, tell him to find me in the Vakarin Plains, on the edge of the Mountain Kingdom. He needs to take some responsibility and come and clean up this little mess that he's made."

Esania glared at Mael. "*Leave.*" Her hand dropped to Imril's wing and she stroked its pale, leathery surface for the first time. It was surprisingly soft and velvety and warm, and up close, she could see the fine network of blood vessels that coursed just beneath the tough, almost-translucent surface.

Mael chuckled.

"Go away, Drakhin." Now more than ever, she felt protective of her fallen Drakhin.

The big guy had defended them. He'd been magnificent; vicious and snarling and undeniably protective.

"I have a proposition," Mael said. "I have no interest at all in you. Clearly, you are *his.*" His gaze settled on Sara. "But *you* suit my needs."

"Needs?" Esania scoffed, beckoning for Sara to come and stand behind her. "And what would those be? If you drain her... her..." she searched for the right word...

"*Vir,*" Mael supplied, one corner of his mouth quirking upwards.

"Yes, *vir.*" So that's what it was called. "If you tap into it now, you might harm her unborn child. She can't afford to go through this endless cycle of strength and fatigue and hypothermia. Not when she's carrying a life inside her. Physically, she's got enough to deal with." Esania brought her hands together in a desperate plea. "*Please,* Mael. Don't do this to her... or the innocent child inside her."

For a moment, Mael was silent. His depthless gaze pierced right through her, making her want to look away. Looking into his eyes was like staring into an abyss.

She'd never believed in the supernatural, but there was something otherworldly about Mael, giving her the sense that he wasn't merely a creature of flesh-and-blood.

Imril felt that way too, sometimes, but with Mael, the feeling was stronger, enough to send a ripple of goosebumps down her arms.

"Hmph," he snorted at last, breaking the hypnotic silence. "Drakhin do not feed from pregnant females."

"Hey, Mael?" Chin jutting out at a stubborn angle, Sara stepped away from the wall. "Can you guarantee me one thing?"

"Sara..." Esania held up a hand, fearing the impulsive human would accidentally provoke him.

"It's okay, ma'am. Remember what you said? We're not in the Serakhine anymore. I can speak for myself." She walked forward, and to Esania's surprise, Mael took two steps back, as if he were trying to avoid her. "I'll ask again. Can you guarantee me one thing, Drakhin?"

"And what might that be?"

"The safety of me and my child. Swear you will protect us at all costs, and I will do whatever you want."

A chill ran down Esania's spine. They had no way of knowing whether this Mael character could be trusted. They didn't know where he came from, or what his place was in this terrifying new world, or what he was truly capable of.

All they knew was that he was strong; strong enough to knock the formidable Imril unconscious.

He didn't *seem* trustworthy. He was all snark and dark threats, with only a little bit of restraint thrown in.

What was Sara thinking?

Beneath her hand, Imril's wings shifted as if in response to her thoughts, but he didn't stir. His massive chest heaved up and down, causing the gunmetal scales of his armor to shimmer in the sunlight.

He reminded her of a sleeping dragon.

Her tormentor.

Her protector.

Impossibly, Mael's expression softened. "That... can be arranged. I will keep you here until you have had the child. Don't be afraid. Despite his foolishness, he is not a complete and utter bastard. He will treat you well, and he is certainly strong enough to ward off the nuisances that currently plague this world."

"You'll *keep* me here..." Sara's eyes narrowed, a hint of stubbornness creeping into her tone. Esania remembered that tone. In her household, Sara had been the kitchenmaster, and she'd run a tight ship.

She might have been an indentured human, bonded to work for Esania until her debts were paid off, but Sara wasn't an idiot.

"Yes." Gathering his cloak of shadows around him, Mael gave her the most intense look. "You and yours will come to no harm from me. I will return."

Suddenly, the entire room went dark. Esania stood up in alarm, but by the time she was on her feet, Mael had disappeared, leaving nothing but a distinct chill in the air.

Sara turned to stare at Esania, her blue eyes wide. "What the hell was *that*?"

"I don't know." Esania looked down at the unconscious Imril and sighed.

If only this planet had a hyperspeed information network like the Serakhine's Orb. She would just enter a search term and know everything in an instant.

No, she had to figure things out the hard way, through small clues and observations. It was maddening, yet intriguing, like putting together a puzzle where half the pieces were were missing.

"It seems those two are brothers," she murmured, studying the elegant lines of Imril's face. Strong brow, strong nose, strong jawline. Luscious pale lips. Skin that was soft yet hard, millions of microscopic scales coalescing to form a dazzling surface that reflected the light in a thousand different ways.

All framed by that magnificent mane of golden hair.

Somehow, he looked like a cross between a dragon and an angel.

"Well yeah, that's how the legend goes. Two brothers were created from the blood of a god and the DNA of a Vradhu woman. One fell to Khira. The other was doomed to stick it out on the sentient ship, the *Hythra,* bonded to her for all eternity. Out of spite, he created the Shadowring, anchoring it to the ship so it would remain even when he left."

"Sounds like exactly that—a legend." Esania stopped just short of running her fingers along the impossibly elegant planes of Imril's face. How could this creature have a god's blood running through his veins? In her tightly regulated world, there were no such things as gods and monsters.

"No, they're the real deal. Think about it, ma'am."

"Esania," she corrected. "Just Esania."

"Esania, then. Think about it. One radiates pure energy, the other darkness. Their appearance is scarily similar to the holograms I saw. They hate each other, and I'm pretty sure the dark one's clinically insane, but they can't kill one another."

"Now you're making me wish I went on that little excursion to the hologram ruins."

"You really missed out. It was fascinating."

"I hate hiking," Esania said dryly. Growing up in the temperature-regulated habitat-domes of Mars, she wasn't used to natural landscapes.

In fact, they scared her a little bit.

"Well, that's all I know anyway. We were only there a short time, and the Vradhu never explain anything to us. If they really *are* Imril and Mael, then they're very scary, and really strong. Better to be on their side, don't you think?"

"Is that why you agreed to Mael's demands so easily?"

"Agreed?" Sara laughed as she ran her hands over her

growing baby bump. "Put it this way. If he wanted to take me, he would have. If he wanted to kill me, he would have. The only thing I have to bargain with is..."

"What?"

"A promise."

"They *do* seem to have some sort of honor system..."

"If they're anything like the Vradhu, then..."

Both Esania and Sara looked down at the unconscious Imril. He lay on his back with his wings splayed across the floor, arms outstretched, his chest moving slowly up and down.

He looked like a fallen angel... with scales.

"Wow, he's... massive. Bigger than Mael, bigger than a Vradhu. Holy moly. Look at those muscles, those claws, that *skin*. I think the legends are real, I really do. When he took me, I couldn't do anything, he's that strong. I seriously thought he was going to kill me."

Esania put a finger to her lips. It was weird to be talking about this larger-than-life Drakhin while he was in such a vulnerable state.

"I wonder what's happened to Calexa and the girls," Sara said quietly. "I hope they're okay. *He* kind of... helped the Vradhu. You should have seen it. He just incinerated the blue guys. They didn't stand a chance." A blank look spread across Sara's face as she shook her head, her eyes glazing over. "I'm not sorry he killed them, though. I get the feeling they wanted to capture us, as if we're somehow valuable to them. Don't know why. You know, it's a weird thing to be looking down on him like this. I feel like he could wake up and any moment and—"

"He *could* wake up at any moment," Esania said. "Perhaps he can even hear you. That's why I want you to go to the other side of the room and sit down.

"What?"

"We wait until he wakes up. I can't predict what he might do." She didn't want Imril to touch Sara's *vir* under any circumstances, mostly for Sara and the baby's sake, but she could admit to herself that there was a selfish reason for it too.

Only she should give Imril *vir*.

"What about you, ma'am?"

"Sara, can you just for once stop asking questions and trust me on this?"

"Yeah, I guess I can. Your instincts have been pretty good so far." Sara started to walk, her boots echoing hollowly on the cold stone floor. "Oh, and Esania?"

"Yes, Sara?"

"Thanks for having my back. *Again*."

Esania shrugged. What else was she supposed to do? As much as Primeans had tried to distance themselves from the ancestral race, humans and Primeans were intrinsically linked, and now more than ever, they needed to stick together.

She of *all* people should know.

Ignoring the fact that Imril had already sucked a torrent of *vir* from her body, Esania reached out and pressed her fingers against his forehead. She could *feel* it now; the flow of her innate energy as it passed into his mysterious body. He was like an empty vessel that could never quite become full, and she was his source.

He *needed* her. It was so damn strange. Even though she was bone-tired and the tips of her fingers were starting to turn cold, there was something slightly addictive about the feeling of being his food source.

Her heartbeat slowed.

Her limbs became loose and relaxed.

A pleasant tingle spread over her scalp and down her back. Part of her was tempted to curl up against him and let him absorb every last drop of her *vir*, but that would mean certain death.

She was slowly becoming addicted to the very thing that could kill her.

"Hey Imril, wake up," she said softly, hating to see him laid low like this. The thought of escaping never really crossed her mind, because really, where would they go?

Into a hostile forest, where blue-skinned aliens in flying ships waited to capture them?

No thanks.

She would rather take her chances with this strange Drakhin.

Something warm and hard closed around her wrist.

His hand!

Golden eyes snapped open, transparent *second* eyelids flicking back and forth as catlike pupils widened then narrowed.

Golden eyes glowed.

And she was completely, utterly captivated, unable to move, unable to do anything but stare into his mesmerizing eyes.

CHAPTER EIGHTEEN

HE SAT UP, and pale wings rose and shifted, creating a rush of cool air around them. Then he drew them together and pulled them tightly against his back, and Esania marveled at the fact that something so massive and powerful could almost disappear, just like that.

"You," he said in impeccable, accent-less Earthian. "I understood you perfectly just now." Armor-encased fingers gently encircled her wrist and pulled her hand away from his face. As soon as the flow of *vir* stopped, Esania blinked, feeling like an ice-cold bucket of water had been thrown over her.

"H-how?"

His lips quirked into a wry smile that was oddly reminiscent of Mael's smirk. "My brother is a sorcerer, conjuring memories out of dead metal. For some reason, *Hythra* logged your language. It seems she already had records of it from before. She *knew* of your kind, human."

"H-how is that even possible?"

"The *Hythra* is ancient. Perhaps she has visited your world once. She is—*was*—a keeper of secrets." His expression became distant. "Now I understand how you came to be on this planet. You were lost..."

"Mael downloaded all that into your brain just now?" A little spooked, Esania spoke in hushed tones.

"Through a tendril of *ilverium*, if you can believe such a thing. The *Hythra's* stored memories are chemicals and electrical impulses, nothing more." His features twisted in disgust. "And now I have a fucking migraine."

He closed his eyes and massaged his temple with his free hand, and it was such a weirdly human seeming gesture that Esania almost forgot about the scales and the armor and the magnificent pale wings...

And the fact that he could learn to speak her language just by absorbing a parasitic drop of liquid metal.

Behind them, Sara watched quietly, wisely staying out of this... whatever *this* was. Esania couldn't imagine how terrifying this must be for her.

Imril looked up, his eyes narrowing. "You are tired." He drew her hand away, staring at her long brown fingers for a moment. "Hm."

"You can tell so easily, huh?"

"I can see your *vir*, Esania. I know when you're refreshed, when you're tired, when you're angry, when you're afraid."

"That's..." she searched for the right word as goosebumps rose on her forearms. *Unsettling.*

"It's only natural for me to be checking on the welfare of my Source. I have taken too much from you these past few days, and you are hurt." He glanced at her arm. The bleeding had stopped quickly, leaving a dark red trail along her arm. "That must be tended to." He looked around, his gaze becoming sharp and demanding. "Rau," he bellowed. The Naaga appeared seconds later, using the servant's entrance even though the massive doors were wide open.

Rau arrived in front of them and bowed deeply. Imril issued a series of rapid-fire orders in yet another language, and the blue alien scurried away without a shred of hesitation.

He hadn't even shown surprise at the fact that Imril was

sitting on the floor with Esania kneeling beside him. Were Naaga servants not allowed to show emotion? For some reason, that didn't sit well with her.

Some Primean citizens—the so-called *Purists*—preferred for their help to remain silent and express no emotions or opinions, but Esania had always thought their attitudes towards humans were a little ridiculous.

What a difference 0.01% of DNA could make, huh?

Imril rose to his feet in a single fluid motion. Despite his impressive size, he moved with the predatory grace of a fighter.

For a moment, Esania just stared up at him, overwhelmed by his sheer presence.

Why was it only now that she was noticing his magnificently honed body? Encased in that form-fitting dark metal armor, every line and contour and chiseled outline of muscle was visible. The reflected light accentuated his broad chest, his pecs, his rippling stomach, his powerful arms.

He extended his hand. Esania closed her mouth and slipped her fingers into his, her bare skin pressing against that strange smooth metal second-skin.

Always, her power flowed into him, even if their skin wasn't in direct contact. When they touched, it was a torrent. When they were close like this but not touching, it was a faint trickle; barely there, but noticeable.

Every time he stepped into her personal space, he was going to drain her, one way or another.

She should run far, far away from a creature like this.

But that was impossible now.

He'd protected her, and now he pulled her up off the floor with the slightest movement of his arm, as if she weighed nothing more than a feather.

"Rau will attend to you both," he rumbled, stroking her palm gently before releasing her. That tiny, almost imperceptible gesture sent a ripple of anticipation down her spine. "Whatever you need to feel comfortable, just ask. You may feed, bathe, dress, and rest." He looked her up and down slowly with a devastating gaze.

Something had *changed* between them.

A strange sensation stirred in her core; a feeling she'd never properly experienced before.

She wasn't naive. She knew what *this* was.

Oh, for Mars's sake, she was attracted to this impossible man. If the Serakhine Thought Monitors could stick their probes inside her brain and map her thinking patterns right now, she would never be allowed back into the Primean colony, *ever*.

Imril shook his head and abruptly stepped away from her, moving backward until she no longer felt the seductive pull of his hunger.

Just like that, her *vir* stopped flowing, and Esania immediately felt a sense of emptiness.

Had he read her thoughts just now? She wouldn't put it past him. In a world where fearsome beings could channel light and shadow, anything was possible.

"I just have one question for you," she said quietly as exhaustion threatened to overwhelm her. "There's supposedly this legend about two brothers with the blood of a god running through their veins, who fell to this planet thousands of years ago..."

Imril laughed, a hollow, bitter sound. "I wouldn't exactly call him a *god*, but—"

"You're the one, then? The Drakhin of legend?"

Golden eyes that had been full of concern for her became inscrutable, impenetrable; layered with a thousand years of experience. "I am."

Esania let out a deep breath. She heard Sara shift on her feet.

This is... insane.

Imril smiled. "But legends are so overrated, aren't they? Rest and refresh yourself, human. I imagine you would like to *talk*. When you are ready, you will find me in the central spire. Rau can show you the way."

Human? Esania stopped just short of correcting him. What did it matter now, anyway?

Before she could respond, Imril turned on his heel and left, his glorious wings folded tightly against his back.

To her surprise, the big doors remained open.

"Whoa," Sara said. "That was intense. He really has a thing for you, huh?"

"I wouldn't know about a *thing*," Esania muttered, feeling strangely out of her depth. She, who had never ever contemplated the possibility of being attracted to someone, who had received the libido-suppressing injections on Mars just like everyone else, was suddenly dealing with a racing heart and feverish thoughts and butterflies in her gut.

Of course, the injection would be wearing off right about now; she couldn't even remember when she was due for her next dose.

"That was a *thing* if I've ever seen one, ma'am. I know your kind think lust and sex and are responsible for fifty percent of Earth's evils... or something like that, and that's why you're all so uptight about letting yourselves feel real emotions, but I've always secretly thought the Primean way of doing things is insane. You can't suppress these things forever. You just can't. It's *nature*."

"Don't make a fuss, Sara. Emotion counters rational thought," Esania said, repeating a mantra that had been drilled into her since childhood.

Sara walked across to the massive bed and sat down. She leaned back on her elbows, her eyes narrowing. "Then why did you save us? Was that your *rational thought* kicking in?" There was irony in her tone, something Esania had never heard from her before.

She shook her head. "No, on my part that move was definitely irrational. A real Primean would have left you to the mercy of the law."

"So you're not a real Primean, then, eh?" There was a slight challenge in Sara's eyes now, and perhaps a hint of anger.

"Let's just say I'm not Primean enough to sentence an unborn child and an innocent woman to death, no matter what the law dictates." She made a gesture of dismissal with her hand. "That's as far as this discussion goes. You've just been through an extremely stressful time, and you're tired. You need to rest."

"O-kay." Perhaps sensing that she'd hit a nerve, Sara flopped down on the bed, her golden hair fanning around her face. She cupped her belly with both hands and closed her eyes. "I'm glad, though. I'm glad that we're here and not on Mars. I'd rather be free than stuck paying off some debt that isn't even mine. No offense, Esania, but the indenture system is fucking bullshit and you know it."

"I know that," Esania said with a sigh. "Why do you think I bought out your debt? Better me than some Fiveways body trader or a robot factory baron who would work you to the bone." All humans who worked in the Serakhine were indentured—wealthy Primeans frequently bought out their debts, saving them from a lifetime of hard work in the toxic industrial zones of Earth. Esania had brought across many such humans over the years—always women, always burdened with massive corporate debts that had been passed down through generations. She was only allowed to take women, because in the Serakhine, male and female servants weren't allowed to mix.

Esania couldn't forgive the debts—that was against Primean law—but she could pay her servants the highest wage allowed, letting them work off their debts in the shortest time possible. Some had already returned to Earth, where they'd reunited with friends, families, even children.

Although Esania never let them know it, many of the

humans grew on her. It was always a little painful when she sent them off, but she'd never shed a tear.

Not until she'd come so close to losing Sara and the precious life she carried.

"Speaking of which," she murmured to herself as Rau appeared, pushing a squeaky metal cart packed with food, water, and folded linens—seriously, where did he find all those things? "I have something I need to discuss with the Drak... uh, Imril."

An idea was forming in her mind.

"But you need to take care of yourself. You look exhausted. The Naaga hasn't even dressed your cut yet. Even *he* said—"

"Later." Esania strode toward the wide open doors, tasting a hint of freedom—and hope. "This is important. Rau will look after you. Don't worry, he won't hurt you."

"I know. Naaga can't fight back. It's in their genetic code... or something." She glared at Rau. "If he tries anything stupid, I'll whoop his skinny blue ass."

"You know more about them than I do, apparently." Esania looked over her shoulder at Sara. The look on the younger human's face was the perfect mixture of naivety and world-weariness. "Eat the berries and nuts," she ordered. "They're perfectly safe. I'll see if Imril can do something about cooking the meat for you."

The girls had lectured her all about human pregnancy and what Sara could and couldn't eat. The task of finding suitable food in the Vradhu forest had been fraught with danger.

"Yeah, figures. He shoots blazing energy from his freaking hands. Nice trick, that."

But before that, there was something else Esania had to convince him to do.

She just hoped the fragile bond that had formed between them was strong enough to extend to the humans in the wilderness.

CHAPTER NINETEEN

"I HAVE A CONFESSION TO MAKE," Imril said, his voice a low rumble as he stared out of the crumbling window. He stood with his back to her, his hands folded behind him.

His armor was gone, replaced with his regular clothes. She got an eyeful of pale arms that rippled with corded muscle. Unless one was very, very close, the tiny, almost microscopic scales that formed his skin weren't visible at all. From where she stood, his skin looked like it was made of velvet.

Barefoot, Esania padded across the stone floor, avoiding the occasional fallen rock or piece of random debris. Strange plants snaked across the crumbling surface; knotted vines and small dark green ferns and tiny tufts of wispy grass.

At one point, her bare foot touched a patch of stunningly vivid purple moss, and she withdrew sharply, fearing it might be poisonous.

Everything on this planet was deceptive. Esania had invented a general rule for Khira: the more beautiful the life-form, the more dangerous it was. Imril was pretty damn beautiful himself, and twice as dangerous, when he wanted to be.

She reached his side and looked out the window. "So the legendary Imril wishes to confess?" From here, the view of the vast lake was spectacular. She was used to the red-dust plan-etscapes of Mars, not wild, verdant forests and cool bodies of water, so to see this in person was a rare treat. "What can you possibly want to confess to *me*?"

"Sarcasm does not suit you, human."

Primean, she wanted to correct him, but what was the point?

He turned to her, looking devastatingly earnest. "The first time I fed from you... the first *proper* feeding, I came so close to killing you. You shouldn't have offered yourself to me like that." There was a hint of reprimand in his voice. He inhaled deeply, locking eyes with her.

Esania went very still as she saw the hunger in his gaze. "You're a little terrifying to be around. I took a calculated risk. I would rather you took from me gently than violently," she admitted, suddenly feeling lightheaded.

"You have nothing to fear from me." Imril said stiffly as he shifted on his feet, moving a few inches away from her. "I'm not as hungry as before. I can control it now."

"Can you?"

"I just did, didn't I?" His wings lifted defensively.

"Hm." Esania stared out across the lake, the wind teasing the ends of her braids. A storm was brewing in the distance, dark clouds gathering ominously. "How long does this last? Until you get so hungry you can't control it any longer... *again*?"

"No. That won't happen. I will make *sure* it doesn't happen."

"Because letting me go isn't an option?"

"You are mine now, Esania. That is not necessarily a bad thing, especially on this planet."

"Your servant," she said dryly, appreciating the irony of the situation. Not too long ago, she'd been the benevolent master. Now she was the helpless one.

"Not a servant," Imril countered.

"Then what?"

"I don't know exactly."

So close, yet just outside of her arm's reach. She wasn't imagining things—she could *feel* his magnetic pull. *What are you, exactly?* She caught a tendril of his scent—spice, earthiness, male musk—and suddenly her heart was racing again, and her arousal spiked, bringing with it a cascade of strange sensations.

Butterflies fluttered in her stomach. Her ears felt warm. Her breath caught, and her lips parted slightly, yearning for something more.

But most powerful of all was the feeling that spread through her core, awakening a part of her that had long been suppressed.

Heat surged between her thighs. She froze, overwhelmed by this... this... *arousal. Is this really happening to me?* Esania fought to keep her expression blank. If the Drakhin ever found out that her body was responding to his presence in such a way...

"After you offered me your *vir*," Imril continued, his voice a low rumble, "I was determined that you wouldn't be my only Source, so I went in search of another."

"And so you abducted Sara, a pregnant woman?"

"I did not know she was with child. Had I known..." He shook his head. "I was wearing full armor. That would have blocked the drift. I did not feed from her."

"I don't understand. You... you wanted to show me that I'm not indispensable? That I can be replaced?"

He went quiet, his golden gaze roaming slowly over every inch of her, which only had the effect of stoking her arousal to new heights.

He mustn't know he has this kind of effect on me.

"I was wrong." A hint of a smile tugged at the corners of his mouth... Stars, did he *know*?

Ba-bump.

"You are unlike any creature I've ever encountered, Drakhin or Vradhu or otherwise."

Ba-bump-ba-bump-ba-bump.

"You're mine now, Esania. Make no mistake, I do not plan on letting you go."

She should be angry at his haughty expression, at his insufferable imperious tone, but all she could do was stare at his face, watching the bright afternoon light play across his pearlescent skin. "You're clearly comfortable with the idea of owning people."

He chuckled a little at that. "It is a fair trade. I don't believe in abusing my Sources. You will be well looked after and given everything you need... everything you desire. You are under my protection now. When I am stronger, I will reclaim my eyrie above the ocean and start to rebuild my House."

House? Eyrie? "Who exactly *are* you on this planet, Imril?"

"I am—*was*—the Overlord. Along with Mael, I was the first of my kind. We are twins, in case you hadn't noticed."

No, I hadn't.

Imril and Mael were polar opposites.

His expression hardened and his eyes became distant, reminding Esania of a statue. Imril took another step backwards, his nostrils flaring as he took a deep breath. "You brought me back to life, Esania. For that I owe you a debt that I fully intend to repay, but I can never let you go. Not now."

Oh. Somehow, she didn't exactly desire freedom from him. Freedom was the wild jungle and living with the Vradhu and hunting and gathering food until the end of her days.

Freedom was washing in cold water collected from small ponds and cooking outside over an open fire, the smell of woodsmoke lingering in one's clothes and hair for days.

Freedom was sleeping in a hut constructed of wood and vines, the unnerving sounds of the forest beasts filtering through the walls at night.

Esania didn't want to go back to that. Here she had food and shelter and clean clothes, and a proper *bed*, not to mention hot water.

It was... *civilized*, and Imril could protect them from the Naaga.

Things were better here.

And he'd just told her he owed her a *debt*.

"Then I want to call in that debt," she said quietly, her heart pounding as she made a decision. "You have to do something for me."

"Oh?" He inclined his head, not promising anything, a half-smile playing across his lips, as if her request was absurd but he would tolerate it anyway.

"You abducted me," Esania accused, taking a step forward. "You started a fight with the Vradhu, seriously injured one of them, took me from my people, and locked me in a tower. You took my... my... *strength* without asking, like some sort of energy vampire."

Imril just stared at her haughtily, not offering any form of apology. He shrugged. "I am not interested in your analysis of what I am. What is your request?"

Esania took a deep breath. "Actually, there are two things. My people. I want to bring them here, along with the Vradhu who protected us—if they choose to come—and I want you to promise to protect them... *us*. Secondly, Sara tells me one of our own might have been taken. If she really is gone, I want you to help find her, and bring her back." She was taking a risk by asking him this, but she had to. The longer the girls stayed out in the wilderness, the more chance they had of getting abducted. The Vradhu were fierce hunters, but the Naaga had technology on their side.

Now more than ever, her people were in danger.

"Vradhu..." Imril's expression darkened. "I will *not* have Vradhu in my eyrie."

"One of my people is mated to a Vradhu... well, *two* of

them." Technically, Calexa Acura wasn't her *people*, but the mercenary had put her life on the line to make sure they all got off the *Hythra* safely, so therefore, she *was* her people, along with the other mercenary women—tough, level-headed Zahra and that firebrand, Mai.

Imril shook his head. "Obviously, a lot has changed since I fell asleep inside Za. Vradhu mating with other species?" He scoffed.

"Get used to it." From the interactions she'd observed between her girls and some of the gruff Vradhu warriors, there were probably going to be a few more of those unions. "I want them here." She adopted the tone she used to use when speaking in the Primean Senate—cool, rational, a little bit conciliatory. "Think about it. You have a whole bunch of humans running around in the forest with their bodies full of that precious energy. Can you afford to let them fall into the hands of your enemies?"

"No," he growled, his wings rising. For a moment, he just glowered at her, radiating tension, his scary eyes glowing. Had she overstepped? "You make a *point*," he said at last, his voice low and dangerous. "I will bring your people to you, *without* the Vradhu."

"If you try and steal them away, the Vradhu will try and fight you."

"I'll incinerate them," he growled.

"And risk injuring my people? I'd never forgive you, especially if you killed one of my girls."

"What do you want, Esania?" His voice deepened to a growl, and she sensed she dancing on the very edge of his patience. But still, this was her one and only *chance*.

"Take me with you. We'll bring them back with or without the Vradhu." Secretly, she fully intended to have the purple-skinned warriors around, but she could try and negotiate that later. This was a *start,* and the situation was fluid. "If they see that I'm unharmed, they'll relax a little. I'll convince them to come."

Imril considered her for a moment, before leaning in close, breathing in her scent, absorbing the faintest amount of her energy. "Very well," he said at last. "We will go and track down your people, but first you need to rest. I will not fly until you are at full strength." He gave her a stern look that made her insides melt a little. *Damn it.* "One favor, Esania. That is all. Actually, it is *two* favors, but I will humor you just this *once.*" He went still, his eyes flicking up and down over her body, studying her with blistering intensity. "Then you will serve me for as long as I need you."

"As long as you *need* me?" Her eyebrow twitched.

"Don't look at me like that, Esania. I'm not some mindless savage. You will be well taken care of."

She shot him a dark look. "In exchange, I just need to provide you with an unlimited supply of my life-force, right?" The thought filled her with a weird mixture of horror and anticipation. "What exactly are you planning, Drakhin?"

Imril folded his arms, the movement accentuating his glorious biceps. He really was a study in power; tall, muscular, radiating a sense of barely contained tension. His closeness put her on edge; she wanted to run from this deadly creature, but at the same time a dark part of her craved his touch.

"I'm going to take back what's left of my world," he said softly. "I made a mistake, and it cost me three hundred revolutions and my empire."

"Mistake?"

"I grew complacent. It seems that the worst kinds of betrayals occur from within."

"Sounds familiar," she said dryly, thinking of Earth's long, checkered history. "Does that have something to do with you flying around naked, looking for a defenseless human to abduct?"

"Huh." He stared at her, his expression unreadable. "I

entered the fray much too late. They had engineered a virus that was fatal to Drakhin, and they unleashed it inside my territory. By the time I reached the battlefield, I was infected. I thought I was dying."

"And you tried to take all of them down with you... A pyrrhic victory, rather than defeat?"

"Am I that predictable, or are you some sort of telepath?"

"Just a scholar of history and a student of character. When you read enough, you get a feeling for how these sorts of things usually pan out."

Surprise flitted across his elegant features. "I did not think war would be common to all worlds. I thought that perhaps my kind were abnormally aggressive."

"Oh, it is, believe me." *Except on Mars.* Through strict behavioral controls, and by limiting the number of people allowed on Mars, the Primean race had managed to keep war and conflict away from the Red Planet for centuries.

But the Serakhine wasn't perfect. Far from it. The orderly exterior hid dark secrets.

She'd found that out the hard way.

"Why didn't the Plague kill you?" she asked, half-fearing the answer.

"I don't know. Maybe because my brother and I are slightly different to the other Drakhin. We are *far* more powerful than the second generation, but we paid a price for that." A bitter laugh escaped his lips. "I don't know much of anything anymore. I don't know what's become of my world since I fell." He moved a fraction closer, and she *swore* she felt the chasm inside him; a hunger that was so deep and complex that she felt she was only scratching the surface.

A hunger he kept oh-so tightly controlled.

His power, his darkness, his unexpected, unpredictable tenderness... it was intoxicating.

"You are my Source," he whispered, a dark smile curving

his pale lips. "I don't want any other. With your power, I am going to take back Khira."

Stars, what have I done? Is this all a terrible mistake?

But she couldn't afford to go back on her plan now. The stakes were too high. Esania stepped forward, her eyes locked on his. "The difference between me cooperating, or having to be dragged kicking and screaming to do your bidding, lies in whether I can trust you." She leaned closer, challenging him. "Is there such a thing as honor in your culture, Drakhin?"

"For the right person," he replied, a ghost of a smile playing across his lips. "Is there such a thing as the willingness to take a *risk* in your culture, Esania? How do you know I won't just go to where your people are and slaughter them all?"

Because you didn't hurt Sara, even when you so easily could have. Because you protected her when Mael came for her.

Because you didn't kill me, even when I practically invited you to.

"You... *wouldn't*," she whispered, unable to take her eyes off his face, particularly his mouth. Those lush, sensual lips were so at odds with the hard lines of his face. His lips parted slightly, revealing a flash of sharp teeth.

"Be a good Source," he murmured, "and perhaps I will give you the world. This little favor you ask of me... it is *nothing* compared to what I can do for you if you please me."

"You can have my *vir*, but I can't guarantee that I'll please you. I can only be myself."

"Maybe that is enough. I will do as you ask of me, human, but do not mistake my cooperation for kindness."

"Fine." Esania carefully concealed her surge of triumph. By using Primean logic, she'd just convinced a incredibly dangerous millennia-old being to protect her people. Was it risky? Sure. But she couldn't stomach the thought of them staying in the wilderness, at constant risk of being attacked and *abducted*.

She considered all the possibilities and came to the conclusion that out of the two options, *this* was by far the better one.

Besides, Imril had the chance to feed from Sara, and he'd held back. Just now, he'd told Esania something profound and more than a little terrifying.

He only wanted *her*.

She was betting he wouldn't try and feed off anyone else. She took a deep breath. "Now, there's this small matter of cooking."

"Cooking?" a look of bemusement spread across Imril's face.

"Cooking." Esania nodded, crossing her arms. "We humans actually prefer our meat cooked by fire instead of eaten raw."

Not that she expected him to understand.

He, who didn't even eat *food*.

She, who had never touched a cooking utensil in her life.

Ha.

She was about to explain the concept to him when her legs started to feel wobbly, and she had to put a hand out against the crumbling windowsill to steady herself. It was as if all the adrenaline had drained from her body in one huge rush, leaving her completely depleted.

"I have used you far too much," Imril murmured, and for the very first time, she saw something else in his eyes—*tenderness*—and it floored her. "I won't touch you again until you are ready. You need to rest."

He stopped just short of apologizing, and Esania secretly wondered if he had ever said sorry to anyone in his life.

"Speaking of food..." He reached into his pocket. "Here."

"Wh-what's this?" Esania reached out and took the item. She stared at it for a moment, not quite comprehending. The sweet, slightly pungent smell of *tchirrin* berries filled the air, and it clicked. This was the pouch she'd dropped when Imril had swooped down and plucked her away from the Vradhu clan. "How did you *find* this?"

One of the ripe fruits rolled out onto her palm. Out of impulse, she popped it into her mouth, and its delicate skin broke, releasing the sweet, soft, gooey, *overripe* flesh.

A cross between kiwifruit and watermelon and pineapple. That's what it tasted like. She wiped her mouth with the back of her hand, leaving a streak of violet across her brown skin.

Then it occurred to her that Imril was staring at her intently, his gaze fixated on her mouth as she chewed.

"Mmhm?" *What?* Suddenly, she felt self-conscious. She swallowed the fruit, and Imril's eyes dropped to her neck, and she could have *sworn* she heard a growling sound coming from deep within his chest.

A warm sensation flooded her body, rising into her cheeks and her ears, spreading right down into her core, seeping between her thighs, awakening something that she hadn't thought even existed.

"You found this in the forest and brought it back... for me?"

Imril nodded. Now he was staring at her hands. Why was every single part of her body suddenly an endless source of fascination for him?

"You dropped it," he murmured. "They should not go to waste."

How unexpectedly... *sweet.* Esania curled her fingers around the pouch, holding onto it as if it were the most valuable gift in the Universe. The taste of *tchirrin* lingered on her tongue, and it was truly the most delicious thing she'd ever eaten.

She could almost feel its energy surging into her, replacing the *vir* Imril had taken.

"But you are tired," Imril growled, "and that cut needs tending to. Rau!" He summoned his servant, switching from intense to tender to bossy to utterly imperious in a heartbeat.

Esania could easily imagine him presiding over a court of equally domineering Drakhin.

Overlord.

Somehow, the title fit him perfectly, but it was just a drop in the ocean of his history.

Who the hell are you, Imril?

CHAPTER TWENTY

THEY DRIFTED OVER THE FOREST, searching, searching, searching. Esania had quickly found out that Imril's vision was much, much sharper than hers; he could spot tiny things on the ground from incredible heights.

Just like a damn eagle.

"Anything?" she asked hopefully as they circled the spot where Imril had abducted Sara, where the Naaga had fought against the Vradhu. It was as good a starting point as any. Esania squirmed in her bonds, trying to get used to the feeling of being thousands of feet above the surface of the planet while tethered to Imril's hard, armor-encased body.

The so-called *harness* was a contraption of Imril's making; a flat, ribbon-like black rope that felt like silk and was apparently incredibly strong. Rau had magicked it from somewhere deep within the ruins of the lake castle, and Imril had quickly and expertly trussed her up, making sure her back was pressed firmly against his torso, as if he'd done this a thousand times before.

It was crude, but it worked. Imril needed to have his hands free, just in case they were attacked, and Esania needed to be safely restrained.

The moment he'd taken off from the spire, jumping out of the crumbling window and getting them airborne with a few powerful strokes of his wings—that had been exhilarating... and terrifying.

And these bindings... she couldn't help but feel that they were just a little bit *naughty*. Imril had assured her he'd tied it in a way that would enable him to release her in a flash just by pulling one of the ends, but to be bound to him in this way, all the while feeling the subtle flow of power from her body to his, feeling the hard planes of his body against her back.

This was a dream. A pleasurable nightmare. Her world had been turned upside down, and she was going crazy.

At least he wore full armor. The scaly barrier between them reduced the drift of *vir* quite significantly. It seemed she wasn't going to end this day completely drained, unless he suddenly needed her power.

A strange thought occurred to her. If skin to skin contact caused him to suck the life right out of her each and every time, how were they ever going to be...

Close?

Her heart beat faster.

Intimate?

As they caught a swirling wind current, Imril wrapped his arms around her. He held her tightly as turbulence hit, swooping to a lower altitude. They shot through a bank of thick cloud, the fine mist turning into moisture as it hit Esania's face, before quickly drying again.

Flying through clouds, held tightly in the arms of a winged alien, thinking about what he looks like underneath all that armor.

So much for her Primean values. She might as well be human.

"Down there," Imril said suddenly, the wind stealing away part of his voice. "That's the spot where I took the pregnant female."

"*Sara*," Esania corrected. "She has a name."

"Yes. She was throwing stones at the Naaga from a distance." Unexpectedly, he laughed. "They did not know how to deal with her."

"Sara is a bit of a spitfire, in case you haven't figured it out by now. Why did you choose *her* out of all the humans you saw?"

"I thought she would make a good alternative Source," he said. "Her *vir* was extremely bright. Now I know why."

"Let me guess. Pregnant women have a certain 'glow' about them?" She wondered if he understood irony.

"Two lives. I didn't realize it at the time. My mistake."

"Ah." She shook her head. Well, at least this obstinate Drakhin admitted to his mistakes and faults.

"That's the place there. We're going down."

"I can't see anything." Trees, trees, and more trees. That was all Esania could see.

Abruptly, Imril angled his wings and they dropped rapidly, causing Esania's stomach to flip.

"I told you not to *do* that," she grumbled, trying to slow her racing heart. No matter how long she stayed up in the air, she would never get used to the feeling of flying.

Imril didn't say a word of apology, but he did slow down a little, easing Esania's fear. "We are going to land and go on foot. I need to track their escape path from the ground."

Phew. Solid ground sounded good right about now. Imril controlled their descent, pulling them into a feet-first position and spreading his wings.

They drifted downward, and the trees became bigger and bigger. Suddenly, she recognized the terrain. They were on the outskirts of their tiny makeshift village, a series of small, water-tight huts that the Vradhu had built out of *sekkhoi* branches.

There was that small freshwater pond—the one they collected rainwater from, since the greater waterways were apparently full of poison. There was the small beaten path and the central fire pit. There was... a shoe. A harvest bag. A piece of torn cloth. A broken war-spear.

Signs of a struggle.

And the village... it was deserted.

They dropped through the canopy, and before Esania knew it, her feet were touching the rocky ground.

How *surreal*.

She didn't even trip or overbalance. Imril had timed their descent perfectly, and she got the feeling he'd done this sort of thing a million times before.

But had he ever taken another *passenger*, besides her?

He was supposed to be thousands of years old. Of course he would have had other passengers, other... *Sources*.

He was the damned *Overlord*, whatever that meant.

A strange emotion rose up inside her, unlike anything she'd ever experienced in her life, and it took Esania a few moments to realize what it was.

Jealousy.

How very un-Primean. What was she turning into? Away from the neat hydro-gardens and atmosphere-controlled domes of Mars; away from the carefully controlled environment of the Serakhine, where emotions were diluted with medication and human behavior was frowned upon, every single thing she'd been taught in her life was being challenged.

And to think most other Primeans had labelled her a *radical*.

Ha.

She'd tried to introduce laws for better treatment of humans on Mars, but most Primeans detested their Earthborn relatives, and thought of them as grossly inferior. Even after all these centuries, humans on Earth were still violent and self-serving and destructive.

But they could also be capable of great kindness and courage and ingenuity.

Most Primeans didn't see that.

No, Esania couldn't treat her *sapiens* cousins as inferior. She just couldn't. After all, her genome wasn't entirely pure. She'd never understood how her mother, Fabra, had managed to keep the details of her conception a secret from the Serakhine authorities, but somehow, she'd been born on Mars and raised as a full Primean.

She never met her father. Primeans didn't have fathers. They were conceived in labs, implanted in surrogates, and raised in the communal *kinderhaus*.

She only found out the truth when she was an adult, just before the incident with Sara.

Her mother had come to her and told her everything.

And her entire world had tilted on its axis.

Shwick.

Esania was jolted out of her thoughts as the silken rope fell away from her body. She spun around and came face-to-face with Imril—all glittering scales and intense golden eyes. He wrapped up the rope in a few swift movements that spoke of years—maybe *centuries*—of practice and stashed it in a small pouch at his waist.

"This way." He removed his helm—a sleek thing of curved metal with small openings for his eyes. Esania half expected his glorious golden hair to tumble out, but then she remembered he'd cut it before they left, in a style that was distinctly military. It was a drastic change, but as she stared at it now, she decided she liked it.

This new style accentuated the elegant angles of his face and made him look even more regal, if such a thing were possible. Losing the hair had caused a subtle change in his demeanor, as if he had now decided to get serious.

It *suited* him.

Oblivious to her scrutiny, Imril pointed up a rocky slope, frowning. "Their retreat was absolute chaos."

"You can tell?"

"I was there." He walked across to a nearby tree and ran

his fingers over a spot on its trunk, taking in some invisible detail. "There's also the *vir*-trail. I can still see the traces, but they are already starting to fade. We must hurry."

Esania strode after Imril as he turned and made his way up the rocky path, his bare feet making barely a sound. In contrast, she crunched whenever she took a step, even though she tried her best to be silent.

Her thick-soled traveling boots didn't help.

Imril had returned them to her, and she wore them over her smooth thermoskin pants, along with the padded golden jacket, which Rau had returned to her freshly laundered and smelling faintly of something lemony. Although the forests here were humid during the day, they could turn chilly at the drop of a hat, especially if a sudden storm or gale blew in, and it was cold up there in the skies, so the jacket was a welcome addition, especially now as a gust of wind tugged at her braids. Thunder rumbled in the distance. The fresh scent of ozone and earth and leaves swirled around them, hinting at the storm that was to come.

Esania hurried after Imril, thankful that she'd stuck to her daily strength and conditioning program back on Mars. Keeping up with his rapid pace was no problem at all.

She took a deep breath. "Why don't you trust the Vradhu?" It was as good a place as any to start. She had so many questions for him, but when picking Imril's brains, she had to be careful. He tolerated her for now, but she wasn't under any illusions that he was suddenly going to drop everything and give her absolute freedom.

They crested a small hill and navigated around a patch of dead bushes, and at one point, Imril actually had to raise his hand and use his power to *burn* through the dead thorny branches. The thicket shriveled into ash in a heartbeat, sending a plume of glowing embers up into the air. One by one, the floating embers blinked out.

Then they were on the move again, and for a while, Imril was silent.

"The Vradhu are the original inhabitants of this planet," he said at last, his deep voice cutting through the stillness. Esania still couldn't quite believe he was speaking Earthian; she'd never heard of technology that could seed a language directly into the recipient's brain.

"And the Drakhin...?"

"We were created. A made race, just like the Naaga. Drakhin is a Vradhu word. It means *treacherous blood.*"

Made race.

Just like the Primeans. Half of Esania's chromosomes came from a heavily edited, artificially enhanced pool.

"Treacherous?" A sliver of unease unwound in the pit of her stomach. "Why would they call you that?"

"Treacherous can refer to danger or betrayal. We are capable of both, and the Vradhu know better than any other species what it means to go to war with us."

"War?"

"We fought, once. They lost."

His words sent a chill through her. "So you're mortal enemies?"

"It is... complicated."

"And you don't want them in your stronghold because of some war that was fought a long time ago."

"Vradhu do not forget. It's highly likely that any one of them could stab me with their cursed tail-barbs and kill me with deadly poison." He guided her through the thorny thicket and into a small clearing carpeted with dead brown plants. Imril looked over his shoulder, his beautiful, inhuman face turning into an inscrutable mask. "Their ancestors died at my hands, as did many Drakhin. They fear me, and they detest me. Why would I trust any of them?"

"You make it sound as if killing people is a regular thing for you."

A hollow laugh escaped him. "Now that my race has all but destroyed itself, perhaps that will change."

They left the clearing and entered a stand of tall trees with slender silver trunks. Small yellow leaves fell from above, and as Esania glanced up, she realized the trees were shedding their leafy crowns.

Part of her wished she'd never asked Imril about the Vradhu.

Now she was left with more questions than answers, and a glimpse of Imril that she hadn't wanted to see—ruthless killer, cynical ancient.

Something monstrous, perhaps.

"They ran," he said, casting his eyes across the leaf-strewn forest floor. "The Vradhu were weakened by poison, and they couldn't fight back. It was the *humans* who came and helped them escape as I took down the Naaga. Strong males and females with weapons."

"Calexa and her crew," Esania said absentmindedly as she looked down and saw a flash of silver. "Wait." She crouched down and plucked a small silver object from the ground.

An earring. She recognized it as belonging to Odessa, one of her horticultural specialists. The tiny thing was shaped like a flower, with glittering pink gemstones in the center.

A distinctly feminine item worn by a woman who was definitely *not* all that feminine.

"They definitely fled," she said, her anxiety growing. Odessa wasn't the sort to just carelessly lose an earring. The woman had a reputation for being meticulous, with never a hair out of place. "What exactly happened here, Imril? You said the Naaga were here, that you blasted them and took off with Sara..." Her eyes narrowed. "Was anyone hurt?"

To her relief, they hadn't seen any bodies.

"The Naaga," Imril said, a chill entering his voice. "I thought I killed them all, but there is no trace of their ships, and no bodies. Someone has come and cleaned up the mess."

"Other Naaga?"

"Perhaps."

"They want us... *humans*... because of our *vir*?"

"Yes," he hissed.

"They feed, just like you do?"

"No. They are Sources too, but their Master is Drakhin." Imril's expression darkened. "Let's move."

He turned away, his wings clasped firmly against his back.

Clearly, that was the end of this discussion.

They walked briskly up the gravelly slope, and Esania started to become short of breath as she kept pace with Imril. That was strange. Usually, this level of physical activity would not have been a problem for her, but she didn't have much time to think about it, because the next thing she knew, a Vradhu war-spear flew past her face and somehow ended up in Imril's clenched fist.

He spun around, his wings raised, his eyes blazing with *vir*, fury creasing his pale features. In a single powerful movement, he spun the spear in his hand and hurled it back in the direction it had come from.

Thunk.

Esania spun around in alarm, searching for their attacker. She saw a flash of violet in the shadows. *Vradhu.* The blade of the war-spear was firmly embedded in the mottled trunk of a tree, but the Vradhu was nowhere to be seen.

"Get behind me." Imril commanded, putting his arm out protectively as he strode forward. He put on his helm, protecting his face. Golden energy crackled from his fingers, giving off a distinct smell of ozone as it dissipated into the air.

Esania started to move, but he made a warning gesture with his hand. "Don't move," he snapped.

He said something in Vradhu, and although Esania couldn't understand the words, the cold fury in his voice was obvious, promising death to her Vradhu attacker.

"Don't kill him," she said, fearing Imril's savage temper.

"He probably thinks you've come back to abduct another one of them. He's Vradhu. Of course he's going to fight."

But he ignored her, becoming a shimmering blur as he darted forward, an ominous hiss erupting from his throat.

It was eerily similar to the primal sound she'd heard the Vradhu make when threatened, and once again, she was struck by the likeness between the two species.

But there was no time to wonder about the uncanny resemblance, because Esania feared Imril was about to kill the Vradhu and ruin her plan to get her humans to safety.

CHAPTER TWENTY-ONE

"TELL me why I should spare you," Imril said softly, speaking in Vradhu as he stalked through the undergrowth, "when you so very nearly killed my Source?"

He trembled with anger, almost losing control of the power that surged through his body. The Vradhu remained hidden, saying nothing, but Imril knew the purple-skinned bastard hadn't gone far. He would be there in the *sekkhoi* thicket, waiting for the right moment to strike and sink his barbed tail into Imril's flesh.

Vradhu had only one shot at harming a Drakhin, but it was *deadly*.

Imril wasn't worried, though. He was wearing scale-armor, and even at a third of his full power, a single Vradhu was no match for him. "I would normally incinerate you for that, but I have made a promise to my human." He grabbed a thorny branch, his hands crackling with power. "Your survival is dependent on your cooperation. I will say this only once. Show yourself, or I will burn you alive."

Esania wisely stayed behind him, but he could feel the anxiety rolling off her in waves. He was glad she didn't speak the language of the Two Clans, because he didn't want her to understand that he was one step away from killing the Vradhu.

The bastard's spear had flown just a hand's breadth from her face, and that was unforgivable. She could have been seriously harmed, or even *killed!* Rage roiled around in his veins, surprising him with its ferocity.

He hadn't appreciated how truly vulnerable Esania was until now. With her soft scale-less skin, limited strength, and seemingly endless supply of *vir*, she was poorly adapted to survive in the wilds of Khira.

And yet she'd been so fearless when trying to protect the pregnant one, Sara.

Humans.

Such fascinating creatures. Where had they come from? Imril knew there were other worlds out there in the endless Universe. His very own father had been from a distant planet.

"Imril," Esania warned, and part of him would do anything for her, as long as she asked him in that sweet, patient, calming voice. It was a balm on his seething, restless soul.

She was beautiful. He couldn't deny it.

But the Drakhin in him couldn't relinquish control. He waited, ready to send his power through the *sekkhoi* thicket at the slightest provocation.

Finally, there was a faint rustle of branches, and the Vradhu emerged, materializing out of the shadows, pulling his war-spear out of the tree trunk. He wore the thick, molded *kratok* armor that was characteristic of their tribe, and he moved with the fluid grace of a seasoned hunter.

A striking pattern of black pigmentation decorated his face, accentuating the fierceness of his glare.

For a moment, he just stared at Imril, not in the least bit intimidated. Then he glanced at Esania, gave her a single nod of recognition, and diverted his attention back to Imril.

"Lightbringer," he hissed. "What do you want?"

Imril nodded in Esania's direction. "The human has asked

for my protection—for her people. I have an eyrie in the Half-green Forest, in the center of Lake—"

"Kunlo's old place. I know it." The Vradhu folded his thick arms and frowned. "Where is the pregnant one? Did you touch her?"

"I did not. You think I would risk the life inside her for a small hit of *vir*?" Imril glowered at the Vradhu. This upstart had no idea about the rules Drakhin had lived by—rules *he* had made. Once, Imril would have thrown the young warrior to the ground and impaled him then and there, just for questioning his integrity.

There was a time, long ago, when Imril had been quick to anger, and he had enforced each and every one of his laws ruthlessly, without question, without argument, striking terror into the hearts of the other Drakhin, never letting them forget the true extent of his power, which vastly eclipsed theirs.

Because only he and Mael were true Drakhin, the sons of Acheros, the monster.

The others... biologically *competent*, but their Drakhin *aum*-genes were diluted.

Those were the old times, the savage times, when the world of Drakhin was still being built, when the Ancestor was still alive, when Imril was the Favored Son.

But then his empire had grown, and the Kingdoms had been formed, and the Drakhin population grew and grew, thanks to the female Vradhu mates, and their civilization had grown complicated and intricate and Imril had learned of certain truths and horrors, and he had started to think: *what the fuck is the point of it all?*

Cynicism was a disease, one that had afflicted him for a very long time.

But now, with Esania standing at his back, silent, watchful, *hopeful*, depending on him for the survival of her people, he started to feel that old fire again.

She had placed her trust in him.

And her *vir* crackled through his veins.

Life. Returned.

He hadn't felt like this in longer than he could remember.

"Where are the humans?" he demanded, feeling strangely protective. All for Esania's sake. What an effect she had on him.

"You will not find them, Lightbringer. Not even *you*. Especially not you."

"You think I can't see their auras from the sky?"

"We know what you're capable of. You won't find them this time." Unexpectedly, the Vradhu smiled, revealing his sharp teeth. "I understand Drakhin law, Overlord. I am a Lord of the Two Clans myself. I also understand that desperate circumstances can make ancient laws seem irrelevant. You Drakhin have caused more death and destruction on this planet in a few thousand rotations than we Vradhu could ever have conceived of, and now your blue *magrel* servants are loose, and they are multiplying and causing chaos, destroying the natural order like you wouldn't believe." His smile was wide, but his eyes were cold, holding a glint of accusation. "How am I supposed to trust you when you have left such chaos in your wake, Overlord?"

Imril shrugged. "You know what I am. I will give you a choice. You can stay in the wilds with your humans and wait for the Naaga to find you, which they have done before, or you can send a scout to my eyrie and see for yourself that the pregnant human is untouched, and you can accept the offer of *my* personal protection, for you and your pack and your human sisters. You see who accompanies me now. Esania is unharmed, and unafraid. It is *she* who asked me to come here."

The Vradhu's black eyes flicked in Esania's direction, and they shared some sort of silent communication.

Esania nodded slowly.

"Both times, I found you easily," Imril said softly. "Their *vir* burns so brightly it is visible from the sky. It will only be a matter of time before others come in search of their power. It's strong, Vradhu. More potent and intoxicating than anything I've ever seen." Even now, he could feel Esania's life-force, and the beast in him wanted to go to her and clamp his hand around her neck and drink until he was filled to the brim with her power.

With great effort, he kept the madness in check.

At least, he tried. His cock was hard again. This had been happening a *lot* of late. He was going to have to do something about it soon, or there would be problems. "Decide for yourself." He waved his hand in dismissal. "Go, Vradhu. Discuss with your pack if you must. You know where to find me."

"I hear you, Lightbringer. Meanwhile, your Naaga are really multiplying like fucking *veppits*. We, would appreciate if you could do something about that. Think of it as a way to court our trust. You will hear from us soon, *Overlord*." The Vradhu gave a mocking bow before making a subtle sign with his left hand. Imril heard faint rustles of movement all throughout the dense, shadowy thicket. *Vradhu.* He was surrounded, but he couldn't see them, and he couldn't sense them. Vradhu males didn't give off *vir* like their female counterparts. Their innate energy was too tightly tethered to their bodies.

The Vradhu Lord disappeared, making barely a sound as he melded with the shadows.

Vradhu were exceptionally good at hiding. Humans, not so much.

That reminded him. They had to leave, *now*. He couldn't leave the eyrie unguarded for too long. Rau had strict instructions to take Sara into Kunlo's underground stronghold at the first sign of danger, but even the thick stone barriers and double-sealed doors would not hold potential invaders off for long, *especially* if they were in possession of Drakhin-tech.

"Esania," he snapped, turning around.

He came face-to-face with a glaring human, her brilliant

green eyes blazing. Furious, she put her hands on her hips. "They're *leaving?* What did you tell them?"

The full force of her anger washed over him, and for the first time, he saw *her*; the real her. She, who was better at hiding her thoughts than a cynical old Drakhin lord, who could make him second-guess himself even when her *vir* was tinged with emotion... Now she faced him with rage and betrayal writ large across her face.

She did not speak Vradhu. She wouldn't have understood the importance of what he'd just discussed with the Clan Lord. She did not understand their culture. Vradhu-Drakhin relations were complicated. The Vradhu had their own customs and laws, and the purple-skinned warriors were notoriously stubborn and secretive.

And even though she was wrong about him, her reaction disturbed him greatly. He did not like her mistrust, her disappointment.

He did not like it when she looked at him like that.

"You'd better have a good explanation for me, Drakhin." Her *vir* was tinged with anger and confusion, but not a shred of fear. She'd eaten and rested before they left the eyrie, and she was almost back to full strength.

She was radiant.

His cock stiffened.

Za's burning hells, what he wanted to do to her.

"Vradhu have their own minds," he slowly, removing his helm as he walked toward her. "They can't be convinced or coerced or forced. I have told the Clan Lord exactly what he needs to know."

"You *threatened* him."

"He threw a *war-spear* at you." Imril's voice grew cold as he remembered how *close* he'd been to killing the insolent wretch.

"Maki wouldn't hurt me. I've seen him in action. His aim

is perfect. He's an exceptional hunter. It was a warning shot, nothing more."

"Oh?" Energy flared from his fingertips as a sliver of jealousy entered his heart. He did not *like* it when she praised another male. He wanted to go after that cursed Maki and burn him to ashes.

"Maki wouldn't hurt me," she repeated stubbornly, and her unshakeable faith in the Vradhu irritated Imril all the more. "You should have let them take me to the others so I could talk to them and convince them that you're not dangerous."

"That would be pointless. They know who I am. The Vradhu will never reveal their hiding place to a Drakhin." The more he said, the angrier she seemed to get, her *vir* turning incandescent. Why was this upsetting her so? He was trying to explain things to her, and he'd never felt that he had to explain himself to anyone before, *ever*.

"My people are in that hiding place, Imril. They don't have poison barbs or spears or fancy armor or impossible powers. They only get one chance on this planet. *I* only get one chance. We can't afford to make a single mistake."

He came to a halt in front of her, and his cock grew even harder as he walked inside the radius of her *vir*. "I *told* you, I gave your Maki all the information he needed to make the right decision. The Vradhu will come to their senses."

"And what if they don't?"

"They *will*." He stared down at her, taking in her perfect features, complete with a smattering of dark pigment spots across her cheeks and the bridge of her nose. He noticed the slight flush in her cheeks and the rapid patter of her pulse, barely visible in her elegant neck. She looked so good in that golden jacket, the one he'd found carefully folded and stored in a chest in one of Kunlo's many rooms.

He breathed in her scent and became obsessed with her luscious pink lips, which glistened with a hint of moisture.

He wanted to devour her. Not just her *vir*, but everything.

"You..." She looked up at him, and there was something else mixed in with her anger. Her eyes were fixed upon his face, and she studied him with great intensity.

He'd seen that look before, countless times, on the faces of the dozens of female Vradhu who had come to Eleia to vie for his affection.

You find me pleasing, don't you, sweet human?

Even when you are angry at me.

In the end, the Vradhu females had always become afraid of him, of *what* he was, and that was the biggest turn-off in the Universe.

And he never heard the song when he was in their presence.

In the end, he had given up trying to search for a mate.

But this *human*...

Her anger, her complete absence of fear... it was glorious, and it turned him on.

"What, Esania?" Their faces were so close. He leaned in just a little bit more and inhaled her sweet scent.

"How can you be so sure they'll come?"

"Because, sweet human, I am the Overlord of Khira. I was here when that upstart Vradhu's ancestors used to roam freely across the Twelve Continents." *I was here when the Vradhu used to walk freely amongst the Drakhin. I was here when the Shadowring fell across our skies. I was here during the First War and during the Great War, and soon you will see what it truly means to be one of my subjects.*

Her lips remained parted, an expression of mild shock flitting across her perfect features before she quickly concealed it.

"What, are you surprised that I am so old?"

"No, I knew that already." The corners of her mouth twisted into a delicious frown, and her anger abated, just a little. She blinked. "*Sweet?*"

Caught in the heady cloud of her aura, Imril nodded.

They were *so close.*

She had no idea how tense he was right now, filled with hunger and lust.

He actually trembled as he nodded slowly, compelled to reach out and touch her. His wings flared. He drowned in her scent, drank in her beautiful form, imagined what it would be like to taste her as she lay before him, naked.

Not just her *vir*, but *all* of her.

"We have to go," he said instead, his voice thrumming with urgency. They'd already been away from the eyrie for too long. Until he got a better feel for what was going on in the Drakhin Territories, he wasn't going to take too many chances.

There would be time to deal with Esania's misunderstandings later.

Later.

Amongst other things.

You are sexually attracted to an alien, Drakhin. You have not even asked her about her world, the place she comes from, her customs, her expectations. Does she even find you attractive?

He *knew* she did... he could feel it in her *vir*. It drove him mad.

Esania exhaled slowly, her anger slowly starting to dissolve. "You'd better be right about this. I don't like the idea of them staying out in the wild."

"The Vradhu are some of the most cautious creatures on this planet, Esania. They won't make the same mistake twice. Do you understand?"

"I... think so." Finally, she relented.

Whatever he was doing, it seemed to be working, because she was starting to calm down. Imril stared at her, torn between wanting to devour her and protect her.

No. He must never take her by force, *ever*. The mere thought of it was enough to put a dampener on his arousal.

"We have to go," he snapped, pulling the *sulak* rope from

his belt-pouch. "Are you coming with me, Esania, or am I going to leave you behind so you can rejoin the Clan?"

"Are you seriously offering to let me go?"

He said nothing as he uncoiled the rope in his hand. Her *vir* was driving him mad. He had the means to restrain her, and the strength to do so. "Are you coming with me, Esania?"

Her eyes widened, and she trembled a little.

That's when he felt it.

Her intoxicating aura flared, giving off a faint hint of...

Arousal.

Thick and sweet. He could smell it, too.

Unable to help himself, Imril leaned in and kissed her.

CHAPTER TWENTY-TWO

ESANIA FROZE as his lips pressed against hers.

Softly at first, then harder and harder, he kissed her. His lips were warm, smooth, sensual, completely at odds with the harsh appearance of his face. He sucked her lower lip gently, running his smooth armor-gloved thumbs over her cheeks, easing his fingers along the braided rows of her hair. He held her in a half-grip, half-caress that was rough yet gentle, and oh-so possessive.

He probed her mouth with his tongue, which was long and pointed at the end. Her tongue connected with his, and Esania's mind was blown.

You can't do this!

That was the first thought that entered her mind, a legacy of years of Primean conditioning, but the intensity of Imril's kiss quickly swept away her reservations.

Her energy surged into him, and even though she was being drained, she didn't care, because a blissful sensation spread throughout her body, relaxing her muscles, filling her with warmth, sending a delicious ache right down into her tender clit.

So *this* was what it felt like to be kissed.

The Primean in her recoiled in horror, but she locked that part of her away, rejecting the culture she'd been raised in.

It wasn't as difficult as she'd thought it would be.

It was surprisingly easy, in fact.

She kissed him back.

Her very first kiss, and it was everything she'd never imagined it could be.

He kissed her harder, his lips crushing against hers. He tasted like sweetness and embers, and she wanted more, even as she slumped against him, the strength leaving her legs.

He pulled back, withdrawing his touch, taking a step back, his golden eyes widening in alarm. "That's enough."

"Imril..."

"Esania." From his lips, her name was a whisper, a growl, a reverent song. Her heart hammered. Her lips tingled with the memory of his kiss. Her desire surged.

What does this mean?

"Let's go," he said gruffly, beckoning to her. "Do you understand now why you need to trust me?"

"You never planned on letting me go, did you?"

He didn't answer her question, but the corner of his mouth turned upwards in a secret little smile. "Come, Esania."

In a trance, she drifted to him, allowing him to place his hands on her shoulders. He slowly spun her around and pulled her against him. "I'm still drinking in your *vir*," he whispered darkly, his voice infused with power and pleasure, "and now I am going to bind you to me."

Unable to even *think* of escaping him, she pressed her back against his rock-hard torso and let him slide the rope across her chest, under her arms, around her waist, even between her legs. Just like last time, he moved quickly and efficiently, but this time, his touch was a caress.

His hands skimmed over her breasts, her waist, her hips, awakening her body.

With their bare skin was separated only by thin barriers of metal and cloth, Esania ached to feel his bare skin against hers.

"I can't stop absorbing your *vir* right now, Esania." His low voice was a soft caress against her ear. "I know it's exhausting, but you don't need to be afraid. I've got you. I will never let you fall."

She couldn't shake off the lingering sensation of his kiss. "And what are we supposed to do now... about all *this?*" His kiss was no accident. The Overlord wanted her.

"There *is* a solution," he murmured. "I did not think I would be suggesting it so soon, but..." His voice trailed off as he unfurled his majestic wings.

"Cryptic as ever, I see," Esania muttered, but her voice was drowned out by the rush of air around them as Imril beat his wings, generating tremendous force.

They rose through the trees, defying the laws of physics as Imril maneuvered this way and that, finding a clear path through the canopy. When leaves and branches blocked their way, he simply blasted them, and they disintegrated into ashes.

Suddenly, they were up above the canopy, and a gust of cool air swirled past, lifting them higher and higher.

They soared, and Imril wrapped his powerful arms around her. All Esania could do was watch the dazzling landscape below as he held her tightly, and she knew without a doubt that he was never going to let her go.

CHAPTER TWENTY-THREE

THEY WERE BEING FOLLOWED. Imril cursed softly under his breath as he detected a presence at the edge of his awareness. He held Esania tightly, wrapping his arms across her chest, soaking in her intoxicating *vir*, although when he wore his scale-armor, he could only drink in a faint trickle.

Not wanting to alarm her, he simply increased his speed, sending a flow of power through his body. He rose higher, higher, until he reached the point where he could go no further without Esania passing out—the air was too thin up here.

"Imril?" she whispered, her voice barely audible above the rush of the wind. "What's going on?"

"Don't worry," he murmured, bringing his wings behind him in a streamlined V. He pushed more power through his body, creating a halo of energy around himself and Esania.

If he were on his own, he would double back immediately and go after their stalker, but he had Esania to think about, and he absolutely could *not* be reckless with her safety.

Suddenly, it dawned on him. This fragile creature was completely dependent on him for protection.

He'd emerged from Za's crater broken, desperate, and defeated, only to find purpose in the form of this delicate human.

Oh, she might be delicate, but she was whip-smart, too. What she lacked in strength, she made up for in cunning.

The fact that he was here in the skies, carrying out her bidding... that was a miracle in itself.

"Something's happening, isn't it?" Her voice was perfectly calm as Imril veered sharply and caught a swift wind current. "But you don't want to scare me, huh? It's okay, Imril. I'm torn between needing to know every minute detail and letting go completely, but I trust you. I'm just going to close my eyes and let you handle this. It's not how I usually operate, but—"

"You are safe with me," he said fiercely as he held her tightly. So strong was his desire to protect her that he didn't even have to think about it. "I'm going to get you home, Esania."

Whoosh.

Something shot overhead, a white and silver blur that reflected a flash of sunlight. Imril knew that outline...

Another Drakhin.

Moving very, very *fast*.

He could go faster if he wanted, but he didn't want to risk it with Esania in his arms.

His heart pounded. A powerful desire to kill rose up inside him, but he restrained himself, mindful of his precious cargo. "I need your *vir*, Esania."

"Take it. Even if I pass out, just take what you need."

This female. Her instant awareness of the situation and her unconditional trust humbled him to the core. Just like that, she disarmed him completely.

He could *never* be cruel to this sweet thing.

Never.

But to their enemies, he would be a nightmare.

He stripped off his scale-glove and curled his fingers around her neck, relishing the instant torrent of power that flowed into him.

Esania gasped.

Below them, the world flew by, becoming a blue and green blur.

He drank from her quickly, becoming intoxicated with power, feeling so fiercely protective that he felt his heart might burst.

"*Hold on,*" he whispered, tucking her head into his chest with his other hand.

A shimmering speck appeared in the distance, coming straight for them. As it neared, he caught the glint of sunlight on its silver helm. The bastard was taunting him, trying to draw him into an attack.

Imril refused to take the bait. He summoned power into his right arm, concentrating pure energy in the palm of his hand, holding it as far away from Esania as possible.

The Drakhin streaked past, wings outstretched, body straight like a spear. Despite his formidable speed, Imril wasn't worried about being hit by a stray bolt of power. This Drakhin didn't radiate power, because he *couldn't.*

Only Imril and Mael—the *first generation*—possessed that ability. The Ancestor had made them in his image; closer to gods than mortal beings. Acheros had created them in a lab, fusing his genetic material with their mother's.

A completely *unnatural* process.

But something had gone wrong. Imril and Mael were immensely powerful, but they were also sterile.

That's why Acheros had created the second generation. The silver ones couldn't even match him in power, but they could reproduce directly with Vradhu females producing live offspring.

A new, viable race.

A monster like Imril... he wasn't even supposed to *exist*.

But he did, and he was going to use every shred of his cursed power to protect this human.

Imril stared into the distance, searching for their stalker, but a thick bank of clouds obscured his vision, hiding the other Drakhin.

"You're an abomination, Imril," a voice called from above. Above the rush of the wind, it was terribly faint, but he recognized it instantly. Nykithus the Betrayer. He was flying above, keeping pace with Imril. "This little creature thinks she can trust you? Keep trying. Sooner or later, she'll realize what a monster you are, and when she is living every moment in fear, she will think of nothing but escape."

Rage coursed through him, but he suppressed it, mindful of Esania. Bound tightly against him with loops of *sulak*, she stiffened, and he caught a trace of fear in her *vir*.

Why? he wanted to ask Nykithus, but he needed to shake the bastard off quickly. This was too risky.

Why did you destroy our world?

"If you don't want to get incinerated, then *leave*," he thundered, raising his hand.

Laughter drifted down to him on the wind; high-pitched, deranged, hateful laughter. "You haven't changed," Lightbringer. Still blind as fuck."

Imril didn't react. Instead, he closed his eyes, listening intently.

The rush of wind.

A body hurtling through the sky.

There.

He clutched Esania tightly with one arm and inverted, coasting on his back for a heartbeat.

Boom!

He released the power from his right hand and heard a satisfying scream of pain.

Got you, you little shit.

He opened his eyes and saw Nykithus clearly for the first time. Clad in silver scale-armor, his wings outstretched, the Drakhin hadn't changed at all.

Clutching his side, Nykithus pulled out a long blade and dropped into a dive. "I can't kill you, but I can destroy your Source," he roared.

No. You will not! Imril inverted again, banking sharply, performing an act of flying that defied the laws of physics.

Esania cried out in fear, but she didn't squirm, didn't try and fight his body's momentum.

Imril thought about hurling another bolt in Nykithus's direction, but decided against it, channelling what was left of his power into the slipstream. He needed all the speed he could get.

Whoosh!

As Nykithus dropped, Imril shot up into the thick clouds, both arms curled tightly around Esania. She curled into his chest, radiating fear, disbelief, and above all, trust.

Cool mist hit them, and suddenly, they were flying through thick clouds.

Faster!

These were rain clouds, pregnant with moisture, soaking them in water. Imril curled himself around Esania as much as possible, shielding her from the fat droplets of water, which felt like tiny pellets when they hit at such high velocity.

He cut a torturous path, one that would make it impossible for Nykithus to follow them. Lightning flashed in the distance, followed by the ominous growl of thunder.

Esania tensed.

"*He won't catch us,*" he rumbled, and unable to resist himself, he planted a gentle kiss on her head, inhaling the soft scent of her hair.

She nodded, and Imril flew on, abandoning his first

instinct—which was to turn around, find Nykithus, and kill him.

There would be time for that later.

But first, he had to get Esania to safety.

CHAPTER TWENTY-FOUR

A WHOLE DAY PASSED, and Esania and Sara were left with nothing to do but eat, rest, and try to figure out how to deal with their strange predicament. Rattled by their encounter with the hostile Drakhin in the skies, Esania retreated into her own thoughts, saying very little, but then Sara would pull her back into the real world, and that wasn't necessarily such a bad thing.

Esania was so exhausted that she spent most of the time sleeping, but when she was awake, she and Sara talked, and she discovered there was a lot more to the human than what she'd thought. Sara was a stubborn, determined, deeply principled woman who hid her hopes and fears behind a half-serious mask.

They didn't see Imril again until he suddenly appeared in the doorway the following afternoon, his expression stern, his golden eyes glowing with an intensity that made her insides melt all over again.

What had he been doing all this time? Hunting for their attacker?

"*Ooh,*" Sara whispered, her voice loaded with irony as she spoke in Modern Galactic, a language Imril definitely wouldn't understand. *"Look who's come to visit. Your not-so-secret admirer."*

Esania resisted the urge to elbow Sara in the side. She wasn't used to being teased.

Imril gave them a pointed look, one golden eyebrow lifting in what *might* be amusement. He might not have understood Sara's words, but he would have understood her sarcastic tone.

Imril ignored her, his golden eyes fixing on Esania. "Come with me." His deep voice was as smooth as silk, threatening to drag her into its dark undertow.

"I've been summoned," she said drily, trying to hide the thrill of anticipation that coursed through her. Following a winged Drakhin through a mysterious abandoned fortress wasn't exactly her idea of *exciting*, but when it was Imril... anything could happen.

Esania rose to her feet and made her way across to where Imril stood. The wide doors stayed perpetually open now, and Imril had given them access to a winding stone staircase that led down into a small, overgrown courtyard where they could sit and enjoy the morning sunshine.

The rest of the fortress, however, was off limits.

Imril kept a safe distance from Sara, obviously not wanting to absorb even a wisp of her energy.

That quiet consideration surprised her a little. Clearly, there was more to this fierce Drakhin than just violence and hunger. He followed a certain set of morals.

They were safe... for now.

Esania nodded and followed him wordlessly, ignoring Sara's curious stare as they left the room and navigated the winding corridors. They ended up a small, sparsely decorated chamber. To one side, a massive open window revealed an impressive view of the glassy lake. There was no glass in the window, just a stone arch through which a cool breeze flowed. The sun was beginning to set, infusing the afternoon light with a hint of crimson.

The room was utterly bare except for a large bed covered in rumpled white sheets that was shoved against a bare wall.

It was so different to their expansive chamber with its fancy ceilings.

Is this where he... sleeps?

Forbidden thoughts entered her mind. "What do you want, Imril?"

When he turned, there was something in his hands—a container of sorts. "Paint my wings." A hint of a smile played across his pale lips.

"What?" Was she hearing correctly? He wanted her to *paint* him?

"This is nightblack. I made it from algae I scraped off the bottom of the lake. You need to coat my wings in the stuff until not a single area of bare skin remains."

The thought of touching the thick, leathery membrane of his wings was strange, but... exciting. For the first time, she became aware of his outfit—a matt-black version of his scaly armor... or was it his original armor, painted? The contrast with his pearl-colored skin was striking. He looked like a character out of some ridiculous Earth film; an otherworldly Hell Knight.

A pale demon.

An emperor without an empire.

Only there wasn't anything remotely ridiculous about him. "What's this all about?" she asked.

"I'm going on a reconnaissance mission."

"This has something to do with the one who attacked us yesterday?"

"I will handle him," Imril said softly, his voice low and dangerously cold. "Do not worry about him, Esania. I won't let him hurt you." He flexed his wings. "Unfortunately, my unique coloring tends to stand out against the night sky. My wings are too visible." He raised them and spread them wide, claw-tipped ends touching the walls on either side of the room.

"This is camouflage." He handed her the container, a small round box with a grey metal lid.

It was surprisingly warm to the touch. Esania opened it and found a blob of some sort of black greasy substance inside. "There's no brush or applicator. How am I supposed to apply this? With my bare hands?"

"Your tongue would also be acceptable." He smirked.

"That's not going to happen." She couldn't stop the heat from rising in her cheeks.

"You do not take well to orders, do you, human?"

"*Primean*, actually," she snapped, correcting him. "And no, I'm not used to taking orders from anyone." It was one thing to lay down her pride and become food-on-tap for this powerful Drakhin, but to be at his beck and call as if she were nothing but a simple servant; to be summoned at his every whim, to be *toyed* with like this...

She was a Primean senator, used to wielding power. Could she really adjust to this new role, where the Drakhin saw her as inferior? The irony of wasn't lost on her. All her life, she'd been treating humans as if they were some sort of lesser species.

That meant nothing here.

Calm down. Esania took a deep breath, reminding herself that Imril had helped her, had protected her, had *kissed* her...

Damn it. Bit by bit, he was wearing down her defenses.

"Primean, then," Imril murmured, his lips curving into an almost-smile. Smug. All-knowing. In control. It infuriated her. "Do you care to enlighten me on what that is, exactly?"

"Does it even matter to you?"

He dropped the smug look then, his expression becoming perfectly serious. "Of course it matters. This is going to be a long-term arrangement, Esania. I need to know everything about you."

"For your own amusement?"

He dipped his head, his expression softening. "I am sorry.

The passage of time has spoiled me. Cynicism is a bad habit of mine. Please continue. I didn't mean to upset you."

When he apologized like *that*, going from asshole to sincere in a heartbeat, how could she be angry with him?

Esania took a deep breath as a warm feeling spread through her, right down to her bare toes. The words started to flow before she even realized what she was doing. "We consider ourselves a different species," she said, reciting what she'd been told from day one. "*Homo primus.* We're descended from humans, but we've inherited highly engineered genes that give us certain advantageous traits. We are smarter, stronger, less vulnerable to disease, and less prone to being influenced by emotion. We live longer. We heal faster. We are..." *Superior.* Esania trailed off as she realized how hollow her words sounded.

The Primean Manifesto was bullshit, and she knew it.

Imril stared at her intently as he brought his wings down, curving them around her. A pale, leathery cage. Or cocoon, depending on one's point of view. "You are a made race, then?"

"You could say that." *Unnatural.* That's what Primeans were. They didn't even reproduce the way nature had intended. They didn't have sex, didn't share intimacy with each other.

They thought they had transcended all that.

"Then we are similar, because I am a made creature too. Come now, Esania. The sun will set soon, and I need as much of the night as I can get. I have a lot of territory to cover." Imril nodded at the container in Esania's hands as she tried to understand what he meant.

Made creature. Huh.

How could something as perfect as Imril be *made*?

"You couldn't just get Rau to do this for you?"

"I could have," he said, that infuriating half-smile playing across his lips once again.

Why were there butterflies in her stomach?

What the hell... here goes.

In her heart of hearts, she *wanted* to do this.

Slowly, Esania dipped her finger into the *nightblack* and traced a line down Imril's wing. The surface was warm, smooth, and slightly velvety, and to her surprise, touching his wing didn't result in a sudden drain of energy from her body to his.

But he tensed, and she could *see* the bulge in his pants.

The thought of his arousal sent a little quiver between her thighs.

Slowly, methodically, she smeared the substance across his wing, painting everything black. Imril said nothing, simply content to watch her as she worked. His intense scrutiny had a strange effect on her.

Her breath caught. Her heart hammered. His scent swirled all around her. She inhaled deeply. His nostrils flared. Once again, she became aware of how big and masculine and imposing he was.

"Keep going." His voice was hoarse.

Esania pressed her palm into the black goo, which was warm. "What am I doing here, Drakhin?"

"What do you think, Esania?"

She already knew the answer, yet part of her couldn't believe she'd just said that. It felt wrong and yet oh-so right.

The *nightblack* slid over her hand like a second skin, and she rubbed it over Imril's wing. It dried instantly, turning his pale skin obsidian.

"I think you're confused," she said, stroking the taut membrane of his wings. Her fingers slid over long bones that formed an elegant framework, and she marveled at how other-worldly he was.

"Oh?" Imril inclined his head, patient, half-amused, his golden eyes smoldering. *Dangerous.*

"Right now, you're having a biological reaction to me. You probably never expected to feel this way about an alien."

"I don't care that you're an alien, Esania. You're my Source."

She said nothing as she ran her hands over his wing, but her heart was hammering wildly.

"It's not just the *vir*," he murmured, his voice dropping to a near-whisper. He gave her that *look* again. All-knowing, all-powerful. His ancient eyes were filled with darkness and secrets.

"I don't understand," she whispered, running her fingers up and down his wing. "We can't touch for too long because you might kill me, we can't biologically reproduce, and we're completely different species, from planets at different ends of the Universe. What do you want from me, Imril?"

"Are you sure you want to ask me that question?"

"I'm asking you, aren't I?"

"One thing you should know about me, Esania. I don't lie." He leaned forward, both menacing and irresistible. "I want *you*."

She stiffened. "You want the energy I give off. Everything else is... *impossible*."

"Your body tells me otherwise."

She tried to fight the heat in her cheeks, tried to fight the warmth surging between her thighs, but it was futile. Her body was in overdrive, her most sensitive organs throbbing with need. How could she ever deny him when he could literally read her emotions?

"Stop this. We're different *species*, Imril. This is unnatural. Biologically, we can't even reproduce. We're not supposed to—"

"Forget logic, Esania. I can feel your *vir*. I can smell your arousal. You can't hide anything from me. Right now, I want to strip you naked. I would burn your clothes right off your body if I could. I want to touch you. I want to feed from you. I want to explore your body, find out where that sweet scent is coming from, and devour it. I am aching to bury my cock inside you."

He raised an eyebrow. "I assume your anatomy permits such things?"

She stiffened as Imril's words washed over her. This impossible male was taking advantage of her vulnerability, and she didn't like that. The power imbalance between them was just too great.

But she couldn't forget the way he'd held her with such possessive tenderness, even as he sucked the very life out of her.

She couldn't forget their kiss in the forest.

She was attracted to a monster, and he knew it.

She *wanted* him to bury his cock inside her, but he would probably kill her.

What kind of fucking torture *was* this?

"What my body is or isn't capable of is none of your business," she growled, peeling her blackened hand away from his wing. "Maybe you should get Rau to finish this job. This is draining for me."

You're such a prude.

That's what Sara had told her the other day.

You Primeans need to get rid of those sticks you've all got shoved so far up your asses. Life is a lot more interesting when you don't take yourselves so seriously all the time. What is even the point of your civilization if you don't know how to enjoy anything? And I mean that in the nicest way possible, ma'am.

Oh, Sara was definitely a lot more free with her tongue now that they weren't trapped within the artificial plas-domes of the Serakhine.

"No," he said softly, curving his wings a little more so there was no way she could back out. She was *trapped*. "Rest assured, Esania, I am not going to mindlessly fuck you as if I were some impulsive youngling. *That* I will not force upon you. Ever. But you are essential to my survival. I need your *vir*. That part is non-negotiable, Esania."

"I'm under no illusions about that, Drakhin." She closed

her eyes. Still, his scent and his overwhelming presence surrounded her, filling her with a strange kind of madness. "I suppose I should be grateful to you for not trying to rape me or kill me." Her voice cracked slightly—a little defensive, a little hurt. She, who had never ever conceived of having any sort of intimate relationship in her lifetime, was suddenly hoping that Imril would turn around and... what?

Set her free?

She couldn't be his slave *and* his concubine. She just couldn't.

Shit. Esania didn't even understand her own emotions right now. Primean life hadn't really prepared her for any of this. She didn't know how to respond to... or *initiate* any sort of intimacy.

"Esania, I would not do any of those things. Ever." Imril's voice was a low rumble as he brushed his wing against her hand. He almost seemed offended. "You *know* what I desire. If you want this, there is a way."

She stared at him, a little shocked. "A way we can... Without you killing me, you mean?"

"Yes. You would have to undergo a transformation. It will be painful, and the changes to your body would be permanent, but the benefits are obvious." He smiled, revealing sharp, brilliant teeth.

This was a revelation to her, but Esania wisely kept her mouth shut and her expression neutral. "Oh," was all she said.

"You only have to say the word, Esania."

Oh. In that instant, something changed between them. The balance of power shifted. No longer were they just master and servant.

It was a lot more complicated than that.

Hiding her confusion, she reached into the pot of night-black and coated her hand in the stuff. Slowly, deliberately, she rubbed it across Imril's wing, and she was a little surprised that her hand wasn't trembling. Inside, her heart was going into overdrive, her body into near-meltdown.

He wanted her.

He wanted to make this thing... *permanent*.

Your mate.

Why did those two words simultaneously blow her mind and terrify her?

And why did this act of rubbing warm black goo over pale, leathery wings feel so damn delicious?

"I... will consider it," she said, trying her very best to sound nonchalant and failing miserably. Imril's wicked smile told her that he'd seen right through her.

CHAPTER TWENTY-FIVE

ESANIA STEPPED BACK, admiring her handiwork. Imril's magnificent wings were now perfectly obsidian, with not a single patch of pale skin remaining. His pale skin, golden hair, and golden eyes contrasted so starkly with all the black, making him look like a beautiful demon.

There was no way anyone would mistake him for an angel, that was for sure.

"Happy now?" she asked, folding her arms. The job had appealed to her meticulous nature, and she'd spent a long time making sure everything was perfect, something Imril seemed to approve of.

The whole time, he was consuming a steady trickle of her *vir,* just enough that she could sense it, but for some reason, she wasn't left feeling as drained as before. Maybe her body was adapting.

As she worked, Imril watched her with a smoldering gaze that radiated power and desire, and despite her earlier reservations, she couldn't help but feel emboldened by his attention.

But not once did he lay his hands on her.

"Impressive," he murmured, his voice a tantalizing rumble. "You are something of a perfectionist, aren't you?"

"I was brought up that way." She couldn't deny it. "Primeans don't accept compromise, and we don't settle for second best."

"We are alike in more ways than you realize." Imril brought his wings down against his back, pulling them so close that they seemed to disappear into his obsidian armor. Before Esania realized what was happening, he took hold of her hands, which were both covered in dried *nightblack*.

"I assume this doesn't just wash off," she muttered, keeping perfectly still as he ran his thumbs over her blackened palms. The *nightblack* had dried, and she wondered if it was ever going to come off.

"Soft hands," he said quietly, studying her long fingers. "Not a worker or a servant. You are intelligent, calculating. Someone who sits in a position of authority."

Esania hoped the heat in her cheeks wasn't showing. So he thought she was *intelligent*, huh?

"Just because I have soft hands doesn't mean I'm not used to hard work. I serve my people, Drakhin." Nothing could make her forget the countless hours she'd spent poring over endless datastreams of Earth law and Primean law as she formulated complicated legal arguments for the Senate.

That had been hard work.

As Imril's scale-covered hands slid over hers, a pleasant shiver ran down her spine. His hands dwarfed hers, and yet he was oh-so gentle with her. What would it be like when they were together in bed, their bare bodies touching for the first time? "I *know* you serve your people, Esania, but you can't deny that I'm right about you."

She loved the way he said her name in that deep, rumbling drawl, as if he were caressing every syllable with his voice.

But at the same time, his arrogance got under her skin. *Typical Imril.* "You think you know everything, don't you, Drakhin?"

"Not everything, but I know most things."

She didn't know whether he was being serious or not. "Then why are you still here, holding the hands of a woman you can't really touch, when your empire is in ruins?"

Imril lifted her blackened hand and kissed it. "Because, my dear *Primean*, I am about to fly into the most dangerous place on the face of Khira, and I do not know what I am getting myself into, so before I do that, I need to feed."

Her palm tingled as his lips touched her skin, as he kissed her hand slowly. His lips were as warm as she remembered them, and his tongue was as devious as ever, tracing small circles on her palm.

The *nightblack* came off as he licked her. "Th-that's not a very good disguise," she gasped.

CHAPTER TWENTY-SIX

"MHMM." Imril ignored her as he drowned in the heady cloud of her *vir*. He didn't tell her that his saliva contained special enzymes that easily broke down the algae's black residue, yet another mystery of his strange biology—probably the Vradhu genes in him. He just kept licking her hand, drawing in her power, cleaning the *nightblack* from her beautiful brown skin in the process.

The more he took from her, the more she relaxed, and he knew that was the effect of his feeding. As a predator, it was easier for him if his victim found the feeding process enjoyable. That was how the Ancestor had designed them. Feeding tapped into neural pathways and released certain chemicals in the brain.

With her right hand licked clean, he took her left, paying homage to the fingers that had painted his wings with such methodical precision.

"Ohh," she sighed, and he wondered what it would be like to hear her cry out when he placed his tongue on her pleasure points.

He was certain her anatomy would be compatible with his.

It *had* to be. They were similar in so many ways; bipedal, two-armed, intelligent...

Besides, he could *smell* her arousal.

Imril sucked on her fingers, imagining that he was pleasuring her below, enjoying the flow of her *vir* as its character changed, becoming deeper, richer.

"You're terrible," she announced in a tone that told him she meant the exact opposite. She made a half-hearted attempt to pull her hand away, relenting when he circled the pad of her thumb with his tongue. "I-I thought you weren't going to force this."

"Mhmm." Imril kept his eyes downcast, fearing he would lose control if he looked at her. His vocal chords started to rumble, a deep, primal sound that surprised even him. He knew of this response, this typically *Vradhu* reaction that could signify both deep desire and satisfaction, but it had never happened to him before.

Unable to help himself, he looked up and saw that her eyes were closed. Her face was upturned, her lips slightly parted, her expression an impossible mixture of serenity and yearning.

She was *ripe*.

But he'd taken enough.

"I have to go," he said hoarsely, turning away. The sun was dipping below the horizon, throwing the deepest shade of violet across the sky.

He glanced over his shoulder, shooting her a final lingering look.

Then he picked up his helm, donned it, and launched himself into the sky, spreading his wings wide as a powerful wind-current carried him away.

"*Be safe.*" Her soft voice drifted after him, and he was grateful for the wind that carried him away, because he almost looped around and turned back to make her his once and for all.

CHAPTER TWENTY-SEVEN

WITH ESANIA'S glorious energy roaring through his *vir*-channels, Imril flew over dark plains and valleys and moon-light-touched streams. He *hated* the thought of leaving her alone even for a moment, but Za's hells, he was spread thin.

Nykithus's sudden appearance had reminded him how vulnerable their position was. Right now, the eyrie was unguarded, and he didn't like that at *all*, but Rau had strict instructions to take the humans into the underground vault at the first sign of danger.

He'd inspected the vault thoroughly, and it was in good working order, connected to two escape tunnels that ran beneath the lake, emerging in secluded thickets on the other side. When it came to defense, Auka technology was infallible.

Hopefully, Esania would never have to use the vault. He would try and get this done as quickly as possible.

Za's burning hells, this was *not* his way of doing things, but Imril had no choice. He had to strike first, to find a way to eliminate the threat before Nykithus found them.

In order to do that, he needed information, and Mael was the only one who could tell him what had happened to the world in his absence.

His brother was as old as he, his existence a mere drop in the lifetime of this planet, but an eternity in the history of their race.

Could he be flying into a trap?

No, Mael had his chance to kill him already. Mael had his chance to take Esania and Sara, and he'd left them in Imril's care.

And Mael would never, ever side with the likes of Nykithus. Mael was a loner, rarely venturing out of his mysterious domain in the frozen southern pole of Khira.

But something had drawn him out, and clearly, he needed Imril's power.

What are you planning, brother of mine?

Imril didn't trust Mael, but right now, he needed him too. How ironic that they were once again forced together—out of necessity. He gritted his teeth. For Esania's sake, he would lay aside old vendettas and work with his twin.

For *her* sake.

She didn't know it yet, but she was his *lukara*—his mate. In the ashes of his empire, Imril had finally found his One, but there was no way he could mate with her unless she accepted his *elgida*. He would kill her otherwise.

What was it that his old friend Tykhe had told him once? Tykhe, who had been happily mated to a Vradhu female, who had given his mate the most stunningly intricate *elgida*, who was the proud father of two healthy Drakhin sons, had thought to advise him on the finer points of mating.

That was such a long time ago, but he remembered it like it was yesterday. They'd just come from a sparring session, and Tykhe was nursing a vicious cut above his left eyebrow.

As usual, Imril didn't have a scratch on him.

"Ah, Lord Imril, you invulnerable bastard. You're more vicious today than usual. What's gotten into you? Maybe you just need to go and get laid."

Imril shot him a baleful look. "Don't you start, Tykhe."

"It will happen, Imril. You might think you're all-powerful now, Overlord, but someday, a female will come along, and she will make you feel like burning your empire to the ground just to have her. You may think you will always be in control, but it will happen quickly, without warning, like a lightning flare from the sky. And you will know without a shadow of a doubt, that she is the One, your one and only lukara, because you won't be able to go a moment without thinking of her." Tykhe laughed. "I can't wait to see you brought to your knees by a female, brother. You might think I'm mad, but one day, you will understand."

But Tykhe was long gone, having left the planet on an Auka escape ship, and he would never meet the female to whom Imril had pledged his *elgida*.

Ah, how he missed the bastard. He really could have used Tykhe's advice right now.

Anger rose up in him as he soared over undulating hills that merged into sand dunes. His body crackled with pent-up energy as he crossed a wide beach and flew over the wild sea. In the distance, a storm raged, spitting lightning from thick black clouds.

He was at perhaps half his full strength now, still hungry, still furious, still horny as fuck, driven half-mad with the thought that he was doing this to himself. Really, he could take Esania at any time. He could force the *elgida* upon her if he wanted to.

But that would be futile.

How could he live with a mate who didn't trust him? She'd already ruined him for *vir*—he just couldn't stomach the thought of feeding from another—and he selfishly demanded her subservience.

Yet he wanted more.

Consumed with thoughts of Esania, Imril flew on until at last he saw what he was looking for.

There.

The darkness below changed, becoming absolute. Not a single ray of moonlight or starlight penetrated here. This was *perfect* darkness, even darker than the night itself, completely obliterating any sight of the vast Kingdom of Ton Malhur.

The *shadowveil* was impressive.

And there was only one being on all of Khira who could construct such a thing.

Twisting his body, angling his wings, Imril caught a downward current and dropped toward the impenetrable darkness. He landed on a windswept rocky outcrop bordered by half-dead grasses and weeds. Power flared from his hands, snapping and crackling against the blackness and silence, the only sign of life in the forlorn, forsaken place.

The Vakarin plains.

The edge of the Mountain Kingdom.

Just as Esania had told him.

Slowly, Imril folded his wings, sat down, and waited for Chaos.

CHAPTER TWENTY-EIGHT

"SO YOU *DO* HAVE some sense left in that thick head of yours."

Imril whirled as Mael materialized out of the darkness. It had always irked him that he couldn't sense Mael, even though Mael could sense him.

But then how did one detect a being that wielded *nothingness* instead of power? Some aspects of his twin's abilities had always remained a mystery, and he still had no idea what new powers Mael might have gained during his bonding with the *Hythra*.

Mael was dangerous, and not to be trusted, and there was a *lot* of bad blood between them.

Imril thought about hurling a bolt of power at the bastard's face, but decided against it. Mael had been decent enough *not* to touch the pregnant human, Sara, so Imril would hear him out. Besides, he needed information.

"What is this, Mael?" His power flared, surrounding him with a cocoon of golden light. "What do you want?"

Mael frowned. "Brother of mine, just this once, can you quit being so *fucking* conspicuous? "

"What are you talking about?" Imril's left eyebrow

twitched in irritation as he rose to his feet, drawing on every shred his self-control just to dampen the tension inside him; anger, violence, lust, surging through his body like an uncontrollable fire.

He couldn't stop thinking about Esania.

Calm down.

Couldn't stop thinking about her.

"Look at you, brother, all lit up like an eyrie's shining beacon in the night. What's up with you? This isn't the age of Drakhin anymore. Try a little stealth before you alert the Naaga to our presence." Mael scoffed. "But subtlety was never your strong point, was it, brother?"

"I've never *needed* to be subtle." Although Imril's voice was laced with scorn, he tempered the power crackling through his *vir* channels, pulling it deep within his body. The light around him disappeared, leaving them in perfect darkness with only the cold wind whistling past. "Since when were you afraid of Naaga?"

"Not afraid, idiot. You've got no idea what has happened while you were having your little three-hundred-revolutions long nap, do you?"

"Care to enlighten me, then? Three hundred revolutions and you couldn't control the situation, Mael? I'm surprised."

A baleful expression crossed Mael's dark features. *"Tch.* I became infected with the virus, just like you. I was weak. *Sick.* It took a hundred revolutions until I was fully healed. In that time, all I could do was contain the area with my shadow. If I let it fall now, I would release them into the world." Mael bared his sharp teeth. *"I'm* not the one who caused this fucking mess. What kind of Overlord ignores infighting between his Lords? You could have stopped it."

Imril went still, anger and lust freezing in his veins as he remembered the events that led up to Nykithus's betrayal.

"I could have," was all he said. *But I grew complacent. I didn't read the signs until it was too late.*

Quick-witted, graceful, charming Nykithus had been his favored Lord, and Imril had gifted him the vast kingdom of Ton Malhur, shocking some of the older Lords who'd had their eyes on the rich highlands for hundreds of revolutions.

Petty politics. Backstabbing. Infighting. Whispers and rumors of a successor. Drakhin Lords all vying for his favor.

How tedious and pointless it had all become.

And slowly, he'd become completely and utterly corrupted by his own power.

"Could have, would have, *should* have," Mael snarled. "The question is, what are you going to do about it now?" He spat on the ground in disgust. "We are still here, and that moron Nykithus has done the unthinkable. He put his cursed seed into a Naaga and spawned an entire race of hybrids. The little lordling continues to rule over them, thinking he's you."

Imril hissed. "I'm surprised you haven't killed him yet, brother." Imril's power flared again as he thought of a hundred different ways he might kill Nykithus the Betrayer. What kind of world had the bastard created in his absence? The younglings—least of all Nykithus—had never respected the old Laws, which he'd created specifically to prevent a situation like this.

One time... just *one* time, Nykithus had spoken of altering the Naaga's DNA; making them stronger, more Drakhin-like, less subservient.

They share our blood, Imril, and there are females amongst them. We are all descendants of the Vradhu. What if we could...

Imril had told him never to speak of it again, on pain of death.

Mael's tail flickered, a sign of his irritation. "You see this shadowveil? It covers all of Ton Malhur, even the Industrial City. Do you know how much concentration it takes to maintain this fucking thing? I don't have the *Hythra* at my disposal to hold it in place while I hunt. In order to attack Nykithus, I would have to let it fall. What do you think happens if I do that?" Mael's black eyes burned, and for a moment, they were twin gateways to the nexus between this dimension and the next. *Shit*. Sometimes even his own brother gave Imril the creeps. "I'm *containing* them, brother. I've held them under siege for three hundred revolutions, but there are thousands of them, and I am only one man, and unlike you, I am wingless." He shot Imril an accusing glare. "It was necessary. They have these cursed new technologies." Mael hissed in disgust. "*Vir* harvesters. Energy weapons. Poisons. Things that can harm even you and me. But now I grow tired of this, Imril. It's time to end it. You need to finish what you started."

Imril stared out at the blackness, at the impossible shadowveil, secretly transfixed by his brother's power. Nobody except Mael really understood how his power worked. Somehow, he killed energy, killed light, turned it into darkness, into *nothing*.

But could his brother be trusted?

"Your madness... is it gone?" he asked finally, staring into eyes that were as black as the infinite Universe. Sometimes, he felt that Mael was changing, becoming closer to what their father was; a spectral creature with a direct link to that *other* dimension.

"It will never be *gone*," Mael said softly, "but I can control it now. The *Hythra* is dead. I have her memories, but she is dead."

"Finally."

"Finally."

Something passed between them then; a moment of shared understanding. Imril went still as hundreds of revolutions of animosity and hatred washed over him. There was a time when they wouldn't have been able to look each other in the eye like this, when they would have tried to tear each other apart. After he broke free of the *Hythra*, Mael had been intent on taking away everything Imril had ruled over.

But now there was nothing. No throne, no empire, no Drakhin.

Bit by bit, Imril's resentment toward Mael faded. It occurred to him that he couldn't remember exactly what they were fighting about. Ages-old feuds had a way of becoming pointless like that.

He might be stubborn, but he wasn't crazy. Imril took a deep breath and closed his eyes, trying to quell the storm that raged inside him. Esania's perfect face swam and crystallized in his memory, her expression capturing a single emotion.

Hope.

Hope for survival.

Hope that he could be trusted. She *wanted* to trust him.

For a while, he said nothing as he listened to the howling wind, to the rhythm of this ancient, mysterious planet, where he and Mael were really nothing more than visitors. Khira was here before they were created, and it would be here when they had long turned into stardust.

He remembered his past life, a time of decadence and cruelty and wanton excess.

He would never want Esania to meet that version of him.

Imril swallowed his pride and made a decision. "What do you want me to do, brother?"

If Mael was surprised, he didn't show it. If the words *I-told-you-so* were running through his mind, he didn't speak them. Imril's twin might be a breath away from madness, but sometimes, he could be surprisingly decent.

"This planet," Mael said softly, "it has and always will belong to the Vradhu. Our *mother's* people. We are the abominations here, the invaders. Or did you somehow forget, brother?"

A sliver of raw pain wound its way through Imril's heart, mixing with his guilt. "No. I did not forget." There was a time when he'd *tried* to forget, when he'd tried to remake his world and erase every trace of the curse that had created them.

Drakhin. *Treacherous blood.* As time went on, he'd come to detest some of his kin.

He thought of Esania and the way she'd so fiercely protected her tribe, putting her own life in danger for the sake of another.

Putting him to shame.

Beyond the skies of Khira, there was life. A sweet, strange creature called Esania had shown him that, and somehow, this small tribe of humans and their determination to survive made all Drakhin grievances and blood-feuds seem so petty.

He didn't want to destroy this world, he wanted to build it again.

For *her.*

"I have held this fucking barrier together for as long as I could, brother. I waited in the hope that you would appear to sort out your own little mess, and it seems you've finally come to your senses. Our mother wouldn't stand for this chaos, Imril."

"No, she wouldn't," Imril said slowly, overcome with sadness and pride as he remembered the magnificent woman who had been his mother. Everything decent in him and Mael was because of *her.* Acheros had allowed Marial to raise them on the *Hythra,* but as they grew older, he started to separate them, playing cruel games with the twins and their mother.

Experiments.

Why did Imril get the feeling they were still stuck in some sort of cruel experiment? "I encountered Nykithus beyond the shadowveil," he growled, studying Mael's face for any sign of deceit.

"That's because my barrier is starting to fall apart. I saw him return. Badly wounded. Desperate. He had no choice. Your doing, obviously. I don't understand why you didn't kill him when you had the chance."

"You do not understand what happened." Imril gritted his teeth. "How did he get out?"

Mael's tail flicked back and forth, the abrupt tempo a clear sign of his irritation. "There are breaches in the veil. The Naaga have been traveling in and out ever since the first hole appeared, and I am tired. I can't hold the form anymore."

"That isn't like you, brother. Has something changed?"

"None of your fucking business, Imril. For once in your life, just listen to me, and do as I say." The Shadowbringer shook his head in frustration. "You need to kill Nykithus. Once you cut the head off the monster, the rest will fall. They tried to take command of the *Hythra*. They poisoned the Ardu-Sai. They are multiplying endlessly, spreading through this world like vermin."

"To what end?" Imril's anger returned in full force as he remembered Nykithus's affinity for power; the way he'd subtly undermined Imril's advisors and pitted the lesser lords against one another.

"That, my brother, is the eternal question. I have my theories, but I won't bore you with the details."

Imril turned, spreading his wings. "Three darklights. That's all I need, and then we will end this once and for all."

"Some sort of strategy would be nice," Mael said, a vicious smile spreading across his face. Now the bastard seemed amused, and Imril thought he detected just a hint of the old madness in the Shadowbringer's eyes. "Can't just go in there and torch the entire place, I suppose."

"Why not?" Imril waved his hand in dismissal. "You leave that to me, brother." He knew Nykithus, that traitorous *bastard*. He knew his strengths, his weaknesses, his deepest desires.

Mael laughed. "You haven't changed, brother."

And no Drakhin wielded power like Imril, no matter how hard they trained. He was one of two truly monstrous beings on this planet. What the second gen lordlings had failed to understand was that none of them—not even Nykithus—had ever seen Imril at his full strength.

They didn't know how much *vir* he could really pack into his monstrous body.

Not even Nykithus, who Imril had once thought of as the son he could never have.

"I will return," he said to his still-smiling brother as he spread his wings wide.

"I'll be waiting."

Imril launched himself into the air and soared, desperate to get back to his Esania. He was about to demand a lot of her, but she was strong enough to handle him, and when she understood what he was about to do, she would give him what he needed.

After all, the survival of her race depended on it.

CHAPTER TWENTY-NINE

IMRIL STOOD on the rocky shore, watching as a small boat sliced across the glassy water like a knife. Mist rose from the surface of the lake, a diaphanous shroud that obscured the forest in the distance.

The Vradhu stood tall on the boat, propelling it across the lake with the aid of a long paddle. His war-spear was strapped to his back, and he stared straight ahead, meeting Imril's gaze without fear or hesitation.

Imril remained perfectly still as the boat slid up on the gravel, coming to a halt. The Vradhu dropped his paddle, jumped out and strode up the shore, moving with the fluid grace of a natural hunter.

He didn't recognize this Vradhu. The warrior sported fierce swirling *ankhata*—those striking black pigmentation marks—on both cheeks, and his hair was braided in the usual Vradhu Hunter fashion. He was youthful, this one, probably no older than twenty revolutions or so. Vradhu lives were short. They usually lived to see about a hundred revolutions, compared with the Drakhin, who didn't seem to age and were usually killed through war or feuding.

For a moment, they just stared at each other, Vradhu and Drakhin, once allies, once mortal enemies, and now...

Something stirred in Imril's blood. Like it or not, his destiny was tied to the violet-skinned ones.

They shared blood, after all.

"Where's your offsider?" Imril narrowed his eyes as he stared at the Vradhu. Hunters always moved in pairs. Why was this one on his own?

"I volunteered to come alone." The warrior crossed his powerful arms, smiling. "We hunt in pairs because of the kratok... but you are no kratok, Imril *Makura.*"

Makura? That was a Vradhu word he definitely didn't understand.

"No, I am not," Imril returned his smile, baring his sharp teeth. "Two of you would not be enough to take me down."

"So you understand why it would be pointless to send another."

"If you fail, it's a suicide mission."

"I'm not afraid of death, Drakhin."

"Don't be so flippant, Vradhu. Your lives are short, and you are still young. Try telling me the same thing when your *ankhata* have turned silver with age."

"You think you know us so well, Lightbringer?" The warrior tensed and bared his teeth, a battle-ready stance if Imril had ever seen one.

"Better than you realize, brat." *A long time ago, I shared meat with your ancestors.* "Has your Clan Lord come to his senses, then?"

"That depends."

"Oh?"

"Take me to the humans."

Imril inclined his head. "Predictably, you want to see if I have kept my word. Is my name held in such little regard in this age?"

"You betrayed us in the past. Trust is not to be taken for granted, *Overlord*."

"I didn't start that war," Imril said quietly, deeply regretting his part in it. As with most of these things, the war had been over females, and it had quickly spiraled out of control.

"But you did your part. How many Vradhu did you kill?"

"It was a Vradhu hunting party that attacked my eyrie." Imril said softly, remembering how the fierce, wily Vradhu had taken him by surprise. Back then, the Vradhu knew how to tame the wild flying Kratok and ride them. A pack of warriors had flown in from the skies, straddling the Kratok, their piercing war-cries echoing through the cold morning air.

They dropped right into the heart of Imril's eyrie.

It was a suicide mission. They knew it, but they were so enraged at what had happened to their clanswoman that they would happily die as long as they took down a few Drakhin with them.

That fool, Brodhiel. Reckless. Arrogant. *Stupid.* Imril had warned him, but he'd gone too far.

"They killed my servants, my Weapons Master, my House Guard..." Imril's voice grew cold as he remembered standing over the lifeless bodies of his men, each with a wound from a Vradhu's deadly poison barb in the center of the chest.

Duhil and Zafikel had been training on the upper landing yard when the Vradhu attacked, taking them by surprise. Furious, Imril had killed the Vradhu warriors that dared to invade his domain. Then he'd taken to the skies and razed the Vradhu settlement, ending the war once and for all.

Driving the Vradhu deep into hiding.

Brodhiel had killed his Source—a Vradhu female—and in doing so, set off a chain of events that would eventually lead to the downfall of the Drakhin race.

"Lord Maki says you killed Kanahe's murderer. Is that true?"

Kanahe. That had been her name, a Vradhu female

promised to Brodhiel in exchange for Drakhin protection and riches. Brodhiel had fed too much, too often.

Imril stared at the young Vradhu, the power coursing through his veins. "What is your name, Vradhu?"

"I am Vanu."

"Vanu. For someone who is at a distinct disadvantage, you presume too much."

The warrior stiffened, glancing warily at the tendrils of power that flickered around Imril's fingers. The Vradhu might be cocky, but he wasn't stupid. *Good.*

"Come now, Vanu. I will show you proof that my word is good. But be warned. If you try anything stupid, anything that causes harm to the ones under my protection, I *will* kill you." He was fairly certain Vanu didn't have any ill intentions toward the humans, but he wasn't taking any chances. Stranger things had happened.

"I-I wouldn't do any such thing," Vanu blurted, appearing a little offended.

"Good," Imril growled. "Welcome to my domain, Vradhu."

It had been several lifetimes since he'd welcomed a Vradhu into his domain.

This, he supposed, was a good place to start.

CHAPTER THIRTY

ESANIA SPUN at the sound of voices.

"What?" She did a double take, shocked to see a Vradhu standing beside Imril in the doorway.

She recognized him. A little shorter than the others, thick, muscular build, the distinctive patterns on his face...

"Hey, it's Vanu." Reclining on the bed, Sara gave him a lazy half-wave, not appearing in the least bit surprised.

How does she do that? Appear so relaxed like that?

Esania felt anything but relaxed.

Vanu stared at them, an expression of shock crossing his proud features. *"Tass tu?"*

Are you okay?

"Tu," Sara assured him. That was about the extent of their Vradhu.

Imril and Vanu exchanged a pointed look.

"Imril," Esania said slowly, walking toward them, taking care to stay just outside Imril's radius, which was about a meter, give or take. "Why is Vanu here?"

"He came to check that I have kept my word; that you and Sara are unharmed. Vradhu don't trust Drakhin."

"Clearly."

Imril turned to Vanu, raising his eyebrows expectantly. They exchanged words in rapid-fire Vradhu, until at last Vanu seemed satisfied.

Imril nodded and signaled to Vanu with an imperious wave of his hand. He turned to Esania, looking decidedly... *Overlordly.* "The Vradhu and the humans have agreed to come to the eyrie."

As if to say: *see? I told you so.*

Relief flooded through her, and even his Drakhin smugness wasn't able to irritate her. "Thank you," she sighed.

Soon, she would see her girls again, along with the fierce mercenary women who had saved them from a terrible fate on Mars.

Imril regarded her with a look that was full of warmth and possessiveness and hunger. She was suddenly tempted to move closer, to feel his inexorable pull, to let him draw on her energy, but she held back, acutely aware that Vanu and Sara were staring at them intently.

Vanu and Sara even exchanged a *look.*

Imril ignored them. "These Vradhu are cut off from their pack. They know they won't last long without my help. It was only a matter of time."

"How did you know?"

One corner of Imril's mouth quirked, his expression softening. "I've been around long enough to get a feel for these things." *How* old was he again? She didn't care anymore. Stars, when he looked at her like that... "They were looking for you, you know. These humans are stubborn... but then again I already knew that. Vanu tells me that despite their warnings, the females were planning to actually fight me to get the two of you back, but on foot, there is only so much they can do." He chuckled softly. "There is no need for them to fight. They know you are mine. All they need to do is accept it. All *you* need to do is accept it."

She heard a deep intake of breath from Sara.

Vanu wore an expression of pure bemusement.

Esania opened her mouth, a sharp rebuke on the tip of her tongue. But then she thought of what he had done.

He'd taken care of them. He'd refrained from taking Sara's *vir*. He'd helped her locate the Vradhu, and somehow, he'd convinced the proud warriors to accept his protection.

You are mine.

She felt it too. She didn't want to fight him anymore.

Imril smiled then, and it was the most glorious thing she'd ever seen. His face transformed, his golden gaze softening, his pale skin shimmering, his sensual lips parting to reveal glittering teeth.

He was *breathtaking*.

And she wanted him to kiss her again.

Esania took a deep breath and stepped closer, entering the invisible ring that surrounded him. As she crossed over into his vortex, he let out a soft, shuddering sigh.

He *looked* like a creature out of some mythical Earth tale—ancient, otherworldly, *perfect*—and she could hardly believe he was real, but when she stepped into his radius, his hard, glittering exterior slipped, just a little.

That was the effect she had on him.

She didn't know how, but she just did.

And she didn't know why, but somehow, this just felt right.

"*Dude,*" she thought she heard Sara whisper in Earthian, "*just go for it.*"

As if she had her own personal cheer squad.

Imril didn't give any sign that he'd heard. His was completely absorbed in her. "Satisfied?" He seemed immensely pleased with himself.

Esania basked in his good mood, feeling triumphant that she'd secured a route to safety for her people. "For now."

But what made her feel even more ecstatic was the fact that he'd kept his word. He hadn't lied to her. He'd gone to great lengths to prove his integrity to her, even though he had more pressing issues to deal with. "You know, you're not as terrible as the legends make you out to be."

"No, I'm not." Imril reached out and stroked the side of her face. For once, he wasn't wearing his armor, and his bare fingers gently coaxed the energy out of her. "These so-called legends make me seem tame. Really, I can be much worse."

There was a strange sort of defiance in his confession, as if he were daring her to see the darkness inside him and accept it.

Right now, she couldn't care less about his past.

A delicious shiver rippled over her as he drank her in with his touch and caressed her with his gaze.

She could *feel* it. It was pleasurable. She wanted *more*.

Science couldn't explain this.

Sara was staring.

Vanu was staring. The poor guy looked absolutely scandalized.

Esania didn't care. Let them stare.

"But for you, I'm nothing like the legends." His voice was deep, mesmerizing, smooth as silk; hinting at a part of him that wasn't quite of this Universe.

Not quite mortal.

Months ago, even weeks ago, she wouldn't have entertained such a thought, but now she was certain of it.

There were things in this Universe that couldn't be explained, and Imril was one of them.

Slowly, he broke the trance, turning to Vanu, his eyes glowing like embers. He said something to the Vradhu in harsh, clipped tones, and the warrior nodded, looking a little bit awestruck.

Then he left without another word, disappearing down the long corridor.

"I'm, uh, going to give you two some privacy." Sara rose up off the bed and slipped out of the room.

Esania barely noticed her go.

CHAPTER THIRTY-ONE

"BEFORE I GO, I need to feed, and before I feed, I want to ask you again. Will you accept my *elgida*, Esania?" He stood with his back against the window, the bright afternoon sunlight streaming in, surrounding him like a halo. His dark scale-armor was gone, replaced with the black sleeveless tunic and pants. With his wings folded neatly against his back, and his cropped golden hair, he looked as sharp as a blade.

They were alone in the tower now. Vanu had left, and Sara had disappeared downstairs, giving them an appraising look as she left.

That Sara.

She understood more than she let on.

Esania paused, as if there were an imaginary line she was about to cross. "It would help if I knew exactly what an *elgida* was, Imril. All you've told me is that it's very painful, and it's permanent. That doesn't exactly make it sound appealing."

His eyes roamed over her body, making her feel naked. "I also told you that it would allow us to consummate our bond without harming you."

Consummate our bond.

This was really happening.

"Does that not sound *appealing* to you, Esania?" Imril raised an eyebrow. He was in his element now; confident, *cocky*, as if he knew exactly what was going on in her body right now.

Wait... that was because he *did*.

Unfair.

And clearly, he wasn't going to stop until he got what he wanted.

"It..." A flush spread through her cheeks as her body came alive once again, reacting to his closeness. *It sounds amazing.* Down there, between her thighs, she was definitely wet, aching to have him inside her. She knew they were compatible. Stars, that first day, when he'd abducted her, he'd been naked. She'd seen him; *all* of him.

And right now, she couldn't get the thought of his impressive cock out of her mind.

The puritanical Primean voice inside her head was completely silent.

"Why are you denying me, Esania? Why do you hesitate?" He traced his bare fingers down her neck, drawing her power into him. Esania didn't even blink. She was used to the feeling by now. The more he took, the more relaxed... and *horny* she felt.

"I'm scared," she admitted, allowing herself to feel vulnerable for the very first time in her life. Gone were the masks and defenses and completely artificial Primean barriers to intimacy.

She was simply a woman.

He, a man.

And she craved him.

Her old existence was gone, and she wanted more in this life.

She wanted to be free.

"What exactly are you afraid of, Esania?"

Oh, that was easy. "The unknown. You're so powerful, Imril. Your body, your abilities, the very being that you are... what you've done and what you're about to do. Do you understand that it's so very hard for my simple mind to comprehend someone like you?"

He shocked her then, because for the briefest moment, so quickly she almost missed it, an expression of pure desperation flashed across his face.

As if he were *lost*.

"I promise, you will know everything. There are to be no secrets between you and me, Esania." He dropped to his knees and unfurled his wings, bringing them around her in a spectacular embrace. "I would never hurt you. I just want to make you mine. The *elgida* is my mark. A seal, of sorts. Once I have inscribed it into your skin, the *elgida* becomes a conduit for my power. As I feed from you, I will be able to replenish your strength."

Now that *definitely* didn't make sense, but Esania had learned not to try and rationalize things on this planet. "A *seal?*"

"It is an ancient Auka technique. Let me lay the groundwork," he urged, placing his hands on her waist. He slid his fingers over the contours of her body and buried his nose between her thighs, inhaling deeply. "Let me in, Esania. Trust me. I will make everything right."

Her breath caught. Hardly believing that he was actually *kneeling* before her, she placed her finger beneath his chin and tilted his head upwards, so she could meet his eyes.

Oh, how she wanted to believe him. Logic flailed around in her mind, warring with her growing desire. "I'm out of my depth here. I don't understand the politics on this planet," she said slowly as she ran her fingers over his jaw, feeling his skin, which was so strange and wonderful. It was perfectly smooth, hard yet soft, velvety yet slippery, made of scales that were so tiny they were almost like cells. "Why are you all alone, Imril, without an empire or an army? What *happened* to you, and why do the Naaga keep attacking?"

"You *need* to know, don't you?"

"I'd feel a lot better if I knew what's going on. I grew up in a world that was based on law and order and structure. This whole thing has been a nightmare for me."

"Not anymore." He ran his hands down her thighs, and Esania resisted the sudden urge to tear off her pants and let him have his way. "This entire situation is my doing. I was a tyrant, thinking I would rule the world forever. I ignored my Lords when they fought, when they started wars, when they began to conspire against me. Absolute power has a way of breeding contempt, and age breeds ennui. I forgot how to value life. Even my own life became pointless."

The thought of an ageless being with almost unlimited power, indifferent to the plight of his own people…

He was the closest thing to a god that she'd ever encountered. She should be terrified of him, and yet here she was, commanding his full attention as he kneeled before her, gently caressing her body.

"How can I be sure that you won't turn into that tyrant again?" Her voice didn't even waver.

"I don't make the same mistake twice." Imril's expression turned fierce. "And I will have you to keep me in check, no?" He took her hand into his and began to trace swirling patterns on her palm with his finger.

Oh, he could be charming. How she wanted to believe him. "What are you doing, Imril?"

"Just thinking of how I will make your *elgida*."

Esania let out a tiny puff of exasperation. She hadn't even accepted yet. "Explain."

"My mark. The knowledge comes from the Ancestors, and the design itself spills from the void between worlds. All Drakhin have one *elgida* to give in their lifetime. It binds us together. It tethers your soul to mine."

Speechless, her heart hammering, her body trembling with need, Esania could only stare at him as he ran his long fingers down her palm, her wrist, her arm, tracing the most intricate pattern. His description of the *elgida* didn't make anything clearer, but his words were utterly enticing.

Stop overanalyzing everything.

"Do you trust me, Esania?"

"I..." She closed her mouth and nodded. *Yes.*

She, the Primean who had been taught to analyze everything dispassionately, to look at the facts, surrendered to an instinct, a gut feeling, a sense that this was *right*.

The second time in her life that she'd given in to that feeling.

"My *elgida* will be the most beautiful, a creation worthy of your beauty. You brought me back to life, Esania. Let me give you my soul."

Stars, when he looked at her like that, his amber eyes glowing, his catlike pupils widening, his lips slightly parted, an expression of perfect longing on his face...

She wanted to surrender.

But this was a delicate exchange, and if she was going to bind herself to him for what sounded like... *forever*, she needed to do it right.

Esania took a deep, trembling breath. "Promise me you'll protect my people. Promise me that we'll be free in this life—on this planet. Promise that whatever you do, there will always be a place for me and my people in your world, and that includes the Vradhu, if they wish."

She'd already calculated the probability of them getting off this planet and successfully reaching their intended destination, Torandor.

It was close to zero.

They probably weren't ever going to get off this planet.

Imril watched her so intensely she thought his blazing eyes would tear a hole right through her. "You put me to shame,

Esania," he said at last, and she didn't entirely understand what he meant. "I told you before, if you accept my *elgida*, I will give you everything."

A promise.

That was all she had in this world.

And Imril could have torn it away from her at any time, but he'd held back. A creature who possessed the power of a god, yet he was oh-so gentle with her.

How earnest he looked right now.

She closed her eyes. "Do it," she whispered.

Her body was on fire. Not in her wildest dreams could she have imagined that it was possible to need someone so badly.

Imril brought her hand to his mouth and kissed her palm. His warm lips sent an electric tingle across her hand and up her arm. He literally *felt* electric. "This is not something I can complete in a single sitting. It will take time, perhaps an entire revolution."

"An entire revolution... around this planet's sun?" *A year? Is that what he means?* Suddenly, she was filled with alarm. How was she going to endure this sweet torture for an entire year? "I don't know what I'm going to do."

Imril chuckled, his voice deep, warm, reverberating through her body, stoking her arousal to new heights even as he continued to draw energy from her in a slow, exquisite trickle.

She didn't mind. His touch made her feel relaxed, euphoric.

It was like being on some sort of drug.

"It might be an entire revolution before I complete my *elgida*, but that doesn't mean we can't mate. As soon as you bear even part of my mark, I can return energy to you. When the *elgida* is big enough, the act of mating won't kill you. Instead, it will energize you."

"Well that's a relief." She, who had always prided herself on being a patient person, was now so terribly impatient.

Imril snorted. "I am old. I've tolerated a lot in my lifetime, but even I wouldn't have lasted an entire revolution. Be strong now, my love. This will be painful."

Feeling giddy, as if she were floating on clouds, Esania dropped to her knees. Imril drew his wings—still painted with nightblack—closer together, forming a dark cocoon around her.

He began to trace her palm, and this time, the tip of his finger emitted a faint golden glow. A dull pain spread through her hand as he drew patterns with his finger.

Strangely, feeling pain only sharpened her arousal.

An intricate design started to appear, burned into her skin with great precision. Swirls, lines, fluid shapes, and mysterious alien characters appeared on her hand.

The markings were deep pink against her brown skin, and they were beautiful, like a grand old piece of Earthian artwork. As Imril continued to work, she looked up at the glittering ceiling.

"That... looks similar to what's up there." Brilliant gemstones winked back at her, and the longer she stared, the more she got the sense that this *was* the Universe; wild, ancient, unfathomable, making her feel as insignificant as a speck of dust.

"It's the song of the void between worlds." Imril's voice stole her attention away from the dazzling ceiling. "It's the flow of life throughout the Universe. It's all around us, ripples of energy that we can't see or feel. I can only see a part of it —your *vir*."

When they were on the *Medusa*, escaping from the Paxnath slavers, they'd entered the Netherverse, a parallel dimension that had spat them out somewhere near this wild, uncharted planet. Could it be that the Netherverse was this so-called *void between worlds*?

Her hand was on fire. Her body was on fire. Pain mingled with pleasure and desire, sending her to the very brink.

Imril didn't relent. Everything she thought she knew about

life and the Universe was turned on its head by this beautiful monster.

Really, Humans and Primeans knew so very little about the Universe.

As Imril worked, the patterns burned into her skin started to glow, turning golden and then fading. She closed her eyes and clenched her teeth, breathing heavily. She cried out as the pain became almost unbearable, tears appearing at the corners of her eyes.

"Just a little more," he said gently, sending a final burst of warmth down her arm. The sensation faded, leaving the most pleasant, tingly afterglow in its place. "There you are." He kissed her bare skin.

Esania didn't feel so drained anymore. She breathed a great sigh of relief.

Gently, Imril released her hand. He studied his handiwork, appearing rather pleased with himself. "I will tell Rau to bring you some *aminac* to rub into the markings. This will heal very nicely."

"That wasn't as bad as I thou—"

Suddenly, she found herself in his arms, being lifted to her feet. Imril's kissed her slowly, tenderly, taking her *vir*. At the same time, he sent a ripple of warm energy down her arm.

She *felt* it. Her body absorbed a little bit of his power, and it was utterly intoxicating.

"This is my power," he whispered, kissing her lips, her cheek, her throat, burying his nose in the hollow of her neck. He inhaled deeply. "With time, as the *elgida* grows, you will be able to take more and more, ."

She still didn't really understand, but right now, she didn't care. Feverishly, she kissed him back. "Does this mean we can..."

"Not yet," he whispered, pressing a finger to her lips. "Still too dangerous. This is just a fraction of what I need to do, but for now, it is enough. I *hate* that it hurts you, but it will all be worth it. But first I need to go and deal with a certain... *problem.*"

"The Naaga," she ventured, taking a wild stab. "I wish there was something I could do to help."

"You just being here is enough." He leaned in and kissed her again, his hot, sensual lips gliding against hers. "The humans and the Vradhu will arrive soon, and Mael is on his way. He will stand guard here while I attack Nykithus's stronghold."

Esania froze. "I thought you didn't trust Mael."

"He's changed. I don't know how, but he is sane again, and I know my brother better than anyone. He would never hurt someone that didn't deserve it. His fight is with me, not with you or Sara or your people."

"Are you saying you *deserved* it when he knocked you out?"

Imril's left eyebrow twitched. "My brother and I have a long and turbulent history. I may have..." He sighed. "The situation is not ideal, but I have no choice. I have to go soon... before the Naaga get too cocky, before Mael's shadowveil collapses. Mael is the second most powerful being on this planet... the *most* powerful in some ways. He's the best person to guard the eyrie while I'm away."

Still warm with the afterglow of his touch, Esania's right arm throbbed. She stepped forward and placed her hand on Imril's chest.

His *glow* became a little brighter.

"Hey," she said softly, feeling his broad, muscular chest through the thin fabric of his tunic. It was sheer torture. She just wanted to pull him onto the bed and have her way with him then and there. "I don't know what's out there, and I'm not going to ask. Just... come back, Imril, and be safe."

He curled his fingers around her wrist. "Esania. Close your eyes. Now, can you feel it?"

There was *something* there, a faint tugging sensation in her heart. She nodded.

"That's me. That's our bond, forming through the *elgida*. If anything ever happens to me, you would know."

"Our *bond*..." Yes, she could definitely feel it now. It was as innate as breathing, or her heartbeat. It was a *feeling*, a part of her, a sixth sense.

This thing... it was going to change her from the inside out.

He kissed her again. "I'm *very* hard to kill, Esania."

So irresistible. So sure of himself. How could he be so certain, and why did a sliver of unease enter her gut just now?

"Just be careful," she whispered, unable to even consider the possibility of losing him. "You got into trouble once because you thought nobody could touch you."

"True. But I never make the same mistake twice." He took a step backward, and Esania reeled. Imril's eyes blazed. Power crackled around his hands. He folded his wings and regarded her with a look of pure hunger. Every line and muscle in his body was taut with tension. He was on the very brink... she could feel it.

How were they doing this to each other?

"You didn't tell me this whole process would involve torture." Esania's voice cracked slightly as she stared at him. She *swore* she could see a faint glow around his body. Either he was becoming more and more powerful, or she was starting to *see* things.

"You think this is easy for me either? Patience, my mate. Soon we will be able to explore one another." He looked her up and down, slowly, hungrily, his eyes bold and dangerous. A certain strangeness came over him. "You smell delicious." He closed his eyes and took a deep breath. "Even your arousal is delicious. I can't leave you like this." Again, he stepped forward, as if temptation were pulling him back and forth. "Come here."

"This isn't going to kill me, is it?" She was just being flippant, but he looked aghast.

"I would *never...*"

"The *waiting* is going to kill me," she whispered as Imril took her into his arms. Without warning, he scooped her up and carried her across to the bed.

She yelped in surprise. "What are you—"

"Shh." He laid her down and stepped back, devouring her with his eyes. "I can't leave you like this."

Esania felt naked under his gaze, even though she was wearing the comfortable white dress he'd given her earlier.

"We can't mate, but there are other ways for me to feed." Imril grinned, sending a wicked shiver through her. Despite her lack of experience in all matters sexual, Esania didn't feel the slightest bit nervous or out of her depth. Imril led the way, she responded, and it felt oh-so natural.

Like they'd known each other for an eternity.

Imril kneeled on the floor and dragged her toward him, spreading her thighs so she straddled him, her lower legs hanging over his shoulders. He pushed the hem of her dress up and planted slow, deep kisses on her thighs. Faint golden light swirled around him, and if Esania concentrated hard enough, she swore it actually looked like the swirling, intricate patterns he'd drawn on her body.

As he kissed her, he drank from her, naturally absorbing her energy, her *life*. The *elgida* on her hand started to feel warm again, but this time, it wasn't painful.

"Ahh..." She sighed as she drowned in a pool of heady sensation. Imril pushed her dress up to her waist, revealing her thighs, her lower belly, and the soft lips of her pussy. He only had to come closer for a wave of blissful sensation to ripple across her bare skin, across her exquisitely tender sex.

Stars, she was so *ready*.

Imril slowly stroked her silken entrance with his finger, sending an insane jolt of pleasure through her. "I almost went insane wondering what secrets you were keeping for me down here. I am *not* disappointed."

"Ah, *Imril*," she squealed as he probed deeper, a playful smile hovering on his lips. She could hardly believe that this was her own voice—excited, high-pitched, breathless. "How do you know so much about my anatomy? You don't know anything about our species."

"Instinct," he replied smugly, watching her face intently as he ran his fingertip over her velvet folds. He thrust deep and she gasped. He withdrew and found the deliciously sensitive pearl of flesh at her entrance.

"So this is sensitive," he murmured, as if he'd just discovered something profound. "If I do this, and this..."

"*Imril!*" Her mind was exploding.

"You want me to stop?"

"No!" Her fingers dug into the soft mattress. "Don't you fucking *dare* stop." Her body tensed. She closed her eyes as he caressed her again and again.

Faster, faster...

"Your *vir* is so sweet right now," he whispered.

Slipping his finger inside her once again, he brought his lips to her entrance and kissed her.

She sighed deeply. Her limbs grew heavy. A feeling of languid euphoria spread through her body as he stole her energy away. They were surrounded by a golden glow; she *definitely* wasn't imagining that.

And even as he drank from her, a trickle of his energy entered her body through the *elgida*, and her strength returned.

He sucked on her clit, gently at first, then harder.

"Oh yesss," she sighed, closing her eyes. She couldn't move. She closed her eyes. Her pleasure was announced in low, breathless moans.

"Mhmm," Imril replied, sounding terribly pleased with

himself. His clever tongue took her pleasure to new heights, with each tremor of sensation breaking yet another barrier.

Just when she thought her pleasure levels had reached their maximum, they went higher and *higher*.

And she whimpered and sighed and cried out, a slave to her desires.

Helpless against his touch.

More!

He gave it to her.

How does he know... how does he do this to me?

Instinct.

As he flicked his tongue again, something incredible happened.

A tidal wave of pleasure hit her. Her eyes snapped open and she stared at the glittering ceiling, drowning in swirls and fractals and starbursts, which flickered with golden energy as her body went into overdrive.

She cried out.

She writhed in pleasure.

A supernova exploded in her mind.

And then...

Release.

Instinct was a powerful thing indeed.

CHAPTER THIRTY-TWO

"CALEXA." Esania stepped forward rather awkwardly and gave the mercenary a hug. She wasn't used to hugging people, but what the hell, she was *learning* how to be human. Funny how this sort of physical contact made her uneasy, and yet with Imril, it was all so natural. "I'm glad you're here."

Calexa's eyes widened, but she didn't say anything. Instead, the mercenary returned the hug, her bionically enhanced arms feeling equally stiff and awkward, the curved swords strapped to her back shifting slightly.

But it was the gesture that counted. Calexa had saved her ass more than once, and now she was placing a *lot* of trust in Esania by coming into a Drakhin's domain.

"You finally found an outpost of civilization in this crazy place, S." Calexa called her by her nickname, the one Esania had given at first, when they'd left the Fiveways and she was still trying to hide her identity. "That's a damn fine looking fortress." She glanced up at the stronghold's smooth dark grey walls. "We sure could use nice thick walls like those to hide behind. The Vradhu are super competent in their natural environment, but they've been cut off from their tribe, and they're not set up to look after a bunch of city-dwellers like us in the wild."

"I know." Ever since she'd sampled the comforts offered by Rau—warm bath, sheets, soft clothes—things she used to take for granted, she'd felt guilty at the thought of leaving her people out in the forest.

The Vradhu took good care of them, but the Vradhu couldn't quite grasp that apart from the merc girls, who were as tough as nails, none of them were accustomed to living in the wild—Esania included.

The forest terrified her.

She wasn't a nature person, and she would never be, no matter how hard she tried.

Calexa smiled. "Proud of you, S. You've turned water into wine."

"Well, let's see." She'd managed to convince Imril to extend his protection to her people, but there was still the small matter of the marauding Naaga. "There's a war on the horizon."

"The Naaga, right? They're making more and more incursions into Vradhu territory. The Vradhu don't know why. I think something's going down in Naaga land. I don't really know much about Vradhu-Naaga-Drakhin politics other than that what Ares told me... that the Naaga went rogue at some point during their history. The last thing I want is for us to get drawn into someone else's war. If Imril's going to use his godlike powers to put this whole thing to bed, then I'm right behind him... just as long as he doesn't turn into an absolute tyrant."

"He won't. Not while I'm around." Esania remembered something. "Where's Rachel?"

Calexa's expression hardened, and Esania's heart sank. "She disappeared into the forest while we were fighting off the Naaga. Ares followed the tracks. It looks like she was dragged off, but at some point, the tracks just disappeared. We think someone might have flown in and picked them up. Whether Drakhin or ship, I don't know. *Fuck*. There's nothing we can even do about it right now. It's *so* frustrating. I wish the *Medusa* was up and running so we could go and search for her, but the left thruster is completely shot." She shook her head. "Monroe's tried—hasn't slept in three days—but he hasn't been able to fix it, and there isn't much that Monroe *can't* fix." A worried look passed over her face, quickly concealed. "We had no choice but to leave the Medusa under mountains of camouflage. Supplies are almost all gone, anyway. The boys will go back there at some point and try to salvage the old girl, but I'm not so sure we'll get her off the ground again. I hate to say this, but I'm at a loss over what we can do for Rachel..."

Esania knew what she was thinking.

If she's still alive.

Neither of them dared to voice the thought.

"If Imril succeeds," she said quietly, "we might have a chance of getting her back. I told him about Rachel. He's the only one who can rescue her."

Calexa let out a deep sigh. "One hell of an ally you've got there, S. I really hope your guy is the real deal. Let's just pray to the nonexistent gods of this planet that he can get her back." Calexa flicked her mahogany braid over her shoulder and flashed her a devil-may-care grin. "From what I've seen of him, I think it's possible. Just gotta keep hoping. You really lucked out with Imril, S."

Typical mercenary. Even in this fraught situation, Calexa managed to find her swagger. And with her deadly combat skills and highly modified physique, why shouldn't she?

But her confidence did nothing to quell Esania's growing unease. She knew Imril was strong, but she didn't know what dangers lay in wait for him out there.

The uncertainty... that was the worst part about it all. When Imril returned, she was going to *demand* to pick his brains until she knew everything about this crazy place.

Several more Vradhu boats slid up onto the shore, the violet-skinned warriors accompanying the girls of Esania's retinue.

Only they weren't her retinue anymore.

They were free.

Her heart swelled as she caught sight of familiar faces. There was quiet Talia, and Sam, the funny one. Clever Aneesa and blunt, outspoken Mirielle.

As they stepped onto the shore, helped out of the boats by the Vradhu, they looked at Esania, then up at Imril's stone-walled fortress with wide eyes.

The first four. Sixteen more to come. Esania saw several Vradhu in the distance, standing tall on their sleek canoes. They sliced across the water, making powerful strokes with a long paddle.

The humans sat in the middle, looking apprehensive. Curious eyes darted around, searching for any sign of danger.

Imril had elected to stay out of sight, predicting that he might antagonize the Vradhu and scare the humans. After their intense encounter, he'd quickly become scarce, leaving her in a mess of tangled sheets and rumpled clothes, suffused with the most heady afterglow.

She couldn't forget the way he'd looked at her as he left.

"I'm going to go now," he growled, his eyes giving off the most unearthly glow. *There was a tension about him that hadn't been there before.* *"You won't see me for a while, but just know that once your people set foot on this island, they will be under my protection."*

"What are you going—"

"Esania. Rest." He cut her off with a look.

The air around him crackled with power.

Somehow, she understood. Maybe it was her subconscious logic kicking in. Maybe it was the mysterious bond that had formed between them.

She understood that he was on the brink of losing it. If he stayed just a little longer... he would *lose it, and he could kill her.*

So she just nodded. Go.

And he disappeared in a blur of dark wings and shimmering skin and golden light.

Leaving her with a completely different perspective on the Universe.

"To be honest, once the Drakhin had you in his arms, I... I didn't know what to do." The sound of Calexa's voice brought her out of her reverie. "I thought about shooting him, but he was moving too fast. It was too risky. Just couldn't afford to accidentally hit you or make him drop you." Calexa placed her hand on Esania's shoulder. "I was praying for a miracle. I'm sorry."

"For what?" With the memory of Imril's touch still lingering on her skin, with the *elgida* snaking across her hand and up her wrist, throbbing slightly, painful but warm, she could only smile faintly. "We're all here, aren't we?"

"Yeah. I knew you were tough. *Smart.* That's why I held out hope that you'd survive. When Maki told us that you came back to the forest with the Drakhin, and that you were totally fine, I knew you'd figured out a way to communicate with him."

I've done more than just communicate. Feeling liberated, she kept that particular secret to herself. "What made you change your mind about him?"

"A few things Ares told me." Strange, how she still spoke of Ares as if he were a single person. "It seems the *Hythra* unwittingly planted a few seeds of memory in his head. He's totally adamant that even if they are what the legends say they are, Imril and Mael don't pose a threat to us. My mate can be stubborn sometimes, and he's pretty fixed on this one."

"Even though he attacked Imril with his venomous barb?"

"Well..." Calexa offered an apologetic shrug. "That was before the memories surfaced. He's convinced now that we need to create an alliance with the Drakhin twins." Her eyes narrowed. "Where *is* the Lightbringer, by the way?"

"Lightbringer?" Esania blinked.

"Imril the Lightbringer. That's what the Vradhu call him. They seem to think all sorts of superstitious things about him. That he's immortal, some sort of demigod. *Huh.*"

"*Imril* is busy." Esania wondered at the truth behind the Vradhu's beliefs. At some point, she and Imril were going to have to sit down and have a big long *chat...* when he was back in control of his lust.

She couldn't imagine the torture he was going through right now... denied the chance to seek his release. All Esania wanted to do was go to him and *give* him what he needed, but she would have to wait.

She had the feeling something massive was about to happen. Imril was quiet, dangerous, and with untold power coursing through his veins. He was preparing to *take back his world*, whatever that meant.

And Mael was about to return.

"I hate to break it to you, Calexa, but there's *two* of them."

"Oh yeah, he supposedly has a twin. Ares told me about Mael. They call him The One Who Brings Shadows. The Chaos." Calexa made a face. "It all sounds very dramatic. I hope you've convinced *Mael* that we don't want to fight him."

Not quite.

But she had to trust Imril.

A shrill whistle split the air, coming from the other side of the lake. Calexa's head snapped in the direction of the noise. "Gotta go. Mai and Zahra should be here any minute. Any trouble happens, they can sort you out."

"Wait, where are you goi—"

But Calexa was already striding away, gesturing to a Vradhu called Kumo, who stood in an empty boat.

"Ares is dealing with a little... uh, *problem* right now. He needs my help," she called over her shoulder, jumping into the boat. "Be back later."

In the distance, Esania heard the faint rumble of thunder. Towering black clouds were starting to gather. A sudden gust of wind whipped at her braids, bringing a chill with it.

Mael's coming.

Ares is going to take back his empire.

Calexa rode away in the direction of the storm, leaving Esania back where she'd started.

With her people.

Only now they were standing on the shore of a rocky island, a crumbling eyrie rising above her, its new lord watching them from one of the high parapets above.

And a storm was brewing.

A sense of dread filled her, until a pair of arms wrapped around her, squeezing her from behind. The faint smell of jasmine surrounded her.

"Hey, ma'am!" It was Alessia, her former aesthetics manager. Loud, generous, larger-than-life Alessia, with her thousand-watt smile. "Thank god you're alive. I thought I never cry, but... god, we were all so worried about you!"

"Th-thanks." Secretly, she felt a little awkward at being hugged, but she turned and returned it anyway, because she was truly glad to see Alessia again. She blinked away unexpected tears. "We have a fortress now, Alessia. That's something, isn't it?"

"Sure is, ma'am, sure is." Alessia stared up at the imposing high towers of the eyrie. "My design colleagues in Milan would have a fit if they saw this place... in a good way, of course. So dark. So *moody*. I don't know how you pulled this off, but I'm not complaining. As much as I adore those Vradhu boys, the jungle life just isn't for me."

Esania was about to say something reassuring, but the words died in her throat as a wall of shadow rose up around them, absolute darkness that blocked out their view of the lake.

A chill entered the air, and in some deep, primal part of her soul, she felt the urge to run and hide.

She pushed that very human instinct aside and stared up at the tall towers of the eyrie. The strangest feeling came over her, raising goosebumps on her arms, sending a ripple down her spine.

The *elgida* on her hand throbbed, and a torrent of emotion washed over her as her skin tingled with the memory of Imril's touch.

He was watching.

A feeling of protectiveness radiated through their bond, and suddenly, she was no longer afraid.

CHAPTER THIRTY-THREE

IMRIL EXHALED DEEPLY as he looked down at the exquisite female that was now his, watching as she directed her people along the rocky shore of the island. Graceful and composed, she gestured at the women around her, speaking firmly but never quite raising her voice.

The humans behaved strangely around her. Some obeyed her right away, while others milled around and chatted, appearing excited rather than anxious.

So these were her people.

Humans.

Strange creatures.

And although she was right amongst them, Esania stood apart—regal, slightly aloof, a fraction taller than the others.

To Imril, humans and these so-called *Primeans* appeared to be one and the same, but he could now appreciate the subtle variations between them.

How different *this* Esania was to the deliciously wanton creature who had squirmed and writhed under his touch, the sound of her low, breathless voice driving him insane.

That version of her was reserved only for him.

Right now, her beautiful features were set in a look of

intense concentration as she chatted with one of the other women. The golden glow of *vir* surrounded every single one of the humans, except for the two males.

And of course, the surly Vradhu stood guard, their deadly tails wrapped around their left legs, eyes darting suspiciously about the place.

Males did not give off *vir*.

Despite the intense energy radiating from the other women, he only had eyes for Esania. With the first tendrils of his *elgida* crowning her right hand, she looked magnificent, and now he could *feel* her through the bond.

It was faint, but the link between them was definitely there.

She was bound to him now, and there was no going back.

He had fed from her, pleasured her, and marked her.

Mine.

Lust pumped through his veins as he watched her, turning him into a savage creature. Power—*her* power—filled him, and it was glorious.

Her *vir* was unlike anything he'd ever tasted in his long life, and he wanted more, *always*.

Imril stared at her longingly, his erection straining against his armor-plate, his teeth clenched, Power radiating from his eyes, his hands.

Patience. You will claim her soon.

He couldn't *bear* to be around her right now. He would lose control, and that would be dangerous... for her.

The thing he wanted most in the Universe was just outside his reach. He had to get away from here before he went insane.

So he would go and attack Ton Malhur, channeling his frustration into violence. He would raze the cursed city into the ground.

That always worked.

Below, Esania and her people started to make their way

toward the South gate. A storm was brewing in the distance, and the wind whipped at her dark braids and fluttered her dress, revealing the sublime outline of her body.

Imril's erection intensified, becoming almost painful.

Ah, fuck.

He'd never experienced this kind of torture in his life. She'd tolerated the *elgida* well. When he returned, he would just have to work faster, to get it to the point where it could absorb enough of his power to protect her from him.

The process of drawing the *elgida* was a highly erotic experience—for both the giver and the receiver, but Esania could only tolerate so much pain in a single session.

For now, he would have to be patient. Like the storm brewing on the horizon, a battle was imminent.

He had to get out of here.

Now if only that bastard Mael would hurry up and get here, so he could leave before he went completely insane.

As if in response to his thoughts, a veil of shadow rose up from below, stretching toward the brilliant sun.

"About time," he muttered. He wasn't going to greet Mael —not when he was like this. Filled with lust and frustration and seething anger, such an encounter would only end in disaster.

So he unfurled his wings and leapt out of the window.

The only way was up.

CHAPTER THIRTY-FOUR

"OH MY GOD!" Alessia looked up at the sky as dark shadows rose up all around them. "What the hell is that?"

"*Mael*," she muttered under her breath, feeling annoyed that Imril hadn't given her any warning.

Imril's power was scary, yes, but at least she knew what to expect with him.

Mael, on the other hand, was downright terrifying.

Where is the bastard?

Laid low by another bout of nausea, Sara was resting in the tower room, *alone*. Mael had already professed his interest in her, but surely Imril wouldn't let him try anything on her in his own domain.

Mael had already pledged to keep his hands off Sara until the baby was born.

Could he be trusted?

Esania wasn't so sure. She had to get back up there.

"Oh my *god!*" Alessia shouted again, and Esania saw a dark figure shoot up into the sky, past the rising shadows, his *nightblack*-ed wings spreading wide.

Imril in his battle-armor.

A terrifying, awe-inspiring sight.

Her right hand throbbed as she stared at him, increasingly aware of the faint golden glow that surrounded him at all times. Somehow, the *elgida* must be allowing her to see his energy.

Was that how she appeared to him all the time? Surrounded by a golden glow as if she were somehow being viewed through the lenses of a heat-sig monitor?

He went higher and higher, until he was just a tiny speck.

Imril the Lightbringer. Ancient, powerful, capable of cruel indifference, able to kill her with a touch if he so desired.

What have you gotten yourself into, Esania?

And he was just about the sweetest, most protective, most desirable creature she'd ever known.

"Let's get everyone inside," she yelled, raising her voice over the rising wind. Mai and Zahra had arrived, along with the reclusive twins, Raphael and Monroe. From their brilliant green eyes —the same as hers—Esania knew they had Primean ancestry, but whether they were pureblooded or half-human, she had no idea.

The twins were secretive, and she didn't blame them.

It didn't matter now anyway, because really, they were all human at the end of the day, weren't they?

"*Kaala!*" she yelled at the Vradhu. *Let's go.*

The violet-skinned warriors turned their dark eyes upon her in unison, regarding her with lazy, insolent stares as if to say: *you dare order us around?*

Esania shrugged. *Suit yourself.*

"Hey, ma'am, are we really going inside? What *is* this place?"

"It's shelter," she said absentmindedly, her eyes drifting toward the sky. *What are you going to do, Imril?* It terrified her a little bit, that he could be capable of terrible violence and destruction; that he could be an enemy to *someone.*

That he was probably going to do very bad things to someone who may or may not deserve it.

But he was the one who had protected her, and now he'd made her his own.

If she concentrated very hard, she could almost *feel* his lust coursing through the tenuous link of their bond, even though he would be very far away by now.

I need to find Mael.

The shadows had all but obliterated the sun by now, plunging them into darkness. Behind her, Zahra flicked on a guide-light which illuminated the stark stone walls of the fortress. "I'm guessing sudden darkness is a regular thing around here, or should I be worried?"

"Let's just get inside." Esania gestured toward the lower entrance, which was wide open. "There's an assembly hall of sorts down the internal corridor, to the right. It's a bit over-grown, but there's plenty of room to settle down. This whole place is abandoned and run down. We're going to have to do a lot of work to get it habitable."

"Good bones, though," Mai added, pushing her way past a frowning Vradhu. Lian. That's what he was called.

He hissed and said something to Mai in Vradhu, although Esania got the sense he was being playful more than anything else.

Mai glared at him, blinked, then returned his taunts with a vulgar sounding Vradhu phrase that Esania had never heard before.

Lian growled, the muscles of his broad violet chest tensing. For a moment Esania thought there would be trouble, but then he just laughed.

Mai stuck out her tongue.

Lian responded in kind.

Amazing. Even in this kind of tense situation, they could... *flirt* like that.

"Let's get inside," she said, not knowing whether to feel giddy or exasperated. "Mai, Zahra, can you please get the

Vradhu to cooperate? I never seem to have much luck with them."

The violet-skinned warriors were wild, secretive, stubborn, primal, violent.

All things she didn't understand, didn't know how to deal with.

"That's because you don't speak the lingo very well," Mai said. I'm surprised, Primean. I thought you'd be all over the language by now. Monroe and Raphael already analyzed it with the scanner. They've developed some neat learning apps."

"I know," she muttered. The truth was that she'd been too shellshocked in those early days to even think of trying to learn the Vradhu tongue.

A fat droplet of rain landed on her forehead, running into her eye. She blinked furiously. Several more droplets fell, hitting the sand with great force.

Pat. Pat. Pat.

"Inside," she said as the shadows around them became thick and impenetrable. An oppressive feeling crept into the atmosphere, as if the darkened sky were pushing down upon them and death was about to creep out from the depths of the lake.

"Uh, that shadow..." Raphael stood at the shore's edge, an Analyzer in his hand. The machine glowed pale blue as it picked up... *something*. "It's an *absence* of energy. It's like a vacuum, only it isn't. It's actively consuming energy, but in a controlled manner." Suddenly, he looked afraid—and Raphael wasn't usually afraid of *anything*. A nervous laugh escaped his lips. "This doesn't make sense. It goes against the basic laws of physics."

"That's because we're on Khira, and nothing makes sense here." Esania said gently. Having witnessed the impossibility that was Imril up close, she'd had a little more time to adjust to that fact. "Maybe, just maybe, the laws of physics that we *thought* we knew don't apply here."

Boom!

A deafening crack of thunder assaulted her ears, so loud that she *swore* the ground itself shook beneath her feet.

But there was no lightning.

Suddenly, everyone fell silent.

For once, the Vradhu didn't look surly.

For once, her people were all quiet.

The skies opened, turning into a vicious downpour.

They *all* ran inside.

CHAPTER THIRTY-FIVE

TO ESANIA'S HORROR, she found Mael up in the tower room with Sara. He sat to one side of the room, on the floor, his legs crossed, eyes closed.

As far away from Sara as possible.

A chill spread through the air. It wasn't just her imagination. The temperature was definitely lower in here.

Almost as if he were meditating, Mael's obsidian hands rested on his knees, and his face appeared smooth and emotionless. His bare chest glistened in the artificial light.

There was a stillness about him that was completely unnerving.

Sara sat in the grand old Drakhin chair on the other side of the room, watching him warily, the way one might look at a sleeping tiger.

But there was also a hint of fascination in her eyes.

Thankfully, Mael was well outside Sara's radius. From that distance, he wouldn't absorb any of her *vir*.

Still, Esania was horrified. They shouldn't be here together... *alone*.

"What are you doing, Mael?" Esania snapped, making large strides across the floor, stopping just outside his radius.

She didn't want *anyone* taking her energy except for Imril, and as terrifying as Mael was, she no longer feared him.

If he and Imril had come to some sort of agreement, then they were safe for now. Besides, if anything happened to her, Imril would be furious.

"Leave." Mael had the audacity to make a dismissive gesture with his hand, even as his eyes remained closed. "Do you *know* how hard it is to try and maintain two *shadowveils* at once?"

"It would help if I actually knew what a *shadowveil* was."

"An extension of my will. My power. A barrier constructed from nothingness, designed to keep out the most irritating intruders. On a good day, I can kill those who come into contact with it by draining their life-force. On a bad day, it becomes patchy, imperfect, full of holes. That's why the Naaga have been appearing in your forests recently. They got out, because I had other, more *pressing issues* to attend to." He sighed. "I can't be everywhere at once. Does that answer your question, human?"

"I..." Irritated by his tone, which was dismissive and bored-sounding, she shook her head. Mael's explanation of his powers was baffling, but also revealing. "I take it Imril has asked you to protect the eyrie in his absence. Do you have to do it from *here*, of all places? There are four other towers to choose from." Her protective instinct kicked in, overriding any sense of caution. Imril had let Mael into his house, so she no longer feared he would harm them, but she didn't trust him... not one bit.

"We were talking," Mael snapped back, sounding equally terse, his brow creasing slightly. In the soft artificial light, his dark face shimmered, making him look like an obsidian statue. Just like Imril, there was a sense of agelessness about him. "We are *still* talking."

Esania definitely felt like the intruder here.

"I'm okay," Sara said softly, and for someone who had been

spending time alone with an irritable immortal shadow-wielding alien, she seemed quite fine. "Mael said I can leave anytime I want. I don't think he's in a position to try anything crazy right now, anyway. He's, uh, got a *lot* on his shoulders."

Calm. Relaxed. *Serene.*

That's how Sara appeared.

The complete opposite of how Esania had had felt when Imril abducted her.

Had Sara fallen under Mael's spell? Was she in the grip of some sort of Stockholm syndrome? No, Sara wasn't the sort to be so easily influenced.

But then Esania remembered all too well how quickly she'd become entranced with Imril. He wasn't aware of how dangerously seductive he was, that strange-yet-irresistible combination of sheer power and arrogance and vulnerability drawing her to him like a fly to honey.

Maybe these ancient Drakhin exuded some sort of aura or glamor that affected humans.

Anything was possible on this planet, after all.

Aware that Mael's eyes were still closed, Esania raised her eyebrows questioningly. Sara frowned and made a gesture with her hand. *It's okay. Go.*

Are you sure?

"*I'll be fine.*" Sara actually mouthed the words. "*Go.*"

"Unlike my brother, I'm not a tyrant," Mael drawled, as if he'd somehow understood their silent communication. "I'm not going to hurt Sara, and I'm *not* going to feed from her either. Leave us, human."

There was the imperious Drakhin. In some ways, he was so similar to his brother, but at the same time, so different.

"I.... *can't* leave you alone with her."

"And what do you think you're going to do? Even with all your weapons and the Vradhu at your side, you still wouldn't be able to stop me if I really wanted to get away with it."

He had a point.

"Enough, human. I'm only tolerating your insolence because my brother likes you..." His eyes snapped open for just a spilt second, revealing twin pools of inky blackness. It wasn't just the iris or pupil that were pure black. The entire orb of each eye had turned into liquid obsidian. "You are fortunate you bear the beginnings of his *elgida*."

But he didn't elaborate. Instead, Mael raised his hand. *Quiet.* His features twisted into a look of intense concentration as he closed his eyes again.

Scary. What was that all about?

It was as if the very darkness he manipulated had infused his soul.

She didn't want to provoke him any further. With a sigh, Esania turned to Sara. *Let's go.* She gestured toward the door.

Sara shook her head. *Nope.*

Are you kidding me? Esania glanced back at Mael. *You want to stay here... with* him?

Sara shrugged. *It's okay.*

Appearing to be in some sort of trance, Mael began to mutter to himself, and the temperature dropped just a little bit more. Sara didn't seem to mind; she had a cozy blanket wrapped around her legs.

Seriously, what was keeping Sara here? How could she be so certain that Mael was trustworthy... that he posed no threat to her or her unborn child?

Just a few days ago, he'd viciously attacked Imril.

Esania thought about physically dragging Sara out of here, but decided against it. Ignoring her screaming instincts, Esania took a deep breath. *Are you sure?*

As if reading her mind, Mael sighed. "I understand why you might be feeling protective of Sara, Esania Lafitte, but she can speak for herself."

"I sure can."

"I *know* that. Wait... how did you know my last na—"

"The *Hythra* told me." Mael unfurled his sinuous black tail, taking it into his left hand. There was a distinct *snap*.

"What are you doi—"

His eyes were still closed. Cerulean blood trickled down his forearm. Something long and sharp protruded from his fist.

His... *barb?*

"Why did you *do* that, Mael?" Sara was on her feet, looking shocked.

"It'll grow back," he said through gritted teeth. "Almost as deadly as a Vradhu's. Imril never had one of these. You need it more than I."

"What the *hell*, Mael?" Sara glared at the Drakhin, but he still didn't open his eyes.

"Your friend doesn't trust me, so I'm giving this to you as a sign of my good intentions. There is enough poison in there to take down even me."

"You're affected by your own poison?"

"A flaw in the Ancestor's design." He sighed and rolled it across the floor. It came to rest at the foot of the chair, just before Sara's boots.

"I don't need that, Mael," Sara protested, looking horrified. "Are you kidding me? I'm not going to stab you with a fucking *poison barb*."

"Take it. My gift to you. You never know when it might come in useful. Khira is a dangerous place."

Esania stared at the barb. It was long and sharp-tipped, made of a smooth, hard material that looked like black ivory. Mael's strange blue blood had already dried, leaving a striking abstract pattern on the hilt-like end.

Gingerly, Sara picked up the barb... literally a *piece* of Mael. "Is this even safe to handle?" She took great care not to touch the tip.

"It's encased in a natural sheath," Mael said calmly. "The poison won't be exposed until the moment of penetration."

"How convenient." Sara stared down at the thing, a look of

bemusement crossing her face. "How... *thoughtful* of you, Mael."

A ghost of a smile played across Mael's lips for just a fraction of a second.

Esania looked at him long and hard. "Mael, why do you have this, and yet Imril doesn't?"

For a long, uncomfortable moment, Mael was silent, and Esania wondered if she'd pushed him too far. With Mael, it was hard to tell.

"I cut it off," Mael said at last, his voice distant, his expression like stone. "During a fight we had, a long time ago. It never grew back. The bastard doesn't need it, anyway. He's too strong for his own good—when he chooses to be."

A chill ran through her. "And this enemy of his, this..."

"*Nykithus,*" Mael hissed. "The Naaga are under his command."

"What are Imril's chances of defeating him? I mean, he's on his own. I assume this Nykithus has resources, an army, weapons at his disposal. Is Imril in danger?" The thought of something happening to him scared the hell out of her. He was so powerful, so sure of himself, but she'd also sensed a kind of desperation in him... beneath the hard, perfect exterior, he was a little unhinged.

Weren't they all?

"*Tch.* I am not worried for my brother *at all.*" Mael opened his eyes again. They were back to normal. "He hasn't explained anything to you, has he?"

"There's a lot to cover," she said tersely. *Besides, he can't... we can't stand to be in each other's presence for too long without going insane.*

Mael clearly didn't understand the exquisite pain of desire; of being close enough to smell, touch, *feel* that person... yet all the while, something—an invisible barrier—forced them apart.

"Fine," Mael snapped. "Just remember this. He is Imril,

son of Acheros. We might be Drakhin, but our father was pure Auka."

Auka? He pronounced the word with a strange inflection, producing a sound that could never be replicated by a human.

The word itself was enough to send a chill down her spine, and she didn't know why.

Sara was being unusually quiet, too.

"You don't even know what that is, do you, human?" Mael's voice was hollow and distant, taking on an otherworldly quality... as if he were caught between two dimensions. "Pray that you never, ever have to find out."

And Imril was half... *Auka.*

It didn't matter.

Esania took a deep breath and concentrated, remembering how it felt to be close to him, to have him trace the *elgida* over her hand with such gentle precision, how he somehow *knew* to pull back just at the right moment, just when it was becoming too much...

And to have him draw on her power, to *need* her, their souls momentarily connected.

She didn't care who—or *what*—had sired him.

Her *elgida* throbbed in response to the memory of his touch. The pink lines had intensified, turning a deep shade of crimson, and her hand was shiny from the *aminac*—a fragrant smelling sap-like substance—that she'd rubbed into it. With time, the swelling would subside, and she would be left with very fine bronze scars.

His *mark.*

She could feel him. He was far, far away, and the sensation was faint, but she could definitely feel him. Anger pulsed through their bond, along with a deep feeling of...

Sadness.

"Imril is my mate," she said softly, glaring at Mael as she rubbed her arms, trying to ward off the cold. "I can't help but worry about him, but if you tell me he can handle this, then that's some small comfort."

Sara's eyes were as wide as saucers at this point. "Fucking *brilliant*," she murmured.

"My brother might be a pompous, arrogant ass, but he has the strength to match." Mael raised his hands, shadows trailing from his fingertips. He began to trace strange symbols in the air, and the very sight of his graceful, slender hand moving in such a manner raised the fine hairs on her arms and the back of her neck. "All will be fine. Now, can you leave us, human? I have been excessively patient with you."

In the past few minutes, Esania's impression of Mael had changed drastically. "Sara?"

"It's cool. Seriously, Es, don't worry. As you said, this isn't the Serakhine."

Esania dipped her head in respectful agreement as she bowed out, leaving pregnant Sara in the company of an irritable Drakhin who was surprisingly honorable, despite his fearsome powers.

Just like his brother.

No, Mael was right. This definitely *wasn't* the Serakhine.

CHAPTER THIRTY-SIX

THE RUSH of cold wind against his body gave Imril little relief from his seething lust as he flew into the setting sun. He crossed mountains and rivers and streams, passing over decaying relics and abandoned cities and the occasional lone eyrie with narrow spires stretching high into the sky, some of them cracked and crumbling.

Abandoned, all of it.

What have you done?

His empire, gone.

It was so long ago, but Imril could still remember Nykithus's calm, smiling face as he raised the metal canister and released the *Deathkiss* virus... only at that time, Imril hadn't known what it was.

"It's already too late," he'd whispered, retreating quickly as Imril rose off his throne, power crackling from his hands. *"I have immunity, but even you won't escape this, Overlord."*

"What is this?" Imril thundered, striding toward Nykithus with blazing hands, ready to wring the whelp's neck if he refused to explain.

"You will see." Nykithus unfurled his black wings as he strode toward an open balcony. Outside, the stars glittered in

the endless sky. "You're too old and too powerful, Overlord. You can't see what is right in front of your face."

Nykithus's expression changed, and for the first time, Imril saw his true heart.

It was full of venom.

Nykithus, the golden child, the favored one, the brilliant scholar, the innovator, the almost-son that Imril had taken under his wing...

His silver eyes burned with pure hatred.

Why?

"You thought to deceive me, Nykithus?" Imril's voice was deceptively quiet.

Nykithus gave him a dark look. Then he turned and jumped, snapping his wings open as he caught a fierce gust of wind.

Instantly, Imril followed, but Nykithus had already disappeared into a thick bank of cloud. Consumed with anger, Imril fired a massive blast of power in his direction. It ripped through the clouds, leaving nothing in its wake. Imril flew on and on, searching for Nykithus, but the bastard had disappeared.

He could have gone in any direction.

Clearly, he'd planned this attack well.

"I'll kill him," Imril growled, coming back into real-time. The depth of Nykithus's betrayal stung more now than ever, now that he'd lost his people, his empire, his identity. He drew some comfort from knowing that at least some of his people had made it off Khira alive, but hundreds of revolutions had passed, and he had no way of finding them now.

But he'd found life in the form of a sweet, soft-skinned female, a *human* called Esania.

And he would lay down his life for her.

He stared down at the world below, watching the landscape fade to grey, the gentle swells of mountains and valleys limned by the silvery moon. Imril tracked north, navigating by memory and instinct rather than sight. After thousands of revolutions, he knew the lay of these lands like the back of his hand.

He flew until he reached the Vakarin Plains, which marked the very edge of the Mountain Kingdom, Ton Malhur.

Here the darkness deepened, snatches and reflections of light disappearing as he reached Mael's shadowveil. A strange tingle rippled over his entire body, the effect of flying so close to a structure that was composed entirely of *nothingness*.

A sense of urgency rose up inside him. He *had* to kill Nykithus before the shadowveil collapsed completely, before the horrors of this dread kingdom were released to the outside world.

Mael's structure was crumbling. Soon it would be no more. As Imril flew, great patches opened up in the darkness, and now and then he would catch sight of a cluster of golden lights far below.

There were settlements down there. If there was one thing Nykithus had always been good at, it was building his kingdom. An obsessive scholar of the Auka manuals and a master planner, Nykithus had seized Ton Malhur from its previous owner, a lazy upstart called Khel. The two Drakhin had engaged in a vicious death-battle from which Nykithus had emerged the victor.

That's when he'd first caught Imril's attention.

And when he received Imril's blessing to keep the lands he'd won, he'd constructed a great civilization on the rolling hills, his new eyrie almost tall and grand enough to match Imril's own.

Back then, Imril had been impressed. He hadn't seen the growing danger.

Cocky. That's what Nykithus was. In all his brilliance, he'd grown arrogant, forgetting who and *what* Imril really was.

Imril swooped through a large hole in the shadowveil, staring straight down. A faint glow crested the horizon, becoming stronger and stronger as he neared.

He realized what it was.

Civilization.

A vast city stretched out before him, hugging imposing hills and deep valleys, networks of blue and white lights glittering in the darkness. The uniform buildings of the low-lying outskirts quickly gave way to a manufacturing zone, where tall towers belched dirty smoke and grey-robed Naaga scurried about in the throughways.

The air here was toxic. His armor shifted and became airtight, protecting him from the noxious vapors. He flew over vast lakes of poisoned water, some glowing in various shades of blue, green, and lurid yellow.

A desolate feeling crept over him.

This is...

This reminded him of his father's way of doing things.

Acheros the scientist.

The explorer.

The creator.

Imril remembered how the Auka would creep into his chamber on the *Hythra,* materializing out of thin air, millions of tiny shadowparticles coalescing into his menacing form.

Acheros took delight in causing fear.

The most frustrating thing about Acheros was his face. One never saw it clearly. It was always changing, always obscured behind a veil of shadow that writhed and shifted, revealing only what he wanted to show.

His sire was dead now, and Imril had never even seen his true face.

Bastard.

Disgust roiled through him. Able to disappear and materialize at will, the Auka were truly terrifying beings. He hoped he would never encounter another in his lifetime.

At last, Imril caught sight of Nykithus's eyrie in the distance.

Built from pale grey stone, it was constructed in the classic style, with four outer spires and a large central spire that rose high above the rest.

This was probably a trap, but Imril didn't care. If things went wrong, he had enough power in his body to raze this entire place off the face of the planet.

As a last resort, he would simply destroy everything.

He pushed on, filled with anger and seething frustration, feeling stronger than he had in a long time.

This level of power... it was dangerous. Nykithus and the other Drakhin had never seen him like this, so full to the brim with power that his eyes turned incandescent white.

Esania's *vir* was so pure and potent that it almost made him drunk, and to his delight, it became even richer when she was aroused. When he'd pleasured her, taking in her sweet nectar for the very first time, following some mysterious instinct that told him *where* and *how* she'd be most sensitive, she'd responded beautifully, surpassing even his wildest dreams.

Imagine what she'd be like when he completed his mark; when she was truly *his*.

Nykithus, you insolent little shit. You do not understand what you have done.

Imril flew toward the central spire, spotting a large window. His entry point. Was Nykithus arrogant enough to be there waiting for him? It didn't matter. One way or another, Imril would kill him.

He dropped silently onto the ledge of the window, his scale-covered feet soundless on the cold stone as he angled his wings, controlling his descent. The window was covered by a thick glass surface. Imril simply pressed his palms against it and channelled power through his hands, melting the surface. He pressed hard and the barrier shattered.

He stepped inside.

Darkness greeted him, so Imril just released a bit more of

his power, obliterating the shadows. He was ablaze in the darkness, a pillar of incandescent light.

Her light.

He felt her in the depths of his soul. She bore his mark now. The song of his power was inscribed into her skin, connecting her to him, connecting them both to the vast energy that flowed between worlds.

Impossibly, at that moment, she reached for him, and he felt her concern radiating through the bond.

Sweet thing. Do not fret. Thanks to you, I am far, far stronger than anything Nykithus can throw at me.

"Show yourself, Nykithus," he thundered, and power flowed through his voice, changing it; making it deeper, more resonant.

More like an Auka's voice.

In response to his command, a Naaga appeared from the shadows. With silent, graceful footsteps, she walked fearlessly into his radius. "The Overlord will see you, but on his terms."

The Naaga possessed the blue skin, pleasing features, and white feathered head-plumage that were typical of her kind. 4507 was the servant-number tattooed into her forehead.

Imril stiffened as her silvery *vir* drifted toward him. Compared to Esania's energy, it was dull, faint, laced with fear and misery, and there was no way for him to stop absorbing it.

"Overlord?" he said softly, one corner of his mouth quirking upward in amusement. "So Nykithus styles himself as my replacement now, does he?" Was it possible to be both irritated and furious at the same time?

The Naaga stared at him blankly, her pale eyes glowing white with the reflection of his power. Her face was expressionless, but her *vir* told him everything.

She was terrified.

Despite his growing irritation, Imril felt a pang of sympathy for the servant, who was utterly defenseless against him. Maybe the time he'd spent with Esania had sensitized him to such things. "He's a coward for sending you up here to face me alone. Where is he?"

Silence.

"Where is he?" Imril thundered. Was this Naaga resistant to his commands too?

"He..." A pained look crossed her face, as if she were torn between two masters.

Imril took a step forward, drawing in more of her *vir*, and not in a pleasant way. The energy he took from her was just a tiny drop to add to the torrent of his power. "You *are* going to disobey your master, Naaga, because if you don't, I will send my power through the walls and floors of this spire, right down into the heart of the eyrie, and everything will be obliterated in an instant, even you. I will ask you one last time. *Where is he?*"

A pause.

A great tremor coursed through the Naaga's body. Her expression grew pained. "U-underground," she whispered at last. "In the vault."

When Imril sounded like *this*, with the cursed power distorting his voice—more Auka than Drakhin, more like his infernal father than ever—no Naaga could resist his commands.

"Hiding already?" Imril scoffed, well aware that this was probably a trap, but not caring in the slightest. Nykithus had gotten the better of him last time, because he'd had the element of surprise, but he was too young to understand what Imril was truly capable of.

"You will take me to him, *now*." He tapped into his power, releasing his tight control *just* a fraction more... until he was surrounded by a halo of white-hot energy. No disease or plague or poison could breach this barrier. Nykithus's old tactics wouldn't work now.

He silently thanked Esania for her generosity, for her willingness, for the exceptional *vir* she'd given him, enabling him to carry out such an impossible feat.

Alarmed, the Naaga stepped back, escaping his radius. "I *can't* disobey..." Again that pained expression flitted across her elegant blue face.

"You can. You just did." *Who are you more afraid of, Naaga?* "Don't test me, Naaga. I will not ask again."

The servant nodded glumly and headed for the door.

Imril followed.

CHAPTER THIRTY-SEVEN

THEY PASSED through dark corridors and silent halls and traversed winding flights of stairs, and the further Imril went into Nykithus's stronghold, the more sensed a *wrongness* about the place.

The halls were deserted.

There was no light.

A foul chemical smell emanated from several rooms, reminding him of the dark labs on his father's ship.

That *smell*... he would never forget it.

A powerful, visceral emotion ripped through him, too dark to put a name to, causing his aura to flare even more brightly. His wings shifted. The Naaga stiffened, but didn't dare look over her shoulder.

He and Mael had probably spent hundreds of revolutions imprisoned in those labs. He didn't know how long it had been —he didn't gain any sense of time until the Ancestor had released him onto Khira—but his memories of being trapped, of being completely at the whim of another, a dark, faceless being that could command the very fabric of space and time and even the walls of the ship itself...

The only one that saved him from giving up on life itself was *her*.

Marial.

His mother.

You are not a monster, Imril. You are my son.

They went down, entering a long, dark, sloping corridor, until they reached a familiar looking entrance.

The triseal of Nykithus's vault. All Drakhin eyries had a vault beneath their high walls, a vast network of chambers and tunnels that were used for storage.

In the event of all-out war or invasion, the vault could also be used as the ultimate bolt-hole.

"Go," Imril said softly, dismissing the Naaga servant with a subtle flick of his fingers. "Get far away from here, as far as you can."

She didn't waste time, shuddering in relief as she fled.

Imril stared at the vault's entrance. Three massive metal barriers stood between him and the Drakhin who had brought his entire world crashing down.

Why?

Before he killed him, Imril wanted to at least ask Nykithus that question.

The vault was supposed to be totally impenetrable, but when Imril was at his full strength, no known substance on Khira could hold him back.

Surely Nykithus knew this. What was the point of all this subterfuge?

He pressed his hands against the metal surface and channelled his power.

Burn.

He drew on all his rage and frustration, on his desire to protect Esania, which was stronger than anything else.

Burn.

The metal started to melt.

I'm coming for you, bastard.

And if Nykithus thought he could lay a trap for him down here, he was a fool, because Imril was at his full strength now, and if pushed, he could blow the whole place apart.

CHAPTER THIRTY-EIGHT

ESANIA SHOWED HER PEOPLE, the Vradhu, and the mercenary crew—with the exception of Calexa and Ares—into a large chamber on the ground floor. High arched windows lined both sides, but with Mael's shadowveil blocking out the sun, the place was dim, with only the soft lights in the ceiling providing a faint golden glow.

Her former servants seemed... *excited.* With its high towers and ornate walls and ceilings and carved archway. The eyrie had a certain charm, she supposed. It was like one of those ancient Earth castles, straight out of a dark fairytale, only eerie and abandoned and filled with mysterious technology.

Esania barely noticed them. The Vradhu stalked around the edges of the hall with dangerous intent, checking for threats. The humans clambered over fallen boulders and cleared away tangled vines, finding various objects of interest amongst the rubble.

In the tower above, Mael and Sara sat across from each other, locked in some strange silent communication.

What the hell are you doing, Sara? I hope you know what you're getting into...

But Esania couldn't intervene. That was Sara's business

now, and she'd known Sara long enough to understand that Sara wasn't a fool.

Esania just had to trust that the woman knew what she was doing. Sara wasn't under her command anymore. She was a free woman. As for Mael, well, he wasn't as terrible as she'd thought. No doubt, he could be terrifying when he wanted, and he was definitely surly and snarky, but he didn't seem to bear any ill will toward Sara at all.

The hubbub of many voices rose to a crescendo as Esania found a quiet corner of the chamber. Unnoticed, she sat down on a worn stone block, letting the sounds of conversation flow around her.

She closed her eyes and focused on the faint feeling of *otherness* inside her. It was *him*. Power and fury and malevolence radiated through to her. The voices in the background became a faint murmur as she desperately tried to cling to his presence.

Where are you, Imril?

The way he felt right now... it scared her.

He felt like he wanted to kill someone... or worse.

What are you doing, Imril?

He was probably a thousand miles away or more, and there was nothing she could do. The delicate markings on her hand started to throb again, and a strange feeling spread through her body—fear, desire, frustration.

The frustration of not knowing, of not being in control, of trusting her fate to a higher power...

It was *maddening*.

And all she could do was wait.

CHAPTER THIRTY-NINE

WITH THE VAULT'S three massive seals completely burned through, Imril strode down the corridor, his incandescent aura lighting up the cavernous space. Still there was no sign of Nykithus, and not a single Naaga in sight. The stillness was unnerving, even for him.

In other circumstances, the silence might have given him pause, but he had no choice now.

Keep moving. Finish this.

The shadowveil was failing, Mael was going mad, and he had to destroy this abomination of a city before its inhabitants ventured into the outside world and ruined everything, before they went after the *vir*-rich humans.

Nykithus thought he was the *Overlord* now?

Imril growled, and the walls around him cracked as his aura flared.

Enough.

He would kill the bastard.

This ended *now*.

"Nykithus!" he roared, losing patience. "Show yourself, or I will burn your fucking eyrie to the ground."

He didn't want to kill the Naaga servants if he could avoid it—they were innocents, after all—but if he had to, he would.

As he rounded a corner, reaching a pair of wide double doors that were decorated with ornate but meaningless stars—hundreds of them, polished so brightly they glittered as if they were in the night sky—he felt a tug at the edge of his consciousness.

Esania.

Her pull was intoxicating, as always. Although their link was faint, she reached out to him, seeking him out with an intensity that made him want to go to her immediately, drop to his knees, and give her his world.

She was his *lukara,* truly.

If only they could do mindspeech.

But that would come later, when their bond was stronger.

Her presence gave him strength. He was doing this not just for revenge, but for Esania and her people... even for the surly Vradhu, who had good reason to despise him.

For the first time in a very long time, Imril wanted to protect his tribe.

Esania had put him to shame, had *shown* him what loyalty meant. Against impossible odds, she'd never given up. Even when he'd offered her sanctuary and safety, she'd never forgotten about her people.

Brave, wily Esania. How had she even *convinced* him to take her back to the forest?

I'm going to finish this, Esania, for you.

This was a remnant of his old life; a consequence of the corruption that lay beneath the deceptively grand surface of his empire. A terrible, familiar emptiness crept into his soul. The Drakhin were an abomination, and this world of theirs... it never should have existed.

He would destroy it before its dark tentacles had a chance to touch her.

He, the tyrant; brutal, all-powerful, despised by his own people... betrayed by the one closest to him.

And now beholden to another.

You are not going to fuck this one up.

Imril slammed his palm against the doors, channelling his power, superheating the metal until it glowed white-hot.

Unexpectedly, they swung open.

Without hesitation, he stepped inside.

And froze.

CHAPTER FORTY

AN ARMY of Naaga stared back at him, their pale, pearlescent eyes glowing in the dim light.

They had weapons.

Behind him, the doors slammed shut with a resounding *thud*.

Imril became furious. "What is the point of this?" he thundered, staring at the strange triangular devices in their hands. "Stand down, or I will burn you all to ashes."

Some of the Naaga stepped back immediately, responding to the command in his voice. Others refused. He was starting to get used to that.

The servant race was diverging; thanks to Nykithus's genes, they had discovered *free will*.

This world was changing; always changing.

Imril walked forward, the halo of power around him flaring. "You know I can kill all of you right now if I want. Your master knows that. Is he the sort of Drakhin who would needlessly sacrifice you for the sake of his misguided ambition?"

Imril thought about releasing all of his power in a single devastating blast. It thrummed through his veins like a wild creature, pummeling at the walls of his self-control, taking all of his energy just to keep it at bay.

He had never felt this powerful, *ever*. Esania's *vir* was just that incredible, and impossibly, the longer she was with him, the more potent her energy became, *especially* when she was aroused. It would take at least a hundred feedings from a hundred different Naaga to try and even touch this level of power.

How utterly humbling. After so many hundreds of revolutions of fighting his way through life, of trying to understand *what* exactly he was, he came to realize that he knew so little about the Universe. How could a creature like Esania contain so much untapped power within her fragile, slender frame? How did she seduce him, challenge him, vex him, all at the same time?

He, who had once been the strongest thing on this planet, so full of cynicism and ennui that he could kill on a whim.

Not anymore.

One of the Naaga lobbed something toward him; a round, circular device that looked like a bomb. Imril pushed his power outwards as the thing exploded, releasing noxious grey gas. His aura burned away the grey cloud before its plumes could reach him. Nothing could touch him now.

The Naaga chattered amongst themselves, clearly agitated.

"Is Nykithus a coward?" Imril asked, raising his wings menacingly as he stalked forward. Unable to stand the heat of his aura, the Naaga scuttled backward. "This confrontation is going to happen sooner or later. Whether it be the next revolution, or in a hundred, I am going to find him, and no virus or poison or weapon is going to be able to touch me. I can kill all of you in a heartbeat." He had Esania now, and she made him invincible. "So I will ask you again. What is the point?"

Cowed by his voice, several of the Naaga had dropped to their knees. The others glared at him defiantly, but he could read fear in their silvery *vir*. The closer he got to them, the more he could taste their energy. It was so *different* to hers; faint, metallic, joyless.

As if they were the twilight, and she, the sunrise.

"Are you going to obey your master? Do you really think you can kill me, *samare*?"

He stepped forward again, lighting up the darkness.

They shrank back.

Fearful eyes.

Indecision.

Silence.

"The Lightbringer is right." A voice rang out in the cavernous chamber, and he recognized it instantly. *Nykithus.* "You are no match for him when he is in this state." A sigh. "There is *almost* nothing that can kill him, and I won't send you to a pointless death. Stand down."

Quickly, almost eagerly, the Naaga fell back, clearing a path toward the center of the room, where a massive throne sat in the center, its carved obsidian wings soaring up toward the roof.

In the throne sat a familiar figure. This was the very being that had almost destroyed Imril's entire existence, and he still didn't understand *why*.

And this was *definitely* a trap.

A growl rose from deep within Imril's throat.

Regardless of the reason, he was going to kill the bastard.

CHAPTER FORTY-ONE

"NYKITHUS," he said softly, staring at the Drakhin sitting in the massive throne. "What have you done?"

Three hundred revolutions had passed since disaster came down upon his world, but it could have been yesterday.

Only Nykithus appeared... *different*.

The dim light reflected off Nykithus's smooth silver skin, burnishing his elegant features—a perfect combination of his Vradhu mother's and Imril's own.

Unable to have offspring of his own, Imril was the prototype, the progenitor, his genetic material harvested by the Ancestor and multiplied a thousand times over in a terrible experiment.

"Imril," Nykithus replied slowly, his voice empty, hollow, a pale imitation of what it had once been. "You think I'm afraid of you, but there are far worse things in the Universe than even you, Lightbringer."

Imril looked into his subject's black eyes and found nothing.

No spark, no emotion, not even anger...
Nothing.

"Are you sure, Nyk?" Imril used the diminutive form of his

name on purpose, a reminder that Nykithus had once been nothing but a common Drakhin without a title.

His voice reverberated with power. Energy rose off his body in waves, turning the air around him into a shimmering inferno.

He was ready to shoot a bolt of pure energy right through Nykithus's heart and be done with it... but he hesitated. As he looked closely, he could see that there was something... *odd* about the other Drakhin. Nykithus's features were unchanged, his sleek black hair arranged in its customary high topknot. He wore a suit of pristine white scale-armor, which contrasted perfectly with his silver skin.

White was such an ostentatious color for a Drakhin. In Imril's court, none had dared wear white for fear of offending him—because of his almost-white skin.

But Nykithus had always been a little bit vain.

"Yes, Imril, I'm sure," he drawled. "You see, I have also seen the face of our Ancestor." Slowly, he stood, unfurling his black wings. Being of the second line, Nykithus possessed the classic coloring of a second gen Drakhin—silver skin, dark hair, black wings.

And yet there was that sense of *wrongness* again—Imril couldn't quite put ins finger on it. "What are you talking about?" he snapped. The Ancestor was dead. Mael had killed him with his bare hands and wrapped him in shadow, thrusting his ephemeral body deep into the belly of the mysterious *Hythra.*

The sentient ship had consumed their father, merging him into her vast consciousness, but now she was melting inside Za's core, and Imril had a strange feeling about Nykithus that he just couldn't shake off.

"He hasn't really seen my face," Acheros said suddenly. ***"He just enjoys taunting you, son. An ambitious one, this youngling."***

That voice... it was the sound of his deepest nightmares.

I am not your son! Imril stiffened, resisting the urge to look around. *How... how are you even alive, bastard?*

How was the monster even *here?* Had he been released during the destruction of the *Hythra?*

Because of course, the Auka's voice came from Nykithus's mouth.

"Acheros," he said quietly, and his voice was ice-cold, without a shred of emotion in it.

Even though he was seething inside.

Even though a sudden panic came over him, because his mate was far, far away, and the source of all evil was here, *inside* Nykithus's body.

"Is that surprise I detect in your expression, my child? You think I am so easy to kill?" The Auka chuckled, a humorless, bone-chilling sound. **"I existed long before this planet was even a speck in the Universe. Time is irrelevant to us. You are still young, but you will learn. The Hythra was merely a container, and now this child has agreed to become my vessel."**

Imril stared at Nykithus's face as it changed, becoming smooth and eerie and *ageless.* He said nothing, anger and help-lessness building up inside him.

Acheros was supposed to be dead.

Foolish Nykithus. Do you even understand what you've agreed to? Were you so desperate to escape Mael's shadowveil that you did a deal with the scourge of the Universe?

The thought of Acheros even *existing* in this world... in Esania's world...

It was unacceptable.

The Auka could *not* be here. Not now, when Imril had found his *lukara*, when he finally had a true sense of purpose in this life.

He started to concentrate every single shred of power in his body, pulling the energy into his chest, building a single bolt of power that could wipe out half the planet if he unleashed it without caution.

Right now, he was dangerous, a live incendiary bomb about to explode. Any ordinary mortal who touched him would be killed instantly.

The desire to kill Acheros was so strong that he began to shake. This was the cruel, vicious alien who had subjected their mother to so many hundreds of revolutions of terrible torture, of cold words and physical pain and imprisonment and long, maddening silences.

And then the bastard would turn it all around and say he loved her.

Torturing her with the promise of kindness, never quite delivered.

Hot and cold.

Darkness and light.

Cruelty and a shred of tenderness, so rarely glimpsed...

But mostly, Acheros was an old, sadistic, cynical bastard who had lived too long for his own good, who knew how to manipulate with terrible skill, who tried to shape his own sons into his image and failed, terribly.

Kuleh.

Evil.

His mother had taught Imril that word, had taught him the meaning of such things. In Drakhin language—the tongue Acheros had invented—there were no words for *good* or *evil*.

As the heat inside Imril's chest grew, he felt something stir.

You.

She was calling to him through their bond.

The female he missed so badly. Her touch, her scent, her sweet calm voice, her green eyes, as calm as a deep lake on a still day, the way she could quell the firestorm inside him with a single measured look.

He loved her.

The Drakhin language had no word for *love*, but the Vradhu did, and he spoke Vradhu just as well.

He *was* half-Vradhu, after all.

Through their bond, Esania reacted to his emotions, radiating concern. He wanted nothing more than to go to her, right now, but he couldn't.

Not when Acheros was here. He would not lead the Dark One to his mate or her people. He would *never* put them in danger like that.

If his father got his hands on that much *vir*... Imril shuddered.

It occurred to him that Nykithus's body didn't radiate any power at all. *Strange.* But then again, Acheros never radiated power either. The Auka was darkness and light in perfect sync.

"I can see that you desire to kill me, son." Nykithus's silver face smiled, but it was Acheros's smile entirely—never reaching the eyes. ***"You're not thinking clearly. Even in this inferior body, I would destroy you."***

"You can try," Imril grated, the energy inside him swelling until it hurt. *But you're weak right now, aren't you, bastard? Mael damaged you. You can't even hold your own form.*

Imril got the feeling that Acheros was bluffing.

The Auka wouldn't have tethered himself to Nykithus's body unless he absolutely had to.

But one niggling doubt remained at the back of his mind. Esania had asked him to look for a missing human called Rachel. What if Nykithus and Acheros were holding the human somewhere and feeding off her?

What if Nykithus/Acheros were hiding some monstrous strength?

It didn't matter. He had to get rid of Acheros before the monster grew even stronger.

One chance.

That's all he had. He had to make this hit count.

Even if it meant destroying half the planet.

As long as he kept Esania safe. That was all that mattered.

"I know what you're thinking, child of mine, but you can't kill me."

Imril said nothing. He closed his eyes and let the powerful wave of hatred wash over him, remembering the first time he'd ever rebelled against his sire.

Not his *father*—no, he would never call Acheros that. Imril might have inherited Acheros's DNA, power, *whatever*, but he was the Auka's offspring in blood only.

When he'd first rebelled—the first of thousands of such incidents—Acheros had locked him in a lightless room, where no sound was able to penetrate. No interaction, no Naaga to feed from, no stimulation whatsoever.

Just Imril and his own silence. How long had he been there? Dozens of revolutions, perhaps.

"You should know this, child. I created you from my own flesh and blood. You are what I am."

Imril sought the place in his mind that he kept so deeply locked away—the place he'd retreated into when he'd been locked inside Acheros's sensory deprivation chamber. He clung to images of all that was *good*, remembering what his mother had taught him. There were rare occasions when Acheros had allowed him and Mael to see their mother, and Imril drank in every single moment of the time spent with her as if it were sweet, precious life-giving *vir*.

After a while, though, those visits stopped.

"Imril, stop this insanity and join me. You and Mael are the only Drakhin with enough power to rule this world. I gave Mael the skies, and you the lands. Is that not enough? Do you yearn for something more?"

For the first time ever, Imril heard a note of frustration in Acheros's voice.

A crack in the impenetrable facade.

He gathered more power, and his scale-armor, made from an alloy that was supposed to be resistant to all temperatures...

It started to melt.

And Acheros chuckled, his voice filled with approval. ***"Finally, you start to fulfill your true potential. Join with me, Imril, and I will give you knowledge that will make you a God in this Universe. Our kind are rare amongst the stars. On some planets, we are even mistaken for Gods."***

Oh, it all sounded so seductive, but Acheros was just saying this because he was weak. He would find a way to use Imril, and as soon as he got what he wanted...

Shut up.

Imril thought of Esania.

He fixed her image in his mind as he became hotter than a thousand suns. His armor was gone, probably vaporized. Perhaps his flesh was burning. Perhaps his solid form was turning into something *else*...

Pure energy.

He felt the pull of the void between worlds. He heard its seductive song. He could so easily turn into *nothing* and drag Acheros and Nykithus kicking and screaming into that place the humans called the *Netherverse*, where time ceased to exist and energy was a state of being.

But he wouldn't survive that either.

He wanted to survive.

He wanted to be with *her*.

He was selfish like that.

Almost there...

But he needed to buy some time, and Acheros was in a rare talkative mood.

"Why did you create us?" he asked, his voice unrecognizable to his own ears. A wave of horror swept through him as he realized that he sounded exactly like an Auka. That was the effect of Esania's powerful *vir*. The energy he'd harvested while she was aroused was greater than he'd realized—*far* greater. "Why did you come to Khira? Why did you choose to breed with the Vradhu?"

So many questions that had never been answered.

Just as he was on the very brink of turning into the same monster as his sire, Imril finally had a chance to understand his existence.

He opened his eyes and met Acheros's steady gaze. Acheros smiled Nykithus's smile and turned his black eyes into dark pools of infinity. ***"Hm. Before you turn us all into stardust, you are entitled to an explanation, at least."***

The stone floor under Imril's feet was melting. He was sinking into the molten rock, but it didn't harm him the way the liquid metal from the *Hythra* had.

He was almost at peak output, and he was momentarily invincible.

Soon.

He would hit Acheros soon, because if he went on like this for too long, he would burn up all his power and fade away into nothing, like a solar flare.

"So explain," he growled, the power roaring in his ears.

"I am a scientist, my child. Our people are few, and we are ancient. You come from a rare line, Imril." He laughed again, a hollow, chilling sound. ***"There was a time when the Auka had finite lifespans just like the Vradhu, but some of us engineered our own immortality. We stole energy from the place between worlds and wove it into our flesh, and when the rest of our people died out, we were the only ones to survive. Alone. Unable to reproduce. So they sent me in search of a vessel, a body that could contain my seed, that could withstand the elgida and all the changes***

needed to bear my young, and I finally found it in Marial."

Imril's pain transformed into something raw, yet very, very old. "That's all she was to you? A *vessel?*"

"No, no, I did feel affection for her on occasion..."

"*Bastard.*" Suddenly, Imril's hand was around Nykithus's neck. Immediately, the Drakhin's silver features melted away, his flesh incinerated, his bones turned to ash, his blood vaporized.

He became dust right before Imril's very eyes...

Is that... it?

Imril's anger surged, and the ceiling started to collapse.

You can't leave without answering—

Acheros materialized across the other side of the room, millions of tiny particles coalescing to form Nykithus's silver body, his dark wings.

Of course, Acheros wouldn't be so easy to kill. Imril stalked forward. "You don't even *get* to speak her name." *Affection? Monster! You tortured her until the end of her existence.* "You killed her." *And I was just a naive stripling, unable to protect her.*

"She had grown old. Weak. She poisoned your minds. You and Mael both. Look at us now. You were supposed to guide and nurture your people, Imril. Thousands of revolutions wasted, and we are back where we started because of her."

Imril didn't want to hear any more. Acheros's cold dismissal of the sacred female who had given them life... it made him sick to his stomach.

I can't allow a creature like you to exist in this Universe. I'll destroy you, even if it means I have to go down with you.

If Nykithus and Acheros and Ton Malhur and its malevolent Naaga were destroyed, at least Esania would have a chance of surviving this. The Vradhu were the true inhabitants of this land, and if there weren't any troublesome Drakhin or Naaga around, they would easily be able to protect the humans.

Even if he wasn't there.

He drew on the darkness inside him, and it gave him strength. "Enough."

He stalked forward, and power rippled down his arms. The air around him felt strange. *He* felt strange, as if he were existing in two places at once.

Imril didn't care. All he wanted to do was obliterate this monster.

He darted forward, becoming an incandescent blur as power surged into his legs, making his movements impossibly fast. Suddenly, he was in front of the monster, wrapping his hands around its neck before it had a chance to retreat.

There was no hesitation.

Imril roared as he channelled power down his arms, into his hands, his body shaking. The walls shook. The floor under his feet was soft. Bits of stone began to fall from the ceiling.

He drew on thousands of revolutions of pain and hatred and the sheer agony of not knowing why, of not even knowing *what* he was.

Of grief at the death of a race that never should have existed.

"Fool," Acheros rasped. **"You would throw away everything I would give you? And for what?"**

For her, I would. Without a second thought. You are no match for her, Acheros.

He released his power in a massive blast, and his hatred burned right through the monster's face...

And everything else.

The air around him turned white-hot.

Burn!

Acheros laughed, his voice distorted by the roar of Imril's

power. His—*Nykithus's*—face seemed to melt, turning into a dark shadow.

No!

He would not give Acheros the chance to tap into his own dark power. Imril poured more and more power into his blast, until he was committed beyond the point of no return.

"Wh-where did you get this power? This is…"

And for the first time in his life, he heard a note of uncertainty in the Auka's voice.

"None of your fucking business," he growled, squeezing his hands around Nykithus's neck. How was the Drakhin's body still in one piece? Of course, that was Acheros, using his monstrous abilities to keep Nykithus alive.

Imril didn't relent, even as Acheros drew on the darkness, absorbing Imril's power… just like Mael. ***"If you cease this now, I might consider not killing you."***

It was Imril's turn to laugh. Acheros was rattled, and he was trying to undermine Imril's confidence, but he had the upper hand.

He was going to finish what Mael had started.

What did it really take to kill an Auka?

He was about to find out.

The shadows rose higher and higher, sucking away his power, creating a swirling vortex in the center of the room. Acheros grabbed Imril's wrists, trying to pull his hands away, his burning face twisting into a grotesque mask.

Consumed with power and hatred, Imril stared at the creature that had tormented him for so many thousands of revolutions, feeling strangely empty.

Suddenly, Acheros looked small, weak; a shadow of the terrifying, godlike Auka he had once been.

And Nykithus was nowhere to be seen, his presence completely absorbed by the malevolent Auka.

"You dare do this to me? I made you."

Dark tendrils of shadow pierced through Imril's energy,

coalescing around his feet, rising up his body, lessening the ferocity of his destructive blast just a fraction.

You think I'm any different to Mael? I just want you dead. Gone.

He wanted freedom.

He wanted to burn everything away and start anew, with her.

Fire could be cleansing, too.

Through their tentative bond, he *felt* her, and she was frantic.

Don't fret, my love. I will come back to you.

He could escape this. He *had* to.

Imril released his grip around Acheros's neck and pressed his hands against his chest, *still* channeling his energy. The Auka's cursed power was weakening him fast.

Finish it.

With a roar, he drew out every single shred of energy in his body, throwing it at the Auka.

Boom!

The shadows retreated.

What was left of Nykithus's body... still moving, it dropped to its knees.

Is this it?

Completely drained of strength, Imril could only dare to hope as he dropped to his knees. As the power left his body, something else replaced it—excruciating pain.

Thud!

"Wha—?" He blinked, his hands dropping to his stomach.

A blade protruded from his belly, buried right up to the hilt.

"There are many ways to kill a Drakhin," Nykithus hissed, his voice coming from that grotesque face—bones protruding, flesh burned away, sharp teeth exposed in a terrible grimace.

Drained of all his power, as weak as the day he'd emerged from Za's burning crater, Imril gasped, hardly able to believe that he'd been brought down by a mere *blade* of all things.

"*Why?*" he gasped.

"Fool. You were soft. You let him get away with too much..." Acheros's voice faded as Nykithus fought for control of his own body, his skeletal face twisting into a terrible grimace.

"We... knew... you would return," Nykithus hissed. "We tried our best to prepare, but fucking Mael and his cursed shadowveil... The Naaga... they just want to be *free*."

He was fading. Acheros, fighting to regain control, was growing weaker. Imril was bleeding out.

Soon they would all be dead.

What does it take to kill an Auka?

A weakened one, apparently, could be killed with an intense blast of power from an Auka halfling.

"Ah..." With great effort, Imril pulled the blade from his belly and flung it away. He placed his hand against the wound and tried to seal it with his power, but the tiny blast he created was weak and lacking in precision.

His power was almost completely depleted.

His brilliant aura flared out, and suddenly they were engulfed in darkness. Shock spread through him. "The... *Naaga?*"

All of this was over that made race of servants? Those submissive blue-skinned ones, who did not speak a word unless bidden, who were physically incapable of defying him... until now?

"They are *not* your slaves anymore," Nykithus whispered, his voice fading. "Their descendants... are also... *my* children..."

How?

Realization struck Imril in the gut, almost flooring him. His shoulders slumped in exhaustion, and the last of his anger drained away. "*You*... you had a mate?"

"She was my *lukara*, and she... was with child," he whispered, his voice a barely audible hiss in the silence of the vast, dark chamber.

"You lie," Imril whispered, shocked to the core. "The Naaga can't sexually reproduce with Drakhin. They are not—"

"No. You do not understand them at all," Nykithus said fiercely, finding a final burst of strength. "Did you ever stop to wonder why there are *male* and *female* Naaga?"

"Wh-what have you done, Nykithus?"

Nykithus had taken a Naaga as his mate. The old Imril would have dismissed the thought as ridiculous, as *wrong*, but as he thought of Esania, of her human fragility and the way she made him want to tear apart the Universe just to keep her safe...

He understood.

He understood so very *well* how Nykithus could have tried to kill him.

Imril grunted in pain as he summoned the very last trace of his power, generating a gentle flare that provided just enough light to see by.

Nykithus stared back at him, a shell of the fierce Drakhin he'd once been. "It's evolution. You can't stop it. You *have* to kill me now, but it doesn't matter anymore, *Overlord*. It is good that I die here under your hand, because I take you and our cursed sire with me into the fucking void. She might be gone, but my... *our* children will survive. You won't." Nykithus slumped forward, and Imril caught him in his arms. The pain in his stomach was excruciating, almost obliterating any awareness of his surroundings. "It's evolution."

A low chuckle escaped Nykithus's nonexistent lips, and it sounded strange; the Drakhin's voice was fused with Acheros's. ***"And so we all go down together, Imril, and over a female, no less..."***

"Fuck you." Digging deep, Imril found the strength to punch *Acheros* in the face. He took a deep breath, trying to wipe away the terrible feeling of regret that welled up inside him.

Because Esania was still there in the back of his consciousness, calling out to him, desperately wanting to be with him, and he could feel the full force of her emotions through her *elgida*.

Humbling him.

He took Nykithus by the hand. The Drakhin was still reeling, his breaths coming in great big gasps.

"Nykithus," Imril said softly, staring into sightless eyes that were burned beyond all recognition. "I am sorry. If only you had come to me first, I would have..."

"Would you really?" Nykithus stared back, somehow finding the strength to grasp Imril's arm with one skeletal hand. "You would have had her executed, because *you* were the biggest nightmare of all, Imril Lightbringer."

What would you have done, Overlord?

The truth was, Imril didn't know. The Drakhin laws he'd created were absolute.

Drakhin-Naaga relationships were forbidden, punishable by death. The law served two purposes. To keep the bloodline pure, and to protect the Naaga.

Their history was filled with cases of Naaga being killed because some foolish Drakhin had taken one to his bed.

Finally, Imril had put a stop to it.

His words, his law.

And now he was dying.

Part of him suspected Nykithus was right.

Cerulean blood spilled through his fingers as he clutched his belly, trying to stem the flow of the bleeding.

Esania was still there in the back of his mind, but she'd gone very, very still, as if she knew something was terribly wrong.

I'm sorry, Esania.

Nykithus gave a great, shuddering gasp. The light in his

charred eyes faded, and he fell backward, his great skeletal wings spreading out on the stone floor behind him, the membranes in between burned away.

Dead.

And there was no sign of Acheros either.

This time, he was gone for good.

A feeling of resignation swept over Imril as he closed his eyes and slumped forward, preparing to enter the Netherverse for eternity.

The song of the place between worlds flowed around him, pumping through his weak heart, carrying him away on its hypnotic, rhythmic beat.

And *still* he could feel her, resolute, unwavering, never quite giving up on him.

Come to me, Esania. I need you.

That was his last thought before he drifted away into the dark, seductive embrace of the void.

CHAPTER FORTY-TWO

SOMETHING WAS WRONG. Esania reached for Imril through their bond. Over the past few minutes, he had been angry, frantic, consumed with hatred, and filled with despair.

And now...

He was fading. She'd felt his power surge and then blink out like a supernova.

Something was *terribly* wrong.

She didn't waste time.

"Hey, Esania, where are you goi—"

She held up a hand, silencing Mai. "Later. I have to go."

She had to find him. She didn't care about whatever danger she might encounter.

There was only one person who could possibly take her there.

Mael.

She headed toward the stairs, leaving a whole bunch of staring humans in her wake.

"Wait, Esania, what are we supposed to do, now that we're—"

"Figure it out," she snapped, breaking into a run. "I have to *go.*"

She ran past fallen pillars and dodged creeping vines. She avoided slippery looking patches of moss and the occasional stray stone. As she reached the wide open double doors, her strides widened, her white dress flapping around her knees, her braids flying. Guided by dim light that came from sconces in the wall, she ascended the crumbling spiral stairs two-by-two and sprinted down the corridor, pumping her arms, going faster and faster as she felt Imril's life-force ebb away.

She was sure of it now.

He was dying.

She pushed the double doors open with both hands and sprinted past a startled Sara, running across the floor until she was just inches away from Mael.

Instantly, her energy drifted toward him, but she didn't care.

"Take me to him," she gasped, her chest heaving up and down from the exertion. "Don't you fucking ask, Mael. It's urgent."

"If I leave here, the shadowveil will fall," Mael said softly, opening his eyes. To her surprise, he looked perfectly earnest. "Are you certain you want to do this, human?"

"Yes." She clasped her hands together in a pleading gesture. "I think something's terribly wrong. He's hurt... perhaps even dying."

"What's going on, S?" Sara was on her feet, hovering at the very edge of Mael's radius.

"Don't take another step," he said softly. "I don't want to feed from you... *yet*."

"I'll explain later," Esania said, her voice rising in pitch as Imril's presence through the bond grew even weaker. "Don't make me get on my knees and beg, Mael. If there's a way to get me there now, just make it happen!"

Mael's dark eyes widened a fraction, but he didn't move.

Sara put her hands on her hips. "Mael, just *do* what the

woman asks." Her eyes narrowed. She actually had the nerve to *boss* him around.

Bless your heart, Sara.

"I can take you there," he said softly, and Esania's heart almost burst in relief. "But the journey will not be without risk to you. Bending the fabric of space-time is incredibly taxing on me, and when we reach Ton Malhur, I wont have much energy left to protect you."

"But I have *vir*," Esania countered. *The stars know he needs it.* The thought that her energy alone could save Imril and give Mael the strength to protect them if needed... it filled her with hope.

She *had* to do this, even if it meant going into a situation where her life might be at risk.

She sent a burst of energy through their bond, trying to pull Imril back. *Damn it, Imril. You're not fucking allowed to die on me.*

Mael turned to Sara, and impossibly, his expression softened. "Go downstairs, Sara. Tell the Vradhu and the humans to get inside the vault. You must be the first to go inside. When I take Esania through to the other side, the shadowveil will fall, and you will be vulnerable until I return."

"The *vault?*" For a moment, Sara looked mildly horrified, but then she managed to pull herself together, a determined look entering her eyes.

"Don't be afraid," Mael said, his voice low and reassuring. "The Vradhu are competent warriors, and they'll have no trouble defending you once you're inside the vault. I will return as soon as possible." For the first time, Esania heard a sliver of worry in his voice. Menacing, intimidating Mael was actually worried enough to let it show. "Go *now*, Sara."

"We have to go," she urged. "He's—"

"I *know*." He rose to his feet, his tail waving behind him. Mael closed his eyes and took a deep breath. As soon as he opened them again, bright sunlight shot through the high windows, bathing them in blinding light. Esania gasped and shielded her eyes.

A deep, shuddering sigh escaped Mael's lips, and it was as if a great weight had been lifted from him. "The shadowveil is gone," he said quietly. "Let's go."

"You better come back, Mael," Sara said forcefully, shooting him a glare before turning toward the exit. "And bring my girl back to me in one piece." She met Esania's eyes for a second, giving her a nod. "Right. The *vault*. I'm out of here. You're coming back with Imril, okay, Esania? You're *coming back*."

"We *are* coming back," Esania repeated, using the words like a mantra, hoping that just by saying them, they would somehow come true.

Mael did something with his hands, a look of intense concentration crossing his features. A tiny speck of shadow appeared in front of him, growing larger and larger until it was just big enough for a person to fit through. Shadows rose all around him, snaking, writhing tendrils of darkness that seemed like they could consume her whole and make her disappear forever.

A ripple of unease crawled over her skin, entering the pit of her belly, sinking deep into her bones. Suddenly, Esania felt cold all over. She could *feel* the flow of her *vir* as Mael drew upon it, using it to create this monstrous dark portal.

He was *feeding* from her, and he felt so different to Imril. Where Imril's touch was warm, gentle, seductive, an irresistible caress, Mael was cold. Forceful. All-consuming. Darkness incarnate. She was being sucked into his endless vortex.

Mael's darkness closed in around her, and suddenly, Esania was terrified. Her breath caught in her throat. Her heart hammered like a butterfly in a cage. Her body was frozen.

Nothing, *nothing* could have prepared her for this.

It was a deep, primal, *human* thing, and all the logic in the Universe couldn't guard against this terrible feeling.

What the hell are you, Mael?

Imril's brother. Wrought from the very same stuff as her lover.

Mael turned to her, beckoning with one hand. **"Come, Imril's *lukara*. I will take you to him."**

Even his voice had changed, becoming deep and powerful and resonant.

The shadows wrapped around her, and everything felt *wrong*. Esania tried to scream, but nothing came out. She forgot who she was, *where* she was.

She was *nothing*, a tiny insignificant speck in the endless Universe.

Nothing.

Mael's arms closed around her, and suddenly they were falling, and Esania started to lose her mind.

She screamed, but her voice was swallowed by the endless void. The only thing tethering her to this reality was the cold fire that burned through her *elgida*.

I'm coming, Imril.

CHAPTER FORTY-THREE

WHOOSH.

There was something hard and cold beneath her. Esania blinked, trying to find her bearings.

Where am I? What just happened?

Darkness surrounded her. She sat up and looked around wildly. Behind her, something—*someone*—let out great shuddering breaths.

He coughed. He gasped.

Mael.

He took me through, I don't know...

A portal? Had Mael created a portal through time? Through space?

Anything was possible on Khira. Just like the *Medusa* had done when it ripped through the Netherverse, they'd *skipped* through time and space, only Mael could somehow accomplish such a thing using his will alone.

But Esania didn't care about all that now.

"Where is he?" she demanded, feeling her way around on the floor, totally blind in the darkness. There was a strange smell in here; the smell of cinder and ash and death. "Imril?"

She could feel his life ebbing away through their bond, but the sensation of closeness was *palpable*.

He was *here!*

"Imril!"

No response.

But a familiar sensation crept over her, even as Mael backed away.

Her *vir* was drifting toward him. Even though he was unresponsive, his body was absorbing her energy. Esania latched onto the sensation and followed it.

Her *elgida* started to throb again.

He's here!

Her bare hands slid over something impossibly smooth and yet hard at the same time, like velvet over steel.

His body.

Cold!

Imril had always felt blissfully warm, and now his body was cold. As she ran her hands over him, guided only by touch, her *vir* flowed into him, becoming a powerful torrent.

Stars, he was weaker than ever. What had happened here?

"Imril, wake up," she pleaded. "Wake *up!*"

In the background, Mael's breathing was harsh and labored, and he groaned deeply, as if in pain. Despite his obvious suffering, he stayed strictly outside her radius, not drawing on her *vir* at all.

Esania barely noticed. She was entirely focused on Imril, on his still, lifeless form. She couldn't detect a heartbeat. He didn't even *breathe.* The only thing giving her hope was the fact that he continued to draw upon her *vir*.

She ran her hands over the powerful contours of his body. He was naked; she couldn't feel any remaining traces of his dark armor. Her fingers met the bony curve of one of his wings. Imril was lying on his side, curled up in the fetal position, his wings outstretched. That was as much as she could make out in the darkness.

Something warm and wet and sticky seeped through the thin fabric of her dress. *Blood? Was this his blood?*

But she couldn't see a thing.

"Mael, help me," she said softly as she found the strong curve of his jaw. Her fingers traced over soft lips, over proud cheekbones and his imposing brow, finally reaching his soft hair. "I need to see what's going on."

There was a pause, then...

"I can't bring the light," Mael whispered, his voice cracking. "Only *he* can. If I come close to you as I am now, I will take all of your energy. He needs it more than I."

Esania's right hand was really throbbing now, the skin under her *elgida* growing hot. The sensation wasn't unpleasant though, just... *strange*.

The silence stretched between them, punctuated only by the quiet sounds of Mael's suffering.

"Traveling through the void really hit you hard, huh?" The words came out as if she were in some sort of surreal trance. She lay down on her side next to Imril, facing him, not caring that his blood seeped through her clothes. Esania placed her hand on his chest, willing her strength into him, even as she grew weaker.

"I've never taken another through the void. Even when I'm on my own, it's a supremely difficult and dangerous feat. I didn't know if it was possible."

"But you took me anyway?" Perhaps Esania should have been angry, but she wasn't.

"I had no choice."

"You would have risked my life... for him?"

"He is my brother."

Perhaps Esania should have felt chilled to the bone that Mael could so easily sacrifice her life, but instead she felt relieved and strangely grateful.

"If my concentration had lapsed even just for the shortest time, I would have been lost, too."

Oh.

Esania ran her fingers over Imril's powerful chest, desperately wanting him to wake up. *We're just fumbling in the dark without you, Imril. Wake up!*

Then his chest moved. Up. Down.

He coughed.

A breath!

Hope surged in her chest.

"He's alive," Mael rasped. There was a note of relief in his voice. "My brother isn't so easily killed."

"When you first encountered each other in the tower room... why did you fight like that? I got the feeling you were trying to kill each other."

Imril's arm twitched. Esania curled her fingers around his powerful biceps. *He's alive!*

"After I escaped the *Hythra*, I was mad. Utterly mad. I did some bad things to my brother and his people."

Imril's arm moved again. Suddenly, it was curled around Esania's body, fitting perfectly into the curve of her waist, squeezing tightly, his muscles flexing.

He's alive.

A soft groan escaped his lips. His head shifted, moving closer to hers. His sensual lips met her forehead, and he kissed her gently. "I think you just redeemed yourself, Mael," he rumbled, and Esania snuggled closer, the flow of her *vir* a rich, unstoppable torrent.

Yours. It's all yours, Imril.

His hand closed around hers, and he sent a gentle stream of power through her *elgida*. Warmth spread through her body, suffusing every part of her, from her hand right down to her toes.

She closed her eyes and sighed in relief as she grew weaker still, as Imril's undeniable need consumed her.

So tired...

So weak, and yet she was ecstatic.

He's alive!

"And you are incredible," he murmured, his powerful arm tightening around her body.

Esania let herself be consumed by him, not caring that her strength was fading away.

He kissed her on the lips; a long, slow, lingering kiss that made her want to surrender everything. His hands were everywhere, velvet-tipped fingers running over her shoulders, her neck, face, her hair.

Gentle. *Reverent.*

He kissed her again, and a soft glow sparked between them, illuminating Imril's face. She stared into golden eyes that held thousands of years of longing.

But there was something else there too, something raw and pure and innocent.

Imril went very still, his gaze piercing right through her. "I've done some terrible things in my life, Esania. I have been merciless and immoral and I've killed far too easily. *This...* what you see here is the aftermath of my ignorance, my recklessness."

"Why are you saying this to me?"

"Because now I understand."

"Oh?"

"The value of an existence."

"You only get one, you know."

"I only *want* one."

Esania's heart fluttered as a thousand and one questions raced through her mind. "That's easy enough for someone as old as you to say. What's the average lifespan of your species, anyway?"

"I don't know." Somehow, he managed to look apologetic. "Our sire only told us what he wanted us to know. There are so many gaps in our knowledge."

"Well, *my* kind only live for a hundred-and-thirty years or so, so you have to make the most of it."

He was going to outlive her, perhaps by thousands of years, and yet here they were, lying on the floor and staring into each other's eyes, contemplating the meaning of their existence.

"No," Imril growled, pulling her closer. "When it's complete, the *elgida* binds your soul to mine. You will live for as long as I do."

So I'll live for thousands of years... perhaps longer?

The thought was both thrilling and terrifying. "You didn't tell me that when you started."

"Is that an objection?"

"No. All of this... it's just a lot to take in."

"Nothing you can't handle, though."

"True." Since landing on Khira, she'd been forced to deal with all kinds of stressful and terrifying situations, and somehow, she'd survived.

And now she had a fierce, fire-wielding Drakhin all to herself.

Hardly able to believe her luck, Esania ran her hand over his chest, her fingers gliding over the smooth surface as she admired his perfectly honed form. Her hand dropped lower, tracing over impossibly well developed abdominal muscles, until she felt...

Blood.

"You're hurt," she whispered, bringing her fingers up to her face. Bright cerulean blood glistened on her fingertips.

"Almost killed me," Imril whispered, a faint smile curving his lips. "Maybe this was the reason I had to start the *elgida* before I left you."

Esania shuddered. "I wouldn't have felt it, otherwise. I wouldn't have known that you were hurt..." *Dying.* Now she understood how he was able to read her so easily. If her *vir* gave away just a fraction of the emotion she felt from him, then she was an open book.

There were no secrets between them.

Not now, not ever.

Imril held her tightly, shifting one massive wing so it curved over her body, enclosing her in a protective cocoon. "*Fate*," he whispered. "You came to me for a reason. You're mine now."

As her energy melded with his, as he drank from her until her limbs grew heavy and her eyelids drooped from sheer exhaustion, Esania closed her eyes and let go, allowing him to possess her completely.

She never thought she'd ever allow another being to have such complete power over her, but right now, she didn't care.

She could *feel* his emotions; a rich, dark, complicated song of shadow and light that radiated from his body, growing stronger and stronger as he drained her *vir*.

He would never hurt her. He would never abuse this power he had over her. She knew it with absolute certainty, because they were bonded.

And the most astonishing thing of all... the most sublime, impossible, wonderful emotion coming from him right now?

Love.

CHAPTER FORTY-FOUR

IMRIL WAS careful not to cast light over Nykithus's charred remains as he guided Esania out of the chamber. She walked slowly but confidently, staying just far enough behind him that he couldn't drink any more of her *vir*.

He'd taken enough from her already, and although he could return some strength to her in the form of power, at this stage the *elgida* wasn't developed enough to be able to truly merge her energy with his.

When he was done with her, she would be a creature of energy and light, able to tap into the vast power he generated from her *vir*, and she would be as long-lived as he.

The science of energy transfer was complicated and mysterious. Acheros had told Imril only the necessary details; that females of certain species were conduits to the rich veins of living energy—*vir*—that ran through the Universe.

Females gave life. They nurtured it. They *were* life itself, and Imril was just a tool, a weapon; able to take her glorious energy, amplify it, and turn it into something physical.

He turned and met her gaze, and she found the strength to smile back at him, even though she was clearly exhausted.

"You're beautiful," he murmured, unable to help himself.

This euphoria... he'd never felt anything like it. They were still deep in the bowels of Nykithus's eyrie. He was weak, recovering from a near-fatal stab wound in his belly, and his scale-armor had burned away, leaving him completely exposed, but he was ecstatic.

He was alive, and he was with his *lukara*. That was all that mattered.

Color rose in her cheeks, a subtle, delicious shade of dusky pink that made her dewy skin look even more appealing.

He just wanted to devour her whole.

Every. Last. Morsel.

"*Imril,*" she whispered, and it was both a plea and a half-hearted protest. "You're hurt. I'm exhausted. We need to find Rachel. We need to get out of here."

"I know that, but can't a man just take a moment to appreciate his good fortune? Don't worry, Mael has already gone in search of your human." Maybe his belly wound had stopped bleeding because all the blood was currently pooling in his cock. He had an erection again, and it was sheer torture.

How much longer did he have to endure this insanity? Imril vowed to finish creating his *elgida* as soon as possible. He could just picture Esania in his mind, his mark decorating every curve and plane of her glorious body, his power filling the intricate channels he'd carved in her skin.

Only then could he truly claim her, taste her, *possess* her.

Esania stopped dead in her tracks and stared at him, her expression unreadable. Being just outside the radius of her *vir*, he couldn't read her so well, but he could feel the undercurrent of her desire through the bond.

It drove him mad. Imril gritted his teeth, his nostrils flaring. He was just going to have to endure it.

"It's driving me crazy too," she said at last, her lips parting to give him a tantalizing glimpse of her sweet pink tongue. "But don't get ahead of yourself, big boy. I'm just glad you're alive."

"Yes." Oh, how he wanted to go to her, to take her into his arms and fly away, to leave this monstrous dark city and its terrible memories behind.

But he couldn't touch her. Not yet. Because he was a monster, and right now his touch would do more harm than good. The *elgida* wasn't strong enough yet.

Imril beckoned to her. *Come.* "I'm yours, Esania. I'll do anything for you. Anything you desire... *anything*."

"Then let's find Rachel, and then... I want you to take me home."

Home.

Now *that* was something he hadn't thought about in a long time. Where was home? In Kunlo's decaying eyrie? In the abandoned halls of *Eleia*, his lofty eyrie above the waves?

"Home is with you," his *lukara* said gently, as if reading his thoughts. With their tenuous bond in place, perhaps she really *did* know what he was thinking.

Not that he minded.

Not at all.

CHAPTER FORTY-FIVE

THEY SPENT a day in the ruins of that strange stronghold—Imril slowly healing, Esania replenishing her strength. Although it was the epicenter of enemy territory, Imril somehow managed to get the remaining Naaga to be at his beck and call, arranging food and warm clothing and a safe, comfortable room where she could rest.

Through some terrible feat of genetic engineering, most of the blue servants were conditioned to obey him without question, however there were a rare few who were immune to the sound of his voice—those, apparently, were Nykithus's descendants.

Esania thought the obey-at-all-costs thing was rather unfair, anyway.

"They might despise me," Imril said, and for a fraction of a second, he looked so terribly lost, "but they are Nykithus's children, and they are a part of this world now. I'm not going to fight them... as long as they leave *my* people alone." His golden eyes flashed, promising certain death to any who threatened his tribe. "If they obey me, I might even offer them my protection."

Stars, her mate could be terrifying.

But not to her.

Never to her.

She could feel him in her blood, her heart, in the beautiful pattern that decorated her right hand, in the inexplicable fabric of the Universe itself, time and energy and *life* melding together to connect them in an endless union.

She *knew* him.

As darkness fell, Imril spoke, his voice tinged with sorrow as he described horrors he'd never shared with anyone before.

Esania learned of the terrifying Auka and of Acheros the monster, who had created Imril and Mael in a lab on the *Hythra* by mixing his genetic material with a Vradhu female's.

Their mother. She was called *Marial*, and when Imril spoke of her, he sounded reverent.

Imril told her about the dark ship *Hythra*, of how she'd been Acheros's creature, how Mael had fought and overpowered their sire, burying the Auka deep inside the fabric of the *Hythra,* only to become consumed by the ship himself.

When Mael had finally broken free of the *Hythra* and reached the surface of Khira, he was completely insane, and Imril had been the Overlord of the Drakhin for hundreds of years.

Chosen by Acheros to rule over the Drakhin, Imril had no idea what had befallen his sibling.

He was an ancient, damaged soul who possessed immense power...

And she was his mate, the voice of reason to his fiery anger, the light against his brooding darkness.

Kind of ironic, considering they called him the Lightbringer.

"What are you thinking, Esania?" Imril reclined on a long stone bench, his wings—they were pale again; the *nightblack* must have worn off—tucked behind him, a simple white tunic covering his powerful torso.

Imril wore a dead man's clothes.

He was a study in pearlescent white, his eyes, his skin, and his sharp teeth glittering in the soft light.

"I was just thinking that I'd like you to hurry up and finish this damn *elgida*." Strangely, even the thought of the exquisite pain that came with the engraving of Imril's *elgida* sent a ripple of arousal through her.

"I would like that too," he rasped, and Esania caught sight of the bulge in his trousers. He made no effort to hide his erection, a devious grin curving his lips as he slowly looked her up and down, undressing her with his eyes. "Very much so... but not here." He stood and held out his hand. "Are you ready, Esania?"

She was strong enough now that she could stand to be inside his radius. She stepped forward, placing her hand in his. He felt deliciously warm.

"Let's go." Imril led her out of the small room, along a light-filled breezeway that was bordered on both sides by elegant stone arches. For a bleak stronghold in the middle of an evil kingdom, this eyrie was strangely charming. Everything about the Drakhin style was oddly familiar-yet-different, reminding her of old-world Earth architecture.

They moved into a wide-open space; a curved stone bowl reminiscent of an amphitheater. Located at the very top of an impossibly tall tower, the ivory walls gave way to wide open windows that offered glimpses of the spectacular countryside below.

Nykithus's eyrie was surrounded by rolling hills and valleys, but where the landscape should have been green, it was painted in shades of grey and brown; a land that had been under shadow for hundreds of years.

But Mael's shadowveil was gone now. Hope and excitement fluttered in her chest, along with apprehension. The danger hadn't entirely passed, but there was a feeling of regeneration, of *renewal,* about this place.

A gust of cold wind whipped past, creating a faint whistling sound as it swirled around.

Esania stared across the wide open space and froze.

A group of around a dozen Naaga stood in the center in a ring formation, speaking quietly amongst themselves. As soon as they caught sight of Imril, they froze, fear written in their eyes, in the stiff lines of their slender bodies.

Maybe it was just her imagination, but she could almost *see* an aura around them; a faint silver glow.

Imril squeezed Esania's shoulder reassuringly. "Wait here. This is *not* going to be a problem. I promise."

"Okay."

As he walked across to the group, Esania couldn't help but admire his powerful form. Even when he was recovering from injury, he radiated power and menace in equal measure. Beautiful, deadly, imperious. *Drakhin.* He was magnificent, and he was all hers. She could see why Acheros had chosen him to rule, but somewhere along the line, the Auka had badly miscalculated.

You didn't just *create* a civilization from scratch.

Humans had fought long and hard to get to where they were now, and as much as they tried to distance themselves from their wild, emotional, illogical, imperfect ancestors, Primeans were just another chapter in the vast human chronicle.

And she was just a tiny byline in that chapter.

She was *human,* damn it. Genetic purity was a con, and Esania was fucking *human*.

"*Tuush tu ve.*" Imril spoke to the Naaga in their language, and although Esania couldn't understand a word he was saying, she knew he was asking about Rachel.

Where is she?

The Naaga in front was slightly taller than the others, her skin shining silvery-blue in the bright sunlight. She stepped aside and the Naaga parted, revealing a slender figure wearing a deep grey cloak.

"Rachel!" Before she realize it, Esania was sprinting forward, her dress fluttering in the wind, her boots pounding the stone floor. She reached the human and wrapped her arms around her, squeezing hard. "I thought you were lost to us. Are you all right?"

"*Alive*," Rachel replied, her voice trembling. Hot tears slid down Esania's cheek, and she wasn't sure whether they were hers or Rachel's. "I didn't think anyone would come for me. I didn't see how it would be possible..."

Esania released her and stepped back, staring into deep brown eyes. Rachel pushed her hood back, revealing gaunt cheeks and a shorn scalp. Her mahogany skin—usually flawless and lustrous—had lost its healthy glow. Esania stifled a gasp. "They did this to you?"

"They just had to go for the hair, damn it," Rachel grumbled, summoning a wry smile in spite of her obvious exhaustion. "After all that effort maintaining it, the 'fro is gone." She shrugged. "It'll grow back. I'm not hurt, though. Just goddamn tired. He... that *thing*... he came every day and every night and put his hands on me, and it was the weirdest thing, but he seemed to be able drain all the strength right out of me. It was like being constantly dosed on hypno-dorm." Her eyes flicked toward Imril, who kept a respectful distance. "Is *he*...?"

"He's with me," Esania said softly, putting her hand on Rachel's shoulder. "He *is* one of them—a Drakhin—but trust me, he won't ever feed from you. I *know* what it's like."

Rachel's eyes widened. "You... you *offer* it to him?"

A feeling of pride and affection surged in Esania's chest. "I do. It's complicated, but it isn't a bad thing. He isn't our enemy."

"If you say so, then I believe you. You know, it's weird, but even though I was chained up and used as food, a couple of the blue guys kinda protected me. I couldn't understand a thing they were saying, but I think they might have just saved my life."

Esania hugged her again. "We're going to get you back to the girls... to the Vradhu, and you'll get plenty of time to rest and regain your strength. You're safe now. You won't have to go through that ever again."

"I could do with a big, long sleep in those warm *eukluk* furs," Rachel murmured, her expression becoming wistful. "Maki made me the *best* bed. Those Vradhu... they're not so bad, really."

"We're going home now," Esania said gently as Rachel nodded, blinking back tears as she let out a deep, shuddering sigh of relief.

"The Naaga have agreed to release her," Imril said. He gave Esania an affectionate look, but didn't make any effort to come closer. She understood. He didn't want to accidentally tap into Rachel's *vir*.

Unexpectedly, he dropped to his knees in front of the group of Naaga, bowing his head. The tall female stepped forward, a look of astonishment crossing her elegant features. Imril said something in Naaga, his voice full of sincerity.

Esania got the feeling something monumental was happening, but she didn't quite understand it.

There was still so much she didn't understand about this strange, wild planet and its inhabitants.

For a moment, everyone was quiet. The Naaga stared down at Imril, looking slightly uncomfortable as the cold wind swirled around them.

"*Toana,*" she said at last, her voice trembling with emotion.

Slowly Imril stood, and he had eyes only for Esania. "I asked for their forgiveness. She said *maybe*. We have many things to work out still, but it is a start."

Esania nodded. A faint roar reached her ears, growing louder and louder until a dark shadow engulfed them.

"That would be Mael," Esania said dryly.

A sleek grey metal ship drifted down from the clouds. Rachel flinched. Esania squeezed her hand reassuringly. "It's okay."

The craft was small, about the size of a basic-level passenger transport. It descended onto a square platform at the edge of the tower, the roar of its engines dropping to perfect silence.

Mael was perched atop the ship, back to his usual menacing self as the dark shadows swirling around him. He seemed to have regained all of his strength, but how he'd managed to do that without *vir*, Esania had no idea. Maybe he was different to the other Drakhin.

"I take it he's not the enemy either?" Rachel backed away slightly, glancing toward the exit.

"Believe it or not, he isn't. That's Mael, Imril's brother, and he's on our side." She thought about Sara and Mael's obsession with her. Esania still didn't quite trust Mael's motives when it came to Sara, but so far, he'd proven himself in every way possible.

For now, they would just have to trust him.

A door opened in the side of the ship, revealing its glowing interior.

"Your transport." Imril gestured toward the ship, nodding his head a fraction. "The pilot is Naaga, one of the first generation. He won't disobey my orders. He *can't*. You're perfectly safe with him."

"We... we're going in *there?*" Rachel stiffened.

Esania nodded, trusting Imril completely. "Just a short trip, Rachel, then we'll be home. This is different to when you were taken."

Rachel looked at Imril, then Mael, then at the Naaga. She gathered her cloak around her body as she stared out at the vast, unfamiliar lands of the kingdom called Ton Malhur. Fear swirled in her eyes, and for a moment, she was utterly frozen. Esania couldn't even begin to imagine what torture she must have gone through, having that Drakhin feed from her, not knowing how to communicate with the Naaga that imprisoned her.

But then she looked at Esania's face, and a steely resolve entered her gaze. *There* was the old Rachel, the tough, persistent woman who had escaped from the squalid women's prison in Nairobi and somehow found her way onto a smuggler's ship... the brave woman who had caught her attention in the Fiveways and begged Esania to take her with them to Torandor.

Small, but wily and tough, not to be underestimated. That was Rachel. She would recover. She was human, after all.

Rachel took a tentative step forward, stealing a quick glance back at the Naaga as she made her way towards the Drakhin ship.

"Thanks," she whispered under her breath.

Esania followed, with Imril bringing up the rear. As they walked up the narrow ramp, Mael materialized at Imril's side.

For the first time, the brothers stood side by side, one Darkness, the other Light, two halves of a dark nightmare, two mysteries, desperately trying to carve out their own truths.

Twins. Impossible, but true. A lot of the male things on this planet seemed to come in pairs, but Imril was more than enough for her.

He was hers, and the other...

Mael probably belonged to Sara.

"Aren't you going to join us?" Esania asked, as Imril flexed his wings.

His eyes burned with desire. "I will fly alongside. Mael will ride on top. The Naaga have agreed to give us clear passage. Nothing will happen to you."

Ah. She understood why he couldn't be inside with her. She felt it too. It was sheer torture, being so close and yet not being able to...

Fuck.

Somewhere in her mind, another barrier crumbled away, and she decided that *fuck* could be a rather useful word. Really, she couldn't believe she'd been such a prude.

"Are you two just going to stand there staring at each other all day?" Mael crossed his powerful arms and frowned, his tail whipping back and forth impatiently. He flicked his head in the direction of the ship. "Hurry up, Esania. I've spent over three hundred revolutions keeping this dismal place under shadow. I do *not* want to waste my time hanging around in this depressing ruin."

"Impatient much?" Esania needled him a little; she couldn't help it. Actually, Mael was turning out to be quite the bossy one.

"What do *you* think?" Mael bristled.

Imril gave them an odd look... was he *smirking?*

"I think I need to keep an eye on you around my precious Sara." She narrowed her eyes. "You hurt that girl in any way, and I'll..."

"You'll *what?*" Mael's shadows rose up, threatening to engulf her. Imril inched closer, his aura flaring, the air around them growing thick with tension.

Danger.

"I'll be *really* pissed, and so will he." Esania might not be able to put a scratch on Mael, but Imril was definitely capable of doing so.

"Hmph. You underestimate me, human. What *exactly* do you think I am?" Mael actually seemed offended.

"I don't know... *yet.*"

"Don't get ahead of yourself, human."

"Ahem..." Awkwardly, Rachel cleared her throat. "Are we going to ride in this thing, or what?"

Instantly, the tension dissolved, and both Drakhin stared at Rachel, as if seeing her for the very first time.

Imril and Mael shared a lightning-quick brotherly glance,

their eyebrows raising simultaneously in a perfect expression of male bemusement.

It was Esania's turn to smirk. After the horrors she'd endured, Rachel had already started to regain her composure. Blunt, outspoken, even abrasive sometimes, this small woman had survived in some of the harshest places on Earth.

She was tough, and so were Esania and the rest of her girls. They were *human*, after all.

These Drakhin didn't know what they were getting themselves into.

Esania smiled sweetly at Imril as she made her way up the ramp. "See you at the eyrie."

He gave her a look that was so intense she thought her ovaries might have melted a little bit.

Her smile melted, too, her lips parting slightly as her jaw threatened to drop. She felt Imril's arousal through their bond, and it floored her.

As if to tease her, he turned and spread his wings wide, displaying them in all their pale, sculptural glory. He broke into a run, making big, powerful strides until he reached the edge of the platform.

Then he jumped.

He disappeared off the edge.

Esania's heart leapt into her throat. She couldn't stop the torrent of worry that flooded her mind. Imril had been terribly wounded. He was still healing. Was he strong enough to fly? What if he...?

Fell?

But then a powerful gust of wind blew past, and he soared up into the brilliant blue sky.

A Drakhin in his element.

Magnificent.

Almost godlike, but utterly flawed...

And now he was showing off, reveling in his abilities, putting on a little display just for her.

He shot up through a bank of clouds, disappearing for a moment. Then he reappeared, circling back to where they stood.

"Show off," Mael muttered, but he didn't sound bitter at all, just amused.

Rachel gasped.

Esania watched her mate soar through the sky, and she was thrilled. She saw the brilliant flash of his smile as he grinned, and her heart nearly burst in her chest.

He was free.

And he was *hers*.

CHAPTER FORTY-SIX

"ARE YOU SURE THIS LOOKS OKAY?" Esania ran a hand over her newly unbraided hair. Soft, curly black waves cascaded down past her shoulders, and for the first time in her life, she allowed herself to feel... *feminine*.

Traditionally, Primeans didn't bother much with trying to make themselves appealing to the other sex. Since direct physical reproduction was forbidden, there was no need. They were designed to be physically attractive by human standards, but that was more for psychological reasons. A strict style code was enforced in the Serakhine, consisting of a neutral palette, minimalist tailoring, and the complete absence of any unnecessary adornments.

Occasionally, Esania and her girls had taken to bending the rules—when they could get away with it.

And now...

She threw those rules out the fucking window. The dress she wore was a bold sheath of deep, vibrant red—almost the color of human blood. It draped over one shoulder and left the other bare, cascading from neck to ankles in impossible waves of lustrous fabric. She wasn't sure what the material was made from, but it felt incredibly luxurious.

One shoulder was left bare, revealing the stunning design that covered her entire left arm and extended all the way down her back. Imril's *elgida* was like an intricate tattoo, only it was comprised of thousands of tiny scars that had faded to a shade of brown slightly darker than her natural skin tone.

Ritual scars.

She bore his mark.

According to the girls, it suited her.

She wasn't sure what she looked like right now, but she felt good.

The Drakhin didn't use mirrors, apparently. There wasn't a single one on the entire planet.

"You look fucking beautiful," Alessia beamed. "I have always wanted to dress you up in something nice, but you Primeans have your *ridiculous* dress code... I've never seen so much grey in my life. What a shame. A planet full of beautiful people, and you all choose to dress in the most boring way possible. *This* is much better."

Esania had chosen the fabric from one of Imril's many storerooms, and using some old-fashioned Earth skills—*magic, really*—Alessia had transformed it into something spectacular. Really, Imril had *too* much stuff lying around this vast eyrie of his, all of it sitting untouched since he'd left this place around three hundred years ago... since his people had succumbed to the horror of the Plague.

She shuddered. Imril never said much about what had happened, but sometimes she could sense his anger and sadness; a dark, seething thing that could turn dangerous if she wasn't there to keep it in check.

It was a secret side of him that only *she* was allowed to see. To the outside world, he was the Overlord; powerful, inscrutable, and terrifying.

Esania sighed as she ran her hands over her dress, wondering how exactly she'd ended up in this glorious mess.

Plucked out of the wild forests of the Ardu-Sai, her new surroundings were luxurious by comparison.

Everything in this grand eyrie was manufactured by the Naaga using highly advanced machines that humankind could only dream of—a legacy of Imril's Auka father.

And the eyrie itself... stars, she'd never seen anything like it. After coming to an agreement with the Vradhu, Imril had given them Kunlo's stronghold. It was theirs to guard and repair and live in for as long as they wished.

He'd brought her here, to *Eleia*, a dazzling construction of pink-hued stone that rose high above the brilliant blue ocean.

Some of the humans, including the mercenaries, and to her surprise, Rachel, had stayed behind, preferring to stick with the Vradhu. But most of them had chosen to follow her here.

"Why the serious face, S?" Sara sat on an ornate footstool that had a padded seat of black velvet-type material and curved ivory legs. Being seven months along, her pregnant belly was round and full now, and according to Raphael, the *Medusa's* enigmatic former navigator—who somehow knew a little bit about human medicine—her size was *consistent with dates*.

That was good. The bub was kicking and active and Sara's terrible nausea had passed, and they were safe in Imril's spectacular castle.

Enough of this eyrie business. It was a *castle*; a big, spectacular castle, something right out of an ancient Earth fairytale.

"I was just thinking," she said quietly, "about whether I did the right thing... I mean, the way we all got off Mars..."

"*What?*" Both Alessia and Sara stared at her as if she were mad.

"Listen, mama wolf," Sara growled, her expression turning fierce. "You're not even allowed to say things like that."

"*Mama wolf?*" Not knowing whether that was a good or

bad thing to be called, Esania made a face. "I'm not that much older than you, Sara."

"Yeah, but you looked out for us when no other Primean would have given a rat's." Sara stared out the window at the dazzling ocean, her blue gaze becoming distant. "You know, at some point, I wanted to try and figure out how to terminate the pregnancy on Mars without anyone knowing. I hated Kivik. *Hated* that asshole. I was trapped. Couldn't even leave the planet, because they would have found out about it on the exit medical."

"What changed?"

"After the initial shock wore off, after I realized what was happening, I started to feel... I don't know, *different.* It was like some sort of instinct came over me. Maybe it's the so-called maternal instinct, I don't know. The more I thought about it, the more I felt this baby was a part of *me*, a precious thing. How could I have even thought of... anything else?" Sara paused, and Esania realized she was blinking away tears. She wiped at her eyes with the edge of her sleeve. "Sorry. Damn pregnancy hormones all over the place. I get so emotional."

"Don't apologize," Esania murmured, completely trans- fixed by Sara's confession. "There's no need."

"It's probably the only chance I'll get in this life to have a child. I don't care if Kivik is the father. This is my baby, and you know what? I *know* what the law is in the Serakhine. You crazy-ass Primeans think you're so far above humans that you can just swat us away like flies, but—"

"I *don't* think that you're inferior." The words were out of Esania's mouth before she could even think. Disgust rose up inside her as she thought of the Serakhine's insane laws. And to think there was a time when she'd actually *accepted* that kind of thinking.

If her mother had accepted it, she wouldn't even be here.

"I wasn't talking about you. You're *normal.* You're the reason we're all here and not dead or slaving away on some mining colony on Kalluq-3. When the girls found out about it, they all convinced me to tell you the truth. They said you were different, that you wouldn't buy into that crap." Sara turned on her side and curled up into a ball, hugging her knees. "They said you'd help. I was terrified at first, but they were right about you. You're all right, Esania."

Esania could only nod as she remembered the frantic night they'd escaped from her villa, aided by an underground group within the Serakhine known only as *The Source*. Would she have done the same if her mother hadn't come to her several days before and revealed the truth about her birth?

Guilt coursed through her.

I'm not as noble as you think, Sara.

A faint tremor shook the walls and floor, followed by another dull *boom*. Whatever was out there, it wasn't relenting.

Hurry up and get back here, Imril. We need you.

"You know, I'm glad we made it here," Sara said quietly as the eerie silence of the cavernous chamber settled around them once again. "I'm glad we got out of the Serakhine. I'm glad we crashed on this crazy planet. Better being alive here than dead on Mars. We're probably the only humans who've ever set foot here, you know?"

"I-I'd never thought of it like that."

"Isn't that *something*, huh?" Sara's voice trembled slightly. "You know, I never got the chance to thank you."

Esania shifted uncomfortably, not used to such familiarity from humans; not used to small pleasantries like *thank you*. And she wasn't used to the warm, fuzzy feeling that spread through her chest, even as the world closed in on them.

"So, Esania, *thanks*. For everything." Sara sat up and met her gaze. "I fucking mean that."

Esania blinked furiously. Were her eyes a little *too* moist? *Tears?* This feeling... what was it called? She'd never experienced it before. "You can thank me when we're all safe," she murmured, trying to hide her emotions, thinking of Calexa and her crew and the girls and Rachel, praying to Mars that they were all going to be okay.

Beyond this crumbling fortress in the middle of the wild forest, there had to be something better out there, a safe place where they could exist without constantly having to look over their shoulders.

And if it didn't exist, she would create it.

"All done." Alessia, who had been silent the whole time, fastened something around Esania's neck and stepped back, admiring her handiwork. "You're stunning, hun. The big, scary Drakhin isn't going to know what hit him."

"I..." *I hope so.* Today was an important milestone in the making of her *elgida.* The intricate markings on her skin had grown over the past two months, each line and swirl and flourish drawn with painstaking care and precision.

Every time he summoned her, every time he lay his hands on her bare skin, he infused a little bit of his power into her, binding them closer and closer together. The process was still excruciatingly painful, but at the same time, she found it maddeningly erotic.

When she had reached her limit, when pain gnawed at the very limits of her endurance, he would go down and give her the most mind-blowing head, and through some serendipitous quirk of biology, her *vir* was actually more delicious to him when she was aroused, so he had extra incentive to keep her happy down *there.*

And that was just the foreplay. They hadn't even fucked yet. She, the educated virgin, who knew so much but had experienced nothing, had been completely undone by this intense, irresistible alien.

"'Hey, Esania?"

"Yes, Alessia?"

"You're blushing."

"I'm *not,*" she protested, even though she knew it was true.

"I don't blame you," Alessia said, a sly smile curving her

cherry-red lips—*where* the woman had found a substance similar to lipstick on this wild planet, she had no idea. "He's very handsome, for an alien. All those muscles, those *exotic* looking eyes, those wicked wings..."

"*Alessia,*" she snapped, feeling embarrassed and jealous and proud all at the same time.

Sara snickered.

"Just admiring from afar. I wouldn't even *dream* of being in your shoes, hun. He's far too much of a scary alien for my liking."

"You've got nothing to fear from him." Now she felt defensive of her mate. "He's been nothing but good to us since we came under his protection."

"Of course. I'll just keep my distance anyway, because you know, the *vir* and all that. Honestly, it creeps me out. You and *you* are probably the only ones crazy enough to take on a pair of Drakhin."

"Hey, for as-yet unknown reasons, Mael came after *me*," Sara growled.

"And hasn't been seen since."

"He has good reason for that." A dangerous glint came into Sara's blue eyes. "Don't you start making assumptions about—"

Esania took a step forward to intervene, but Alessia threw up her hands in surrender. "Sorry. None of my business, I know. Look, I wasn't trying to be an asshole. I've just had bad experiences with guys who don't stick around."

"You're assuming that I actually want anything to do with him in *that* way. I don't. But he's different to how the stories make him out to be. *Misunderstood.*" Sara put her hands on her belly, wincing. "God, this little one's really got a kick on him. *Ouch!* Settle down, little dude."

"*Dude?*"

"It's a he. Mael said so." She beamed, then winced. "Ugh."

"I'm not even going to try and understand how he knows that without some sort of medical scan." Alessia looked a little spooked. "I guess this is just..." she shrugged, "the *new* world, huh?"

"The new world," Esania agreed, taking a few steps forward on bare feet. Her crimson dress swayed against her legs, making her feel... *sexy*.

Ha.

Imril was going to go nuts.

This whole thing—dressing up, doing her hair, making herself look *nice* for him—it was her idea. Today was the day the bond between them would become strong enough.

After months of excruciating temptation, they could finally be together.

Properly.

Just the thought sent a thrill of excitement down her spine and a surge of warmth into her pussy. She took a deep, quivering breath. "I'm going."

"Enjoy," Sara said. "It's good to see you like this."

"Like what?" Esania glanced over her shoulder as she passed through an elegant curving archway.

"You actually seem happy."

"*Huh,*" Esania whispered under her breath. It had only taken a trip to a wild, uncharted planet from there was no escape for her to feel this way.

Happy.

Who would have thought?

CHAPTER FORTY-SEVEN

HE SAT in his grand throne, unblinking, unmoving, his wings curled behind him, golden eyes blazing.

A sight to behold.

Imril could have been a statue for all Esania knew, and yet here he was, living, breathing, and ancient.

A golden glow surrounded him; she could see it so much better now, and her *elgida* throbbed in response, her body yearning to join with his.

On the threshold, she paused.

Beneath them the waves crashed against the vast foundations of the eyrie, the rhythmic, seductive sounds lulling her into a kind of trance.

Esania drank in the scene before her, feeling as if she were in the midst of some fantastic dream. Imril's command room was spectacular, a study in vastness and light and elegant lines.

In comparison to Kunlo's eyrie, Imril's stronghold was surprisingly minimalist. There were no ornate carvings or statues or brilliant patterns inscribed into the ceilings. The lack of embellishment was a statement in itself—he didn't *need* to try and impress with lavish displays of wealth. Imril's supreme power had been undisputed.

And now there was nobody to challenge him, because apart from Mael, all the Drakhin were dead or gone.

Imril's throne was massive. Made of ivory stone, it had a high, curving back that dipped outward to accommodate his pale wings. Broad armrests stretched down to the polished floor, seamlessly joining the reflective surface.

It was a fluid, organic thing, designed to frame but not outdo the man sitting in it. But then what could outshine Imril, who wore his power so effortlessly, who drew attention to himself without even realizing it?

"Esania," he growled, his deep voice echoing through the vast chamber, sending a thrill of anticipation down her spine. He held out his hand, beckoning her. *Come.*

Her heartbeat went into overdrive. She walked forward, her bare feet silent on the cold stone floor.

This is it.

There was no turning back now.

As if drawn by some irresistible force, she stepped into his radius, that invisible circle where he could tap into her energy. For all his flaws and vulnerabilities, for all his mistakes, he was still half Auka, and she'd since learned that the Auka were possibly the most terrifying beings in existence in the entire Universe.

Ancient beings, older than the Earth and the sun, the Auka had discovered the secret to immortality.

They had transcended physical existence.

They were gods, or perhaps monsters, and their dark, magical blood ran through Imril's cerulean veins.

"You," he rasped, desire rolling off his body in waves. "You look incredible, my *lukara*. I... I wasn't expecting this."

Suddenly aware of the power she held over him, Esania smiled as she reached him, placing her hand into his. A surge of golden energy flowed from his fingertips and danced up her arm, sending liquid fire through the intricate markings on her body.

The patterns lit up, turning golden, as if someone had filled them with skeins of electricity.

His power, which came from *her,* spread through her body, and it was pure ecstasy. She felt lighter, younger, more alert, each sound and sight and sensation coming to her in crystal clear detail.

It felt as if she'd been given a shot of some highly addictive narcotic. She stared down at Imril and drank him in, hardly believing that this powerful, dangerous man was all hers.

Being close to him no longer drained her. Every time she was in his presence, he gave her an injection of his power, and it filled her *elgida*. Channelled through the symbols and patterns of the *song*, his energy turned into life itself.

Esania was the Source of raw *vir*, nothing more. Imril drew it into his body and converted it into something else entirely. *He* was the catalyst, producing a reaction that defied all logic and science—something that Raphael had tried to analyze, only to fail miserably.

Esania had a word for what he did—for what he *was.*

Magic.

Imril was a sorcerer.

She didn't completely understand him or *what* exactly he was—she probably never would—but Esania didn't care. Imril had kept his word, and since they'd returned from Ton Malhur, he'd treated her with nothing but patience and tenderness, showing a very different side to him.

Her incessant questioning... he found it entertaining.

Her constant need for rules and structure... he was amused by it.

And her obsession with protecting her tribe... he *admired* it.

"Well, today is special. I wanted to surprise you."

He cocked his head, dark eyebrows rising questioningly. "This is your Primean custom? To dress in such a way?"

"Not Primean. Dressing up... is very much a human thing."

"So are you human, or Primean?"

"I'm *both*." She edged closer and closer, until Imril took her hand and dragged her into his lap. He wore nothing but a simple robe; a swath of cloth that revealed the broad muscles of his chest, tapering to a vee over his well defined six-pack.

Actually, it was more of a *ten-pack*, if one wanted to be specific. Since Imril was a Drakhin and all Drakhin were actually half-Vradhu, his physique was almost identical to the powerful bodies of the violet-skinned warriors, except he had the added advantage of those glorious pale wings.

He was *ripped*, as Sara might say.

"Well," Esania said slowly, sliding around in his arms until she felt his *very* conspicuous erection against her thigh, "what do you think?"

"It is a good custom," he rumbled, his golden energy swirling around them. "A *very* good custom." Even as he took her *vir*, he returned it in a constant stream of warmth, so Esania never felt drained.

That was the power of the *elgida*. It allowed her, a mere mortal, to join with this creature of darkness and light; this pale-skinned demigod.

She was human, but she wasn't anymore. She was possibly going to outlive all of her people, and perhaps their descendants too.

How would she deal with that?

If she thought about it too much, she might go insane. She'd never *asked* for any of this, but at least her people were safe. They had a future now, and with Drakhin technology, perhaps they even had a way off this planet... if they wished.

Imril ran his hand up the back of her neck, turning her head so she she faced him. His warm fingertips were like liquid velvet, his touch electric. "You are the most beautiful thing I have ever seen." He kissed her lips slowly, tenderly, savoring her. "I'm a lucky wretch indeed."

"Lucky, huh?"

"That you would choose this existence with me, after everything you've learned."

"I see the *man* in you," she said as she stared into his mesmerizing golden eyes. A complex tangle of emotions filtered through their bond. Lust, protectiveness, remorse, reverence, sadness. A trace of anger, too. There was *always* a fierceness about him, even when he was at his most gentle. "You could have taken me by force, but you held back. You could have ignored my requests to save my people, but you brought them under your protection. You could have started a war with the Vradhu, but you put past vendettas aside. What changed in you, Imril?"

"That's true," he murmured, stroking her hair. "There was a time when I would have done all those things, when I was young and vicious and eager to please my sire." A bitter chuckle escaped his lips. "It only took a thousand revolutions and a colossal fall from grace for me to understand what I had lost. When I fell into Za's crater, I was the Overlord of the Drakhin. When I woke, I was *nothing*... until I found you."

"We're really not so different, you and I." Esania had lost everything too—her position, her estate, her status as a Primean.

But in return, she'd found her tribe.

She'd found her mate.

"And yet we're *completely* different." Imril teased the dress off her shoulders, running his fingers over her neck, her back. "When you first encountered me, I'd been taught how to live from a creature that had forgotten how to exist. That was all I knew. You, on the other hand..."

"I was trying to survive," Esania said quietly. "That was all."

"And now?"

"There's room to breathe," she admitted. "I feel safe. *You* make me feel safe."

"Good." Appearing pleased with himself, he kissed her again, tasting of spice and sweetness and a hint of ash. He traced tiny patterns on her back with his finger, sending a ripple of desire through her. "Are you ready, Esania?"

Esania's body was on fire. She couldn't stand it any longer. "Do it. I can't believe you've waited this long."

"Only with great difficulty." A hint of strain entered his voice as he started to engrave the intricate *elgida* into her skin with his bare hands. That familiar, exquisite agony engulfed her once again, and Esania gasped.

"Be still, my love. Not much more to go." He kissed her as he worked, closing his eyes. Esania closed her eyes too, surrendering to the feeling of his warmth, his closeness, his delicious masculine scent. "This is one of the few good things he taught me."

"Your father?"

"*Sire,*" he corrected. "Even Auka take mates, or at least they used to. This is one of their traditions; a necessity more than anything else."

"There isn't an easier way?" Esania winced as Imril concentrated on the delicate patch of skin just above her left shoulder blade. For the last two months, they'd done this twice a day, and she'd found it easy to endure, because she knew there was a big reward at the end.

Now the *elgida* was almost half done, and it covered both her arms and extended the length of her back. In some ways, it reminded her of the intricate ritual tattoos favored by some Earth-dwelling humans.

"If there's an easier way, I don't know it." He stopped, lifting his finger and kissing the area he'd just marked. His warm lips were a welcome salve, obliterating the pain. "That's it. We can finally..." His voice grew hoarse. "The *elgida* is strong enough. It will hold."

"Oh. That's it?"

"That's *it*," he growled, and suddenly, she became acutely aware of his erection. "I have been dreaming of this moment ever since you came to me."

"I don't know how you even—"

"Shh. No more words." He tugged gently on her legs, and Esania got the idea, shifting so that she was straddling him. Imril tore her dress away with a savage flick of his arm, leaving her completely naked, her curly hair cascading over her breasts. He leaned forward and inhaled deeply, burying his nose in her hair. "*Stunning,*" he rasped.

"I thought you said no more words," she whispered as she stared back, unable to take her eyes off him. She whipped away the slender belt that held his robes together. They fell away, revealing the Drakhin in all his shimmering glory.

Imril grinned, seemingly aware of how damn spectacular he was. He wore his arrogance like a second skin; it was as much a part of him as his wings and the almost microscopic scales of his skin.

Stunning.

That rock hard abdomen, those powerful, muscular thighs. His erection, proud and massive, rising between his thighs, teasing her with its almost-human appearance.

Esania put her hand on his chest, the *elgida* on her arm glowing intensely. She rose up on her knees as a fierce torrent of need surged through her, turning her into a wanton thing.

Imril was beneath her, completely transfixed, the catlike slits of his pupils dilating as he ran his hands over his work, gently massaging her soft, aching skin. His power danced across her body, seeping into her muscles and bones, making her feel alive in a way that she never could have imagined.

Esania listened to her body, to the song in her heart, to the rhythm pounding through her veins.

This was what she was made for.

As heat rose inside her, a faint sheen of sweat broke out on her body, and her hair stuck to her skin. Imril ran his fingers through her dark, curly tresses, admiring them.

The smile faded from his lips, and his expression turned fierce. He inhaled deeply, his nostrils flaring.

Esania shivered in anticipation. "I can't believe you held back for *this* long."

Two months. Sixty days since they'd left the nightmare of Ton Malhur, and he'd been with her constantly, feeding from her, working on the *elgida*, pleasuring her in the most fantastic of ways, but taking none for himself.

"I'm Drakhin," he said simply, as if that explained everything, but his voice was strained, and his eyes glowed with lust.

Esania nodded, words deserting her as her arousal flared. She couldn't hold back any longer. She *needed* him inside her.

Imril ran his hands down her waist, her hips, her ass, her thighs, teasing out her energy, filling her with his own power. "Look at you. *Beautiful.* More than anything I could have ever imagined."

She leaned in and wrapped her arms around his neck. His wings shifted reflexively.

This is it.

Slowly, deliberately, she lowered herself, and Imril groaned as the tip of his cock grazed her slick entrance. His large hands settled on her ass, and he pulled her closer, controlling her movements.

His massive shaft glided against her throbbing flesh, entering her, stretching her, and at first she felt a twinge of pain, but then a torrent of white-hot pleasure surged through her as Imril buried himself up to the hilt.

He growled, a low, rumbling, *primal* sound that resonated in her bones. His power flared, surrounding them in a halo of golden light.

Strong arms wrapped around her, pulling her against him, their bodies melding together. Esania's *vir* became Imril's power, and he returned it to her as quickly as he took it, their energies becoming one.

"Fuck me, Esania," he whispered, guiding her hips.

She obliged, moving in small circles at first. Imril closed his eyes and groaned. Delighted at his response, she moved faster and faster, guided by blissful sensation. Power coursed over her *elgida*, her arms glowing with brilliant tendrils as she moved back and forth. She closed her eyes and fucked him, her slick hair whipping back and forth, her body becoming an extension of his.

He encouraged her, his large, powerful hands guiding her this way and that, caressing her breasts, her neck, her cheeks, his thumb entering her mouth...

She bit down, and tasted something sweet.

His... *blood?*

Imril grunted. Esania moaned. She writhed back and forth, sliding her hands over Imril's shoulders, down his back, finding the points where his wings emerged from his shoulder blades.

She grabbed the bases of his wings, holding on tightly as she moved faster, faster, a delicious tension winding its way around her core.

His wings rose, and suddenly she found herself being lowered to the floor, her back pressed gently against the smooth cold surface. The whole time, Imril kept his cock inside her.

Her eyes snapped open. Overwhelmed by the ferocity of her need for him, she cried out, her voice trembling.

Imril began to thrust, his wings curving over them like a canopy, his eyes glowing with power as he threaded his fingers through her hair.

He kissed her as he fucked her, again and again and again. Esania was in a world of pure bliss.

"You're mine now," he rasped. Their bodies became one,

moving to the rhythm of a Universe that was far beyond their understanding. "I have waited *so long* for you, Esania."

"Was I ever anything but yours?"

"No," he groaned, thrusting deeper. "You just didn't know it yet."

"Ah..." she tried to think of a coherent reply, but her brain had turned into blissful mush, and right then Imril hit a certain point, a threshold, and pleasure started rolling over her in waves, from the center of her chest right down to the throbbing tip of her clit.

The waves grew bigger and bigger; deep, shuddering sensations that were beyond her control.

She'd lost control a long time ago.

Now, she totally abandoned it, and it felt so *good*.

"A-ah," she cried, her voice rising an octave. "*Ah!*"

Imril slammed into her with the full force of a Drakhin male, with the full force of a man who had starved himself for far too long. Now he drank long and hard, completely consuming her.

Every. Last. Drop.

The waves grew bigger, until they weren't waves any more, but a single stream of insane pleasure...

And then something burst...

And her world shattered into a million brilliant fragments.

Of light.

CHAPTER FORTY-EIGHT

AFTERWARDS, she lay in his arms naked as he reclined in his throne, the *elgida* on her arms pulsing softly. "Satisfied?" she asked, tracing one finger up and down his broad forearm.

"More than," he rumbled, pulling her closer, dipping his nose into her hair. He took a deep breath. "You are my first and only."

"First?" Esania tried to conceal her surprise and failed miserably.

"Do not get me wrong. There was plenty of interest. There was a time when the Vradhu wanted to forge alliances with us, when a union would have been highly desirable..."

"But?" It was unreasonable to expect that a being like Imril would have stayed pure for thousands of years, but Esania still managed to feel a pang of irrational jealousy toward any female who might have caught his eye.

"The song did not come. In order to mate, I needed to draw the *elgida*, but I never saw it. Not until you appeared." His smile held a trace of bitterness. "The science of attraction is complicated, no? Acheros could never have predicted that *you* would be a part of his design."

"It seems there's a lot more than science to our... to *this*," she said breathlessly, Imril's warmth and the constant gentle pull on her *vir* threatening to lull her into sleep.

"The Universe works in mysterious ways," Imril agreed. "Before you fall asleep here, I want to show you something." He stood, lifting her effortlessly in his muscular arms, placing her gently on her bare feet. Imril picked up her discarded red dress and draped it across her shoulders, fashioning it into a kind-of cloak. "It gets cold up there."

"Up where?"

"Come, Esania." The smile never left his lips. Imril pressed his hand against the seamless wall. Suddenly, an edge appeared, then a part of the stone wall slid away, revealing an entrance beyond which lay a spiral staircase.

He looked over his shoulder. "My private sanctuary. It was in disrepair when I came, but I have been preparing it for you."

"I see." Her heart racing, Esania followed, taking the steps two at a time to match Imril's big strides. As they climbed, she heard a muted roar—the pounding of the big waves below, the rush of the wind.

She followed Imril all the way to the top, and suddenly she was drenched in glorious light. The vast blue sky of Khira stretched above them, so similar to Earth's, and yet just a few shades more vivid; hyper-real.

But maybe that was just the effect of Imril's power on her body. Every time he sent his energy through her, her senses became heightened.

Esania gasped as she stepped out into a circular courtyard of sorts. The salty ocean air caressed her naked body, carrying just a hint of a chill with it, and she drew the sumptuous fabric of her dress around herself, covering her bare breasts. Imril put his arm around her shoulder, pulling her close so that she was surrounded by his natural warmth. The exchange of energy between them was fluid now, a constant process without beginning or end.

They were bound together in an eternal loop.

A low parapet ran along the edge of the courtyard, and beyond it was a spectacular three hundred and sixty degrees view of the shimmering ocean. There was not a single cloud in the sky, and no land in sight.

Everything was shades of blue.

Just inside the parapet, low shrubs with leaves of deepest green grew amongst stout-trunked trees that seemed designed to withstand the formidable ocean winds. Violet flowers bloomed amongst the bushes, and underfoot, a carpet of silvery moss caressed her bare feet.

"This is... magnificent." Surrounded by the waves and the wind and the intoxicating scent of wild blooms with her mate standing beside her, his arm curled protectively around her shoulders, Esania stared out at the world below.

His world.

Their world.

Unbidden, tears pricked her eyes. How different this place was from the cold, sterile environment she'd been raised in. How different she *felt*, as if her true self had been awakened.

"This is Khira," Imril whispered, his warm breath feathering her ear. "I was supposed to rule over this planet, to build a great new civilization." A soft, bitter laugh escaped his lips. "I failed. I was a fool. We Drakhin did not know it, but at the time of our inception, Acheros's grand plan was already doomed. That is just our nature. To fight. To destroy. To exist without meaning. But now I have you, Esania."

"I'm not so special," she murmured, leaning against him, closing her eyes. "I'm just an ordinary human."

"No," he said gently, taking her into his arms. "You are *exceptional*. You are brave and righteous and perfect for a fiend like me. I *need* you, Esania. I will rebuild my world—*our* world—but this time I will do it right, and when the void in me threatens to take over, you will be there to keep me in check. Your people are my people now."

Faced with the magnitude of the task ahead of her, Esania

wasn't fazed. The warmth and love flowing from Imril through their bond obliterated any doubt in her mind. "I trust you," was all she said.

He leaned in and kissed her, his scent, his warmth, his intoxicating power engulfing her completely. She was totally consumed by this powerful, seductive creature. "I will not disappoint you," he whispered, and he sounded so earnest that her heart melted all over again. The wind dropped momentarily as he held her tightly, and they simply stood there, reveling in each other's presence. "Welcome to Khira, my *lukara*."

Knowing the full weight of what that really meant, Esania didn't shy away from the responsibility. Somehow, it was as if every event in her entire life had been in preparation for this. She leaned into him, putting her arms around his neck, embracing her future. "I'm home," she said, then kissed him fiercely.

Not once did the thought of leaving Khira enter her mind. Even if they found the means to escape, she would never go.

Not now. Not when she'd found Imril.

Her heart was here, with the Drakhin who had shown her what it meant to be human.

To be alive.